THE CRYSTAL CRYPT

THE CRYSTAL CRYPT

POPPY DENBY
INVESTIGATES

BOOK 6

Fiona Veitch Smith

LION FICTION

Published by **Lion Fiction**
www.lionhudson.com
Part of the SPCK Group
SPCK, 36 Causton Street, London, SW1P 4ST

ISBN 978 1 78264 359 3
e-ISBN 978 1 78264 360 9

First edition 2021

Acknowledgments
Excerpts on pages 12 and 65 from *Married Love*, Marie Stopes, 1918
© Galton Institute London

A catalogue record for this book is available from the British Library

For the forgotten and overlooked women of science.

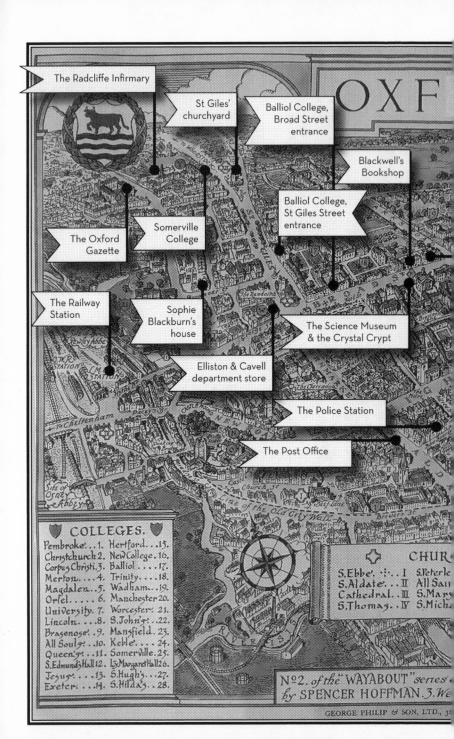

The Radcliffe Infirmary

St Giles' churchyard

Balliol College, Broad Street entrance

Blackwell's Bookshop

Balliol College, St Giles Street entrance

The Oxford Gazette

Somerville College

The Railway Station

Sophie Blackburn's house

The Science Museum & the Crystal Crypt

Elliston & Cavell department store

The Police Station

The Post Office

OXF

COLLEGES.

Pembroke...1. Hertford...15.
Christchurch 2. NewCollege.16.
Corpus Christi.3. Balliol....17.
Merton....4. Trinity....18.
Magdalen..5. Wadham...19.
Oriel.....6. Manchester 20.
University. 7. Worcester. 21.
Lincoln....8. S.John's:..22.
Brasenose'.9. Mansfield.23.
All Souls'..10. Keble'....24.
Queen's:..11. Somerville.25.
S.Edmund's Hall 12. Ly Margaret Hall 26.
Jesus:....13. S.Hugh's...27.
Exeter:...14. S.Hilda's..28.

CHUR

S.Ebbe'. .:.. I S.Peterle
S.Aldate:..II All Sain
Cathedral..III S.Mary
S.Thomas..IV S.Micha

No 2. of the "WAYABOUT" series
by SPENCER HOFFMAN. 3. We

GEORGE PHILIP & SON, LTD., 3

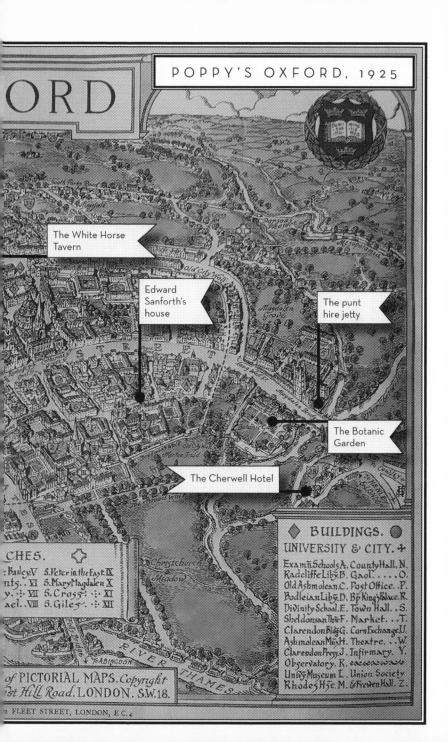

POPPY'S OXFORD, 1925

ORD

The White Horse Tavern

Edward Sanforth's house

The punt hire jetty

The Botanic Garden

The Cherwell Hotel

CHES.

: Baley.V S.Peter in the East.IX
nts.. XI S.MaryMagdalen X
y. .∴ VII S.Cross∴ .∴ XI
ael. .VIII S.Giles∴. .∴ XII

of PICTORIAL MAPS. Copyright
st Hill Road, LONDON. S.W.18.

2 FLEET STREET, LONDON, E.C.4

◆ BUILDINGS. ●

UNIVERSITY & CITY. ✦

Examñ Schools A. County Hall. N.
Radcliffe Libŷ B. Gaol. . . . . O.
Old Ashmolean. C. Post Office. . P.
Bodleian Libŷ. D. Bp Kingŷ Place. R.
Divinity School. E. Town Hall. . S.
Sheldonian Thŷ F. Market. . .T.
Clarendon Bldg G. Corn Exchange U.
Ashmolean Muŷ H. Theatre. . . W.
Clarendon Preŷ. J. Infirmary. Y.
Observatory. K. ∿∿∿∿∿∿∿
Unŷ Museum L. Union Society
Rhodeŷ Hŷe. M. & Freûen Hall. Z.

Acknowledgments

I started writing The Crystal Crypt in January 2020 before I, like most other people in the world, knew that our personal and professional lives would be severely curtailed by a global pandemic. Fortunately, I managed to get in a research trip to Oxford for a few freezing days in January, intending to visit again later in the year. In August, a few hotels and restaurants managed to reopen, so I squeezed in another visit; but unfortunately all the buildings I hoped to go into were still shut due to lockdown restrictions. Nonetheless, I was still able to walk the streets where Poppy walked (and cycled), and even visit the Botanic Garden. I would like to offer my thanks to the very helpful staff at the History of Science Museum who, in January, showed me where Dorothy Hodgkin had her laboratory, and the intersecting basement rooms – now part of the museum's displays – which would house the fictional Crystal Crypt.

I shall explain how the Nobel Prize-winning scientist Dorothy Hodgkin inspired the writing of this book in the historical notes at the end, but here I would like to express my thanks to her and other leading women of science, for their incredible work. Not least of these, the women and men of Dr Sarah Gilbert's team at Oxford University, who, unbeknownst to me when I visited in January 2020, were already working on a vaccine against Covid-19. As I write this today, in March 2021, my arm is aching slightly from receiving that very vaccine, and I hope that by the time this book hits bookshelves later this year, the world will be a brighter, healthier, and more open place.

Thanks, too, go to Paul Gitsham for helping me get my head around some of the science in this book.

As always, I would like to thank the team at Lion Hudson, for helping to bring this book to Poppy's readers, not least my erstwhile editor, Julie Frederick. A particular word of thanks to my former editor, Jess Gladwell, who, although no longer with Lion, continues to encourage me. I was able to meet her in person, in Oxford, in both January and August, where we put the world to rights in the White Horse, as do Poppy and Sophie in the book.

Finally, my thanks, as always, to my family, who due to the pandemic have been at home far more than usual. And to you, the reader, who gave me reason to write another Poppy Denby adventure.

Character List

London

Poppy Denby – arts and entertainment editor for *The Daily Globe*; amateur detective.

Daniel Rokeby – a photographer on *The Daily Globe*; Poppy's beau.

Rollo Rolandson – owner and managing editor of *The Daily Globe;* Poppy's boss.

Yasmin Rolandson (née Reece-Lansdale), KC – a barrister; Rollo Rolandson's wife.

Delilah Marconi – actress, flapper, and socialite; Poppy's best friend.

Ike Garfield – senior journalist at *The Daily Globe*.

Ivan Molanov – archivist at *The Daily Globe*.

Mavis Bradshaw – receptionist at *The Daily Globe*.

Lionel Saunders – reporter with *The London Courier*, rival of *The Daily Globe*.

Richard Easling – disgraced former Detective Chief Inspector of the Metropolitan Police.

Lord Melvyn Dorchester – disgraced peer and industrialist serving time in Pentonville Prison.

Bert Isaacs – (deceased 1920) former senior journalist at *The Daily Globe*.

Roger Leighton – a jeweller; June Leighton's father.

Mrs Leighton – a former medical student; June Leighton's mother.

Larry Leighton – a jeweller; June Leighton's brother.

Dot Denby – radio actress and former suffragette; Poppy's aunt.

Dr Theo Dorowitz – psychiatrist at Willow Park Asylum.

Oxford

Dr June Leighton – DSc graduate in chemistry; recently deceased.

Sophie Blackburn – lab assistant and former suffragette; former fiancée of Bert Isaacs.

Reg Guthrie – lab assistant.

Professor James Sinclair – senior research fellow in chemistry.

Dr Bill Raines – senior researcher, physics.

Dr Miles Mackintosh – DSc graduate student to Dr Raines.

Dr Gertrude Fuller – principal of Somerville College; PhD in linguistics.

Annabel Seymour – Dr Fuller's assistant.

Edward Sanforth – member of the Sanforth Foundation funding scientific research in Oxford.

Mrs Mary Sanforth – head of the Sanforth Foundation; mother of Edward.

George Lewis – editor of *The Oxford Gazette*.

WPC Rosie Winter – only woman police officer in the Oxford City Police.

Chief Constable Fenchurch – head of the Oxford City Police.

Detective Chief Inspector Birch – head of detection at the Oxford City Police.

Dr Dickie Mortimer – pathologist for the Oxford City Police.

Mr Cooper – porter at Somerville College.

"While modern marriage is tending to give ever more and more freedom to each of the partners, there is at the same time a unity of work and interest growing up which brings them together on a higher plane than the purely domestic one which was so confining to the women and so dull to the men. Every year one sees a widening of the independence and the range of the pursuits of women; but still, far too often, marriage puts an end to woman's intellectual life. Marriage can never reach its full stature until women possess as much intellectual freedom and freedom of opportunity within it as do their partners. That at present the majority of women neither desire freedom for creative work, nor would know how to use it, is only a sign that we are still living in the shadow of the coercive and dwarfing influences of the past."

From *Married Love*, Marie Stopes, 1918

Chapter 1

Thursday 16 April 1925, London

Two bright young women, arm in arm, strode out of Piccadilly Circus Tube Station and headed down Piccadilly Road. Both were wearing fashionably cut coats and the latest in Paris millinery. One sported a flamboyant headscarf in lilac, with a black ostrich feather; the other, a slightly more restrained red and black velvet cloche hat. The taller blonde and the shorter brunette laughed at a shared joke, giving off the air of a pair of thoroughly modern misses. Their Cuban heels clicked on the pavement as they headed past the imposing triple-arched gateway to Burlington House, home to the Royal Academy of Arts, which was currently hosting an exhibition, in memoriam, of the late post-impressionist artist Agnes Robson.

They paused for a moment as the dark-haired girl with the lilac headscarf took out a cigarette and lit it, endangering the ostrich feather as it brushed perilously close to the flame.

"Careful, Delilah!" warned the blonde. "You'll set yourself alight!"

Delilah giggled, wafting away the smoke and the warning with a delicately gloved hand.

"Not to worry, Poppy. I shall live to embrace another day! Unlike poor Agnes..."

A shadow passed over Poppy's face as she looked towards the entrance to the Robson exhibition, where, under the watchful stone stares of Leonardo, Titian, and Michelangelo, a queue of people waited for the final entry of the day.

"We must still go, Delilah. I just haven't been able to summon up the courage yet."

Delilah put her arm around her friend's waist. "Give it time, Poppy. Grief takes a while to work through." And then, as if she were on stage in one of her theatre productions, she switched mood, splashed on a smile, and said, "Chin-chin, old bean, let's not get all glum. We've got a night of revels to enjoy!"

Poppy laughed and linked arms again with her friend. "I wouldn't exactly call a scientific lecture at the Royal Institution a 'revel', but you're right. Let's try to enjoy ourselves anyway. Besides, it might actually be interesting."

Delilah wrinkled up her nose. "I doubt it. But thank you for coming with me anyway."

Poppy smiled indulgently. "You're welcome. But you still haven't told me exactly *why* you have to come. And I'm sorry, old girl, but I don't buy the tale that it's because you want to be able to impress your Uncle Elmo next time you see him."

Delilah's great-uncle was the famous radio pioneer Guglielmo Marconi, who frequently berated his niece for her lack of attention to matters of the mind.

Poppy and Delilah resumed their stroll westwards along Piccadilly as a number 9 omnibus trundled past in the opposite direction on the way to the theatre district of Covent Garden. A few moments later, the ladies both nodded in acknowledgment when a gentleman, alighting from a hackney carriage, raised his hat to them before ascending the steps of a private gentlemen's club.

Then, suddenly, Delilah steered her friend towards the right into Old Bond Street.

"It's not this one, is it? Albemarle Street's the next."

Delilah took a long drag on her cigarette, blew it away from Poppy, and said, "I thought we'd have a little peek in a window. You might get some inspiration."

"For what?"

Delilah shook her head in despair. "Oh, don't be coy, Popsicle! You know exactly what." Then, clenching her elbow down on Poppy's arm so there was no option of a quick escape, she led her friend to the window of one of the most exclusive jewellery shops in London: "William Lawes & Co. (Established 1783)." Delilah pressed her nose against the glass and Poppy peered over her shoulder.

"Oooh, look at that one. That huge pink diamond in the ruby setting!" cooed Delilah.

"Hmm, not really my style. And it looks like it would cost a fortune anyway."

"If Danny Boy wants the hand of the delightful Miss Denby, he'll find the money."

"Pity the delightful Miss Denby doesn't care about such things."

Delilah peeled her nose away from the window, ignoring a glare from the shop assistant on the other side. "I know, Poppy; I was just pulling your leg. Not your style at all. Which one do you like?"

Poppy took out her hanky and rubbed the smudge off the window to appease the proprietor. Then, she appraised the exquisite selection of rings, earrings, necklaces, and brooches. Eventually her eyes fell on a delicate sapphire nestled in a swirl of tiny diamonds. "That one is lovely."

"Which one? The little dress ring? Well, yes, that *is* nice; but it's not really an engagement ring, is it?"

"Well, I'm not really engaged, am I?"

"Not yet... but we all know Danny Boy is going to pop the question sooner or later."

"Do we?"

"Of course!" Then Delilah took a step back, startled. "Heavens, Poppy, you don't think he's getting cold feet, do you? He did say he wants to spend the rest of his life with you, didn't he? Do you think he's changing his mind?"

Poppy felt a stone drop to the bottom of her stomach. Daniel, a widower with two children, had indeed said that. But he'd also said that he just needed to get his children settled in their new schools after returning from two and a half years in Africa. And he also needed to square things with his in-laws, the children's maternal grandparents, who were not too happy that he was thinking of marrying again, even though their daughter had been dead nigh on seven years.

It was, unfortunately, sounding all too familiar. Poppy had thought she and the press photographer would have married three years earlier. But instead of popping the question, he had told her he was taking a job on a newspaper in South Africa so his children could live with his sister, who had raised them since their mother died of the Spanish Flu.

But then, last October, he had returned, proclaiming his love and his intention to spend the rest of his life with her. Since then, she had waited patiently for him to formally "pop the question", but as autumn turned into winter, and winter into spring, Poppy was beginning to worry that once again it might not happen. She had not voiced her inner fears to anyone. Nor did she intend to. If Daniel needed time, she would give him time. And if he was going to change his mind, well...

She put a smile on her face and turned to her friend. "Of course he hasn't changed his mind. I'm sure it won't be long now. Don't worry, Delilah, you'll be the first to know when he does."

Poppy linked her arm through her friend's and drew her away from the window and into the swish and very upmarket Royal Arcade, which linked Old Bond and Albemarle Streets. A few moments later they were standing outside the august Royal Institution of Great Britain, dedicated to scientific research and education, and joined a line of far more conservatively dressed Londoners.

Poppy and Delilah emerged from the lecture auditorium into a foyer filled with animated folk sharing their views on a fascinating talk about a new field of science called X-ray Crystallography. It had been given by Professor William Henry Bragg, Director of the Davey Faraday Research Laboratory (housed in the basement of the building), and ably demonstrated by a young female scientist called Kathleen Yardley. Poppy's heart always warmed when she saw young women forging careers in fields normally dominated by men. She thought that Miss Yardley would be a perfect subject for her new monthly column for *The Daily Globe* – Women in the Workplace – and tried to find her in the crowded room. Ah, there she was: holding court to a circle of gentlemen, while nibbling on a jam tart. Poppy would have to wait until she could catch her alone. Perhaps in the ladies' cloakroom…

The lecture attendees were being treated to complimentary tea and cake, so Poppy and Delilah stood in a queue, waiting their turn. But Delilah appeared distracted, craning her neck left and right.

"What's wrong, Delilah? Are you looking for someone?"

The young woman sighed. "Yes. But I don't think he's here. I thought perhaps I'd just missed him in the auditorium, but I can't see him here either."

"Him? Oh… so that's why we're here. Why didn't you tell me?"

Delilah shrugged and gave a sheepish grin. "Sorry. I should have. But I wasn't sure you'd come with me if I did."

Poppy looked curiously at her friend. "Why on earth would

you think that? You know I've always been supportive of your quest to find the perfect beau."

"I know you have, but I thought you might not approve of me moving on so quickly after Peter."

Peter MacMahon was a reporter for the *Newcastle Daily Journal*. Delilah had met him when she was up in the northern city on a theatre tour in the autumn. But the relationship had not survived Delilah's return to London.

"Well, it's hard to make long-distance relationships work, Delilah; I should know that better than most. So no, I don't think harshly of you for it. I just want you to be happy. So tell me, who is this new beau?"

Delilah looked around again and turned, disappointed, back to her friend. "His name's Samuel Wessel. He's a young German physicist – if that's the correct word. I met him at a dinner party hosted by Uncle Elmo. Oh, Poppy, he's frightfully handsome and awfully clever! He asked me if I ever attended lectures here. And of course, I fibbed! But then he told me about this one and asked if I was going. I said, 'Of course! You couldn't keep me away from a talk about X-rays and crystals with a bargepole! I'll see you there!' And he said he'd see me here too. But" – her shoulders slumped – "I can't see him."

Poppy gave her friend a sympathetic pat on the shoulder. "So sorry. But at least you'll be clued up on what those crystals and X-rays do the next time you see him at Uncle Elmo's."

Delilah gave a melodramatic sigh. "Golly, Poppy, you expect me to remember all that?"

"Golly, Delilah," said Poppy, matching the actress's tone, "you manage to remember entire Shakespearean monologues; I'm sure a little science isn't beyond you."

The women edged forward towards the tea table, and as they did they came face to face with a strongly built woman in her early forties, holding a cup and saucer with a pair of macaroons perched precariously on the side.

"Good heavens!" said Poppy. "If it isn't Sophie Blackburn!"

The older woman peered at her from behind a pair of tortoiseshell-rimmed spectacles. "My word, Poppy Denby! And" – she squinted short-sightedly at Delilah – "is that Delilah Marconi? I haven't seen you since... well... since you know when."

"Sophie? Oh Sophie, is that really you?" Delilah threw her arms around the woman, spilling tea down both of them.

"Careful!" Sophie extracted herself from Delilah just in time to save her macaroons from falling.

"Sorry! But oh, Sophie, I can't believe it's you. You haven't changed a bit!"

The older woman smiled sadly, as she took a handkerchief from Poppy and dabbed at her blouse. "Thank you, Delilah, but my mirror tells a different story. Let's just say the last twelve years have treated you far better than they have treated me." She appraised the beautiful young actress. "You've grown up to look so much like your mother. How old are you now?"

"I'm twenty-six. I think I was only fourteen when I last saw you." And then, quietly, "At mother's funeral."

"Yes," said Sophie. "That was the last time. Since then I've been living in Paris. Working for Marie Curie at the Radium Institute. But I expect you know that." She embraced Poppy with her gaze. "When was it you came to see me, Poppy?"

"The summer of 1920."

"Goodness," said Sophie. "That long ago?"

"Yes, it seems like an age. So, what are you doing in London, Sophie?"

Sophie indicated that the two young women should help themselves to tea. As they did, she explained, "I'm just visiting London. I'm down from Oxford, where I live now. I wanted to hear Professor Bragg's lecture. Because I'm in a similar field, you know. I learned all about X-rays at the Radium Institute. Now I work as a laboratory assistant. We also work with crystals."

"It's fascinating stuff," said Poppy, her eyes flitting between Sophie and the sugar cubes she was popping in her tea. "I had no idea that so many things were made of crystals. Like these sugar cubes!"

Sophie smiled briefly. Poppy wasn't sure if it was with good-natured humour or condescension. The last time Poppy had seen Sophie she had been interrogating her as a witness in a case she was investigating, relating to the death of Sophie's fiancé. The two women had not initially got on, but by the end of the case, a grudging respect had developed between them.

As if reading her thoughts, Sophie asked, "So, Poppy, are you still doing your detective work?"

Poppy nodded. "Sort of. I'm still working at the paper as a reporter – that's my full-time job – but I do a bit of sleuthing now and then."

Delilah's eyes widened in pride. "Oh Poppy, don't be so modest! Poppy has solved dozens of cases that have baffled the police."

"Well, hardly dozens, Delilah... a few."

"A few really important ones! Did you hear about the stolen Fabergé eggs and the murdered Romanov princess?"

Sophie nodded.

"Well, that was Poppy! And the archaeologist who dropped dead at the auction of the Death Mask of Nefertiti?"

Poppy put her hand on Delilah's arm. "I'm sure Sophie doesn't want to hear my entire resumé."

"Oh, to the contrary," said Sophie, handing back a neatly folded handkerchief to Poppy. "I would very much like to hear about it. Because, you see, I might have a little detecting job for you."

"A job?" asked Poppy and Delilah in unison.

"Yes," said Sophie, looking to left and right and lowering her voice. "That's if you agree to take it. But I do hope you will. You see, I think one of my colleagues in Oxford might have been murdered. Everyone else thinks it was an accident. As do the authorities. However, I don't. So, while I was in London, I was hoping to look you up, Poppy. But – as it turns out – here you are!"

Delilah was fit to burst with excitement. "A murder investigation? That's just up Poppy's street! Of course she'll take it, won't you, Popsicle?"

Oh dear, thought Poppy. *What am I getting dragged into now?*

Chapter 2

Poppy and Delilah waved goodbye to Sophie as they walked up Albemarle Street and into Mayfair, heading towards Grosvenor Square. Poppy had invited Sophie to accompany them, but the older woman had instantly declined the offer when she heard where they were going and who was going to be there.

Poppy wasn't really surprised. She knew the disdain with which Sophie regarded her aunt Dot Denby and her companion, Grace Wilson, and the bad blood that flowed between them from their days when they all belonged to a militant suffragette cell known as the Chelsea Six. Delilah's mother, Gloria, had been a member too, before her untimely death. And as for Poppy's editor, Rollo Rolandson, Sophie said she had nothing against him per se, but seeing him again would remind her too much of her late fiancé, Bert.

Bert Isaacs had been the political editor of *The Daily Globe*, the newspaper which Poppy worked for. He had died under mysterious circumstances on Poppy's very first day on the job in 1920. It was his death that led Poppy to take up her first case as a reporter sleuth and ultimately secured her a permanent position on the paper and a reputation with the London Metropolitan Police as both a newshound and bloodhound.

It was eight o'clock when Poppy and Delilah arrived outside a very well-appointed townhouse on Grosvenor Square. The whitewashed walls, sparkling in the streetlamps, housed six floors of luxury flats. Rollo Rolandson, Esq., and his wife, Yasmin

Reece-Lansdale, KC, were comfortably ensconced in the four-bedroomed penthouse, spread over two floors, including access to a three-bedroomed attic flat for their servants. The ladies were greeted by a smart doorman in full livery who raised his top hat at their approach.

"Miss Denby. Miss Marconi. Good evening. Mr and Mrs Rolandson are expecting you. Please go up."

"Thank you, Jackman," said Poppy. "And how is your little one doing? The last time we spoke you said he was down with mumps."

The doorman smiled. "He is much better, Miss Denby. Thank you for remembering." He then rang the bell for the penthouse, to alert the Rolandsons that people were on the way up, and ushered the ladies in. Inside they were greeted by an elevator attendant, in equally splendid livery. Without being told, he pressed the button for the top floor.

Poppy and Delilah stepped out into a private vestibule which was a paean to the most contemporary and modern style. The black and white floor was like a chessboard, overlooked by Egyptian statuettes in alcoves. Under each alcove was a brass light bowl illuminating the divine occupants. A large fern in the corner was positioned under a light well, which Poppy knew during the day filtered the real sun through a stained-glass effigy in the oculus. Poppy also knew that the style was not a slavish reproduction of the latest fad sweeping the design world since the discovery of King Tut's tomb, but that Yasmin – who was half-Egyptian – had been ahead of the game all along. However, now that clubs and hotels across London were jumping on the bandwagon, Yasmin was planning a redesign in the summer.

The door to the penthouse opened before either Poppy or Delilah knocked. They were greeted by a handsome dwarfish man in a black butler's suit. Gosper had been Rollo Rolandson's butler before he married Yasmin Reece-Lansdale, and he had moved into the Grosvenor Square penthouse along with his employer, two and a half years earlier. Poppy knew that Rollo had hired him not only for his skill with the clothes iron and the cocktail shaker, but for his stature. Rollo too was a dwarf and knew how difficult it was for men of such short stature to be taken seriously in professions outside of the entertainment industry.

"Good evening, ladies. And how was the lecture?"

"Fascinating!" said Poppy and Delilah in unison: the former seriously, the latter with irony. They met each other's eyes and laughed, bringing a smile to Gosper's normally neutral face. The butler stepped aside to usher the ladies in, then supervised as their hats and coats were received by a maid.

Betty, the maid, gave a little curtsey and greeted them in her Geordie accent. Poppy returned the greeting with a warm smile. "Good evening, Betty. How are you finding London?"

"It's grand, Miss Poppy, just grand. Me mam can hardly believe I've come all this way. Thanks again for putting in a word for me. You and Miss Dot."

Poppy smiled. "It was no trouble at all. My aunt and I were very impressed with you up in Newcastle. How is Betty doing, Gosper?"

The butler raised a brow. "She's got a bit to learn yet, Miss Denby, but not bad. Not bad at all. Now, girl, hurry along and hang up the ladies' coats. Before you turn into a clothes horse." Betty flushed, curtsied, and did as she was told.

Gosper nodded with approval then ushered Poppy and Delilah towards the drawing room, from which spilled the hubbub of a small but lively party.

Rollo Rolandson was standing beside the fireplace – a tumbler of whiskey in hand – in animated conversation with a tall, powerfully built Trinidadian man. This was Ike Garfield, the *Globe*'s senior reporter, who had taken the place of Bert Isaacs after his untimely death. On the other side of the room, seated in the window alcove, was his wife Doreen – an amply proportioned West Indian woman in her forties – who was chatting quietly with two other women: the slim, bony figure of Grace Wilson, a former bookkeeper of the Women's Suffrage and Political Union; and the impeccably turned-out Marjorie Reynolds, MP, rumoured to be a member of the Secret Service. Then, over by the wireless, was Marjorie's son, Oscar, a man in his thirties wearing a dandy suit and monocle, through which he was squinting at the radio dial. He was being directed from a wicker wheelchair by a woman in her sixties, wearing a voluminous gown in peach chiffon, who was referring to a copy of the *Radio Times*.

"Have you got it yet, Oscar?" asked the woman, Poppy's aunt.

"Not yet, Dot. Reception's a bit iffy."

"Oh bother! I hope it won't be when I'm on the show next week!" Dot Denby, before her accident with a police horse at a suffragette demonstration in 1910, had been a doyenne of the West End stage. In recent years, with the advent of live radio and the founding of the British Broadcasting Company in 1922, she had resurrected her career as a voice artist and was now one of the rising stars of the BBC. She spotted Poppy and Delilah and waved. "Girls! You've made it! How was the lecture?" But before Poppy could answer, her aunt chipped in, "Thank heavens you're here, Delilah. Can you give your Uncle Marconi a ring? His wireless isn't working properly."

Delilah giggled. "It's not *his* wireless, Dot. He owns the company, but he can't do much about your squiffy contraption. Here, let me help." Delilah joined Oscar and Dot in their efforts to tune into the live broadcast, leaving Poppy to be greeted by the lady of the house, the tall, elegant Anglo-Egyptian barrister Yasmin Reece-Lansdale, otherwise known as Mrs Rollo Rolandson.

Yasmin drew Poppy towards her and gave her a kiss on each cheek.

"So glad you could make it, Poppy. How was the lecture?"

For once, someone actually listened as Poppy gave a brief but effusive summary of the talk on X-rays and crystals.

"Sounds fascinating!" said Yasmin, with sincerity.

Poppy noticed dark rings under Yasmin's eyes, unsuccessfully hidden by make-up. "You look tired, Yazzie. Are the children behaving themselves?"

Yasmin gave a weary laugh. "Who knew two-year-old twins could cause such devastation?"

Poppy nodded in sympathy. Yasmin had surprised the whole of London society by announcing two and a half years ago that she was expecting – at the grand old age of forty-five. However, with her and Rollo's substantial joint income they could afford two nannies – one for the day and one for the night. Nonetheless, Poppy felt for the older woman, trying to balance her professional and domestic life.

"Are they asleep?" she asked.

Yasmin let out a relieved sigh. "Finally. Now what can I get you to drink?"

"A glass of pink champagne, if you have it."

Yasmin chuckled. "Of course we have it, darling. Gosper!" The butler was there in an instant and returned a few moments later with two glasses of pale pink bubbly.

"So, who else was at the lecture? Anyone I might know?"

"Well actually," said Poppy, "Delilah and I bumped into Sophie Blackburn."

"Good heavens, really? I thought she was in Paris. Rollo! Ike! You wouldn't believe who Poppy and Delilah met at the Royal Institution…"

"Who?" asked Rollo as the two ladies joined him and Ike at the fireplace.

"Good evening, Poppy," said Ike and gave a gentlemanly nod.

"Good evening, Ike. Evening, Rollo. Well, as I was saying to Yasmin, Delilah and I saw Sophie Blackburn."

"Bert Isaacs' fiancée?" asked Ike.

"Yes. Did you ever meet her?"

"Not personally, but Rollo has told me all about her. I thought she was in Paris."

"Just what I thought," said Yasmin.

Poppy took a sip of her champagne, wondering how much of her conversation with Sophie she should share with her colleagues. It had, after all, been rather bizarre. Eventually she said, "Well, apparently she's been back for a while. Not sure how long. But she says she's got a job now in Oxford at a laboratory there. And, well, this is the odd thing – she has asked me to come up to Oxford to help her with something. Something, well, something quite unexpected..." Poppy trailed off and took another sip of champagne.

Rollo looked at her curiously. "Well, spit it out, Miz Denby: what does she want you to do?"

Poppy swallowed her drink and cleared her throat. "She wants me to investigate a mysterious death."

Rollo's eyelids shot up to meet his shaggy red brows. "Really? Don't tell me she wants you to look into Bert's death."

"No, not that. It's someone who died in her laboratory. A young lady scientist."

"I think I heard about that," said Ike. "It was a few weeks ago, wasn't it? I read about it in *The Times*. But I thought it was an accident. Death by electrocution, I think."

Poppy nodded. "Yes, that's what Sophie said. But she thinks there's more to it."

"Like what?" asked Yasmin.

Poppy shrugged. "I don't know. She said if I'd come up to Oxford on Saturday she would tell me."

"Will you go?" asked the barrister.

"I think I will, yes. I must say she has piqued my curiosity. Is it all right if I go, Rollo? I'm not booked in to work this weekend, but if there's anything you need me to do?"

The editor pursed his lips. "No, nothing that I can think of. But do be careful, Poppy. Miz Blackburn is not all there." He gave a twirl of his finger to his temple.

"What do you mean? She seemed to have all her faculties intact."

Rollo passed his tumbler to the butler, who, without being told, headed to the drinks cabinet to pour his employer another.

"Well, there's something I haven't told you. When you were up in Newcastle last year – just before Yazzie and I came up to join you – I had a visit at the paper from Sophie Blackburn. Let's just say she wasn't very well. Her nerves were on edge, and I heard through one of my sources that she'd been seeing a psychiatrist. In fact, she'd spent some time in Willow Park Asylum."

"You didn't tell me this, Rollo!" said his wife.

Rollo shrugged. "I was going to, but then the Agnes Robson story took off and it got pushed aside. Anyway, I'm telling you now. Sophie wanted to know if I could give her any more information about Bert's death. I told her all I knew – which is not much more than what is already in the public domain. That Bert hadn't been well – his heart – and that it was believed he had felt faint walking up the stairs that day. And as you all know – and I'll never forgive myself for it – the bannister was broken, awaiting repair. Bert leaned on it and it didn't hold his weight."

Poppy nodded. "Yes, I remember." She closed her eyes and shuddered, recalling the horror she had witnessed as Bert fell to his death onto the floor of the newspaper building's foyer.

"The official finding was accidental death," said Yasmin.

"It was," agreed Rollo, "but Sophie, it seems, can't accept

that. She believes there was a cover-up and that Lionel Saunders pushed Bert to his death."

Ike grunted. "Well, that's the rumour I heard."

"And what most of us at the paper believed – none of us had any time for Saunders, not after what he tried to do to Poppy – but there was no evidence to back that up. And that's what I told Sophie."

"How did she take it?" asked Poppy, dismissing the awful memory of being chased through the newspaper building by Lionel Saunders, fearing for her life.

"Not well," said Rollo. "She was in a bit of a state. I offered to call a taxi, but she refused and left on her own; I don't know where to. I was going to mention it to y'all, but then I got the call about Agnes Robson's murder, and..." He shrugged and took a sip of his whiskey.

"So," said Yasmin, "are you suggesting that she might have another agenda for asking Poppy to visit her in Oxford?"

Rollo lowered his whiskey glass and looked up at the two women. "I don't know. But I'd be careful if I were you, Poppy. There seems to be a pattern here: Sophie believing accidental deaths were not accidents. I'm no shrink, but I think there might be something in that."

"Are you saying I shouldn't go to Oxford?"

Rollo shook his head. "No, I'm not saying that. You're a big girl and you can make up your own mind. But being forewarned is being forearmed, don't you think?"

Poppy nodded her agreement and took a sip of champagne.

CHAPTER 3

SATURDAY 18 APRIL 1925, OXFORD

Daffodils nodded their drooping heads as the motorbike roared past on its way from London to Oxford. As they approached the ancient university city, Poppy looked up through her motoring goggles and took in the handsome, determined jaw of Daniel Rokeby, who was deftly steering the bike and its sidecar over Magdalen Bridge and onto Oxford High Street. On their right were the medieval spires of Magdalen College and on their left, the beautiful Botanic Garden, bursting with the joys of spring.

This was the first time Poppy had been to Oxford, and although she could have come up on the train, she was grateful that Daniel had said that he would run her up on the motorbike instead. His children were spending the weekend with their grandparents, and it was the first weekend in over a month that he and Poppy were both off work at the same time.

It was a glorious sunny day, and representatives of both Town and Gown were out and about doing their Saturday morning shopping. Poppy had never seen so many bicycles in one place in her life, and Daniel had to slow to a snail's pace to join the flow. Poppy didn't mind, as it gave her an opportunity to look left and right and appreciate the beauty of the city she had only previously read about. On the left were the famous Examination Halls where students took their exams, although all was quiet there today as it was still the Easter break, when the university took its breath between the Hilary and Trinity terms. Approaching on the right was the ancient church of St Mary the Virgin, and Daniel turned into a worryingly narrow lane. Poppy's bones jarred as the sidecar bounced over the cobbles, and she inadvertently held her breath as they squeezed between the walls of All Souls College and St Mary's. She was relieved as the bike and sidecar emerged into an open quadrangle, with the exquisitely domed circular Radcliffe Camera library in the middle. Poppy craned her neck to take it all in as they passed the historic splendour of the Bodleian Library and then took a left into Broad Street. Daniel found a parking spot near a long line of bicycles outside the Sheldonian Theatre and grinned down at Poppy as he turned off the engine and pushed up his goggles onto his leather helmet.

Poppy chuckled at the red welts around his eyes, making him look like a giant panda, before realizing she would look just the same.

"Welcome to Oxford, m'lady. I hope you were pleased with your sturdy steed."

"Well thank you, good sir; the sturdy steed performed admirably."

Poppy unstrapped her leather helmet and replaced it with her cloche hat that she'd kept in the footwell. She adjusted the belt on her red spring mackintosh and smoothed down her white cotton skirt.

Daniel pointed across the road. "There's the White Horse there. Next door to Blackwell's." Poppy's ears twitched at the mention of the famous bookshop. She promised herself that she'd pop in after her meeting with Sophie.

The couple waited for half a dozen cyclists to pass before heading towards the pub. Daniel had to duck his head under the low-slung beams as they entered the centuries-old public house. Poppy scanned the small, busy interior and spotted Sophie at a table near the back. She waved and Sophie waved back, while staring with open curiosity at Daniel.

A few moments later introductions were made.

"I didn't expect you to bring anyone with you, Poppy."

"Oh? I didn't think you'd mind. Mr Rokeby and I are…" Poppy was just about to say "almost engaged to be married" but stopped herself in time. "… workmates. He works on the newspaper."

Sophie nodded. "Yes, I remember Bert spoke very highly of you, Mr Rokeby."

"And Bert was a fine journalist," said Daniel in reply. "However, if you'd prefer I wasn't here, I can grab a pint and wait for you at the bar."

Sophie smiled tightly. "No, that's all right. Take a seat."

The waitress approached and recommended the day's special of fish and chips. They all agreed to have it; then Daniel asked for a pint of bitter, Poppy a lemonade, and Sophie a refill of her Bee's Knees – a cocktail of gin, lemon juice, and honey.

Poppy readied herself for a bit of small talk but was not entirely surprised when the straight-talking woman she'd first met in Paris wanted to get right down to business. Sophie took out a photograph and laid it on the table. It was of a group of six people in white laboratory coats, standing in what Poppy assumed to be a laboratory. There were four men and two women. One of them was Sophie.

"This is the team that works in the crystallography laboratory over the road."

Poppy looked towards the window overlooking Broad Street. "Your laboratory is over the road?"

"Yes, in the old Ashmolean. It now houses the Science Museum. We work in the basement. This photo was taken in

January, soon after I started work there." She pointed. "That's me, of course, and that older, bald gentleman with the pipe is Professor Sinclair. He's the senior research fellow in chemistry. The other chap next to him is Doctor Raines, a physicist. And the chap next to me – the one with the glasses – is Reg Guthrie, the other lab assistant. The two young folk are the DSc graduate students Miles Mackintosh and June Leighton. Technically, they should be called 'Doctor' too, but no one bothers. June" – Sophie's finger traced the outline of a dark-haired young woman, a few years younger than Poppy, whose profile looked a little like that of the novelist Virginia Woolf – "is the girl who died."

Poppy took a moment to study the image. It seemed like an ordinary workplace photograph – the kind that might perhaps appear in a yearbook. There was nothing she could glean about the relationships between the people depicted, nor much of their personalities; although Professor Sinclair looked a tad austere... However, none of them were smiling in the photograph, so it was hard to tell. Eventually, Poppy spoke: "She looks like a lovely young woman. Such a tragedy that she died with so much life ahead of her. My colleague Ike Garfield told me that he remembered reading about the accident. So, I looked it up. It doesn't fall within the *Globe*'s circulation, but *The Times* covered it."

Poppy opened her notebook and removed a newspaper cutting and spread it on the table.

The Times

5th April 1925

LADY SCIENTIST ELECTROCUTED IN LABORATORY

OXFORD – A young, female DSc graduate from Somerville College has been found dead in the basement of the Old Ashmolean Museum.

A statement from the Oxford City Police said that laboratory assistant Mr Reginald Guthrie found the body of twenty-four-year-old Dr June Leighton on Monday morning. According to Mr Guthrie's statement to the police, Dr Leighton was entangled in wires and lying on the broken glass of smashed apparatus.

Mr Guthrie attempted to resuscitate Dr Leighton but was unable to do so.

On examination of the body and the scene the police pathologist determined the death to have been caused by electrocution.

The head of the laboratory, Professor James Sinclair, the eminent Oxford chemist, told the police that Dr Leighton had been working late on Sunday evening on an experiment involving electricity and that she had not taken adequate precautions.

"Dr Leighton should not have attempted such a complex experiment on her own, out of hours," Prof Sinclair said. "Sadly, her youthful exuberance and feminine stubbornness have led to her untimely and tragic death. Our thoughts are with her family."

* * *

"Youthful exuberance and feminine stubbornness," observed Daniel, taking a sip of his beer. "Well, that puts her in her place, doesn't it?"

"Quite," said Sophie, her demeanour visibly softening towards Daniel.

Poppy nodded her agreement. "Yes, it's in poor taste, but it's only evidence of an unfortunate attitude towards women, nothing more. I expect there's more coverage in the local Oxford paper."

"There was," said Sophie. "Extensively. But the conclusion they came to was the same: June Leighton died in a tragic accident. And yes, 'youthful exuberance and feminine stubbornness' are mentioned there too."

"But you don't believe that's the case."

"No. June was passionate about her work – exuberantly and stubbornly – but those are positive qualities in my book. They were not what killed her."

"Well, that appears to be electrocution. Do you dispute that?" asked Poppy.

Sophie looked around at the luncheon diners and lowered her voice. "No, I don't. I saw the body soon after Reg found it. It looked like electrocution to me. But I don't believe it was an accident. I don't believe June's carelessness caused this. She was a meticulous scientist. I have worked with plenty of them in my time, and although young, she could hold her own against any of them – male or female."

Poppy smiled sympathetically at Sophie, appreciative of her efforts to protect the reputation of the deceased woman. "But accidents can still happen. Perhaps it wasn't her fault? Perhaps there was something out of her control, something she couldn't have foreseen..."

"Like someone plotting to kill her?"

Poppy tensed. Here it was. Sophie's paranoia... Rollo's

warning words rang in her ears. However, she settled her face into a neutral expression and asked, "What evidence do you have of that?"

Sophie shrugged. "I have none. That's why I asked you to come here, Poppy. So you can find the evidence."

Poppy sucked in her breath, willing herself to stay calm. "I think we're missing a few steps here, Sophie. Firstly, I can't investigate something when there is no indication that it wasn't an accident, and secondly—"

"I didn't say there was no indication; I just said there was no evidence – as yet. But there *are* indications. There are definitely indications that this wasn't an accident."

"Such as…?" Poppy opened her hands on the table, palms up.

"Such as…" Sophie again scanned the pub before continuing, "a series of arguments between June and the men. As I said, I only came in January, but I can tell you that girl did not have an easy time of it."

Poppy shrugged. "That's par for the course for women in most professions." She flicked a quick glance at Daniel. "Fortunately, not for me, of course. All my male colleagues have been very supportive. But both you and I know, Sophie, that animosity from men towards women in the workplace is not that uncommon."

Sophie nodded. "I agree. But there seemed to be more to it than that. Miles – the other DSc graduate – appeared to be jealous of her, and he was always trying to get her into trouble with Raines."

"The opinionated professor?"

Sophie shook her head briskly. "No, that's Prof Sinclair. He's old-fashioned in his views in some ways – hence the youthful exuberance and feminine stubbornness – but he genuinely respected June's abilities. And mine. He had no hesitation in giving me a job when he saw my qualifications. No, it's his second in command." Sophie pointed to the handsome middle-aged man in the photograph, with a full head of hair. "Dr Bill Raines. Young Miles is his protégé, and he always defended him whenever June complained about harassment."

"Harassment? What kind of harassment?"

Sophie shrugged. "I'm not sure. I just overheard a heated discussion one day behind closed doors in which June accused Miles of harassment, Miles denied it, and Doc Raines backed him up. I wish I'd prompted June to tell me what it was. One woman to another. But we didn't have that kind of relationship. I was new on the job, older than she, not an academic. Reg and I are treated like servants – best seen and not heard – you know the thing..."

Poppy did.

"Anyway," Sophie continued, "let's just say that when June's body was found, neither Miles nor Raines appeared to be too shocked. Of course, it could just have been the old British stiff upper lip, but it was odd, very odd. So that, on top of me knowing that June was a meticulous practitioner and not the type to make dangerous mistakes, has led me to think that this might not have been an accident."

Sophie picked up her glass and had a sip of her gin. Eventually, she said, "So, will you take the case?"

Poppy let out a sigh. "I'm sorry, Sophie, but while I appreciate your view that June had a difficult work life, there still isn't enough to suggest foul play. And I'm sure the police have looked into it..."

Sophie snorted. "The *police*? Here in Oxford? Do you know that the university have their own security agents known as proctors? Well, they're not officially police, not anymore, but they're still more than just campus security. They have power to investigate offences on university property."

"But surely a death would not fall under their ambit?" observed Daniel.

"Not officially, no. But they would have been the first to be called. And then they would call the city police after that. The proctors always try to protect the university's reputation. And so do the city police. And that's what they've done here."

Poppy tensed. There it was again: Sophie's "they're-all-out-to-get-us" interpretation of events. "I'm sorry, there needs to be a bit more than that."

Sophie's eyes narrowed. "I thought better of you, Poppy. I thought you'd be prepared to look beyond the obvious. I never took you to be an establishment lackey."

That stung, but Poppy would not be goaded. She was no longer the cub reporter whom Sophie had first met in Paris, and so had no need to try to impress her.

"I'm not. But you must understand that as Oxford is not in my newspaper's circulation, I would need a good reason to convince Rollo to let me investigate this. And so far, I don't have enough. I'm sorry, Sophie, but you'll need to give me a bit more."

Sophie's face dropped and she drummed her fingers on the table. Suddenly, she stopped and looked up, directly into Poppy's eyes. "What if I told you that I think Miles might have stolen June's research and passed it off as his own?"

Poppy inclined her head. "I'm listening..."

"Well, you see, the time when I overheard June complaining about harassment was not the only time I listened in on a conversation. There were quite a few heated discussions, and one of them was when Miles had just had his first paper published in *Nature* – that's a scientific journal. We had a few drinks over here to celebrate, and I overheard June say to Doc Raines that there wasn't an original idea in there that she hadn't thought of first and that she had the evidence to prove it."

"And what did Raines say to that?" asked Poppy.

"Nothing," said Sophie. "He just got up and walked to the bar as if he didn't hear her. June looked embarrassed. I tried to catch her eye, but she got up then and left. She was fuming."

Daniel leaned into the conversation. "Are you suggesting June accused this student – Miles – of plagiarism?"

"Plagiarism. Yes, that's the word. And yes, that's exactly what I'm suggesting, Mr Rokeby. And I think June was going to expose it. It was a week later that she died." Sophie pursed and then unpursed her lips, her eyes boldly holding Daniel's. "So now do you think I've got grounds for suspicion?"

Daniel looked at Poppy; Poppy nodded. "Well, that is a bit stronger. Not necessarily of murder – I think we're a long way off that still – but I think there's certainly a story here if this Miles did steal June's ideas and his boss covered it up. That's a story in itself. I'll tell you what, Sophie, let me run this by Rollo and see if he'll allow me a few days to see if it's got legs. Is that all right?"

Sophie nodded, visibly relieved, and took another sip of her gin. "Thank you, Poppy. Thank you very much."

Poppy smiled at the older woman. "You're welcome. However, there's one more thing: I really need to try to find a London connection. As I say, Oxford is not in our circulation area. If I'm going to use work time, there needs to be something in it to interest our readers."

"Won't they be interested in a murder?"

"Of course, but we don't know it's a murder."

Sophie thrust out her chin.

Poppy raised her hand to silence her. "Like it or not, as it stands this is a story about a male scientist possibly trying to take credit for a woman's work. Which could fit very well into my Women in the Workplace column – and I would love to write something for that – but it still needs a London connection..."

"Well, June was *from* London."

"Was she?"

"As far as I know, yes. And she also had a fiancé who apparently had a flat in London. Or an almost-fiancé – I never quite got to the bottom of that. She only mentioned him once in passing. And she never wore a ring... But she was definitely from London. Does that make a difference?"

"It very well might," smiled Poppy. "I'll talk to Rollo about it and then let you know."

CHAPTER 4

Half an hour later, Poppy and Daniel left the White Horse, promising Sophie that Poppy would be in touch again as soon as they'd got permission from Rollo to go ahead with the investigation. They then popped into Blackwell's Bookshop. Ten minutes later, in the classic novel section, Daniel whispered in her ear: "Choose your book, Poppy; I don't want to miss the afternoon sun."

Poppy was surprised. Daniel enjoyed reading as much as she did, but he didn't seem in the least interested in the rows of Walter Scotts or Jules Vernes that would normally attract his attention. So she hurriedly selected the latest Agatha Christie, *The Secret of Chimneys*, and paid the teller.

Back out on Broad Street, Daniel offered her his arm, suggesting, "Should we head down to the river?"

She smiled up at him. "If you know the way..."

After a leisurely stroll through the streets of old Oxford, they arrived at the gateway to the Botanic Garden. It was a beautiful day to be surrounded by such horticultural beauty, and Poppy was glad Daniel had suggested it. They wandered, slowly, through the walled gardens, imbibing the scent of hyacinths and stopping to admire the tulips. They decided not to go into the glasshouses – too full already with folk – but had a peek through the window at the waterlilies in the pond. They passed the medicinal plants – grown to treat everything from heart problems to gout – then made their way through the stone arch into the fruit garden.

Ducking under the low-swung branches of the apple trees, blousy with blossom, they eventually made their way to the banks of the River Cherwell. To their left was Magdalen Bridge, with punts drifting lazily downstream, while on the other bank, a cricket match was under way, punctuated by gentle applause as willow connected with leather. Daniel led them to a wooden bench, brushed the seat clear of some dried cut grass, and encouraged them both to sit.

They watched in companionable silence as a young man in shirt and braces, wearing a boater hat, pushed his punt along, while his lady companion leaned back on a pile of cushions, dribbling her fingers through the water.

"That looks fun!" said Poppy.

Daniel took off his hat and wiped at his brow with a handkerchief. "Would you like to have a go? I can find out where to hire one, if you like?"

Poppy chuckled. "Best not. It looks a bit tricky. I wouldn't want to capsize!"

Daniel gave a look of mock offence. "Are you saying you don't think I'm man enough?"

Poppy wrinkled up her nose. "Of course not!" She stopped herself before adding, *you're man enough for me...*

Poppy leaned back on the bench, enjoying the feel of her shoulder against Daniel's and the warmth of the sun through the light cotton of her dress.

Daniel, however, seemed stiff and ill at ease.

"What is it, Daniel?" she asked. "You seem a bit out of sorts."

"Do I? Well, I'm not. I couldn't be happier than I am now. Here with you. But..."

Oh no, thought Poppy. *Here it comes...* "But what?"

Daniel shifted along the bench so their shoulders were no longer touching and turned his face towards her.

"I have something to tell you, Poppy. Something to confess."

"Oh?" Her voice was small and fearful.

"Well, do you remember last weekend when I had to work out of town?"

"Yes. Rollo asked you to go down to Southampton and get some snaps of a new ocean liner that was being launched."

"That's right; he did. But I didn't go."

Poppy's eyes widened in surprise. Daniel was one of the most diligent people she knew. If he had agreed to do something, he would. "Why ever not?"

"Because..." He wiped again at his brow and Poppy could see that he was sweating profusely, far more profusely than was warranted by the April sunshine. "Because there was someone I needed to see. Someone at the other end of the country."

"Oh," said Poppy again, not knowing what else to say. A cheer went up from the cricketers over the river and Poppy wished they would all just pipe down.

"You see, I took the train up to Northumberland to see your parents."

Poppy felt like someone had just knocked her for six. "Why on earth would you do that?"

Daniel shrugged, looking like a shy schoolboy. "Don't you know, Poppy?"

And then, suddenly, it dawned on her. "Oh my. Oh my, oh my. Did you really? What did Daddy say?"

A sheepish grin spread from ear to ear. "He said yes, Poppy. Absolutely yes. I wasn't sure if he would, you know, me being an atheist and all, but he said that didn't matter; he believed that to be merely a temporary state of affairs – which was a bit cheeky of him, really, but I let it go, him being a clergyman and all. And then your mother came in and I asked her too, and she was quiet for a while – which worried me of course – but then she said that if you were happy she would be happy, and" – he looked at her intently – "well, are you?"

Poppy's heart was beating nineteen to the dozen. "Well, I am! I am happy! At least I will be... when you ask me."

Daniel laughed, then reached into the inside pocket of his jacket and brought out a little black velvet box as Poppy quivered with excitement.

He took a deep breath and opened the box.

Poppy gasped. Inside was the pretty little ring she'd seen in the jewellery shop window the other evening: the blue sapphire set in a swirl of tiny diamonds.

"Oh Daniel, how did you...?"

"Shhh," said Daniel, putting his finger to her lips. "It's still my turn." Then he straightened his tie, cleared his throat, and said, "Miss Poppy Denby. Will you do me the greatest honour and become my wife?"

"Oh Daniel! Yes! Yes! Absolutely yes!" And then, oblivious to who was watching, she threw her arms around him, knocking her hat from her head.

A cheer went up from the crowd on the opposite bank.

Game, set, and match, thought Poppy, not caring for a second that she'd got the wrong sport.

CHAPTER 5

MONDAY 20 APRIL 1925, LONDON

Poppy got off the bus at the bottom of Fleet Street and stepped onto Cloud Nine. She could not wait to get to the office, take off her glove, and flash her ring finger at anyone who might be the slightest bit interested. She was still coming to terms with the fact that it had actually happened: Daniel had finally proposed. They had returned from Oxford to tell his children and their grandparents. Little Amy was delighted, demanding to be a flower girl and insisting that she design both her and Poppy's dresses. Young Arthur – a quiet and thoughtful boy of eleven – expressed his concern that their house in Croydon didn't have enough bedrooms for Poppy to live with them. When he was told that Poppy would stay in the same bedroom as his father, he nodded sagely and said, "That will work." Poppy, who had been bracing herself for questions about whether or not she would be replacing their mother, was relieved that the size of the house and who would design the dresses were the children's greatest concerns. Mr and Mrs Boxton, the late Lydia Rokeby's parents, were measured and polite in their response. Poppy hadn't expected much more from them and was grateful that that was the sum of it.

Aunt Dot, on the other hand, was over the moon. She booked them all a table at Oscar's Jazz Club and, with only an hour's notice, managed to get word to a dozen friends and well-wishers. Champagne and congratulations flowed in equal measure. Delilah, who was performing at Oscar's that night, gleefully admitted that she and Daniel had been in cahoots when she lured Poppy to the jewellery shop window to ascertain her taste in rings. "I knew you wouldn't have come if I'd told you why, so I came up with the plan to go to the science lecture."

Poppy laughed. "So your German physicist who was supposed to meet you there was a fabrication?"

Delilah chuckled. "Of course! Do you think someone would really stand me up?"

Daniel shimmied in on their conversation to ask, "So, did I get the right one? I only had a couple of hours on Friday to get it when I found out you needed a lift to Oxford. I thought it would be the perfect time to propose."

"And it was!" said Poppy, raising her hand to admire her ring and then leaning her head on her fiancé's shoulder. "It's all perfect. Thank you."

"Do you want to dance?" he whispered as the band slipped into a slow, sultry number.

"I'd love to," she whispered in return and slipped into his arms.

Poppy hummed the tune to herself as she strode along Fleet Street, greeting the flower sellers and newspaper vendors at their usual spots, before crossing the road outside Ye Olde Cock Tavern and skipping up the steps of *The Daily Globe*.

As expected, the receptionist, Mavis Bradshaw, had already heard of the engagement and leaped out from behind her desk to demand a look at the ring. A couple of printers on the way down to the basement raised their caps to her and passed on their congratulations. "Rokeby's a lucky fella!" was the general consensus.

On the way up to the newsroom, Poppy was tempted to stop off on the second floor and see if Daniel was in the photography department. But she knew if she did she'd want to bask in his presence longer than she should and she'd be late in getting her work started. Instead, she blew a silent kiss as the lift passed by. On the fourth floor she pushed open the newsroom door and was embarrassed, but not surprised, to receive a chorus of wolf whistles and a round of applause.

"I see the news has got out already," she retorted, hanging her satchel over the back of her chair.

"What else did you expect from a yellow rag like this?" quipped Ike Garfield at the next desk. "Well done, Poppy. I don't know why it took the boy so long."

"Thanks, Ike." She smiled back at her colleague.

"Oh, Rollo wants to see you."

Poppy rolled her eyes. "I bet he does." She picked up her notebook and pencil and headed to her boss's office.

As she approached – relaxed and filled with confidence – she remembered how different it had been on her first day five years earlier. She was applying for a job as an editorial assistant – which she later found out was really just the title of a glorified maid. Rollo Rolandson – in danger of being crushed to death under piles of unfiled papers, books, and cuttings – hired her after only the briefest of interviews in which he seemed more concerned with finding out her views on alcohol and temperance than whether or not she could type. As it turned out, she could type, and she put it to good use when, on the spur of the moment, she offered to provide a story to fill a gap in the paper when the then arts and entertainment editor, Lionel Saunders, failed to turn up for work.

She remembered too how the very same Lionel Saunders had attacked her one night while she was alone in Rollo's office, but quickly dismissed the thought from her mind. Instead, she chose to remember when she had first seen Daniel with his beautiful grey eyes walk into the same office. She smiled as the now familiar warm glow replaced the chill of the more disturbing memories. Then, she knocked on the door.

"Come in," came the voice in the same New York accent she had heard all those years ago.

She pushed open the door to see Rollo's red head barely visible over a pile of precariously perched files. A series of "editorial assistants" had come and gone over the last five years, each of them failing to tame the editor's chaotic work habits. But, Poppy knew, it did not affect his razor-sharp mind or the quality of journalism he presided over.

"Ah, Miz Denby! Or should that be Mrs Daniel Rokeby-to-be?" He grinned and came around his desk.

"May I?" he asked, tilting back his head and puckering his lips.

"You may," said Poppy, lowering her head so he could give her a kiss on the cheek.

"Congratulations, young lady! Rokeby had better do you right or he'll have me to answer to."

"Oh, I'm sure he will," said Poppy, sinking into the seat Rollo had cleared of debris.

They spent the next few minutes discussing the ring, Daniel's in-laws, the children's and her parents' reaction to the engagement, and chuckling about how Aunt Dot would be totally giddy in the run-up to the wedding scheduled for the summer. Poppy assumed that Daniel would ask Rollo to be his best man, and she of course would ask Delilah to be her chief bridesmaid.

But Rollo soon moved the conversation on to professional matters.

"So, Oxford. Engagement aside, what news do you have? What happened with Sophie Blackburn? Is there a story in it?"

Poppy caught herself twirling her ring and stopped. She had always found it annoying when other young brides-to-be did it, now here she was doing it herself – and at twenty-seven, she wasn't that young anymore, either. "I do think there's a story, but I'm not sure it's a murder. Sophie seems to think that the scientist who was electrocuted a few weeks ago was killed by one or more of her male colleagues who were trying to silence her."

"Why were they trying to silence her?" Rollo grinned and added, "Allegedly."

"Sophie thinks that June, the victim" – she smiled wryly at Rollo – "*alleged* victim, suspected one of them of stealing her research and presenting it as his own."

"And she has evidence of that?"

"Evidence of June's suspicion, yes. Sophie overheard a couple of conversations to that effect."

"Then, hearsay."

"True, but we've started following up stories on hearsay before—"

"We have, but not in Oxford. Not when I have to pay for your train fare and possible hotel bills when you're there."

Poppy leaned back in her chair and looked at her editor curiously. "Why are you blowing hot and cold on this, Rollo? On Thursday night you were warning me that Sophie might be mentally unwell and that she could be imagining this murder because of her anger and grief that no one was convicted in connection with Bert's death. Then, just a minute ago, you were excited that there might be a story in it. Now you're worried about the train fare." She opened her hands in mock exasperation and smiled.

Rollo, on the other hand, frowned and templed his fingers in front of him. "I know Poppy, I know. I must confess I haven't stopped thinking about Sophie since you mentioned her on

Thursday. I've been feeling real bad about her since she came to see me last fall. I wish I could have done more for her. She's broken up about Bert. It was five years ago now, but she's not over it. Not in her head and not in her heart. I want to help her, if I can. Bert was not just an employee; he was a good friend. He deserved more."

Poppy was surprised. She knew Rollo to be a compassionate man – on the inside – but he rarely let it be seen through his brash New York persona. She bit her lip, chewing on what she'd just heard, then asked, "Do you think Sophie's right – that Bert was murdered? That he didn't just fall by accident?"

Rollo let out a long, painful sigh and then opened the cigar box on his desk. "I don't know, Poppy, I really don't. As we know, the timing of it was very peculiar. He had his tragic accident on the very same day he received a letter tying one of the most powerful men in the country to a criminal conspiracy. And we all now know that Lionel Saunders was in the pay of that same powerful man. But Melvyn Dorchester never admitted to telling Saunders to kill Bert, and we have no evidence that he was even in the building the day Bert died. But this is old territory we've been over before." He snipped off the end of his cigar, sniffed it, then flicked a lighter.

Poppy nodded. Yes, it was old territory. The only punishment Lionel Saunders received was to be sacked from his job – and Poppy had replaced him. But he soon got work with the *Globe*'s rival, the *Courier*, and had been a professional and personal thorn in Poppy's side ever since. "So, what are your thoughts about this story in Oxford?" asked Poppy. "As I say, Sophie didn't present me with any evidence of murder, and it seems the police there didn't think there was anything to pursue, but I still think there might be an article in it. June Leighton was a London girl. Apparently, her parents don't live too far from you in Mayfair."

"Really?" asked Rollo, withdrawing the now-lit cigar from his mouth.

"That's what Sophie said. And apparently there might have been a fiancé too. Also London-based. Or perhaps he just owns a flat here; Sophie's not sure. Still, I thought that might be enough to justify a story. Even if there was no murder, the story of the life of a young, promising female scientist, cut tragically short, might be worth a few column inches, don't you think?"

Rollo nodded. "Yes, I think it is." Then, he grinned; the old Rollo was back. "Not sure it's worth more than a couple of train rides to Oxford though – the budget won't stretch that far."

Poppy smiled. "I shall try to keep expenses to the minimum. In fact, I think I can get started on this right here in London. Before I go any further, I probably need to speak to June's parents, and, if possible, her fiancé. I'll try to ascertain whether or not they think there is more to her death than just an accident, and if not, then I'll just head down the 'promising career cut short' route. How does that sound?"

Rollo rolled smoke around his mouth, then exhaled. "I think that's a good plan, Poppy. When you have it, give me the parents' address too, and I'll see if any of the neighbours know anything about them. Leighton, you say?"

Poppy nodded.

"Can't say I've heard of them. But there are plenty of busybodies around who might."

CHAPTER 6

Armed with Mr and Mrs Roger Leighton's address, which she got from the London AZ Telephone Directory, Poppy caught a bus to Mayfair. She had rung ahead to see if the Leightons were in and, if so, would be prepared to talk to her about their daughter. Mr Leighton was at work, but the lady of the house was in and received her call. Poppy introduced herself and was surprised (and pleased) that Mrs Leighton said she was a regular reader of the Women in the Workplace column and would be happy to speak about June and her career. So, Poppy dropped off the address with Rollo so he could make enquiries with the neighbours, and then headed off to meet Mrs Leighton for eleven o'clock tea.

The Leightons lived in a four-storey townhouse off Berkeley Square. A maid answered the door and ushered Poppy through the house and into the small, walled back garden where the black-clad figure of Mrs Leighton waited. "I thought we'd have tea in the garden. It's such a lovely sunny day," she said, as she greeted Poppy.

Poppy shook the grieving mother's cold hand and decided not to remove her coat.

"That will be lovely, thank you."

After the maid served them tea and fruit cake, Mrs Leighton said, "So, Miss Denby, where did you hear about my June, and why do you want to feature her in your column?"

Poppy wiped away some crumbs from her fingertips and answered, "Firstly, Mrs Leighton, may I say how sorry I am for your loss. And thank you for agreeing to see me. Where did I hear about June? It was through a mutual acquaintance – Sophie Blackburn – who worked with June in Oxford. Did you ever meet Sophie?"

Mrs Leighton thought for a moment and said, "A strongly built woman in her forties? Brown hair? Spectacles?"

Poppy nodded. "Yes, that's Sophie."

Mrs Leighton nodded in return. "I think she was at the funeral, yes. There was a woman of that description who came with Professor Sinclair. She introduced herself, but" – she gave a wan smile –"there were lots of faces and names and, well, I wasn't at my best."

Poppy smiled kindly. "That's totally understandable, Mrs Leighton. But yes, that sounds like Sophie. She is an acquaintance of my aunt, Dorothy Denby. I met her again – after not seeing her for a few years – at a lecture the other evening at the Royal Institution. She" – Poppy paused for a moment, remembering that she had decided not to mention the accusation of murder, and considered her phrasing – "she invited me up to Oxford to see her new workplace. And it was there that she mentioned June and her terrible accident. She'd only worked with her since January, but she tells me she had immense respect for your daughter and said she was a meticulous and gifted scientist. And she would know. You see, she previously worked with Madame Curie in Paris."

Mrs Leighton perked up at the mention of Marie Curie. "My word, that is impressive. Is your friend a chemist or a physicist?"

Poppy wasn't quite sure of the difference between the two. "I must confess, I don't know. I am not familiar with the different scientific terms. But I do know she's a laboratory assistant."

Mrs Leighton looked momentarily disappointed. "Ah, so not degreed then."

Poppy shook her head. "No, I don't think so. She was a nurse in London – before the war – then worked out on the Western

Front, I think. It was there that she met Madame Curie and her mobile X-ray machines on the battlefields. After the war, she moved to Paris to help Madame Curie. She learned on the job at the Radium Institute. I visited her there once. And I got the impression that she's very experienced and knows her onions. I believe Professor Sinclair thinks very highly of her. Just like he did of June..." She trailed off, hoping to redirect Mrs Leighton's attention away from Sophie's lack of academic credentials.

The mother took a sip of tea, put down the cup, and said, "I suppose it's not your friend's fault. Not many of us ladies have had the opportunity to read at university. And it's only very recently that they started conferring degrees... which is why I was so proud of June... and why, no doubt, you want to write about her."

Relieved, Poppy let out the breath she hadn't realized she'd been holding. *Good.* Mrs Leighton was coming back on track.

"Exactly that," said Poppy brightly, then realized her tone was perhaps a little too cheerful for the circumstances. She moderated it and said, "Yes, I'm always interested to highlight successful women where I can. And – although June is sadly no longer with us – I still thought she would make a very interesting subject for my column."

Mrs Leighton smiled weakly, her pale green eyes lit for a moment with a flicker of remembrance. "June would have wanted to, I think. Oh, she would have been shy – she was always reluctant to push herself forward – but at the bottom of her she was ambitious and proud of it. I know it's not considered a desirable feminine trait, Miss Denby, but I think ambition is something that should be encouraged in young women, don't you?"

"Most definitely," said Poppy, relieved that on this subject she was speaking to a kindred spirit. She looked around for a moment at the beautifully kept garden and wondered what ambitions Mrs Leighton might have harboured as a young woman. "So," she said, "why did June go into science? Did she inherit her interest from you?"

Mrs Leighton sat up straight and proud. "Actually, yes. My father was a physician. And my grandfather an apothecary. I was always fascinated with the chemicals in his shop when I was a little girl. My governess, though, only taught the so-called 'feminine' subjects like French, art, and music. However, my brother had a tutor who taught him mathematics and the sciences. I would sneak into his lessons and soak up as much knowledge as I could. When my father found out, he was cross at first, but then discovered that I had much more of an aptitude for it than my brother. He then formally employed the tutor to teach me too. I was so good at it that he encouraged me to take the entrance exam for the London School of Medicine for Women, at the Royal Free Hospital. I got in!"

Poppy's eyes lit up. "So you're a doctor! I'm sorry; I didn't realize. I should be interviewing you for the article too."

Mrs Leighton sighed, leaned over the table, and topped up their teacups. "Unfortunately not. You see, after my first term of study I met my husband-to-be, Mr Leighton, and when we got engaged, it was agreed that I should no longer pursue my studies or my profession."

Poppy's heart sank with disappointment. "And you were happy to go along with that?"

Mrs Leighton looked at Poppy through a stray strand of hair that had escaped from her bun. "Not happy, no. But it was a different age, Miss Denby. I didn't really have a choice. Which is why I encouraged June to follow an academic path as far as it would take her."

"And Mr Leighton? Did he approve of June's chosen field?"

Mrs Leighton plucked a sugar cube from the bowl with a pair of ornately engraved silver tongs. "He did not mind. June, like me, has – had – an older brother. Larry has followed his father into the family business. June, I'm afraid, was surplus to requirements. He always allowed me to indulge her – as he put it – while he focused all of his attention on our son."

Poppy was beginning to sense a whole well of frustration in Mrs Leighton, despite her outer poise. "I see," she said. "So, you encouraged June in her interest in science and then, no doubt, to take the entrance exam to Oxford. Tell me what happened then." Poppy reached a hand into her satchel to grab a pencil, then stopped herself and asked, "Do you mind if I take notes?"

Mrs Leighton agreed and then proceeded to tell Poppy all about June's illustrious time at Oxford. How she earned a place at Somerville College. How she studied under the best tutors and professors. How she outshone the few women science students and nearly all the men. How chemistry was her forte. How she achieved a distinction in her final schools. How she went on to be recruited by the world-famous Professor Sinclair as his graduate student, and how she was so passionate about the new and exciting field of crystallography.

When she was finished, Poppy took out the photograph Sophie had given her of the crystallography team and laid it on the table. "My friend, Miss Blackburn, gave me this." She pointed to Sophie. "That's her there."

"Yes," said Mrs Leighton, "that's the woman I saw at the funeral."

"And that is Professor Sinclair?" asked Poppy, pointing to the oldest man in the photograph.

"It is," said Mrs Leighton. "He had a choice of six top graduates, and he chose June."

"That must have made you very proud," said Poppy. "So, it must have been a little upsetting when he said what he said to the newspaper..." Poppy took out the clipping from *The Times* and offered it to Mrs Leighton.

The older woman looked down the bridge of her nose but didn't take the clipping in hand. No doubt she already knew what it said. "Yes, it was a little upsetting. I expected that from Raines," she pointed to the other senior scientist, "but not from Sinclair. He had always been so very supportive of June. And held her work in very high regard. He wouldn't have taken her on otherwise."

Poppy nodded sympathetically. "Perhaps just a slip of the tongue."

Mrs Leighton smiled tightly. "Perhaps."

Poppy turned a page in her notebook, then crossed and recrossed her legs. "So... you said you expected that from Dr Raines. Why is that?"

Mrs Leighton looked up sharply. "Why do you ask?"

"Oh, no reason. It's just that you are the second person to tell me that. Miss Blackburn also mentioned that Dr Raines – and his assistant – were not always on the same page as June."

Mrs Leighton's eyes narrowed. "She did? Why would she say that?"

Poppy sensed the growing tension and realized she needed to quell it. Quickly. "Oh, no reason really. She was just telling me how much she – and Professor Sinclair – respected June's abilities. And how regretful she was that Dr Raines didn't seem to appreciate June's worth. Which is why she suggested I might do an article on her. She mentioned in passing that there might have been a bit of jealousy from some of the other men. Which – I'm sure you know, Mrs Leighton – is not unusual when women manage to show some aptitude in a normally male-dominated field."

Mrs Leighton's shoulders relaxed. "You're right, Miss Denby; it's not unusual."

"Did it bother June much? Did she mention it to you – this animosity at work?"

Mrs Leighton shrugged. "Now and then. She said she thought that Miles – the other graduate student – was lazy and sometimes took credit for her work."

"Yes, I heard that too. Did she mention anything about an article in the journal *Nature*?"

The older woman's eyes narrowed again. "She did, actually. You seem to know an awful lot about this, Miss Denby."

Poppy gave what she hoped was a winsome and trustworthy smile. "I like to do my research."

A chill wind whipped up the edge of the tablecloth. Mrs Leighton looked at her wristwatch. "Well, hopefully, Miss Denby, I've given you everything you need to write a fulsome article in June's memory. Now, if that is all..."

Poppy realized she was being dismissed. But she still had one more question.

"It is. Almost. I was just wondering why you have not mentioned June's fiancé?"

Mrs Leighton's eyes opened in surprise. "Fiancé? June was not engaged to be married. Who told you that?"

"Oh, gosh, I'm sorry; I must have misunderstood. Miss Blackburn told me there was a fiancé. A young man, possibly from around here..."

Mrs Leighton stood up, waiting for Poppy to do the same. "No, absolutely not. Your friend must have been mistaken. Now, thank you for your time, Miss Denby. I look forward to seeing the article when it's finished. Would you like a portrait photograph of June? I'm sure I have something more suitable than that one."

"Yes, thank you. I'd appreciate that very much." Then, Poppy snapped her notebook shut.

CHAPTER 7

Poppy returned to the office, her mind swirling with questions. Why had Mrs Leighton denied the existence of a fiancé? She had seemed almost offended by the question and, in Poppy's estimation, was definitely not telling the entire truth. What did she have to hide? On the bus ride back to Fleet Street, Poppy had considered that Sophie might have been wrong about the fiancé, but so far everything else the laboratory assistant had told her (other than the possibly nefarious circumstances around June's death) had been confirmed by the grieving mother. Poppy had chosen not to broach the subject of the means of death, feeling it would have been crass to do so. However, she had hoped that Mrs Leighton herself might have mentioned the cause of the accident and was disappointed that she had not. So, Poppy was no wiser about whether or not Sophie's suspicions were well founded or even shared by June's family. She had, though, been right about the tension between June and her male colleagues and the deceased woman's belief that her fellow graduate student had stolen (or at least copied) her work. Poppy now felt more justified to pursue this angle.

But what about the non-fiancé? Assuming that Sophie had not just imagined it or got the wrong end of the stick, why had June told her she was engaged? Or perhaps told someone else who had told Sophie... Was June engaged or not? And if she was, why had her mother denied it? Had the young scientist kept it secret from her mother, perhaps worried about how she might react? Poppy had got the distinct impression that Mrs Leighton regretted giving up her medical studies to get married and would not want June to do the same.

Poppy felt the ring on her finger with the edge of her thumb. She was grateful she didn't have to worry about that anymore. She knew that it was still expected that professional ladies would give up their jobs when they got married. In fact, in some key professions, like teaching, it was legally mandated that they did so by a "marriage bar". Which was why, she was well aware, there were so many spinster schoolteachers – women who had chosen their jobs over marriage. It saddened her that they had been forced to make that choice. She would have to do some checking, but as far as she was aware, the marriage bar didn't apply to laboratories or universities. Not legally, anyway. And of course, she smiled, as she stepped out of the lift on the second floor of *The Daily Globe* building, no one had thought of extending it to journalism.

She and Daniel had finally worked out their differences on this some time ago. When she had first met him, he had held more traditional views about women and work, which had led to a fair bit of conflict in their relationship. But once he had come to terms with the fact that she actually wanted to carry on working if or when they got married – and, eventually, had come around to wanting her to as well – there was still the complication of who would look after his young children. She had always felt that she would be expected to. However, five years later, the children, now eight and eleven, did not need such close attention, and besides, she and Daniel now both earned enough to pay for a housekeeper and a nanny. That would free her to keep on working. At least until she became pregnant. *Golly*, thought Poppy, *when might that be?* Poppy honestly did not know what she would do then. On the one hand, she had the example of Rollo's wife Yasmin, who had gone straight back to work as soon as she could, but she was not

Yasmin. She felt that she might like to stay home with the children for a while... How long that while might be she wouldn't know until she got there. But for now, she wouldn't have to worry about it. And if she could successfully apply the anti-conception advice she'd been gleaning from Marie Stopes' books *Married Love* and *Wise Parenthood*, she wouldn't have to worry about it for a lot longer yet.

Poppy giggled to herself, remembering some of the racier chapters of *Married Love*, as she opened the door to the art and photography department just as Daniel stepped out of the dark room at the rear of the office. "And what are you smiling at, Miss Denby?" he asked.

"Nothing!" She flushed. Fortunately, her embarrassment was soon swept away on a wave of congratulations from Daniel's colleagues, including some good-natured ribbing of the groom-to-be. Once it settled, Daniel ushered Poppy to his desk in the far corner near the dark room, surrounded on three sides by shelves of camera equipment. On his desk, overlooking a scatter of photographs and newspaper flatplans, was a photograph of his two children, Arthur and Amy, with their mother Lydia. It had been taken when Amy was only a few months old, and, only a few months after that, Lydia was to die of the Spanish Flu. Poppy did not resent Lydia's presence on Daniel's desk or in his memories, but she did hope that one day she too might be framed and given pride of place. Daniel had taken many photographs of her, but none, as yet, had made it to public display. She imagined that now they were officially engaged, that might change. Or perhaps after their wedding... She pulled herself back to the present. There was work to do. And this was first and foremost a workplace.

She took a seat and retrieved the photograph of June Leighton given to her by Mrs Leighton. It was taken on the day of the young scientist's graduation, and she stood smartly and proudly in her academic gown, clutching her scroll. "Are you able to make a couple of prints of this, please?" asked Poppy. "I've just been to see June's mother, and she has loaned this to me but wants it back as soon as possible."

"You've just been there now?" asked Daniel.

Poppy said she had and proceeded to tell Daniel what she had found out.

Daniel nodded encouragingly. "It sounds like you've got enough to justify a story, don't you think?"

Poppy agreed. "Yes, I think there's more than enough for the Women in the Workplace column. I'll just have to run it past Rollo first, but I think he'll agree. I'm also intrigued about this 'missing' fiancé too."

"Yes, that does sound curious," observed Daniel. "Someone's not telling the truth: either June or her mother. Either way, it suggests there's something worth digging into."

"I agree," said Poppy. "Or, alternatively, Sophie could have got the wrong end of the stick, or..." She paused, feeling guilty for contemplating what she was about to say, but knowing that it must still be said. "We cannot discount the possibility that Sophie might be getting her own situation mixed up with June's. Emotionally."

"Meaning?" asked Daniel.

"Meaning, that if there was no fiancé, and if June had not misled her, then Sophie could have been getting her own life and that of June confused. Let's not forget that she spent some time in Willow Park Asylum – if what Rollo told us was correct. She might still be suffering the after-effects of her nervous breakdown. We all know that she is still hurting about Bert's death. But if I recall, it's more complicated than that. Hadn't their engagement been broken off *before* his death? And hadn't she been trying to rekindle their relationship with him just before he died?"

Daniel nodded. "Yes, I think that's what happened. But we don't know for sure. And it turns out that everything else she told us on Saturday was true."

"Everything?" asked Poppy.

"Well, not the murder."

"Not *necessarily* the murder," said Poppy.

Daniel leaned back in his chair and tapped his finger to his chin. "Are you saying you believe her, Poppy? That June was murdered? But at the same time, you're contemplating that Sophie might have made up an imaginary fiancé?"

Poppy sighed, remembering the earnestness with which Sophie had shared her suspicions about the young scientist's death. "I don't know, Daniel. But I have a sense, particularly after speaking to June's mother, that there is more to this story. Whether it will lead to anything as sensational as a murder, I don't know yet, but there's something there. And I think Sophie's instincts on this – that there might be more to June's death than the official findings – might prove to be true. And I also know that just because someone has had nervous or mental problems, it doesn't mean everything they say and do should be dismissed. But we do have to be careful to unpick what's true and what's imagined. To be honest, I don't know enough about Sophie or her condition to be sure she's *not* telling the truth. But I think I know enough about her to believe that she might be. Does that make any sense?"

Daniel leaned forward until their foreheads were nearly touching, then lowered his voice to an intimate whisper. "Oh yes, Poppy, it does. And I know enough about you to know that you *will* manage to unpick this. And that's one of the very many things I love about you."

"Oi, lovebirds! Get back to work!" came the voice of one of Daniel's colleagues, accompanied by laughter from the rest of the office.

Poppy and Daniel pulled apart.

"Right," said Daniel. "I'll see what I can do with this photograph."

"Thank you," said Poppy, standing up and smoothing down her skirt. "Can you bring it upstairs when you're finished?"

"It will be my pleasure, my lady."

CHAPTER 8

TUESDAY 21 APRIL 1925, OXFORD

The general ground plan of our physiology is told to us in youth because it, so obviously, is right for us to know it accurately and in a clean scientific way, rather than to be perpetually perplexed by fantastic imaginings. But the physiology of our most profoundly disturbing functions is ignored – in my opinion, criminally ignored. To describe the essentials, simple, direct and scientific language is necessary, though it may surprise those who are accustomed only to the hazy vagueness which has led to so much mis-apprehension of the truth. Every mating man and woman should know the following. . .

"Next stop Oxford, ladies and gentlemen! Oxford next stop!"

Poppy slammed shut her copy of *Married Love*, disguised inside the dust jacket of Charles Dickens' *Great Expectations*. She took a deep breath, hoping the heightened colour in her cheeks would not cause her fellow passengers to suspect she was any more than stirred by the great novelist's prose.

Half an hour later, and quite exhausted from carting her suitcase all the way across town, she was checking into the Cherwell Hotel. Poppy hadn't realized that the train station was on the far side of Oxford from where the hotel – which she had first noticed on the day Daniel proposed to her – was situated. The well-to-do Victorian establishment, on the opposite bank to the Botanic Garden, was at the end of Cowley Place, next door to St Hilda's College. She and Daniel had gone there together for a celebratory glass of champagne after the big moment and sat on the terrace to watch the final overs of the cricket match. So, when she and Rollo had discussed that she should spend a few days in Oxford following up the Leighton story – and that the paper would be prepared to foot the bill for moderately priced accommodation – she knew exactly where she would stay.

However, in retrospect, when she remembered that her main inquiries were to be centred around the heart of the city and university – a fair walk from where she was – she chastised herself for allowing her heart to override her head. But a solution was to be found in the line of bicycles outside the ivy-clad building and the framed notice in reception that the two-wheeled vehicles could be hired for the duration of her stay.

Poppy had only recently learned to ride a bicycle on a fun-filled weekend with Daniel and the children. Daniel and the two youngsters took to it like ducks to water, but Poppy needed hours more practice before she could keep the contraption in a steady line. Not to mention, she remembered with a wince, that her undercarriage had protested for days. Nonetheless, seeing nearly everyone else in Oxford rode one, Poppy thought she'd give it another go. So, after depositing her suitcase in her room, having a spot of lunch on the terrace, and listening to the tuneful bells of Magdalen Tower, she paid her dues and hired a bike.

The bike keeper watched, half-amused and half-alarmed, as she wobbled up and down Cowley Place before she finally felt confident enough to head off into town. The hotel had provided her with a map and the bike keeper had given her verbal directions, so she felt fairly confident of where she was going. Over the bridge the High

Street was busier than she had hoped it would be, and her heart was in her mouth on more than one occasion, before she managed to turn into the quieter alleys of the old university. She followed the route that Daniel had taken the previous Saturday and this time stopped to admire the breathtaking Radcliffe Camera library and the exquisite spires of All Souls College, with the famous sundial by Sir Christopher Wren. Thereafter, she pushed her bicycle through the hallowed pathways of the Bodleian Library until she was on Broad Street, being observed from above by the stern gaze of the stone Caesar heads circling the Sheldonian Theatre.

Across the road was Blackwell's Bookshop and the White Horse Tavern, and next door to the Sheldonian, the Old Ashmolean Museum, which, Sophie had told her, housed the laboratory where June Leighton had worked. Poppy found a space to park her bicycle, making sure she memorized its shape and colour so she wouldn't lose it in the throng; but then, for good measure, she tied a red ribbon from her hair to the handlebars.

Yesterday afternoon, after deciding with Rollo that she would come up, she had sent a telegram to Professor Sinclair at the Old Ashmolean, informing him to expect a visit from her. She had not waited for a reply so had no idea how she would be received. She and Rollo had decided that she should continue writing the article for the Women in the Workplace column until or unless further information emerged that justified writing another kind of story.

Poppy straightened her skirt and walked up the stone steps to the main entrance of the museum. Sophie had told her that the Ashmolean collection had been moved many years ago and that up until recently, the old building had been used as spare office space for the publishers of the Oxford English Dictionary. But the previous year it had been refurbished and opened as the Museum of the History of Science. The artefacts were housed on the first and second floors, while the ground floor was used for public lectures and talks. The basement, however, was used for laboratory space. Apparently, in less enlightened times it had been utilized by medical students to study the anatomy of corpses, until students and librarians in the nearby Bodleian had complained about the smell and shut the practice down. These days, according to Sophie, the place was nicknamed "the Crystal Crypt" by the scientists who worked there, due to the tomb-like stone walls and the crystallography work that went on within its confines.

Inside the museum entrance hall, she was greeted by a bored-looking porter behind a desk who asked her for a shilling donation for the upkeep of the museum. She paid it, telling him that she wasn't actually there to visit the museum, but Professor Sinclair. She braced herself, ready to justify why she wanted to speak to the scientist, but the porter didn't seem to care. He pointed her through some doors and told her to go down the stairs, before returning to his newspaper.

Poppy made her way through the double doors at the back of the foyer and into the sun-soaked stairwell. The light was coming from an exquisite stained-glass window but dimmed as Poppy descended into the bowels of the building. A series of stone-flagged rooms, bare of the wood panelling of the upstairs halls, presented themselves to Poppy at the bottom of the stairs. Directly in front of her was one with an inscription above the door in medieval lettering: OFFICINA CHEMICA. Poppy didn't know much Latin, but she assumed that it had something to do with chemistry.

She stepped through the doorway into what was obviously a laboratory, full of scientific apparatus and a number of people in white coats. One of them, a wide-eyed Sophie Blackburn, stepped towards her. Poppy was just about to say "Hello, Sophie" when Sophie whipped her finger to her lips and said, "Good afternoon, miss. Are you lost? If you're looking for the museum, it's upstairs."

Poppy immediately got the message that Sophie did not want their association to be known and played along. "Good afternoon. No, I'm not lost. At least I hope I'm not. I'm looking for Professor Sinclair. I sent a telegram yesterday informing him that I would be visiting."

The other occupants of the laboratory, all men, stopped working and listened in on the conversation.

"Ah, then this way, please; I'll take you to him." Poppy meekly followed Sophie out of the laboratory, back into the stairwell. Each step of the way she was aware of the men watching her go. There was something disturbing, almost predatory about it, as if she were a small animal who had accidentally stumbled into a carnivore's lair. As they rounded the corner, Sophie hissed, "What are you doing here?"

"I'm following up on the story. I thought you'd be pleased," Poppy whispered.

"You should have told me. I would have made arrangements."

"I'm sorry. I didn't realize I needed to. I said I'd ask Rollo if I could continue working on the story and he said yes. I was just about to tell you now. I hadn't realized you would want to keep it all a secret."

Sophie stopped, her back against the wall, out of sight of the men in the laboratory. "For a renowned investigator, you're rather dim. Why would I want my work colleagues to know that I suspect them of murder?"

Poppy bristled. "For heaven's sake, Sophie, give me some credit. I wasn't going to mention the murder – or even the suspicion of murder. I am here to write an article for my Women in the Workplace column. I've spoken to June's mother and this is a follow-up on that. If anything more comes of it, well and good, but for now that's all I'm here for. And that's what I told Professor Sinclair in my telegram yesterday. It's an article in memoriam."

"Fine," hissed Sophie, but clearly it was anything but fine. "Prof Sinclair's through there. I'll meet you at five o'clock in St Giles' churchyard. You can find out for yourself where it is if you're such a hotshot detective. And make sure no one follows you."

Poppy sighed. "Fine," she said, matching Sophie's tone. Sophie glared at her and returned to the laboratory.

Professor Sinclair was seated at a desk in another stone-flagged room that had been converted into an office. Above him, a wrought-iron spiral staircase wound its way up to a wooden balcony which surrounded the small room, housing leather-clad books and shelves of microscopes and other fancy brass instruments. Light came from a single window on the mezzanine above. James Sinclair was a man in his sixties, of medium build, with stooped shoulders and a bald pate as shiny as the brass of his scientific instruments. He pushed back his spectacles to rest like antennae on his head and stood as Poppy appeared in his doorway. His clothes appeared a size too big for him, as if he had recently lost weight.

"Ah, Miss Denby, I assume. I got your telegram. I have just replied asking if you would rather come next week, as we're a tad busy. But obviously it's missed you."

"Good afternoon, Professor Sinclair. Poppy Denby of *The Daily Globe*. I'm sorry if I've inconvenienced you."

"Not at all, not at all. I'll just juggle things around a bit." He looked over his shoulder at his desk with a slightly rueful expression, before turning back to Poppy with a polite, welcoming smile.

Poppy smiled in return as Professor Sinclair pulled out a seat for her and gave it a flourish with his handkerchief, like an old-world gentleman. She took the seat, putting her satchel on the floor beside her.

"Your telegram said you'd spoken to Mrs Leighton and you want to do an article in June's memory. Is that correct?"

"It is. I write a monthly column for the *Globe* called Women in the Workplace, and when I heard about June I knew she would make a perfect feature. I'm only sorry I heard about her after her tragic death. How terrible for one so young."

The professor nodded in sympathetic agreement. "Yes, it was – a terrible tragedy. June had such immense potential. She had a fine scientific mind. Made even more remarkable by her being of the fairer sex."

Poppy remembered what Sophie had said about Sinclair: he had some old-fashioned ideas but was still supportive of women. "Do you mind if I take notes?" asked Poppy.

Sinclair nodded. "Not at all. The more forensic, the better."

"So," said Poppy, with pencil poised, "why did you hire June Leighton as your research assistant? I believe you were her DSc supervisor too. Is that correct?"

"It is," said Sinclair. "She was in some of my undergraduate lectures and stood out from the class by her intelligent questions. Then, I was asked to take her on for tutorials. Now, I'm not sure if you know how the college system works here, Miss Denby, but it is not very common for academics from one college to supervise students from another. Although it's not unheard of. I am from Balliol – that's just down the road here – and June is – *was* – a Somerville girl. Somerville is one of the four ladies' colleges here at Oxford, and it has only been since 1920 that the girls could be conferred with a degree. It only has a couple of science tutors – both competent academics and more than adequate for your average science undergrad – but June was far from average. So, the Principal of Somerville asked me if I would take her on. Now some fellows here – I mean that in both a male and faculty sense – refuse to take women on. By Jove, some of them are still spitting teeth that the ladies were admitted to Convocation at all!"

Poppy had no idea what "Convocation" was but wrote it down phonetically the best she could. Sinclair was on a roll and she didn't want to interrupt his flow. She nodded to him encouragingly to continue. "So, you took June on?"

He nodded. "Yes, halfway through her second year. Then saw her through her third year and schools. She graduated, unsurprisingly, with an uncontested first. The best *viva voce* I've ever heard!" Sinclair glowed like a proud parent.

Poppy smiled. "She sounds like a remarkable young woman. I'm not surprised you had no hesitation taking her on in the laboratory."

Sinclair frowned, picking at a splodge of ink on his blotting pad with a fingernail. "Well, it wouldn't be entirely true to say I had 'no hesitation'. To be frank, I did have some."

"Oh?"

"Yes, there's one thing to support a woman in an academic environment, but another out in the professional world. You see, Miss Denby, there is still a lot of ill-feeling and, dare I say, unfounded prejudice against ladies in science. Even though the likes of Marie Curie and Martha Whitely have done well – one of them won a Nobel Prize, for heaven's sake – there is still a reluctance to employ them in laboratories or to allow them on research teams. After all, scientific advancement requires funding. Funding needs to be applied for. And if there is prejudice against women team members, then that funding might not be forthcoming. So, I must confess to being in two minds about taking June on. There were a number of male candidates in consideration too; candidates who would not have raised as many eyebrows with the funders. But in the end, I decided to go with her. She was working on some groundbreaking ideas. I wanted to see that come to fruition."

Poppy circled the word "prejudice" on her notepad. She was wondering whether or not to raise the issue of the professor's chauvinistic comments in the news report she'd read. She didn't want to antagonize him, as he was freely sharing information with her, but it was something that was nagging at her gut. And if Poppy had learned anything in her years as an investigator, it was to listen to her gut. She cleared her throat and adopted a non-judgmental air. "That is lovely to hear, Professor Sinclair. You clearly hold June – and other talented women – in high regard. Which is why, if you don't mind me saying, I was surprised to read your comments in *The Times* about the accident being caused by her 'youthful exuberance and feminine stubbornness'. What exactly did you mean by that?"

The professor lowered his head so Poppy had a good view of his polished pate, renewing his interest in the ink splodge. Then, he sighed and looked up at Poppy, shame written all over his face. "I'm afraid, Miss Denby, I would give a thousand pounds to take those words back. They didn't translate well to the page."

"Are you saying you were misquoted?"

Sinclair shook his head. "I'm afraid not. But I was misconstrued. I meant it as a compliment. June was youthful and exuberant in her work. And stubborn. But those were qualities that invigorated her approach to science. If she hadn't been so passionate and dedicated – on reflection the words I *should* have used in that interview – she might not be dead now."

Poppy nodded. *Yes*, she thought, *they would have been better words. But hindsight is a wonderful thing.* "All right, I understand that. It's difficult sometimes to get the right words on the spur of the moment. And under such fraught circumstances. Perhaps, though, you might consider a letter to the editor to clarify your comments? Mrs Leighton, I know, is a little hurt by them."

Sinclair's jowls dropped, making him look even more shamefaced. Eventually, he cleared his throat and said, "That is a very good suggestion, Miss Denby. I might do that. Now, if there is nothing else..."

Poppy shook herself. How silly of her to knock him off topic like that. Yes, it would be nice of him to correct the misunderstanding, but it wouldn't help her get to the bottom of the incident. And now he was calling time on the interview.

"Well, actually, Professor, there are a couple more things. When you say that it was her passion and dedication that got June killed, what do you mean?"

Sinclair jutted out his chin. "I didn't say that, Miss Denby. I suggest you check your notes. I said she might not be dead now."

Poppy did check her scribbled shorthand. "You're correct, Professor; that is what you said. But it means the same thing."

"It does *not* mean the same thing. Forensic accuracy is important. I used the incorrect words last time I spoke to a journalist and I shall not make the same mistake again."

Poppy smiled tightly, her lips compressing into a straight line. "All right, point taken. Nonetheless, that does not clarify what you meant by your comment. In what way did June's passion and dedication contribute to her death?"

Sinclair's fingernail was once more worrying the ink spot. "I only meant that if she had not been so dedicated to her work, with a positively feminine sense of devotion, and fuelled with the energy of youth, she might not have been working on a Sunday night when everyone else was at home. She would not have been here alone."

Poppy nodded, making a good show of taking *forensic* notes. "I see. And what, may I ask, actually caused the accident? What were the physical circumstances around it?"

Sinclair's hands clenched into fists and then released. "Nothing more than was reported in the press. A surge of electricity. June was electrocuted."

Poppy made another note, although she did not need to. Then she tapped her pencil on her pad. "But what *caused* the surge, and how did June become the victim of it?"

Sinclair cocked his head to the side. "Why does that matter to you, Miss Denby? I thought this was an article about ladies in the workplace – an homage to June's professional accomplishments – not a blow-by-blow account of her death. What newspaper did you say you work for again?"

"*The Daily Globe.*"

"A tabloid."

"Yes, a tabloid. So, you were saying, there was a surge of electricity and..."

Sinclair slapped his hands down onto the ink pad. "I think, Miss Denby, that's all I have to say. As I mentioned earlier, we are very busy. Thank you for coming to see me and good luck with your article. I'll see you out." He stood, his body language brooking no disagreement.

Poppy slipped her pencil into her notebook and closed it, picking up her satchel as she stood. There was no use pushing her luck any further. Besides, she had already got more than she needed from the interview – not so much in what Sinclair *had* said, but what he hadn't.

Poppy's newshound nose twitched.

CHAPTER 9

Poppy left the Crystal Crypt without popping her head back into the laboratory – although sorely tempted. Sophie had made her discomfort in being identified as an "associate" of Poppy clear. Just as well she hadn't mentioned the lab assistant in her telegram to Professor Sinclair! So, Poppy decided, she would do as Sophie asked and meet her at five o'clock in St Giles' churchyard. It was a pity, though, as Poppy would have liked an opportunity to speak to the other members of the laboratory team who both Sophie and Mrs Leighton had suggested had been antagonistic towards June. She would just have to find another way to do so when Sophie wasn't there. They could discuss tactics later.

Poppy collected her bicycle with the red ribbon tied to the handlebars and, after consulting her map, made her way to the Post Office on St Aldates Street. She was growing more confident riding the contraption and arrived at her destination – without incident – just as the clock on Tom Tower struck four o'clock. Poppy parked her bicycle, booked a telephone booth, then put in a call to Rollo in London. She explained to him what had transpired in the interview with the professor, as well as Sophie's continued erratic behaviour.

"So," said Rollo, "despite her being a bit off her rocker, you still think she's on to something about June's death? That it might not have been an accident?"

"I do," said Poppy. "The professor was evasive when I asked him how June died, and a bit defensive. He seemed genuine enough in his regret that she'd died, but I got the feeling that he was covering something up."

"Do you think he did it?" asked Rollo.

"I wouldn't go that far, no, and it still might be the case that no one actually 'did it'. But I do think he knows more about the circumstances of the accident than he's letting on. I'd be interested to see what he actually said to the police in his interview. As well as the pathologist's report. Do you have any inside contacts I could use here?"

"I don't, sorry Poppy. Definitely not with the local constabulary. I have met the *Oxford Gazette* editor, briefly, but I believe he's just retired and headed off to sunnier climes. I'll make a couple of calls, but there's no guarantee I'll get anywhere. But I'll give it a go. For now, though, you're on your own."

Poppy perked up. "Does that mean I can stay on?"

"I'll give you another day. If you don't have anything concrete by close of play Wednesday, then come back down to London. Is that a deal?"

Poppy nodded into the phone, as if Rollo could see her. "That's fair enough. I'll see what I can do. Oh, by the way, have you made any progress finding out about June's fiancé from the neighbours?"

"Not yet," said Rollo. "I'm still on it. But I have made some progress finding out about Sophie's time at Willow Park Asylum."

"Oh?"

"Yes. I'm meeting with someone for lunch tomorrow."

Poppy frowned to herself. "Is that *ethical,* Rollo? Getting someone to talk about a patient's private medical record."

"Probably not." Poppy could almost hear the shrug in her editor's voice.

She sighed. "All right. But I'm not sure what difference it will make. Even if Sophie is 'off her rocker', as you call it, I still think she might be on to something here."

"Then prove it," said Rollo. "And keep in touch."

Rollo hung up before Poppy had a chance to ask him if Daniel was around. It had been a whole day since she'd seen him, and she was missing him already. She consoled her sorrows with a cream tea in a cafe next door to the Post Office until it was time to get on her bicycle and head up to St Giles. If she read the map correctly it was on the same road as St Aldate's, past the new Ashmolean Museum and near Somerville College. *Somerville College?* Wasn't that where June had been a student? *Hmm, interesting.*

St Giles' churchyard was crammed into a triangular area where St Aldates Street – which then became Cornmarket, then Magdalen Street, then St Giles Street – forked into Woodstock and Banbury Roads. She parked her bicycle along with a dozen or so others against the railings on the Woodstock side and headed towards the entrance of the twelfth-century Norman church as its bells rang to call the faithful to Tuesday evensong. Poppy stepped aside so as not to be swept into the chancel and looked around the grounds to see if she could spot Sophie. And there she was, smoking a cigarette while seated on a stone bench under a darkly brooding yew. One or two of the parishioners cast disapproving glances at the smoking woman, but Sophie was unmoved. Poppy walked over to join her.

"Good afternoon, Sophie."

"Afternoon. You find it all right?"

"I did, thank you. The hotel concierge was kind enough to give me a map."

"I see you're on a bike. Best be careful you don't get knocked off."

Poppy thought this was stating the obvious but nodded her agreement anyway.

"So," she said, "I've spoken to Rollo on the telephone at the Post Office, and we've agreed that I can give it another day. I need to give him some proof of foul play in June's death by this time tomorrow evening or else I must head back to London."

Sophie pursed her lips so tightly around the cigarette that Poppy thought she might have to prise them loose. She eventually released her grip, exhaling the smoke in an explosive puff.

"So, my word isn't enough?"

Poppy spotted a black smudge on her stocking that looked like bicycle oil and frowned. "Unfortunately not. But after my chat with Professor Sinclair, I think you are right to be suspicious."

Sophie didn't quite smile, but there was a slight twitch at the corner of her mouth.

Poppy waited for her to speak, but all she got was a frank stare, suggesting an unspoken *go on*.

"So," continued Poppy, "as I said to Rollo, Sinclair seemed to be genuinely distressed at June's death and regretful of his comments to the newspaper, which he tried to justify—"

"He would do," interjected Sophie.

"But he was evasive and defensive when I asked him to describe the circumstances of June's accident. Unnecessarily so, I thought. If it was an accident, then why not just say what happened?"

"Why indeed." Sophie stubbed out her cigarette, then reached into the pocket of her grey mac and pulled out another one.

Poppy waited for her to light up and then continued. "So, I've decided that I need to find out more about that to see whether or not there's anything concrete to go on. I want to try to get a look at the police pathologist's report. Is that something you can help me with?"

Sophie shook her head brusquely.

"All right, I'll go to the police station tomorrow. Do you know the name of the investigating officer?"

Sophie shook her head again.

Poppy sighed. "It should be in the local news report. I'll go to the library tomorrow morning and read a copy. Then I'll go to the police station. Do you know where the public library is? Not the university library, the one for ordinary folk?"

"Corner of Aldates and Blue Boar Lane." Sophie jutted her cigarette in the direction from which Poppy had ridden her bike. "If you know where the Post Office is, it's near there. Opposite side of the road. Attached to the City Hall."

"And the police station?"

"Back end of the City Hall. Entrance further down Blue Boar Lane. Easy to find."

"Well, that's convenient."

Sophie rewarded Poppy with a flicker of a smile.

"Good. Then I'll go there tomorrow morning. I'll also need to speak to someone at Somerville College who might have known June. I assume that's where she lived?"

Sophie nodded. "Yes, she still had rooms there. Not many postgraduates do – they're normally expected to move into their own digs to make room for the new girls – but June did a bit of tutoring work in the college, so they let her stay on."

"Well, that's good. I'll go there tomorrow as well. Whom should I speak to? Any idea?"

Sophie took a drag on her cigarette and exhaled. "The principal is a woman called Gertrude Fuller. Dr Gertrude Fuller."

"What is she a doctor of?"

Sophie shrugged. "Nothing important. Foreign languages I think."

Poppy, who, apart from a smattering of French tourist phrases, did not speak any foreign languages herself – and always admired people who did – thought this rude and dismissive but by now was unsurprised by Sophie's demeanour. She had been much the same the first time they had met in Paris five years earlier. Poppy had wondered for a while if Sophie had become like this due to the grief of losing her fiancé Bert, but Aunt Dot, who had known Sophie for nearly twenty years, assured Poppy that she had always been direct and forthright, bordering on rude.

Poppy took out her notebook and wrote down the name Gertrude Fuller.

"Right," said Poppy, "that should keep me going for a while." With her notebook open she perused the notes from her meeting with Professor Sinclair, stopping at a circled note. "Sophie, how exactly *did* June die? I know you said electrocution, and that's what it said in the newspaper, but I'd like to know exactly *how* it happened. That's what I was hoping Sinclair would tell me, and that's when he got defensive. Do you know any more about it? Anything?"

Sophie took another drag on her cigarette. "Not much, really. It was on a Sunday night, when the Crystal Crypt was closed."

"How did she get in then?"

"There are a few keys circulating between the scientists. Keys to the outside basement doors, not the museum proper. All four of them would come in at different times if they were working on experiments. Sometimes in the middle of the night if they couldn't sleep. Or early in the morning."

"So, it wasn't unusual that she was there on a Sunday night?"

"It was, in that none of the current experiments were at a crucial enough stage to warrant out-of-hours visits. Nothing that warranted overtime."

"What was she working on?"

"She'd been investigating the molecular structure of thallium dialkyl halides."

"What's that?"

Sophie gave her a withering look. "It's a chemical compound."

"Oh," said Poppy, no more enlightened than she had been before. "So, was June doing an experiment with this – this – compound when she died?"

Sophie shook her head. "No, that was the strange thing. She had been growing thallium crystals and X-raying them, but when her body was found there was a diamond in the tube, not thallium."

"A *diamond*?" said Poppy, her voice rising with excitement.

Sophie shook her head dismissively. "It's not as exciting as you think. Diamonds are often used in crystallography laboratories. It's one of the first compounds that students work on, under supervision of course. It's a simple form. Which is why it's so strange. Why would June – a DSc graduate and an already very experienced scientist – be X-raying a simple diamond?"

Sophie looked enquiringly into Poppy's eyes.

Why indeed? thought Poppy. "Was there anything special about this diamond?"

Sophie shrugged. "Not that I could tell. But I didn't get a proper look at it."

"Where are they normally kept?"

"In Professor Sinclair's office, I think. He has a strongbox. But they aren't very expensive diamonds. They are really just diamond chips. Industrial grade. No use for jewellery."

"Still worth a bit though."

"Well, yes, but if you're thinking jewellery heist here as a motive, you'd be on the wrong track."

"All right," said Poppy, hiding her disappointment. Yes, she *had* been thinking jewellery heist...

She gathered herself and refocused. "All right, so it's not the value of the diamond that's of interest, but the simplicity of it in scientific terms. Is that correct?"

Sophie raised an eyebrow, and once again Poppy discerned a flicker of a smile. "That's right. Sinclair suggested that she might have been preparing a lecture for the new term but wasn't sure why she needed to take X-rays, as there were already plenty of plates available to show students. And why she had to come in on a Sunday evening to do so – a month before the new term started – no one could fathom."

Poppy nodded and made some notes. She didn't understand the science stuff here, but she did understand that something was out of the ordinary. And in her experience, something out of the ordinary always demanded further investigation.

"So," she said eventually, "her actual death. How did the electrocution take place?"

Sophie leaned back and stretched her neck, twisting it from side to side, then pushed up her spectacles onto the bridge of her nose. "Somehow she got tangled in the cables that plugged the X-ray machine into the wall. The cable was torn out of the machine. The exposed wires were found burned into the palm of her hand."

"She grasped the exposed wires while they were still plugged into the wall? Why would she do that?"

"My question exactly, Poppy. Sinclair and the police seem to believe that she got tangled, fell, ripped out the cable, and grasped the wires in a panic."

"And you don't?"

"Why would I? It's a stupid thing to do. And June was not stupid."

"No, from what everyone has told me about her, she was anything but that."

Sophie finished her cigarette and stubbed it out on the churchyard path with her heel just as St Giles' choir burst into four-part harmony. "I'm glad you're beginning to believe me, Poppy. Hopefully you'll be able to find out more than I have. Have you got somewhere to stay?"

Poppy was pleased at the softening of Sophie's tone. "Yes. I'm booked into the Cherwell, thank you. I was going to stay overnight anyway. But I might extend it depending on what I find out tomorrow. Do you live nearby?"

"Not far," said Sophie. "But I don't have room for guests." Her tone was once again terse.

"That's not a problem. As I said, I've got a room in a hotel. Do you want to meet again tomorrow?"

"Yes. Here at the same time."

"That sounds good. Do you have plans for dinner?"

"I do. Goodbye." Sophie stood up abruptly and walked off.

Poppy chuckled to herself, shaking her head.

CHAPTER 10

WEDNESDAY 22 APRIL 1925, LONDON

Rollo Rolandson cursed colourfully and loudly as an omnibus ploughed through a puddle and drenched him from the knees down. The umbrella he carried to ward off April showers had saved his top half, but his trousers and shoes were well and truly soaked. He contemplated going back to his office to change but decided against it. Dr Theo Dorowitz had told him he only had an hour to spare, as he was due back at his Harley Street practice for an appointment with a society heiress who was having trouble with her nerves.

Dorowitz was a German Jew who had done his postgraduate medical studies at Harvard – Rollo's alma mater. Dorowitz's mother was British and he held dual German/British citizenship. After the war he had settled in London and set up a psychiatric practice on the prestigious Harley Street, bringing with him the new techniques of psychotherapy that were so popular in his native Germany. He also worked part-time at Willow Park mental hospital where he studied some of the more extreme cases of mental disorders, which provided material for his research.

Rollo had met Dorowitz at his London club back in '22, and the two men had bonded over their love of whiskey, their weakness for poker, and their reminiscences of Harvard. Rollo had not initially intended to court Dorowitz as a source, but when discovering that after having a few drinks the psychiatrist often let slip some juicy titbits about his celebrity clients – never mentioning names but giving enough clues that anyone who followed society gossip could figure out who was meant – Rollo realized his friend was a rich vein of information for a tabloid journalist's stock in trade.

Rollo waited for a gap in the traffic, careful to step well back from the puddle that had just caught him, and crossed the road to Ye Olde Cock Tavern, where he and Dorowitz had agreed to have lunch. He took a moment to squeeze out the turn-ups of his trousers, wishing it was winter so he could sit near a fire to dry out, before pushing open the door of his favourite watering hole.

The barman nodded to him as he entered. "Your usual, Mr Rolandson?"

"Thanks, James. Not this time. I'll just have a pint of bitter – and a towel." He gestured to his wet trousers as he took off his mackintosh, lifted it on the point of his umbrella, and hung it on the coat rack that towered above him. He then did the same with his bowler hat.

He spotted Theo Dorowitz at the back of the tavern, then scooped up the towel the barman passed to him and dabbed at his trousers while waiting for his pint.

"Don't worry, Mr Rolandson; I'll bring it over. Dr Dorowitz is having a beef and onion sandwich. What can I get you?"

"The same, James, but double up on the beef."

Slightly dryer, and looking forward to his beer and beef sandwich, Rollo sauntered over to join Theo at the table. The doctor wiped away some mustard from his mouth with a napkin, then stood and thrust out his hand. Rollo noted, not for the first time, the psychiatrist's impeccably manicured nails, so different from his own cracked and inked fingertips. The men shook hands warmly and Rollo climbed up on the vacant chair.

Theo gestured to his half-eaten platter. "Sorry, old man; I thought I'd get a head start. I've got to be strict on time today." He spoke English with a mixed German and American accent. Rollo suspected the American twang was exaggerated in his company.

"That's all right, old sport; I've got work to do myself. But thanks for agreeing to see me at such short notice. I could really do with your help."

Theo gave him a chastising look. "I hope you're not going to try and pump me for information on who I'm seeing this afternoon. My clients pay me to help them get their heads straight, not to get into the papers. And after that last little slip of mine at the club – too much whiskey, I'm afraid – I have to be more careful."

Rollo gave him a wide-eyed innocent look that fooled neither of them. Then he grinned. "Well, in your defence, Theo, you never actually used Lady Langford's name."

"And yet somehow you knew who I was talking about."

Rollo laughed. "I'd make a great psychoanalyst."

Theo laughed in return. "You would indeed. Before we know it, you'll be telling me everything's your mother's fault."

Rollo, who actually did have problems with his mother – a eugenicist who had never forgiven him for being born a dwarf – took the comment with a pinch of his customary salt. As he'd never spoken to Theo about his childhood, he very much doubted the comment had any subtext. So, he just grinned, adding, "Or that it's all about sex."

Theo chuckled. If the psychiatrist realized he'd struck a nerve, he gave no indication. "Seriously Rollo, I can't do it again. My clients will stop trusting me."

Rollo waited a moment for the barman to put down his pint and beef sandwich, took a sip of the head, then wiped away the froth from his upper lip with his inky forefinger. "And I'm not asking you to. What I'm asking is personal, nothing to do with the paper. Well, not entirely. It's got something to do with someone who used to work for the paper. Someone who died that I feel responsible for. Call it unresolved guilt, if you will. And your client will not get into the paper, I swear. Unless she wants to."

"She?"

"Sophie Blackburn."

Theo leaned back in his chair. "Sophie Blackburn? Really? Well, she's not actually my client. Not a paying client, anyway."

Rollo leaned forward, fixing his friend with his best interrogative stare. "But she was a patient. You treated her; I know you did."

Theo threw up his hands. "All right, all right. Yes, she was a patient. A ward of the state. I was asked to treat her at Willow Park. How did you know I've worked with her though?"

Rollo leaned back and shrugged. "A newspaperman never reveals his sources."

Theo looked suddenly nervous. "Dammit, Rolandson, I didn't say anything the other night at the club, did I? I hadn't drunk *that* much..."

Rollo grinned, tempted to play his friend along, but realizing time was ticking away. "No old sport, you didn't. But I pay one of the cleaners at Willow Park to tell me who she sees going in and out of there. And one of the names that came up – oh, a good few months back now – was Sophie Blackburn. And she told me she was one of your patients. I never mentioned it before because I never had need to, but now I do. Because I think she might be in trouble – or is causing trouble that might do her harm in the long run – and I owe it to my old pal Bert to keep an eye on her."

Theo's eyes narrowed. "Why, what's she done now?"

Rollo went on to tell Theo about the visit he'd received from Sophie the previous fall, how disturbed and distressed she still was about Bert's unsolved death, and how she had recently resurfaced again to rope his star reporter into a possibly imagined murder investigation.

"So, what I need to know from you, Theo, is how crazy she really is. Do you think it's possible she could have fantasized this whole Oxford murder to somehow compensate for Bert's killer never being found?"

Theo finished chewing the last of his sandwich before answering. "You mean, is it transference."

"If that's the psycho lingo, then yes. Could it be transference?"

Theo brushed the crumbs off his fingers with his napkin, then took another sip of his beer.

"It's possible, yes. When I first met Sophie, she was under restraint. The police had brought her in under court order. She had been stalking someone for a few months – sending him threatening letters, following him in the street, turning up at his office and demanding he 'tell the truth' about what happened to your pal Bert."

Rollo's eyes widened. "Is this someone, by any chance, a fella called Lionel Saunders? A reporter who works for *The Courier*?"

Theo nodded. "Yes. He's the man she blames for Bert's death."

"I know."

"Well, it seems she finally snuck into his flat and threatened him. He was saved by his neighbour across the street who saw her through the window – behaving erratically – and alerted the police. Saunders is a weedy fella and Sophie's a big woman. When the police got there, she didn't go down without a fight."

Rollo shook his head. "I can't believe this. It was never in the papers."

"Saunders didn't want it in the papers. In fact, he didn't even want to lay charges. He told the police and the magistrate that she was delusional and needed to be put in an asylum, not prison."

Rollo raised his shaggy eyebrows in surprise. "And the magistrate agreed with him?"

"Yes, he issued a court order to have her sent to Willow Park for treatment."

"For how long?"

Theo templed his fingers in front of him. "Just for three months. But this would have been extended if her psychiatrist recommended it."

Rollo cocked his head to the side. "And you didn't."

"No. She made sufficient progress in that time for me to think she was no longer a threat to herself or Saunders. And as she was there as a ward of the state, there were limited funds to pay for her upkeep."

"So, it was a financial decision to release her?"

Theo shrugged. "Partially, yes, but I wouldn't have let her go if I thought she was a genuine danger. Also, her release was conditional. If she was seen within ten feet of Saunders again, she would be arrested."

Rollo took this in. "All right, can you tell me then why you thought she was well enough to be let go, but now you think she might be confused enough to make up an imaginary murder?"

Theo drummed his fingers on the table, contemplating how best to phrase his response. After a while, he said, "Have you heard of a psychiatrist called Eugene Bleuler?"

Rollo shook his head.

"Well, Bleuler worked with patients who were schizophrenic – commonly referred to as 'split personality'. Back in 1912 he produced a paper in which he referred to a certain set of symptoms as 'autism' – from the Greek to mean 'caught up in the self'. He noticed some patients, during their quiet, withdrawn state, to be emotionally cut off from people, finding it difficult to socially relate or understand other people's emotions."

"Are you saying Sophie is schizophrenic – that she has different personalities?"

Theo shook his head briskly. "Not at all. If anything, Sophie is very fixed in her personality. Almost inflexibly so. You see, I haven't published anything on this or done extensive research, but I have seen other people like Sophie in my time in asylums – people who I don't believe are schizophrenic but who display some of the same fixed, inflexible personality traits, with the same difficulties in social situations. What Bleuler called 'autistic' behaviour. They come in varying degrees of severity – some of them, particularly children, can be almost completely non-verbal, unable to speak. Others, like Sophie, are able to communicate, are sometimes uncannily clever, but are burdened with difficulties establishing and maintaining relationships. They become obsessive about things. And most of them – on the milder end of it – have a tendency to be fixated on the need for justice. If they believe something is unjust, they just cannot let it go. They crave order in the world, which makes them feel secure, and an unresolved injustice knocks their world out of order. Justice must be enacted in order for equilibrium to be restored.

"Now, a lot more work will need to be done on this, and frankly I don't have the time. But for now, I will give you this poor man's diagnosis. I think Sophie is one of these people. She's not schizophrenic; she does not have *splits*, as it were, in her personality, but she does show these 'autistic' characteristics. And I think it's the lack of justice that is driving her, and will continue to drive her."

Rollo finished his beer, raised his glass to the barman to indicate a refill, then turned back to Theo. "Very interesting.

Yes, I know exactly what you mean about her being fixed and inflexible. And yes, I see the drive for justice in her. But that's not always a bad thing, is it? My reporter, Poppy Denby, has the same compulsion, and she's not mentally imbalanced."

Theo raised his forefinger. "Ah, I didn't say Sophie is mentally imbalanced. I honestly don't think she is. Which is why I agreed to have her released. But she does sometimes struggle to let go of things. And yes, a quest for justice can be seen in lots of different kinds of people. But in Sophie, with her particular personality make-up, it can be self-destructive."

"Self-destructive? Not destructive of others? You don't think she'd try to destroy another person? Even though she threatened Saunders?"

Theo shrugged. "I don't think so. She wanted to get him to confess, but she didn't want to kill him. And Saunders himself didn't feel threatened enough to lay charges."

"Are you sure about that, Theo?"

Theo shrugged again. "I wouldn't bet my mother's life on it, but that's my hypothesis. I didn't have that much time with her. It was a pro bono case. She was a ward of the state." The psychiatrist looked pointedly at his watch.

Rollo understood. Theo was offering him an educated guess, not a definitive diagnosis. "All right," he said, "thanks for your help. But just one more thing before you go. You said you think she might have made the Oxford murder up."

Theo shook his head. "Not fabricated it, no. But she could have inferred meaning where there was none. She might have read something into the situation that she wanted to see, rather than what was really there. She might have been frustrated in her attempts to lay Bert's death to rest, so is seeking closure another way. But I can't say for definite without speaking to her again. Or knowing all the details of this Oxford death." He looked at his watch again and stood up. "Sorry, Rollo, but I've got to go."

Rollo nodded and stood too. The men shook hands.

"Thanks for your time, Theo. You've given me lots to think about. And don't worry, I'll pick up the tab."

Theo grinned. "Well, that'll be a first!"

Rollo chuckled as his friend left the tavern. But as he settled down to drink his second pint and mull over what he'd just heard, he couldn't shake the feeling that there might be a lot more going on in Oxford than either he or Poppy realized. And that worried him. It worried him a lot.

CHAPTER 11

WEDNESDAY 22 APRIL 1925, OXFORD

Poppy called to the waiter to ask for a refill of tea. She had just finished her kippers and poached egg and was rounding off her breakfast with a slice of marmalade on toast. She was one of a dozen guests in the breakfast room of the Cherwell Hotel, with ceiling to floor windows overlooking a sloping lawn that led down to the River Cherwell. On the riverbank, the boatswain, who had been busily cleaning down the punts with a mop, stopped to look up at the sky. The clouds over Oxford were darkening – it looked like it might soon rain. Poppy decided to wait and see how the weather developed before heading out for her first appointment. Rollo had sent a telegram first thing this morning to say he'd been in touch with *The Oxford Gazette* and the new editor, a Mr George Lewis. Mr Lewis had said he would be happy to receive her any time before lunch. So that left most of the morning free.

Consulting her map, she discovered that the *Gazette*'s offices were on Walton Street, in the Clarendon Press buildings, which was in the general vicinity of Somerville College. She could telephone ahead to Somerville and ask to see the principal on her way to the newspaper office. What was the name of the principal again…? Poppy consulted the notes she'd made during her meeting with Sophie the previous evening. Ah, there it was – Fuller, Dr

Gertrude Fuller. Yes, Poppy needed to speak to Dr Fuller. But she also needed to speak to the police pathologist. She doubted she could just wander into the police station and demand to see him. Perhaps the *Gazette* editor could make introductions for her?

Poppy made a few notes relating to the order of interviews she needed to conduct, then turned her attention to June Leighton's laboratory colleagues. She really needed to speak to Miles Mackintosh, the other DSc student, as well as his supervisor, Dr Raines. So far, they seemed to be the people with the most animosity towards June, and if Sophie were correct, and foul play had occurred, then they were top of the list of "most likely suspects". Of course, Sophie might be quite wrong, and Poppy was keeping an open mind about it all. Still, it would be very useful to speak to Mackintosh and Raines.

Oh bother, thought Poppy. *I should have thought this through a bit more before blundering in there yesterday. Now I don't have a good reason to interview the other men.* Poppy was furious with herself. She realized that she had been distracted, thinking more about Daniel and fantasizing their future together than giving serious thought to how she should conduct herself professionally. Sophie was right – she really should have talked it through with her in advance. Now she wondered how on earth she was going to manage it all and couldn't quite see a way through. She sighed. *Focus on what you can do, old thing*, she chided herself and finished her toast and tea.

After breakfast, Poppy asked the concierge to put through a call to Somerville College. She was encouraged that Dr Fuller not only was in and available but said she would be honoured to speak about June for Poppy's Women in the Workplace column. Poppy had decided that that was still the best cover for her investigation, largely because it was true. She *did* intend to write something about June as a professional woman. If it turned out that the story became bigger, then so be it. But for now, it was best that she hide in plain sight.

After putting down the telephone, Poppy checked the weather and decided that the light drizzle should not deter her from riding her bicycle. Fortunately, the weather had put off some of the other cyclists, and the roads were much clearer than they had been the previous day. Twenty minutes later, arriving at Somerville College, Poppy realized why. Her stockings and the hem of her skirt were sodden and muddy, and her shoes squelched as she walked. *Oh bother.*

The porter at the gate greeted her politely and asked her if she had mislaid her galoshes. She bit her tongue and huffed to herself. *Another thing I never thought of in advance...*

The porter led the way through the portico and into a quadrangle, carrying a large golfing umbrella that protected them both from the now persistent rain. Poppy imagined the green lawns on a sunny day, speckled with young women talking and reading. Poppy had never considered higher education for herself. She wasn't sure why. Perhaps it had been that back then she had never personally known anyone, other than her father, who held a degree. Perhaps it was because it wasn't the sort of thing most women did – although that hadn't stopped her getting a job as a journalist. Perhaps it was that when she finished school when she was sixteen (two years later than many of her female peers), almost none of the pupils at her school were going on to tertiary education – not even the boys. It was 1914 and the universities were losing most of their students to the war effort. Including her brother. Christopher had been accepted to read Law (as their father had once done) at Durham University. But he never took up his place. He never lived to do so.

Poppy wondered for a moment what she might have read if she'd had the opportunity to be accepted into such a prestigious institution as Somerville College. Certainly not science, like June Leighton. She had never been very good at mathematical thinking – although she was curious, very curious, and from what she'd learned so far about scientists, that was an essential characteristic. Perhaps English literature. Hadn't the novelist Dorothy L. Sayers studied here? Poppy did enjoy reading books. And writing. But what would she *do* with a degree? Teach? She shuddered at the thought. No, she did not regret one bit not following an academic path. Her job at the newspaper was a perfect fit for her, and she was eternally grateful to have it.

Dr Gertrude Fuller, housed in a spacious, book-lined suite of rooms in the far corner of the quadrangle, welcomed her with a concerned look and a warm smile.

"Goodness, Miss Denby, you look like a drowned rat! Come in, come in!"

Ten minutes later Poppy was sitting cradling a mug of hot cocoa with a blanket over her knees, while her skirt, stockings, and shoes were drying in front of a small single-bar electric heater. Dr Fuller's swift action upon seeing the sodden woman at her door suggested a caring, motherly attitude. Poppy was pleased: firstly for herself, as she'd feared an intimidating, intellectually superior character, but also for June. She hoped the young woman's years at the college had been happy ones and, for the purposes of the investigation at hand, that the young scientist might have confided in the college principal.

"Thanks awfully for drying me out, Dr Fuller. Seems I came out quite unprepared!"

"Not at all, Miss Denby." She had a slight Northern Irish lilt. "Now, what can I tell you about June?"

Poppy felt herself relax. After the difficult start to the investigation, first dealing with Sophie then with Professor Sinclair yesterday, she'd felt more than a bit rained on. And of course, the interview with Mrs Leighton had not been a walk in the park either.

She smiled appreciatively, put down her mug on the little side table, and then reached into her satchel to retrieve her notepad and pencil. "Well, Dr Fuller, as I said on the telephone, I'm doing an article on June for a column I write for *The Daily Globe* in London. In it I like to highlight the achievements of professional women. I heard about June – sadly, only posthumously – but I thought she was a remarkable young woman whose achievements needed to be known more widely."

Dr Fuller, a plump red-headed lady in her early sixties, with large, tawny eyes behind round spectacles, smiled sadly. "Yes, she is greatly missed by us all. She was just at the start of a very promising career. In years to come, I wouldn't have been surprised if she were mentioned in the same breath as Marie Curie. She was that brilliant."

Poppy nodded. "Yes, that's what Professor Sinclair suggested too. He said she was one of the most remarkable students he'd ever had."

Dr Fuller cocked her head to one side. "You've spoken to James Sinclair?"

Poppy paused a moment, trying to read the principal's tone. She wasn't sure of it, so decided to proceed cautiously. The warmth of the fire and the hot cocoa should not lull her into complacency.

"Yes, I have. I saw him yesterday."

"Hmmm."

Poppy raised an eyebrow, inviting further comment. Nothing came.

"He was very complimentary of her."

"Was he now?" That was better, there was a definite "tone" now. A tone that suggested, "I don't believe a word you're saying."

Poppy leaned forward. "You sound like you don't believe me, Dr Fuller."

The academic held her hands together as if in prayer. "Oh no, Miss Denby, not you. It is not you I don't believe; it is Professor Sinclair. If he told you how much he supported June, then he's a barefaced liar."

"Oh? Why is that? As I said, he was very complimentary of her, and even her mother – Mrs Leighton – said that he had opened doors for her. I'd be curious to know why you feel differently."

Dr Fuller rested her hands against her ample belly, like a mother protecting her unborn child. "Well, Mrs Leighton is right; he did open doors for her. He coached her through her undergraduate degree and then took a great risk by taking her on as his DSc student, when there were a number of male candidates for the position."

"Candidates that would have pleased the laboratory's financial backers?"

Dr Fuller once again cocked her head to the side, her large eyes behind the round spectacles reminding Poppy of a tawny owl. "I see you've been doing your research. Yes. There were a number of male candidates whom the Sanforth Foundation would have preferred."

Poppy made a note of the name of the Foundation. It was the first time she'd heard it. She would need to follow up on that, but for now, she wanted to press Dr Fuller more on Professor Sinclair's attitude to June.

"I see," she said. "And yet you hold that he didn't support her. Why is that?"

Dr Fuller pursed her lips. "Because, Miss Denby, he chose to overlook considerable bullying at the laboratory. I cannot tell you how many times June sat in that very chair, drinking cocoa from that very cup, telling me how awful those men were to her."

"Those men?"

"Raines and Mackintosh."

"And Sinclair?"

Dr Fuller shook her head. "No, he wasn't unkind to her. But he didn't help her either. Academically, he did, of course. But not personally. And not professionally. She put in numerous complaints to him about their behaviour and he failed to act. And now she's dead. He has to take responsibility for that."

"Are you saying, Dr Fuller, that Raines' and Mackintosh's bullying led to June's death?"

"I am. If June had not been so harassed by them, day in and day out, she would not have felt the need to work in the laboratory after hours to avoid them. She would not have been on her own. And if she hadn't been there on her own, someone might have been able to save her. She wouldn't have..." Dr Fuller's voice cracked with emotion. "Oh dear, I'm sorry."

Poppy reached out her hand and placed it on the older woman's shoulder. "That's all right. I understand. June was very fortunate to have someone like you looking out for her."

Dr Fuller shook her head. "No, no she wasn't. I didn't do enough for her. She was a Somerville girl. One of *my* girls. I should have taken it higher than Sinclair. I should have done more to protect her."

Poppy nodded sympathetically, then said, "I understand how you're feeling. But perhaps you can do something now."

"What do you mean?"

Poppy tapped her pencil on her pad, wondering how to phrase her next comments. Eventually she said, "Perhaps, Dr Fuller, we could use this article to bring the bullying to light. Is that something you think you could help me with?"

Dr Fuller composed herself and looked Poppy straight in the eye. "What do you have in mind, Miss Denby?"

"Two things. Firstly, would you be able to write down some of June's complaints? What she told you happened with the bullying?"

Dr Fuller shook her head. "No need to. I have carbon copies of the letters I sent to Professor Sinclair on June's behalf. The letters he failed to act upon. I'll get them for you in a moment. And the second thing?"

"The second thing is that I need to speak to Miles Mackintosh and Dr Raines. But I'm not sure how to go about it. You see, I gave Professor Sinclair the impression that I was simply writing an obituary of June, and that at the end of our interview, there was nothing more I needed. It was silly of me. I should have thought it through better in advance, but it was only when I spoke to him that I got the impression that there might be more to the story. And that's why I'm still here in Oxford."

"Oh?" Dr Fuller's eyes narrowed behind her spectacles. "What more do you think there might be?"

Poppy, who had already decided not to mention Sophie, or her suspicion of murder, still felt she could entrust the college principal with more information. "Well," she said, "Mrs Leighton told me that June had accused Mackintosh of plagiarism. That he'd stolen her ideas. But Professor Sinclair didn't mention that when I spoke to him and became very defensive when I tried to probe deeper into the manner of June's death. Were you aware of the plagiarism accusation, Dr Fuller?"

Fuller nodded. "I was. In fact, I was busy helping June formulate an official complaint to the Academic Disciplinary Panel at Mackintosh's college – Balliol – before she died."

Poppy raised her eyebrow. "Really? Had you submitted it?"

Fuller shook her head. "Unfortunately not. We hadn't got that far. June blew hot and cold about it. Initially, when she read his paper in *Nature* and realized it was based largely on her own work, she went to Sinclair, who tried to dissuade her from taking it any further. He said the laboratory didn't need the drama of two feuding DSc graduates. He said he would have a word with Raines and Mackintosh to ensure it didn't happen again and assured June that she would have further opportunities to publish her research under her own name. June was angry that he wasn't going to back her, but said that she felt that without his help she wouldn't get far with her complaint. And she was right. I spoke to Sinclair myself, but he wouldn't budge from his position. But then, about a week before she died, she came to me and asked me to help her put in a formal complaint after all. I said I would, but I was very busy at the time and hadn't made much progress."

"Why did she suddenly change her mind?"

Dr Fuller shrugged. "She didn't say. But she was very upset about something. Very upset indeed. So naturally, I agreed."

"But you didn't actually file the complaint?"

The principal's shoulders sagged. "No. There was no point after she died."

This surprised Poppy. "Really? Why not? Surely she could still receive credit for her work posthumously."

Dr Fuller sighed. "Yes, she should. But it will be hard to do that without her testimony to the Panel."

Poppy nodded her understanding. "I see that. Which makes me want to write this article even more. But I will need to speak to Mackintosh and Raines. Do you have any idea how I might go about that? Could you make introductions on my behalf?"

"I'm afraid as June's mentor I am persona non grata with those two. They know that I tried to help her with the plagiarism complaint. However" – Dr Fuller tapped a plump forefinger against her lips – "I think I might have an idea. But I don't think you're going to like it very much, Miss Denby."

"And why's that?"

The principal looked embarrassed. "You are a very attractive woman, Miss Denby, with your blonde hair and blue eyes and lovely figure. And I'm sorry to typecast you like this, but you appear – on the outside – to be just the type of woman that men like Mackintosh and Raines would find appealing."

Poppy blinked in disbelief. "Good heavens, Dr Fuller, are you suggesting I use myself as bait?"

"Yes. That's exactly what I'm suggesting. You see, this evening there's a formal dinner dance at Balliol. I am invited but I was not going to attend. However, I could still go. And the invitation specifies that I may bring a partner. The assumption is, of course, that it would be a male partner, but if you don't mind causing a bit of a scandal, you could accompany me instead."

Poppy grinned, imagining the scene. "Golly, Dr Fuller, that *would* be scandalous. But I'm game if you are."

The principal of Somerville College grinned back at the young woman. "Oh yes, I'm game. And please, call me Gertrude."

Chapter 12

Oxford smelled freshly washed as the limestone buildings shook off the last droplets of rain. The downpour had stopped by the time Poppy collected her bicycle from the porter's lodge at Somerville College. She confirmed with the gentleman the best route to her next appointment, which took her round the block and onto Walton Street, a mere two minutes' ride away. Poppy was careful to avoid puddles, so by the time she entered the foyer of *The Oxford Gazette* she did not look like a drowned rat.

She gave her name to the receptionist and a few minutes later was seated in the editor's office. She smiled to herself, comforted by the messy piles of newspapers, scattered flatplans, and photographs. She sniffed in the acrid smell of newsprint and let out a contented sigh. This was familiar territory. And although Poppy had never met George Lewis, the editor, he too was a familiar sight. His grey shirt sleeves were pushed up at the elbows by arm garters, his faded tie, once – possibly – navy blue, was off-centre, and Poppy could see one of his shirt buttons was missing. His black braces clung valiantly to a pair of charcoal flannel trousers which sported a limp white handkerchief dangling from one pocket. He grinned at Poppy, wiped his hand on his trousers, and thrust it towards her.

"Miss Denby, I presume." He spoke with an Edinburgh accent.

"Mr Lewis, thank you for agreeing to see me."

The two shook hands warmly and the editor indicated she should take a seat.

"Not a problem at all. Got a good few hours to deadline yet.

Your editor – Mr Rolandson – is a bit of a legend in the trade. We've not met yet, but I hope to rectify that soon enough. I'll be down in London for the Press Association dinner next month and hope to bump into him."

"I'm sure he'd be delighted to meet you. He'll be the fella with the whiskey tumbler."

"Scotch?"

"Of course!"

"Good man!" Lewis chuckled, his salt and pepper moustache bouncing up and down on his top lip, before settling back down. "Now then, Miss Denby, how may I help you? Rolandson said you are writing a story on June Leighton."

"That's correct," she said. "I write a monthly column called Women in the Workplace and I heard about June's tragic death. As she is originally from London – and her parents still live there – I thought it worth writing something about her as an aspirational career woman."

Lewis raised a sardonic brow. "A bit off your patch for a women's column. Does your editor usually let you travel out of town for days on end to get copy for it?"

"Not usually. But we thought the circumstances of June's death made it a bit more newsworthy."

George Lewis' eyes sparkled. "Aha. So there *is* more to the story. I suspected as much. You don't get phone calls from Rollo Rolandson unless there's something sensational afoot. So, what's your angle, Miss Denby?"

Poppy shrugged, trying to appear nonchalant. "Nothing more than I've told you, Mr Lewis. It's a simple article for a monthly column."

Lewis leaned forward, his amiable smile disappearing under a frown. "Oh, I very much doubt that, Miss Denby, and if you want my help you will have to come clean."

Well then, thought Poppy, *you've got another thing coming, Mr Lewis. I don't need your help that much.* However, she realized that antagonizing the editor would not help her cause either. So she said, with her most charming smile, "All right Mr Lewis, you've got me. There is a touch more to it. But I can't tell you just yet. I'll tell you what, though – I promise to share any information with you that pertains to Oxford or the university so that we can have a simultaneous release of stories. I'll obviously have to pass that with Mr Rolandson, but I'm sure he can be persuaded. How does that sound?"

Lewis' smile was back. "It sounds like you're stonewalling me, Miss Denby, but I'll go along with it for now. If it weren't for the fact that we have separate readerships so are not in direct competition, I would not be so accommodating. I hope you understand that."

"Oh, I do, Mr Lewis. I certainly do. And I would never try to tread on your turf – as the Americans would say."

Lewis nodded his approval. "I'm very glad to hear that." He leaned back in his chair and gestured around the messy office. "The thing is, Miss Denby, I've only been on the job two weeks. The June Leighton story was the last one my predecessor worked on before he left. I got the feeling that it was a rushed job. That he could have done more with it, but I didn't feel that it would have been politic for me to say so at the time. Harris was on his way out – and let's just say his motivation had retired long before his body. Now don't get me wrong, he was a good newspaperman in his day, but during the war the paper lost its edge. It was not thought patriotic to be too critical of anything. And that carried on after the war too. Oxford – as a town and as a university – almost shut down. Most of our halls were turned into hospitals. So, when the war was over there was a sense that we all needed to work together to rebuild. Harris was on board with that, and the *Gazette* became a cheerleader for Town and Gown working together for the greater good. Nothing wrong with that, of course, but the result was that sometimes stories that might reflect poorly on the university were swept under the carpet, or diluted in some way."

Poppy nodded her understanding. "And you think that's what happened here? That it was swept under the carpet?"

Lewis shrugged. "I can't say that for sure. But I do think that if there were anything, it would have been missed in the hurried way it was reported and then spiked. I mean, it's not every day that a scientist – and a female scientist at that – is electrocuted to death in a laboratory nicknamed the Crystal Crypt, now is it?" He grinned.

"You should be working for a tabloid, Mr Lewis," chuckled Poppy. "But sensational headlines aside, do you think there was anything substantial that was overlooked in Mr Harris' reportage?"

Lewis stood up and walked across his office to a filing cabinet. He opened it, riffled through some folders, and pulled one out – a very slim one. He passed it across the desk to Poppy. "You tell me, Miss Denby. Feel free to look through Harris' file on it – for what it's worth. I must confess to not having done so myself. It's been one of those things niggling at the back of my mind, though. And when Rolandson rang me this morning, I wasn't entirely surprised that it was June Leighton he was asking about. But I *will* hold you to your promise."

"And I shall keep it," said Poppy.

An hour later and Poppy left the *Gazette*'s office with a page full of notes. The Harris file had been a rehash of what she'd already seen in the press – mainly quoting Professor Sinclair, blaming June's youthful exuberance for the accident, and all but absolving the university or the laboratory of any responsibility. There was also an interview with the head of Somerville Old Girls (an alumni group), which was just a string of platitudes of how proud they had been of June and how saddened they were to have lost one of their own. There were brief notes on an interview with Dr Gertrude Fuller, saying much of what Poppy had heard that morning about the bullying June endured – and a circled note next to it saying, "axe to grind, ignore". Only one quote from Dr Fuller made the final story: "June Leighton was Somerville's Marie Curie. She is a huge loss to the college, the university, and the field of research science."

There were brief notes about June's academic background – what she studied, when she graduated, and so forth, as well as which extra-mural societies she participated in (chess and photography). However, two things caught Poppy's interest. The first was a note that the police pathologist, a Dr Dickie Mortimer, had smelled strongly of liquor when Harris spoke to him outside the Crystal Crypt and was a tad unsteady on his feet. Poppy wondered if the pathologist had been drunk when he examined the scene. And if so, what had he missed?

The second thing was just a single sentence: "Funding issues: are the Sanforth Foundation at it again?" *At what again?* Poppy wondered and resolved to find out more. Gertrude Fuller had also mentioned the Sanforth Foundation. She would ask the principal more about it at the dinner this evening. *Golly!* thought Poppy. *I have nothing to wear to dinner!* So, she decided to take a spin past some dress shops before returning to the hotel for lunch. She had remembered passing a large department store opposite St Mary Magdalen's Church on the ride up to Somerville that morning. She checked her map to confirm directions and within a short time had arrived outside Elliston & Cavell Ltd. It had a similar feel to Selfridge's in London where she sometimes shopped, and she noted with approval the price tags on some of the frocks modelled in the window displays. Good quality, but not priced beyond her means. She parked her bicycle against the railings of St Mary Magdalen's and crossed the road.

Half an hour later Poppy came out of the shop, happily carrying a parcel wrapped in brown paper and string. She put it in her handlebar basket, climbed on, and headed along Broad Street towards her hotel for lunch. As she passed the Science Museum, she spotted Professor Sinclair and another gentleman waiting to cross the road towards the White Horse Tavern. She didn't attempt to wave, partly because she was not confident enough on the bicycle to do a one-hander, and partly because she wasn't exactly on first-wave terms with him. As she approached the intersection with Catte Street, she had a sense that there was someone else on a bicycle behind her. Being a new rider, she felt an inexplicable clench in her stomach, worried she would be judged on her cycling ability and etiquette. She made an overt gesture with her hand, indicating a right-hand turn, and was inordinately relieved that she made it through the intersection without incident. Letting out a long breath, she chided herself for her silliness.

Five minutes later she was approaching Magdalen Bridge with the entrance to the steep cobbled slipway down to the river on her left. She began visualizing the luncheon menu: a nice piece of trout and new potatoes with lashings of butter and a side of spinach and carrots... Suddenly she felt the bike lurch into a small pothole. She lost balance, corrected herself, then realized she was off the road and heading down the slipway towards the river – and a collection of punts moored to a jetty. She tried to brake but nothing happened. With growing terror, she faced the stark choice of throwing herself off the bicycle and doing herself an injury on the cobbles, or getting a good soaking in the river. She chose the latter.

As she flew off the edge of the jetty she let go of the bicycle and landed unceremoniously in the thigh-deep water, narrowly avoiding a bobbing boat. She let out a gasp; then, as soon as she realized she was not about to drown – or die of hypothermia – she checked that her hat was still on and splodged towards the ill-fated bicycle to snatch the brown paper package before it sank in the shallows. "My new dress! Got you!"

"Good heavens, miss, are you all right?"

Poppy looked up to see a woman in a police uniform peering at her from the jetty.

"Golly, I don't know! I seem to have lost my balance. I'm not very good on a bike. I'm – I – well—"

"Hold on, miss!" The police officer scrambled around and found a bargepole.

A few moments later, Poppy was sitting on the edge of the jetty, clutching the brown paper parcel and her satchel that was still safely slung over her chest. As it was made of thick leather, the contents had not been in the water long enough to get wet.

As Poppy caught her breath, the policewoman used the pole to hook the bicycle and drag it to the side, then she heaved it out of the water. Kneeling over the contraption, she checked for damage before turning back to Poppy. "Are you sure you're all right, miss?"

"Yes I am, thank you. Nothing broken. I just got a fright. And" – taking handfuls of her skirt to wring out – "a tad wet. Thank heavens you came by. Looks like the boat hire man has gone to lunch." She nodded to the locked boathouse.

"Then I'm very glad I did. It doesn't look like you were about to drown, but it could have been much nastier if you had landed on one of the punts – or hit your head on the side of the jetty."

"Golly, yes! I was a bit worried for a moment when I couldn't stop. My life flashed before my eyes!"

The policewoman frowned, her face awash with concern. "You couldn't stop, you say?"

Poppy shook her head. "Not at all. I tried the brake and nothing happened."

"Well, miss, that doesn't surprise me at all," said the policewoman, pointing to the dripping bicycle. "Because it looks like your brakes have been tampered with."

Poppy was stunned. "On *purpose*?"

"Well, I can't say that for sure, but it appears that someone – very recently – may have taken a hacksaw to your bicycle."

"By Jove!" said Poppy, her blue eyes wide with fright. "Whoever could have done that?"

CHAPTER 13

WEDNESDAY 22 APRIL 1925, LONDON

Rollo Rolandson picked the last of the sandwich crumbs out of his stubble, asked James the barman to put the meal on his tab, and plucked his hat and coat down from the hatstand with his umbrella. Theo Dorowitz had given him a lot to think about – and a lot to do. Grateful that the rain had finally stopped, he popped across the road to let the *Globe* receptionist know that he would be out for the rest of the afternoon, then hailed a cab. His first stop was a jewellery shop in Mayfair. He wondered at the coincidence of it as this – according to Daniel Rokeby – had been the very shop where he'd bought Poppy's ring.

However, his visit had nothing to do with Daniel and Poppy's engagement, although it did – tangentially – involve Poppy. Just as he'd promised, he had made enquiries in the neighbourhood about the Leighton family and this morning had been informed by his building's doorman that the Leightons were in fact the current owners of William Lawes & Co. (Established 1783). When Poppy had spoken to Mrs Leighton, the conversation had not turned to what Mr Leighton did for a living, only that his son worked with him in the family business. Rollo thought it worth his while that he pay the male members of the family a visit.

He entered the shop and sauntered over to one of the display cabinets. While he was there, he thought, he probably ought to get a little something for Yasmin. He'd been working late a lot the last few months, literally leaving her holding the babies. Yes, they had two nannies – a daytime one and a night-time one – but as the mother Yasmin still had a lot to do. And while, in principle, he agreed with her newfangled notion that fathers should be just as involved in looking after children as mothers, in practice, well... What would his friends at the club say if he couldn't attend a poker game because he was changing diapers? Hopefully, as the children got older, he'd have to worry about this sort of thing less frequently, but for now, perhaps an emerald and diamond necklace would suffice.

A young man in his late twenties – whom Rollo hoped was Leighton Junior – approached him politely. "Good afternoon, sir. How may I be of assistance today?"

"G'day. I'm looking for something for the little lady. Is that a unique piece or a factory line?"

The young man's upper lip twitched. "Our pieces are all unique, sir. As an American, perhaps you are unaware that William Lawes & Co. is one of the most exclusive jewellery shops in London. We are nearly one hundred and fifty years old."

"No sir, I did not know that. But great to hear. Are you Mr Lawes?"

"No sir, my name is Leighton. Mr Larry Leighton. Lawes was my grandmother's family name. My grandfather, Henry Leighton, married into the family. But if you trace us back through the Lawes line then the shop has been in my family for six generations."

Rollo grinned. "That's nearly as long as we Americans have been independent."

Larry Leighton did not return the grin. "Quite. So, are you interested in this piece? As I said, it's unique. We import jewels directly from the colonies and have them designed and made up here. There are a dozen handcrafted emeralds – three carats apiece – interspersed with two-carat diamonds – in a fourteen-karat gold setting."

Rollo thought it would look beautiful around Yasmin's exquisite neck. "Yes, I'll take it. How much do you want for it?"

Rollo balked at the four-figure sum but did not show it. "Banker's cheque?"

Larry said that would be acceptable and passed a gold embossed pen to Rollo. On receipt of the cheque, his eyes widened. "Rollo Rolandson? Heavens, I'm sorry, Mr Rolandson; I didn't recognize you. I believe you don't live far from us."

Rollo grinned again, wondering how an American dwarf wandering into a shop in Mayfair, where he lived, could possibly not be recognized. "That's right. Rollo Rolandson. I am pleased to make your acquaintance." He stood on tiptoes and reached his hand across the counter. Larry shook it, looking embarrassed that he had not earlier identified his customer.

"I'll get this boxed up for you, sir. Will there be anything else?"

Rollo smiled inwardly. He knew the tone. Larry wanted to make up for his perceived earlier rudeness. *Only the Brits!*

"No, I don't think so. Although perhaps you could pass on my condolences to your father."

"Your condolences?" asked Larry as he proceeded to package the necklace.

"For your sister's death."

Larry's face dropped. "Ah, yes. Thank you, Mr Rolandson. I shall."

"That must have been quite a shock for you." *No pun intended*, he wanted to add but stopped himself in time.

"Yes, it was. Totally unexpected, of course."

"Such a wasted life. I heard your sister was a genius scientist. That it was just a matter of time until she won a Nobel Prize."

"Well, that might be over-egging it a bit. Although everyone did say she was very clever."

Rollo detected another tone. And if it had a colour, it would be as green as the emeralds in the necklace. Rollo decided to poke the hornet's nest further. "Did you never think of following in her footsteps?" he asked innocently.

Larry's eyes narrowed and his lips pursed. "Not in the least. It is I who is the elder."

"So, she never thought of following you then?"

"It was not expected of her. William Lawes & Co. has always been run by the men of the family."

"Even though it was owned by your grandmother?"

Larry's lip twitched again. "It was never hers. It was passed to my grandfather on their marriage."

"Ah, I see," said Rollo, with an admirable lack of sarcasm. "A traditional family set-up. Well, as I said, please pass on my condolences. I believe my reporter has already passed on hers to your mother."

Larry's eyes widened. "Your reporter?"

"Yes, didn't you know? We are doing a story on your sister for *The Daily Globe* and my reporter, Miz Denby, interviewed your mother about it on Monday."

"No," said Larry tersely, "she never mentioned it." He handed a velvet case over the counter to Rollo, who took it with thanks, slipped it into his inside pocket, raised his hat, and wished the young jeweller good day.

As the door closed behind him, he noticed an older man emerge from the back of the shop – Leighton Senior, he assumed. *Damn, I should have stuck around to see him... That's what you get, old sport, for insisting on leaving on a killer line.*

Rollo asked his cab driver to drop him on the other end of Fleet Street to *The Daily Globe*. *The London Courier*'s head office was a building of a similar size to the *Globe*'s. Both were tabloids, trying to cater to a slightly less fuddy-duddy readership than the all-conquering *Times* and *Evening Standard*. Both had an eye on celebrities. But – and this was a crucial distinction in Rollo's mind – the *Globe* wasn't just a gossip rag; it made an effort to challenge the self-importance of the ruling class, give a voice to ordinary people, and, with its daring investigative journalism, be a thorn in the side of the establishment. And Poppy Denby, who had worked for him now for five years, was his ace investigative journalist.

What a remarkable girl she was. *No*, he chastised himself, *not a girl. Woman. She's grown into a remarkable woman.* When he'd first met her – nervous and uncertain in his office – he hadn't thought she'd last the day, never mind be here five years later, having written thousands of articles and solved a host of crimes. He had hired her out of desperation – he simply needed someone to tidy his office – but in a very short space of time she'd shown her mettle. Underneath the pretty blonde fluff was a girl – a woman – with a razor-sharp mind and a backbone of steel. And yet, her heart always remained soft. Danny Boy Rokeby was one lucky man. And he'd better do her proud.

Lionel Saunders, on the other hand, was the opposite of Poppy – and not just because of his sex. Lionel had Poppy's job before she arrived. Rollo had – unfortunately – inherited him when he took over the paper in 1917. By 1920, when Poppy arrived, the former arts and entertainment editor had proven himself to be unreliable and a bit of a lush. Now, Rollo didn't judge him for his drinking habits – he himself had chosen to live in London because he couldn't abide living under prohibition in his native New York City – but he never let his alcohol consumption impinge on his professional life. Lionel, on the other hand, frequently didn't come into work after a late-night bender. Once again, Rollo had extended him a bit of grace. On the arts and entertainment beat, the journalist would often work until the early hours and couldn't be expected in the newsroom bright-eyed and bushy-tailed at nine o'clock in the morning. But it *was* expected that the journalist would still file copy in time for deadline. And this Lionel frequently failed to do. Which was why, on Poppy's first day in the office, an interview she managed to do with the director of a West End theatre production – arranged by her friend, the ever-delightful Delilah Marconi – was able to fill Lionel's slot and put him to shame. Lionel never forgave her for it. Then, when it became apparent that Lionel was in the pocket of the notoriously corrupt politician and industrialist Lord Melvyn Dorchester, and his equally dastardly son Alfie, Rollo and Poppy had him clearly in their crosshairs.

Both Rollo and Poppy believed that Lionel was responsible for Bert Isaacs' death. Bert had been in contact with Melvyn Dorchester's daughter Elizabeth, who had been incarcerated in Willow Park Asylum – the same asylum within which Bert's fiancée, Sophie, would years later be a patient. It turned out that Elizabeth had been locked away to prevent her from revealing damning information about her father's business affairs. Rollo and Poppy believed that this was what ultimately led to Bert's death – an apparently accidental fall from the third floor of *The Daily Globe* to the marble floor of the foyer. However, despite the Dorchesters being indicted for their crimes (though Alfie was later to escape), the police could find no tangible proof that Lionel had pushed Bert to his death.

And then, even though Lionel had physically attacked Poppy in Rollo's office, chasing her through the building after she had fought him off, the police once again had failed to lay charges against him. So here he was, five years later, a free man, working for the rival of *The Daily Globe*.

Rollo straightened his bow tie and walked into the building.

The *Courier's* newsroom was much the same as the *Globe's*. Around a dozen newspapermen – and they were all men – were variously bashing out stories on their typewriters, shouting into gooseneck telephones, or, in the case of Lionel Saunders, staring into space through a plume of cigarette smoke as he leaned back on his chair, bracing his feet against his desk.

"Sorry to interrupt your hard work, Saunders. Pushing a deadline as always, I see."

Lionel flashed a venomous look at his unexpected visitor. "Rolandson. How did you get in? We have a height restriction in these parts."

"But not a moral one." Rollo shoved Lionel's feet off the desk, knocking him off balance, before clambering up on a spare chair.

"Whatya want, Rolandson? I have work to do."

"Then I'll cut to the chase. Two words: Sophie Blackburn."

Lionel's ferret-like eyes narrowed. "What about her?"

"Just what I'd like to know. I have it on good authority that you failed to lay charges against her when she broke into your home and threatened you last year. Why's that? Scared that it be known that you got beat up by a girl?"

Lionel's lip curled back from his yellowed teeth. "None of your damn business, Rolandson. Now get the hell out of here before I call security and tell them you're here conducting industrial espionage."

Rollo threw back his head and laughed. "Righto. As if the *Globe* ever needed to steal ideas from this yellow rag. So, are you going to answer me or not? Why didn't you lay charges against

Sophie Blackburn? Was it because you knew that if you did, all her evidence against you for Bert's death would come out in open court?"

Lionel grabbed Rollo by the braces, leaned forward, and hissed. "Get the hell out of here. That loon has got nothing on me. Nothing." Then, loudly, so the other journalists could hear, "Boys, show the Yankee Dwarf the door. We don't let rats in our newsroom."

Two minutes later Rollo was picking himself up from the pavement and dusting off his hat. He wasn't hurt; he'd just lost his balance as he was shoved out of the building. And whatever mild humiliation he might have felt by being the subject of pitiful stares from Fleet Street pedestrians was outstripped by the knowledge that he'd struck a nerve with Lionel Saunders. His suspicion that Sophie might actually have some evidence that Lionel had been responsible for Bert's death had been confirmed. Or, if not actual evidence, she was close to something. But no one would believe a madwoman. Having her incarcerated in Willow Park instead of laying charges was, rather than a mercy, a way of silencing her. He needed to do some more investigating.

Chapter 14

Wednesday 22 April 1925, Oxford

Poppy and the kind policewoman – who introduced herself as WPC Winter – carried the wet and broken bicycle up the bank between them. Poppy told the WPC which hotel she was staying at and together they made their way there. The bicycle manager from the hotel spotted them as they turned into Cowley Place and he rushed to help them. On examining the damage, he confirmed the policewoman's suspicions. "Aye miss, it does look like someone has cut through the brake rod. See here," he said, pointing to the sharp edges of the now bent and buckled rod that attached the front wheel brake to the lever on the handlebars.

Poppy shook her head, puzzled. "But the brake was working when I was riding. I stopped at at least two intersections."

"Then you were lucky, miss. It doesn't look as if it was cut all the way through in the first go. Just enough to weaken it. But it would be just a matter of time until it gave way. If this had happened when you were in a busy intersection you could have been hit by a motor car. Lucky for you, you only landed in the shallows. The good Lord must have sent his angels to look out for you, miss."

"It certainly looks that way," said WPC Winter, before sending Poppy into the hotel to get changed. "I'll finish taking this gentleman's statement, then I'll wait for you in the lobby."

Poppy, still shaken, did what she was told. There was something very comforting in the presence of the woman police constable.

Half an hour later, a much dryer Poppy and WPC Winter were sharing a luncheon table.

"So, let me get this straight," said WPC Winter. "You are here in Oxford to write an article about the late June Leighton?"

"That's right," said Poppy, after swallowing a mouthful of trout. While getting changed and cleaned up, Poppy had decided to not tell the kind policewoman about any of the more sensational suspicions around June's death. From past experience, it was never a good idea to bring the police on board too soon into an investigation lest they try to take over – or worse, shut it down. And, apart from Sophie, there was no one in Oxford who knew her true reasons for being there, so, if it came to it, her story could easily be corroborated. Besides, after what George Lewis, the editor of *The Oxford Gazette*, had told her, it appeared as if the police – or at least the police pathologist – might not have applied due diligence when they investigated the scientist's death. Poppy was unsure what, if anything, WPC Winter knew about the Leighton case, but she doubted it was much.

Women constables were a rare breed and, from Poppy's experience, were never given any meaningful role on a police force. They were only ever used to deal with domestic issues and to accompany their male colleagues if it were thought a female suspect or victim might become hysterical. Apart from that, they were just glorified clerical helpers. Poppy appraised her new companion with sympathy. She was in her early thirties – and taller than Poppy, with broad shoulders and large, agricultural hands. She had ruddy cheeks and a square face with dark blue eyes. Her brown hair was pinned away from her face. In the old days, she would have been described as having "peasant" looks – strong, plain, and pleasant.

"So, who do you think is unhappy that you're asking questions about Miss Leighton?" asked the policewoman, before piercing a carrot with her fork.

Poppy's eyes widened in surprise. "Why do you think anyone is unhappy with me asking questions?" asked Poppy. "So far, everyone I've spoken to has been willing to talk to me. June Leighton was a well-regarded young woman." She waited for WPC Winter to finish chewing before receiving an answer.

"Come now, Miss Denby, we are not in the back of beyond. We have heard of you here in Oxford. Your detective work in London – and on your travels – has not gone unnoticed. And you are hardly here in disguise, are you? Word has got out that the famous and beautiful Miss Poppy Denby – journalist and amateur detective – is in town, asking questions about the death of June Leighton."

Good heavens, thought Poppy, *am I really famous?* However, she chose not to comment on it, not wanting to appear falsely modest or to knock the line of enquiry off track. So she said, "I am asking questions about her life, not her death. I am writing an article in honour of her achievements as a scientist and a professional woman."

Winter's dark eyes twinkled. "Of course you are."

Poppy didn't quite know what to say to that. It seemed that she had been wrong in her first appraisal of the policewoman. Or perhaps, to her shame, she had allowed her preconceived ideas and prejudices against women police officers to get in the way.

"So," said Poppy, "when you say 'word has got out' – to whom? Who do you know that is aware that I'm in town?"

"You mean, apart from the police?"

Poppy blinked. "Well, yes, but let's start with the police. Did you know I was here?"

Winter nodded. "Yes, it was discussed at this morning's briefing."

"Why on earth would it be discussed at a police briefing?"

The policewoman shrugged. "I'm not sure, Miss Denby, but it was. We were asked to keep an eye out for you. It was said – and I'm sorry to inform you of this – that where Poppy Denby goes, trouble is sure to follow. And, well, sure enough—"

"You were following me?"

Winter's eyes widened. "Heavens no! But I was heading over to your hotel to see if I could meet with you."

"On orders from whom?"

"On orders from nobody. I was on my lunch break. And I thought it would be marvellous to make your acquaintance. And then, as luck would have it, you literally landed right in front of me!"

Winter laughed – a loud "peasant" laugh that brought stares from the other diners.

Poppy was confused. Was this woman telling her that she was under police surveillance or not? And if she was, why on earth was Winter telling her? She looked around and noticed the other diners' conversation had quietened, and the two women were receiving curious glances.

Poppy leaned in and said quietly, "Look, let's finish up here and take coffee on the terrace. It's more private there."

WPC Winter agreed, and five minutes later they were settled at the far end of the hotel terrace, out of earshot of the curious luncheon guests.

"All right," said Poppy, cutting to the chase. "So, tell me why you want to make my acquaintance if you haven't been instructed to do so by a commanding officer."

Winter stirred some milk into her coffee, then clinked her teaspoon three times on the edge of her cup. She looked up at Poppy and smiled. "Because, Miss Denby, I admire you immensely. You are doing what I joined the police to do."

"And what is that?" asked Poppy, stirring her own black brew.

"Solving murders, of course." The smile faded from Winter's face. "I always wanted to be a detective. You see, my husband was one. He was a member of the Oxfordshire CID. I used to help him in the evenings with his paperwork. It wasn't really allowed, but he trusted me. He always struggled with writing and reading – getting his letters the right way round – it took him three goes before he was able to pass the police exams. But he eventually did. And he was a good detective, with the practical stuff. He just needed help writing up his reports."

Poppy listened carefully, imagining the domestic scene of the then Mrs Winter helping write up her husband's reports. *The then Mrs Winter?* "You are speaking in the past tense, WPC Winter. Has your husband passed? If so, please accept my condolences."

Winter smiled gently. "Yes, he has. Right at the end of the war. He didn't actually serve on the front – he had broken a knee on duty. He walked well enough to do his job back home, but not to serve. So, we thought he'd got off lightly. But unfortunately, he died in a motor accident in 1918."

"Oh," said Poppy quietly. "I'm awfully sorry."

"Thank you, Poppy. May I call you Poppy?"

"You may."

"Good. Then I am Rosie. Rosie Winter." She reached her hand across the table. Poppy took it, feeling her small hand enveloped in a larger one. As expected, Rosie had a strong grip.

Poppy smiled again, once more feeling that her first impressions of this woman were right, even if she had underestimated her. "So, how did you end up a policewoman?"

"Well," said Rosie, "five years ago the Oxford City Police put an advertisement in the newspaper asking for women volunteers. Three of us got through. But I'm the only one left on the job. The others gave up. One got married, the other pregnant, so that just left me. I've already been married – and have no plans to be so again – and after seven years of marriage, I think it's safe to say that I am unable to have children."

Poppy raised an eyebrow, surprised that Rosie was sharing such personal information with a relative stranger. But there was something intimate about their conversation. Something almost confessional, as if Rosie were finally unburdening herself to someone she thought might understand. Poppy didn't want to disappoint her. Then, she remembered something she'd recently read in *Married Love* – that women normally got the blame for infertility. "Or perhaps it was your husband who was unable to father children?" she offered.

"Perhaps," said Rosie, shrugging away the burden of blame. "It doesn't matter. I have none. So, I decided to try to become a professional policewoman, with the hope of eventually becoming a detective."

Poppy was impressed. Here was another candidate for her Women in the Workplace column. "Are you on track to becoming a police detective now?"

Rosie let out one of her loud laughs, but this time there were no other guests to worry about. "Hardly. I wish I were. After five years on the job, my rose-tinted spectacles have been removed. There is no chance I'll ever become a detective. There is no chance, in fact, that I will even get a promotion. No woman has ever risen above the rank of constable, and no woman, I believe, ever will."

Rosie, for a moment, looked desperately sad. Poppy's heart reached out to her. "Golly, Rosie, that's not fair."

"No," said Rosie, "it's not." And then her smile was back. "But you, Poppy, have done what I always dreamed of doing. And that's why I wanted to meet you."

Poppy cocked her head to the side. "Are you sure you haven't been asked to keep an eye on me?"

Rosie laughed, her humour rising again. "Well, not more than any of my fellow officers. As I told you, we were briefed this morning that you were in town and asked to keep an eye open for you. I was being polite earlier when I told you that. What was actually said was, 'That blighted woman is in town. She's nothing but trouble. Watch out for her.' Naturally, I was delighted to hear that the blighted woman was here, and hence my visit to you."

Poppy finished off the last of her coffee. "Well thank you, Rosie. I'm honoured to know you hold me in such high regard. Not that any of it is deserved, of course. Most of my detective work is just luck. And I certainly couldn't do it all on my own. I would never dream of taking all the credit. However, that aside, I'm still curious as to how your police colleagues found out about me being here."

Rosie nodded. "I agree; it is curious. No one explained to me why. But that doesn't surprise me. No one ever does. But what makes me more curious is who took a hacksaw to your bicycle. And why? You claim, Poppy, that your reason for being in Oxford is to write a simple article about a dead scientist. But clearly someone doesn't like that you're here. Do you have any idea who that might be? And where and when someone would have been able to tamper with your bicycle? Do you have any idea, Poppy, who might wish to harm you?"

It was Poppy's turn to laugh. But there was little mirth in her voice. "Oh Rosie, where do I start?"

CHAPTER 15

It was nearly four o'clock when Poppy and Rosie arrived at St Aldates Street. They parted ways, with Rosie turning down Blue Boar Lane to the police station and Poppy crossing the road to the Post Office. Poppy had already decided – after her meeting with George Lewis – that there was sufficient reason to justify staying longer in Oxford, and her time with Rosie had confirmed it. Poppy, still circumspect, had not told the policewoman about Sophie's suspicions of murder, but she had told her what George Lewis had said about there perhaps being more to the scientist's death than met the eye, and that he feared that his predecessor at the paper – as well as the police – had failed to apply due diligence to the investigation. Rosie had agreed with her. She confirmed to Poppy that the police pathologist had been the worse for wear for drink when he arrived at the scene, and it hadn't been the first time it had happened.

"He's only got a year until retirement, so no one wants to challenge him," explained the WPC. Rosie said that she had not personally attended the scene of death but had heard talk of it in the station. She said that she would try to get a look at June Leighton's case file to see if there was anything that had been overlooked or not followed up properly.

Poppy was in two minds about Rosie's offer of help. On the one hand, it would be very useful to have someone on the "inside". Rollo, she knew, had a number of "tame cops" (as he referred to them), and Poppy had always felt uneasy about the ethics of it.

But she couldn't deny that tame cops could be useful. She had just never thought that she would have one of her own. It made her uncomfortable. However, she trusted her instinct about people, and she honestly believed Rosie's primary motivation for offering help was to vicariously pursue the type of career she had always dreamed of with the police, and which she realized would now never happen. There was, of course, the possibility that Rosie was a "plant" from the powers that be on the Oxford force, sent to befriend her, to find out what she was up to. But Poppy doubted it. She lived with actresses, and as far as she could see, Rosie was not playing a role. However, she could be wrong. And because she could not dismiss that possibility entirely, she had chosen not to tell Rosie everything.

She had also decided not to formally report the apparent tampering with her bicycle. Rosie was not happy with her decision and suggested that she would have to file a report anyway, particularly since she had already taken a statement from the man at the hotel who looked after the bikes. But Poppy asked her to delay doing so.

"If a report is filed, then someone will be sent to investigate, and it will probably not be you. Is that correct?"

Rosie had frowned her agreement. "Correct. They will take anything mildly interesting off my hands immediately. But I can't pretend it didn't happen, Poppy; then I'm doing exactly what we're accusing my male colleagues of doing: sweeping things under the carpet."

"A bit of vandalism is hardly the same as the death of a woman though, right?"

"But was it just a bit of vandalism? What if someone intended the death – or serious injury – of another woman? In other words, you."

"Or it could have been some young scallywags having a lark."

Rosie nodded. "It could have been. But even then, it could have had serious consequences and should be investigated. Even if it is to just give some young scallywags a rap over the knuckles."

Poppy agreed but asked Rosie to hold out on filing the report for a while longer. Rosie reluctantly agreed. Poppy was relieved, but she knew she had only bought herself a bit of time. She also knew that Rosie was right; there was every possibility someone had done it deliberately and that she – specifically – was the target. But who could it have been? She reconsidered her movements of the morning. She had picked up the bicycle after breakfast and headed into town. The rain had got heavier, and by the time she reached Somerville College she was drenched. She had left her bicycle in the porter's lodge while she interviewed Dr Fuller. She had been in there for around an hour: plenty of time for the porter, or someone else, to tamper with the machine. But who? From there she had ridden around the corner to the newspaper office. Again, she had spent around an hour inside. While she was there, she had left the bicycle leaning against a wall outside the entrance – once more, plenty of time for someone to do something. Although she wondered if anyone would be brazen enough to take a hacksaw to a bicycle in full view of passers-by. The same applied to the next stop she made: the Elliston & Cavell department store. The bicycle man had said that it looked like it had been only partly sawn through and had taken a while to break properly. Was that deliberate, to delay the inevitable accident, or because the culprit had run out of time to finish the job? She wasn't sure. But if Rosie was correct and she had been specifically targeted, the question was, by whom? She had no doubt of the "why" – it was because she was sniffing around June Leighton's death, which confirmed to her all the more that there was something worth investigating in Oxford.

She went into the Post Office and commandeered a telephone booth. She put in a call to the *Globe* office in London and waited for the operator to connect her. She smiled as she heard the friendly voice of the receptionist, Mavis Bradshaw.

"Mavis! Hello! It's Poppy."

"Poppy! You sound like you're just next door. Good line. How's Oxford?"

"Very interesting. I think there's definitely a story to follow up here. Is Rollo there?"

"Sorry Poppy, he isn't. He went out at lunch to meet someone in the Cock, then popped back in, briefly, to tell me he'd be out for the rest of the afternoon and didn't know when he'd be back. He did say, though, if you rang, to tell you to carry on doing what you're doing and that he'd try to get hold of you at your hotel this evening."

"Oh," said Poppy, disappointed. "I was hoping he'd be in. And I'm going out this evening so won't be at the hotel."

"Oooooh, anywhere nice?"

"A dinner dance."

"How lovely!"

Poppy then went on to tell Mavis about the new dress she had bought but declined to mention the accident that had nearly lost the dress before she'd had a chance to wear it. After giving Mavis a few more details about the hotel – what her room was like, the view, the social standing of her fellow guests, and so on – she turned the conversation back to the business at hand.

"So that's all Rollo said? That he'd try to call me later and that I should carry on doing what I'm doing?"

"That's it, I'm afraid. Oh, and he asked me to pass on a message to Ivan too."

"Oh?"

Mavis chuckled. "The message was for Ivan, not for you, Poppy." Ivan Molanov was the archivist at *The Daily Globe*. He kept files of every story covered by the newspaper in its thirty-year history. He also kept records of other newspapers. If there was any background research needed by *Globe* journalists, Ivan was the man to ask.

"Oh, come on, Mavis..." Poppy teased.

"All right. It's to do with your story anyway. He asked Ivan to find anything he could on the Leighton family. Seems like they own a jewellery shop in Mayfair."

"Really? Now that *is* interesting."

"Speaking of jewellery, would you like to speak to your fiancé? He's just walked in."

"Oh yes, please!" said Poppy, flushing with excitement. "But first, would you mind asking Ivan to do something on my behalf too?" Poppy opened her notebook to the notes she'd taken at the newspaper office. "Can you please ask him to do a search for anything on the Sanforth Foundation or anyone connected to it? They are funding some scientific research in Oxford, but I don't know anything else about them. Anything he can find will be appreciated. Oh, and Mavis, can you get him one of those chocolate cakes he likes from the bakery to sweeten him up? I'll give you the money when I get back."

Mavis chuckled as she took down Poppy's instructions, then passed the telephone to Daniel. "Your lady awaits."

"Thanks Mavis... Hello sweetheart, how are you?"

"Missing you," said Poppy, and she then went on to give Daniel a sanitized precis of her adventures – excluding, of course, her accident on the bike.

"Golly," said Daniel, "it does sound like there's more to this than meets the eye. Anything yet that confirms Sophie's suspicion of murder?"

"Not yet," said Poppy. "And there may never be. But I think there's more than enough to suggest that her death wasn't properly investigated, and that in itself is a scandal."

"Yes, it is. Do be careful, Poppy, won't you?"

"Of course!" said Poppy, feeling a pang of guilt that she had failed to mention that someone might have tried to injure her earlier in the day. But best Daniel didn't know. He'd be up to Oxford like a shot, and while it would be lovely to see him, she didn't want him trying to stop her doing her job because he was worried about her. It had always been an issue between them. In fact, they had broken off their courtship once because of it: he, in her mind, being overprotective, and she, in his, being reckless. Since he'd returned from South Africa, he had made much more of an effort to not restrain her. But she hadn't been involved in a potential murder investigation since he'd been back. This was quite a different kettle of fish.

Instead, she told him about the dinner dance that evening and that she was going as Dr Fuller's partner. "Best you only dance with Dr Fuller then," he said teasingly. "I don't want you swept off your feet by an amorous gentleman scholar."

Poppy laughed. "Don't worry, amorous gentlemen scholars are not my cup of tea."

He lowered his voice. "But amorous gentlemen photographers are?"

She lowered her voice in turn. "I can think of only one." Poppy could almost feel his glow down the telephone line. They spoke until her money ran out and the operator called time.

"Give my love to the children. And tell Rollo to call me tomorrow morning at the hotel, not this evening."

"Come home soon, darling," said Daniel, and then they were cut off.

Poppy held the receiver to her ear even after the line was dead, trying to keep the connection with her fiancé for as long as possible, but a knock on the side of the booth and the realization that someone else was waiting in line shook her out of her reverie. She apologized and withdrew.

Poppy visited the tea shop next door – succumbing once more to the full cream tea – and dreamed for a while about wedding dresses. However, after her second cup, she put thoughts of her upcoming nuptials aside and turned once more to the case at hand. It was time to meet Sophie in the churchyard to bring her up to date with the investigations and to tell her about the dinner that evening where she hoped to meet Dr Bill Raines and his assistant, Miles Mackintosh. She had of course failed to tell Daniel that Gertrude Fuller had suggested she might be "just the type of woman they would be attracted to".

She also wanted to ask Sophie what she knew about the Sanforth Foundation and its connection to the laboratory, and what the former editor's note about them "being at it again" might mean. However, when Poppy got to St Giles' Church, Sophie wasn't there. She waited for half an hour, but the lab assistant didn't show up. Poppy considered going to Sophie's house but then realized that she didn't have her address. And the Post Office was now closed, so she couldn't look it up in the directory. *Oh well*, thought Poppy. *I'll just have to try to find her tomorrow. Now I have to get back to the hotel to get dressed.*

CHAPTER 16

The maid arrived at Poppy's hotel room with an evening dress draped over her arm. Poppy thanked her and gave her a generous tip, declining the offer of help to get dressed. Poppy had never had a ladies' maid, nor would she. She had grown up managing to dress herself, and she would continue doing so, even though she now earned enough money to pay for the symbol of social status. But she was glad that she could ask the hotel concierge to arrange for her slightly damp dress to be cleaned.

She hung it up on a hanger and appraised it with satisfaction. What a bargain! It was a Lucien Lelong cocktail dress – one of Poppy's favourite designers – in mauve georgette crêpe. The calf-length skirt was gathered up on one side and tied to a scarf at the hips, causing the soft fabric to hang in flattering drapes. The bodice was loose, as was the current fashion, and sleeveless, with a cape of georgette flowing down the back to the waist. It was from Lelong's 1924 spring collection – something she knew because Delilah travelled to Paris every year to see the new designs – and was now cut-price because it was a year old. Poppy didn't care. It was new enough for her, and it was beautiful. She caressed the fabric, allowing it to cascade through her fingers and over her engagement ring. *Daniel will love it*, she thought.

She had also bought a pair of burgundy shoes that were on sale, as well as a string of waist-length beads made from wood and coated in a burgundy lacquer to match her shoes. They were nowhere near as nice as the Prince of Wales' pearls that Aunt Dot had given her for her birthday one year, but she hadn't thought to pack the pearls for her short trip to Oxford. Her ensemble was completed by a burgundy satin hairband, to which, using a diamanté paste pin, was attached a feather. The feather was a little worse for wear after the brief dip in the Cherwell, and despite an hour in front of the coal fire and attempts to comb it through, it still looked limp and crestfallen. Poppy decided to remove it. Besides, she was beginning to wonder if a formal dinner dance at a medieval college was quite the place to sport a feather in one's hair. Was it even the place to sport a Lucien Lelong cocktail dress? She wasn't sure, but it was too late now.

After a gloriously hot bath, she tamed her short crop of damp curls with Brillantine then applied her make-up. Again, thoughts of the potentially austere nature of the event moderated her application; this was not going to be a night at Oscar's Jazz Club with Delilah. She then pulled on a clean pair of silk stockings, attached them to a pair of garters on the thighs, and slipped into her dress. It fell over her gently curved figure like a waterfall. She appraised herself in the mirror: elegant and sophisticated. It was hard to believe this was the same young woman who got off the train from Northumberland five years ago wearing a smart but dull twin set that she'd bought at a church jumble sale.

She wished she'd quizzed Dr Fuller more regarding what to expect this evening. She had never been to a function at a university, but she had been to receptions at diplomatic embassies and various government dos. This outfit would fit in well there. She tried on the hairband and immediately decided against it: *jazzy, far too jazzy.* The burgundy beads, though, were a must. The ensemble didn't hang together properly without them. And if the dons and their guests at Balliol thought them too flighty, then so be it. Besides, the plan for this evening was to attract *some* attention – specifically from Dr Bill Raines and his graduate student, Miles Mackintosh. What was it Gertrude Fuller had said? "... *you appear to be just the type of woman that men like Mackintosh and Raines would find alluring.*"

Yes, she was deliberately setting herself up as bait. Poppy felt a bit sick thinking about it, but if she were honest with herself, it wasn't the first time she'd done it. It was just the first time that she'd done it so overtly. Poppy was not falsely modest. She knew she was attractive. Not drop-dead gorgeous like Delilah, but she was aware that she was considered very pretty and could not ignore the fact that heads often turned when she walked into a room. It was something that she found annoying, realizing that people judged her on her looks and assumed she was just a bit of pretty blonde fluff. However, over the years in her work, she had discovered that that could be used to her advantage. Men, particularly, could be put off guard, assuming she was just Rollo Rolandson's pretty little assistant without much going on between the ears. Nonetheless, she would sometimes play the dumb blonde, using people's prejudice against them, while behind the guileless disguise her sharp mind would be gathering evidence and information. This was what she intended to do tonight, although she wondered how successful her ploy would be. She was concerned about what WPC Rosie Winter had told her: that her reputation had preceded her. How had she achieved the status of "renowned reporter sleuth"? She really hadn't been aware that she had. But, after Rosie's admission today that the policewoman admired her and wanted to meet her, Poppy realized that her investigations in Oxford – and perhaps elsewhere where her name had become known – might be hampered.

Goodness, she thought. *Have I really become infamous?* Delilah and Aunt Dot would be tickled pink by the idea, but Poppy wasn't so pleased. She wondered how she might proceed – professionally – in future. Might she have to start adopting disguises like the famous private detective Maud West?

Well, it was too late now. She would just have to tackle this investigation as herself. She shook her head, checking that the Brillantine had now set, then applied a touch of perfume behind each ear. She finished off her toilette with some fresh lipstick and went down to the foyer to await Gertrude Fuller.

Balliol College Great Hall, built in the mid-1800s, was a relatively new addition to the six-centuries-old college, but was designed to fit in with the medieval ambiance. Poppy and Gertrude entered the college grounds via the back gate from Magdalen Street, rather than through the main entrance on Broad. Poppy wouldn't have minded seeing all of the beautiful buildings and gardens, but Gertrude – who no doubt had seen them all many times before – was not playing tour guide and asked for their taxi to drop them at the closest entrance to the hall.

Inside the hall, laid out like a medieval banqueting hall, the ladies were led to their seats at one of the long dining tables. Gertrude mentioned that the platform at one end of the hall was usually reserved for the "high table", where the college's top dons and their guests dined, but this evening it had been cleared to make room for a dance floor. To the side was a string quartet, playing sedately while the scholarly guests ate and conversed. Poppy hoped they would up their tempo for the dancing later in the evening but wasn't holding her breath. Oscar's Jazz Club it was not.

Nonetheless, the room was abuzz with animated conversation. The academics arrived in their gowns – including Dr Fuller – but Poppy was assured that those who were brave enough to indulge in the dancing later would "disrobe". Poppy stood out like a mauve sail on a black sea. She was not the only person there not wearing academic dress, but she was certainly the brightest. *Thank heavens I left the feather behind!* Gertrude assured her she looked perfectly splendid and not in the least bit garish. Poppy was sure the doctor of linguistics (as Poppy had discovered she was) was just being kind.

She and Gertrude were also the only pair of ladies. Not all the gentlemen had female partners with them, but no other women were "unaccompanied". Gertrude didn't seem to mind and walked through the wood-panelled room, ignoring the portraits of the leading men of Balliol through the centuries staring accusingly at her. Poppy imagined that as one of the very first women to earn a doctorate at the esteemed university, Gertrude Fuller was well practised in shrugging off criticism, condescension, and judgment. Poppy felt like a baby bird protected by its mother on its first outing from the nest, surrounded by black-winged predators. Not all the guests showed animosity though; Gertrude obviously had a number of friends and allies in the academy. She stopped here and there to greet them and to introduce her friend, Miss Poppy Denby, who, she said, was a journalist from London writing an article on some leading alumni of Somerville College. This was close enough to the truth for Poppy to relax into.

The ladies were to be seated with some gentlemen and their partners from the history department, but Gertrude whispered something to the steward, who nodded and led them instead further down the hall. The steward pulled out a vacant chair, first for Poppy, then for Dr Fuller. The gentlemen at the table all rose as the ladies were seated. As the gentlemen took their seats, Poppy noted that none of them had female partners. As she'd already ascertained, this wasn't unusual, but it did make her and Gertrude more conspicuous. She wondered if this had been Gertrude's plan. And then, she suddenly recognized one of the gentlemen, just as he, in turn, recognized her.

Professor James Sinclair inclined his bald head. "Well, good evening, Miss Denby; this is a surprise. Good evening, Gertrude."

"Good evening, James," said Gertrude. "I believe you and Miss Denby have met."

"We have," said Professor Sinclair. "I hadn't realized you were still in town, Miss Denby."

Poppy smiled politely at the scientist. "I decided to stay on. After speaking to Dr Fuller here about June, I realized there was a lot more I needed to find out."

"Is that so?" a gentleman to Poppy's left interjected. Poppy turned towards him. There was something vaguely familiar about him. He was in his mid-forties: very handsome and debonair. Under his gown she could see that he was wearing a tuxedo.

"Yes, it is. I'm writing an article on June Leighton, mister—"

"Doctor," said the man with the flicker of a smile. "*Doctor* Bill Raines."

Dr Raines! That's why Poppy thought he was familiar. She remembered now the man in the photograph that Sophie had pointed out. *And that*, she thought, flashing a quick glance at a younger man in his twenties on the opposite side of the table, *is Miles Mackintosh*. Gertrude smiled benignly. *Thanks Gertrude – straight into the lion's den.*

"Bill, this is Miss Poppy Denby, the lady journalist who came to visit me in the lab yesterday. She's writing an article about June for a London newspaper. I forget which one..."

"*The Daily Globe*," said Poppy. "I do a monthly column about exceptional women."

"Exceptional *dead* women?" asked Mackintosh, without an accompanying smile to soften the crass comment.

A flurry of discomfort was conducted around the table.

Poppy shrugged it off. "Not usually. Most of the subjects of my column are very much alive and making a mark on the world. Unfortunately, I only heard about June after her tragic death but still thought she should be featured."

"She's a worthy subject in life or death," said Gertrude, fixing her gaze on Mackintosh.

Mackintosh shrugged. "For the readers of a tabloid newspaper, perhaps."

"Now, now, Mackintosh; there's no need to be rude. The young lady is just doing her job," said Raines, as his eyes ranged up and down her torso. Eventually, he looked at her face and smiled. "I'm sorry, Miss Denby; we are all still quite shaken by Miss Leighton's accident. I can assure you Dr Mackintosh meant no disrespect. An apology is in order, young sir."

Mackintosh's eyes narrowed, but disapproving glances from Professor Sinclair and the other gentlemen at the table compelled him to eventually say, "My apologies, Miss Denby. Miss Fuller."

Miss Fuller. Not Doctor. An oversight? Poppy imagined not. But before Gertrude could reply to the jibe, the room was called to order. A gentleman (who, Gertrude whispered, was the Master of Balliol College) welcomed everyone to the dinner, which, he reminded them, was being given in thanks for a large donation made to the college by the Sanforth Foundation.

Poppy's ears pricked at the name.

The Master went on to ask everyone to stand as he proposed a toast to Mrs Mary Sanforth, a dignified grey-haired woman to his right, who remained seated and nodded beneficently to the guests. The Master proceeded to say grace, then wished everyone a hearty meal and an enjoyable evening.

Poppy was grateful he kept the formalities short, not just because she was hungry, but because she was dying to ask Gertrude about the Sanforth Foundation. As the soup was being served, she lowered her voice and made her enquiry.

"That's Mary Sanforth," explained Gertrude. "And the man on her right is her son, Edward. Mary is the widow of the late

American industrialist Edward Sanforth III. When he died, she set up the Sanforth Foundation in his name. The Foundation provides funding for academic research – mainly in the sciences." She grinned. "Let's just say my linguistics department has never been a beneficiary."

Poppy smiled, then turned to Bill Raines. "And you, Dr Raines, has your laboratory benefited from Mrs Sanforth's generosity?" Poppy made sure her look and tone were honest and open rather than interrogative, as if she were engaging in normal dinner conversation.

Raines smiled back, lowering his eyeline to her chest before raising it again to her face. "We have indeed, Miss Denby. Mrs Sanforth has been most generous."

Poppy smiled as prettily as she could. "That is heartening to hear. And what, pray tell, is it you do in the laboratory that has caught Mrs Sanforth's attention?"

Raines looked at her indulgently, as if she were a five-year-old asking him to show her how to tie her shoelaces. "Well, Miss Denby, we take pictures of crystals. Just like those pretty stones in your ring there."

Poppy smiled again. "And why would Mrs Sanforth be interested in pretty stones?"

Gertrude laughed.

Raines' smile slipped for a moment, then returned. "Well, it's not the stones she's interested in. I was just using that as an example. To help you understand."

Poppy realized she needed to raise his assessment of her mental capabilities just a tad, or she'd never get him to divulge the information she required.

"Yes, I believe the molecular structure of diamonds is one of the first things crystallography students are introduced to."

Raines dropped his spoon into his soup. "Goodness, Miss Denby, how do you know that?" he asked, before retrieving his spoon and cleaning up the splatter with his napkin.

Better not drop Sophie into it, thought Poppy. "Oh, I attended a lecture by Professor Bragg at the Royal Institution last week. That's how I first heard about June Leighton and what a remarkable young woman she was."

Raines' eyes widened in surprise. "Bragg spoke about June in his lecture?"

Poppy had to think quickly. "No – no, it wasn't him. It was in the reception afterwards. A few people were talking and they mentioned June. I listened in and thought she would make a wonderful subject for the column."

"Who were these people?" asked Miles Mackintosh from across the table.

Professor Sinclair was in conversation with someone further down the table so wasn't – apparently – listening. Yesterday Poppy had told him that it had been June's mother who had suggested she do the article. Or, if she hadn't said that exactly, it was certainly implied. Best she keep to the same story. "Oh, I didn't catch all their names. But one of them was Mrs Leighton, June's mother. She lives not far from the Institute."

"I'm surprised she felt able to listen to such a lecture so soon after her daughter's death," said Mackintosh.

Poppy looked at him, her face neutral. But inside she was churning. *Oh, what a tangled web we weave when first we practise to deceive...* However, she had promised Sophie, and she intended to keep that promise.

"Yes, I was a little surprised too. But she is very proud of her daughter and her achievements." Poppy was on firmer ground now. She allowed herself to relax slightly and turned back to Bill Raines, who appeared more susceptible to her charms than the twenty-something graduate student. "So, Dr Raines, if Mrs Sanforth is not financing your research into diamonds, what is she financing?"

Raines was just about to answer when Professor Sinclair chipped in: "That, I'm afraid, is confidential, Miss Denby. And far beyond the scope of your article, I'm sure."

Poppy smiled at him, nodding her understanding.

Drat and double drat. This isn't going well. She wracked her brain for a phrase she'd written down during her meeting with Sophie yesterday. Then it came to her and she said, "June, according to her mother, had been working on something to do with a chemical called thallium, is that right?"

"Sort of," said Dr Raines. "But more specifically, thallium dialkyl halides." He rolled the words off his tongue at a rapid rate, then grinned, adding, "I know, it's bamboozling, isn't it?"

"Golly, yes. Hard for us non-scientifically trained people to remember. What did her research involve? Thallium is used in rat poisoning, isn't it?"

Mackintosh, who was already on his second glass of wine since Poppy and Gertrude had sat down, rolled his eyes and said, "Ah yes, thallium poisoning. The stuff of tabloid headlines. But June wasn't poisoned, she was electrocuted. Accidentally. Best you get that straight in your article, Miss Denby." He took another sip of wine and stared at her.

Professor Sinclair cleared his throat and intervened. "That's enough, Mackintosh – of the comments and the booze, I think. Miss Denby, to save you any more time digging, let me tell you what you want to know. June was studying the molecular structure of thallium dialkyl halides, which are used in the production of optical lenses. However, young Mackintosh here was simultaneously and – I might add – *independently* working in the same area and beat her to publication. I believe Dr Fuller here might have mentioned that to you, as it has been a – how should I say – bone of contention between us. But I can assure you – and Dr Raines here will back me up on this – Mackintosh's work in no way drew on Miss Leighton's. It was pure coincidence that two great young minds were wandering down the same avenues. However, as soon as it was realized that research was being duplicated, June started work on a new project – the project that the Sanforth Foundation is financing, and which, I have already stated, I am not at liberty to divulge. Particularly to a lady from the press. Now, if you don't mind, I wish no more to be said on the matter. Come. The second course is about to arrive. Let's stop talking shop and enjoy it."

"Hear, hear!" said Raines. Mackintosh just smirked and raised his glass.

"Well, that's you told," muttered Gertrude.

Poppy nodded graciously. Actually, she didn't mind being shut down. She'd got quite a lot from the conversation already. She smiled at Gertrude, then finished her soup.

CHAPTER 17

The final savoury course of the sumptuous banquet – roast goose with oodles of port cherry sauce – had been followed by plates of pavlova. This was a bridge too far for Poppy, who just managed a couple of spoonfuls. Gertrude offered to finish the rest. As the last of the pudding plates were taken away, the guests all leaned back in their chairs and lit cigarettes while the quartet struck up a moderately paced foxtrot. It was far from the Black Bottom or the Charleston, but certainly enough to get the toes tapping. A few of the younger guests took to the dance floor.

"Would you care to dance, Miss Denby?" asked Bill Raines, slipping out of his gown and draping it over his chair. He presented a fine manly figure in the sharply cut tuxedo.

Poppy, who was so full she feared she could barely walk, did not care to dance; however, an opportunity to get Bill Raines on his own – in a chaperoned environment – was too good to miss.

"I would love to dance, Dr Raines."

Raines flashed a smile at the other gentlemen at the table, then stood to claim his prize. Poppy smiled back and accepted his hand as he led her to the raised platform and joined the other couples. Poppy was a competent dancer, having learned the steps from Delilah. Over the years she'd had many opportunities to practise, including, once, a memorable night dancing in the arms of Rasputin's assassin during an investigation into the murder of a Russian princess. As she took Raines' hand and slipped into hold, she wondered whose arms she was dancing in tonight.

Poppy and Raines soon got into the slow, slow, quick, quick rhythm, with the scientist leading her confidently. The foxtrot hold was not as intimate as that for the waltz, and Poppy was grateful, appreciating the small gap between them. She accepted that she was using herself as bait, but she was still an engaged lady and did not want to betray Daniel's trust. She smiled to herself as she remembered his comment about amorous gentlemen scholars. That notwithstanding, she still had a job to do. "You are a very good dancer, Dr Raines. Do you and your colleagues have much opportunity to socialize outside of the laboratory?"

"We see each other a fair bit. In a town like this, most of the social events are linked to the university and you see the same people doing the rounds."

"Did June Leighton meet her fiancé at the university?"

"Fiancé? I didn't know she was engaged. Who told you that?"

"Oh," said Poppy, still determined to keep Sophie out of it. "Someone I spoke to in London."

"Well, it's the first I've heard of it. She wasn't a very friendly girl around the lab. She didn't talk about much other than her work."

"Would she have come to a do like this?"

"She might have. Occasionally."

"And did you ever dance with her?"

Poppy felt his right hand stiffen on her left shoulder. "Once or twice. She was not as light on her feet as you, Miss Denby. A gangly girl, really. Not my type."

"But a brilliant scientist."

"Is that what you've heard?"

"It's what everyone says."

"Not everyone," he said, his words tinged with disdain.

Poppy took a few moments to consider her reply. Slow, slow, quick, quick... Slow, slow, quick, quick...

"So, who will replace her in the laboratory? Another woman?"

"By Jove, I hope not! No offence intended, Miss Denby, but women do not do very well in the scientific world."

"What about Madame Curie?"

"The key is in the 'madame'. She achieved what she did because of her husband. Without him, she would have not got where she is."

Poppy tensed but brought herself under control. Getting into an argument with her dance partner about women's capabilities would not help her achieve her goal.

Slow, slow, quick, quick... Slow, slow, quick, quick...

"I bow to your greater knowledge of the world of science," she said eventually.

Raines chuckled. "If only all ladies did!"

"So, not another woman in your laboratory. Who will replace her?"

"That's for Sinclair to decide. It is he who is missing a graduate student. But it has already been decided that it should be a man. The Sanforth grant is contingent upon it."

"Goodness. Really?"

"Yes. And I'm very pleased that it is."

Again, Poppy chose not to take the bait. Slow, slow, quick, quick... Slow, slow, quick, quick...

Poppy could hear that the foxtrot was approaching its final bars. She didn't have much time. She had one more question, and she'd better make it count.

"So," she said, "why was June X-raying a diamond on the night she died?"

Raines stopped abruptly, causing one of the other couples to almost bump into them. But he still held Poppy firmly in hold. "What kind of article are you writing, Miss Denby? Fess up. We don't like naughty girls here, so tell the truth now."

Poppy looked him straight in the eye, all pretence of a smile gone. "The truth, Dr Raines, is exactly what I intend to write. And now, if you don't mind, will you please release my hand."

Raines met her stare, his hand tightening on hers until it began to hurt. Poppy pulled back but was unable to break free. She was just about to yell at him – not caring if it were the done thing or not – when the music came to a stop and the other dancers applauded the band.

"Come on, Raines," said one of them, "you're hogging the floor."

Raines spun his head to see who had spoken to him. Then, he fixed a rakish grin on his face, released Poppy from his hold, and gave her an elaborate bow.

Poppy couldn't bring herself to feign a response. She turned on her heel and walked away, leaving the scientist to deal with the mocking laughter of the other male dancers.

Poppy emerged from the ladies' cloakroom feeling a tad calmer. She was just about to go back into the dining hall to rejoin Gertrude at the table when she spotted a gentleman leaving the hall, going outside, and lighting up a cigarette. If she were not mistaken, it was Mrs Sanforth's son. What had Gertrude said his name was? Edward?

It was not considered appropriate for an unaccompanied lady to approach an unintroduced gentleman, but Poppy had had enough of doing the appropriate thing for one night. She hurried to the door and followed Edward Sanforth out into the garden.

A tall, thin man with dark blonde hair slicked back from a sharply featured face, he stood with one foot resting on a low wall surrounding an ornamental flower bed as he inhaled, then exhaled, his smoke. Poppy guessed he was in his early thirties.

Poppy approached him from the side, giving him plenty of opportunity to see her, so she would not appear to be sneaking up on him. But he was lost in thought.

She cleared her throat. "Ahem. Excuse me. Sorry to bother you, but are you Edward Sanforth?"

Sanforth turned towards her. He took a few moments before verbally acknowledging her, as if it took some effort to drag his thoughts back to the present. He had a faraway look that she sometimes noticed on Grace Wilson, her Aunt Dot's companion, who spent much of her time cloaked in memories of past failings and the deaths of friends and comrades.

"Er, yes, I'm Edward Sanforth."

His voice was middle-English. She had assumed it would be American.

"I'm sorry to bother you, but I was wondering if I could talk to you for a few moments. My name is Poppy Denby and I'm a journalist for *The Daily Globe* in London. I'm writing an article on a lady scientist called June Leighton who worked at one of the laboratories your company sponsors."

Sanforth gave a tight smile. "You were the lady dancing with Raines. Did you enjoy it?"

What a curious question, thought Poppy. "Er, yes, I have just danced with Dr Raines."

"Did you enjoy it?" he asked, more pointedly.

Not in the least! she thought, but moderated her answer to, "As much as one enjoys these sorts of formal dances with a partner one has just barely met."

Sanforth grinned, suddenly making his unremarkable face light up with good humour. "I'll take that as a *no* then."

Poppy, despite herself, grinned too.

He chuckled. "Well, I'm pleased to meet you, Miss Denby. But I'm not sure how I can be of help to you. The Sanforth Foundation is, firstly, not a company – that would be Sanforth Industries – and secondly, neither the company nor the Foundation is mine. My father was the majority shareholder of the company, but now my mother holds those shares, and she is the one holding the reins at the Foundation too. I am merely here to hold her wrap and pull out her chair."

"Ah," said Poppy.

"Ah," Sanforth said and took another pull on his cigarette. "Would you like one?" he asked, slipping his hand into his jacket pocket.

"No thank you," said Poppy. "So," she said, "not your company or your foundation, but it does bear your name, so I imagine you know a little about it."

He shrugged. "A little. What do you want to know?"

"Well, as I said, I'm doing an article on June Leighton. Have you heard of her?"

Sanforth sighed deeply. "I have. Did you know her?"

Poppy shook her head. "Unfortunately not. But she seemed like a remarkable woman. I am writing a posthumous article on her... With full permission of her mother," she decided to add.

"I never met her mother before the funeral."

"You knew June then? You'd met her?"

"Oh yes. And as you rightly say, she was a remarkable woman."

Poppy heard the door to the hall open and close behind her, allowing a few bars of music to escape into the night. She'd better not take too long, or Gertrude would be looking for her. "That's good to know. Could you tell me then what work the Sanforth Foundation was – or is – sponsoring in June's laboratory? I've been told that she was just about to start work on a new project with Sanforth funding – before she died."

Sanforth flicked his cigarette to the ground and stubbed it out with his shoe. "That's not true." There was anger in his voice.

Poppy took a step back.

He noticed and his voice softened. "I'm sorry, Miss Denby. I didn't mean to alarm you. However, I don't want any untruths to slip into your article."

"Neither do I, Mr Sanforth, so perhaps you can clarify what you mean. What, exactly, is not true?"

The door to the hall opened again. Sanforth flicked a glance towards it, then turned to her and said quickly, "It's not true that June was about to start work on a Sanforth project. She would never agree to that. And that's why she was—"

"Ah Sanforth, there you are. Your mother's waiting for you. She's ready to go."

Poppy turned to see a gentleman in an academic robe. She recognized him as one of those who had sat at the "high table".

"Thanks, Wilson. I'll be right there."

Wilson waited expectantly. Sanforth gave him a pointed look. He took a few steps back but didn't leave. Sanforth pursed his lips.

"May I contact you tomorrow, Miss Denby? I'm afraid I need to go. But I would dearly like to continue our conversation."

I would dearly like that too. "Of course, Mr Sanforth. I'm staying at the Cherwell."

Sanforth nodded. "I'll be in touch in the morning, then. Good evening, miss." He gave a little bow and accompanied the scholar back into the hall.

As the door closed, Poppy was all alone in the garden. If it were the middle of the day, she might have stayed there, but she did not care to allow the shadows a foothold in her imagination. The previous autumn, during the Agnes Robson murder investigation, she had been attacked on the edge of a park on a night very much like this. Fortunately, she and Delilah had recently taken self-defence and ju-jitsu classes, so she had managed to fend off the assailant until help came. But the memory still sent shivers down her spine. She rubbed her arms in her sleeveless Lucien Lelong gown. *Yes, it's getting decidedly chilly out here...*

"What do you know about Edward Sanforth IV?" asked Poppy as she and Gertrude waited for their taxi outside the Magdalen Street gate. It was ten o'clock and they were in a line of guests who had spilled out from the Balliol dinner.

"I've only met him a couple of times," answered Gertrude, "so I can't vouch for his character. He is notorious though."

"Notorious for what?" asked Poppy, thinking that, unlike Bill Raines, Edward Sanforth had acted like a perfect gentleman. She shuddered at the thought of what Raines might have done if she'd had the misfortune of being in the garden alone with him.

Gertrude waved to a group of black-cloaked guests as they climbed into a taxi ahead of them. "He's a conchie," she said, turning back to Poppy.

"Goodness! Really?"

"Yes. He refused to serve. Much to the embarrassment of his parents, if I recall. Even though his father was American, his mother – and he – are British by birth. So, he was eligible for the draft. He could have moved to the States for the duration of the war, but he didn't; he chose to stay here and make a point of his objections. I believe he was forced to serve in an armaments factory. Ironically enough – or perhaps it was deliberate – one co-owned by Sanforth Industries."

Poppy stepped back to avoid a swaying scholar, who appeared the worse for wear for drink. "Interesting. So Sanforth Industries are into armaments?"

"Amongst other things. But yes, they have a few armaments factories on both sides of the pond. Which was why it was such an embarrassment to them that Edward turned out to be a pacifist – and a socialist."

Poppy took this all in. A socialist she could identify with – her father and aunt were both socialists (although her aunt more on the champagne side) – but she had never met a conscientious objector in the flesh. She'd met pacifists – those who had lived through the horrors of the war and declared "never again", and those who had been too old to go to war but objected strongly from the sidelines – but no one of conscription age who had actually refused to go.

"Do you know how he became a pacifist?"

"He got in with the wrong crowd here at Oxford, apparently. I always thought that was more of a Cambridge thing, but there you go."

"He was at Oxford?"

"Yes, before the war. His grandfather on his mother's side was a professor emeritus – in the sciences – and managed to get him in. Apparently, Edward was quite unremarkable. He didn't finish his degree – because of the war – but I'd heard he was on track for a third-class pass at best. So overall, quite a disappointment to the family. Not sure what he does now. He accompanies his mother on Foundation business, but I don't know what he actually *does*."

"He seems like quite a nice man, actually."

Gertrude looked up at Poppy, her round face flushed red with wine. "You spoke to him?"

"Yes, I bumped into him on the way back from the cloakroom. And he said he's going to come to my hotel tomorrow. I'm hoping to find out a bit more about what June was working on before she died. For the article. Edward – Mr Sanforth – seemed to suggest that he might know something about the project she was working on."

Gertrude nodded. "Well, he would probably know what research they're sponsoring. Funny how Sinclair didn't want to talk about that, isn't it?"

"It is," said Poppy. "All very top secret and hush-hush. June didn't say anything to you about it, did she?"

Gertrude shook her head. "No, she didn't. But she didn't talk to me about her actual work – the science of it. Not my field, you see. She only told me about how horrible Raines and the Mackintosh boy were to her. And of course, the issue of him stealing her work. After meeting them both tonight, I imagine you are not in the least surprised that they behaved so abominably towards her."

Poppy frowned, remembering Raines' painful squeeze of her hand and Mackintosh's dismissive behaviour. "Not in the least. But thank you for inviting me. It has given me a lot more material to work with."

"Do you have enough for the article now? You have those transcripts of June's complaints, don't you? Have you had a chance to look at them yet?"

"Not yet," said Poppy. "But I will. What I would like, though, is to speak to someone more sympathetic to June who might know about her work. Did she have any friends in the sciences she might have spoken to? Anyone at Somerville?"

Gertrude thought for a moment and shook her head. "Not really. June didn't have many friends. She worked day and night. There were a few girls she sat with at meals and such, but they've gone up now after their degrees. There's no one I can think of who is still here. Oh!" Gertrude turned to Poppy, her face lighting up. "What about that woman who works in the Crystal Crypt? The lab assistant. June mentioned her a few times. What was her name? Sylvie someone?"

"Sophie," said Poppy. "Sophie Blackburn. Yes, I've spoken to her briefly but perhaps I should do so again." Poppy, still nervous about letting on that it was actually Sophie who had invited her to Oxford in the first place, kept her voice neutral. "I'll see if I can speak to her tomorrow."

A taxi pulled up. Gertrude instructed the driver to take Poppy back to the Cherwell.

"Aren't you coming too?" asked Poppy.

"No," said the academic. "It's just a short walk up to Somerville from here. Do pop by for tea before you go back to London, Poppy; it's been delightful meeting you. And I very much look forward to reading your article."

You might get a very big surprise when you do, thought Poppy, before waving goodbye.

CHAPTER 18

WEDNESDAY 22 APRIL 1925, LONDON

Rollo stepped out of Mark Lane Tube Station and headed down Great Tower Hill. To his left were the ancient hulking walls of the Tower of London, and before him the dark grey swell of the Thames. There were boats and barges on the water, ferrying goods to sustain the heaving population of the metropolis, while on the opposite bank, a trio of cranes was building yet another edifice of modernity. He turned left as he reached the river, heading towards the docks, marking, with some dread, the yellow-green fog creeping over the stone embankment and onto the cobbled towpath. *That's all we need*, thought Rollo, *another London particular.* He sniffed the air and recoiled at the sharp sulphuric stench, then whipped out his handkerchief and covered his nose and mouth as he hurried towards his destination. A few minutes later, he reached it. The Old George Tavern was shoe-horned between a dilapidated warehouse and tannery and looked as foul as it smelled. Rollo cursed Richard Easling for choosing it as their meeting place.

Easling was a disgraced copper. Formerly a high-ranking officer in the Metropolitan Police, he had been stripped of his rank and kicked out of the force when it came to light that he had been in the pay of Lord Melvyn Dorchester, who was currently serving seven years for a multitude of crimes, including the attempted murder of his own daughter, Elizabeth. It was Rollo and Poppy who had broken the story leading to Dorchester's conviction and Easling's defrocking. And yet, Easling didn't hold a grudge against the American dwarf. At least not a big one. Rollo knew that much of it had to do with Easling's new "career" as a purveyor of information for profit – known more colloquially as a snitch. Easling's years on the force and his easy-going relations with the criminal underworld meant that he knew an awful lot about an awful lot, and as long as you were prepared to pay him – as Rollo was – he didn't care who you were. So, while the former police officer's respectability as one of London's finest had suffered in his fall from grace, his bank balance had not.

He could certainly afford to meet in a better-class establishment than the Old George, but, Rollo knew, he was no longer welcome in those more fashionable clubs. Easling, although earning enough on which to retire well in another city in another part of the world that did not know or care about his past indiscretions, was for now a social pariah.

Once inside the pub, Rollo edged his way past a heavily tattooed seaman staring at the sagging breasts of an ageing prostitute, and found Easling nursing a warm beer the colour of urine.

"Easling."

"Rolandson."

Rollo pulled out a stool, sticky with the residue of a spilt beer, laid his handkerchief on it, and clambered up. He caught the eye of the weary barmaid, and without being asked she pulled a pint of the same lavatorial beer. *The house special*, thought Rollo, as he fetched a shilling from his coin pouch and gave it to the woman. She took it without thanks.

Rollo took a tentative sip: it was as unpleasant as he had expected.

"So, what do you want?" asked Easling, not bothering with small talk. Rollo didn't mind; the less time he spent with this man in this place, the better. He had other people to see today.

He slipped a wadge of ten-shilling notes out of his wallet and tucked them under an old jam jar lid that was being used as an ashtray. "Sophie Blackburn and Lionel Saunders. What have you heard?"

Easling stubbed out his cigarette and picked up the cash, counting it like a bank teller.

"Nothing recent."

"How about last year?"

Easling stared at him.

Rollo stared back. He did have more money, but he didn't want to bring it out just yet.

Easling shrugged and took another sip of his beer. "A home invasion. She broke into his flat and threatened him. She had a knife."

Rollo hadn't heard about the knife.

"Did she hurt him?"

"No. Just threatened him."

"What did she want?"

Easling lit another cigarette. He didn't bother offering one to Rollo. "She said she wanted him to admit that he'd killed Isaacs – your reporter – or if he hadn't, to tell her who did."

"And did he?"

Easling grinned, showing a broken front tooth. "Did he kill Isaacs, or did he tell her he did?"

"Either."

Easling shrugged. "I don't know. A neighbour saw what was going on and called the lads."

"The lads", Rollo knew, meant the police. "And Saunders didn't lay charges?"

"No."

"And why's that?"

Easling grinned again. "Why do you think?"

Rollo took a sip of his own beer – not because he was thirsty, but because it gave him an air of nonchalance. These sorts of meetings had a certain theatricality to them, and the formalities needed to be observed. Eventually he said, "Because he fears that if Sophie goes to court, she'll repeat her allegations in front of a judge and that maybe she's got a bit more evidence than was available back in '20. And he doesn't want that coming out. So, he was happy to drop charges in exchange for her being locked up in the loony bin to discredit her mental state. Am I right?"

Easling ran his thumb through the wad of cash and said nothing.

Rollo reached into his wallet, took out some more bills, and placed them on the table.

Easling picked them up and said, "You're right."

"What's the new information?"

"That I don't know."

Rollo raised a shaggy eyebrow.

Easling shrugged and in an exaggerated Cockney accent said, "I swear guvnor, I don't know nuffing." Then, in his normal voice, added, "Why don't you ask her yourself?"

"Sophie?"

"Yeah, you're in touch with her. Or at least that Denby girl is."

Rollo was not easily startled, but he was now. But years of practice disguised it. "How do you know that?"

Easling shrugged. "I have friends on the Oxford City Police. Not everyone thought tossing me out on my arse was the right thing to do."

"And what else do these friends say?"

Easling took a drag on his cigarette and exhaled, blowing the cloud of smoke over the table. It settled on Rollo's beer. "That she'd better be careful. She's making trouble for the lads."

"Which lads?"

"The ones that did a perfectly good job investigating an accidental death that should be laid to rest. But as usual, your girl is sticking her nose in where it doesn't belong."

Easling sucked again on his fag.

"And?"

"And what?"

"And what are your lads planning on doing about it?"

Easling laughed. It was as unpleasant as Rollo's beer. "What are you suggesting, Rolandson? That the best of blue, sworn to protect and serve, would hurt a young girl?"

"No. Not the best of blue. But not all of them are the best. You know that as well as I do." Rollo grabbed Easling's wrist. His grip was surprisingly strong for such a small man. "Tell them to back off her, Easling."

Easling shook himself free. "Or what? Whatya gonna do about it, little fella?"

Rollo forced himself to calm down. He gave Easling a humourless smile. "You're not the only one who deals in information, Easling; I have an entire archive of it. And more besides. You never did any time after Dorchester went down. But I know for a fact that the extent of your true involvement never came out. But if anything happens to Poppy Denby – or to me – it will. So let the lads know that."

Rollo climbed down from his stool, his head now level with Easling's chest. "Oh, and in case you didn't know – but I'm sure you do – Dorchester is due for a parole hearing soon. And while you, and Saunders, have been protecting him all this time, he may be offered a reduction on his sentence in exchange for information on his former associates. So beware, Easling: your back might not be as well covered as you think."

Easling lurched in an attempt to grab Rollo by the shirt front. But he was impaired by his large belly wedged against the table. Rollo made a hasty retreat before the big man could rally. As he passed the sailor, he slipped him a half-crown and whispered something in the man's ear. The sailor stood, and as Rollo opened the tavern door, he heard the man say, "Oi, leave the little fella alone." Rollo did not wait to hear Easling's reply but hurried out to be embraced by the London particular.

Rollo got off the train at Temple Station and made his way up through Mid-Temple to Fleet Street. The higher up the hill he climbed, the more his heart pounded. Rollo knew that he needed to get to Oxford. Easling was right; he should speak to Sophie himself. But he wasn't aware that she had a telephone, and it was best that he spoke to her in person. And he also wanted to keep an eye on Poppy. He knew she had handled herself in difficult situations before and he wasn't one to mollycoddle her, but he had a sense that this might be more than she could deal with. She normally had friends and allies with her, but in Oxford, as far as he knew, she was on her own. He would head up there first thing in the morning. He would go on the train, as he couldn't drive himself and he didn't want to worry Danny Rokeby. Unlike Rollo, he did mollycoddle Poppy, and it was the one thing that worried Rollo about their upcoming marriage. Yes, he could understand a man wanting to protect the woman he loved – God knew he would do anything to protect Yasmin – but Rollo feared that Poppy's wings might be clipped. So no, he wouldn't be telling Danny Boy what he'd heard.

By the time he got back to the office, Mavis Bradshaw had locked up reception and gone home. He checked his messages and saw that Poppy had called at four o'clock and all was well. Good. He could relax a little more. She was going to an academic dinner tonight with the principal of Somerville College – a woman – so that should be safe enough. She'd asked him to ring her at the hotel in the morning. He'd do better than that and go and see her. He also saw that she'd asked Ivan Molanov to dig out anything he could find on the Sanforth Foundation. The name rang a bell, but he couldn't place it. There was some vague association with the interminable charity balls he tried to avoid.

Rollo greeted a young sports reporter on the way out of the newsroom.

"Just posted my copy, Mr Rolandson."

"Good lad. Is Ike still in?"

"No. I'm the last to leave, sir. Everyone else seemed to meet deadline before me."

Rollo grinned up at the lad. "They'd damned better have!"

The reporter grinned back, raised his hat, and left. Rollo pushed the door into the newsroom and made his way through the overflowing wastepaper baskets to his office at the end of the room. He really should bring up the issue of housekeeping at the next editorial meeting. But, he thought, as he pushed open his own door, he didn't really have a leg to stand on. He just needed to pick up some papers and he'd be heading home. He still had the necklace he'd bought in his inside pocket and smiled to himself, thinking how much Yazzie would love it. Then he chastised himself for carrying it with him down to the docks. If he'd been mugged, that would be a lot of money down the tubes, and Yazzie wouldn't thank him for that.

He got the papers he needed from his desk and then noticed a file placed on top of his typewriter. On the front was pinned a note written in Ivan Molanov's bold script: "Rollo, give to Miss Denby as per her request." Rollo opened the file and found a typed summary entitled "Sanforth Foundation / Sanforth Industries".

He gave it a quick scan and noted that it indexed various articles in the file: Sanforth Foundation Donates to Oxford Lab; Sanforth Industries in MOD Wrangle; Sanforth Industries Wins Big Defence Contract; Sanforth Industries Criticized for Weimar Investments; Sanforth Foundation Withdraws Funding from Cambridge – Pacifists to Blame; Sanforth Industries in Hostile Takeover of Diamond Mine in German South West Africa...

Suddenly, a shadow fell over the file, blocking Rollo's light. Then came a crushing blow to the back of his head. The file fell from Rollo's hands as he slumped to the ground. His assailant stepped over his body, retrieved the file, then turned out the light, closing the door on the way out.

Chapter 19

Thursday 23 April 1925, Oxford

Poppy dropped two lumps of sugar into her tea and stirred. It was a particularly palatable brew – one she'd never had before – and she reminded herself to ask the waiter the name of the blend. She was once again having a hot cooked breakfast, rather than the slice of toast she normally snatched on the way to the office, thinking ruefully about her waistline. However, she – or at least the newspaper – was paying for the breakfast as part of her hotel package, so she didn't want to let it go to waste.

She took her mind off her figure – and the wedding dress it needed to fit into – and instead contemplated the day ahead. She was very much looking forward to the promised visit by Edward Sanforth but was perturbed that they hadn't agreed to a time. How silly of her not to have asked. She couldn't wait in all day. He had said "the morning" – but when? She had a lot to do. She needed to track down Sophie. She needed to try to find out what was in June's police pathology report. She needed to find out what Ivan Molanov had managed to pull out of the archives on the Sanforth Foundation. And of course, she needed to speak to Rollo. Her encounter with Bill Raines last night – with his barely disguised violence – made her all the more inclined to believe that June might indeed have been the victim of foul play. Although her death could still have been a tragic accident, there was very little doubt in her mind that Dr Bill Raines was the type of man who was capable of physically hurting a woman.

That view had been confirmed by her reading last night of the complaints June had made to the faculty. They documented verbal put-downs from both Raines and Mackintosh, efforts to undermine her ability to work by childish pranks like hiding her equipment and samples, and, worst of all, a disturbing report of inappropriate sexual behaviour when a drunken Raines had grabbed and fondled her at an after-work function. All of these incidents had been dismissed by Professor Sinclair as "boys will be boys", with a platitudinous sop that he would "have a quiet word with them". Poor June. It sounded like the Crystal Crypt was a *terrible* place for a woman. *She must have loved her professional work an awful lot to put up with that nonsense*, thought Poppy. But even that came under threat when Mackintosh stole her research and published it as his own.

A tight ball of rage was forming in Poppy's belly. How dare those men treat June that way? Whether or not the scientist had been murdered, there were wrongs that needed to be righted, and Poppy decided she would not stop until the whole sordid affair was exposed. Oh yes, she would write an article at the end of all this. And it would be a damning one on the way a young woman had been hounded to her death.

As she finished her tea, she was surprised to see a serious-looking WPC Rosie Winter being shown to her table. The other guests looked on curiously. Poppy could imagine their thoughts: *This is the second time this young, unchaperoned woman has received a visit from the local constabulary. And did you see her stagger in here yesterday, like a drowned rat? Not to mention coming back last night – on her own – in a taxi, with alcohol on her breath and looking like she'd just stepped off a Paris runway...*

Poppy smiled at the elderly couple at the next table. The gentleman with the impressive handlebar moustache smiled back. The lady glowered, first at her, then her husband, who lowered his eyes and cleared his throat. *Oh dear...* She turned to greet the policewoman.

"Morning, Rosie. I wasn't expecting you. Sorry, I've just finished breakfast, but would you like anything?"

"No thank you," said Rosie, stepping anxiously from foot to foot. "I'm sorry to bother you so early, Poppy, but I thought you would want to know: last night on the way back from the Balliol dinner, Dr Fuller may have been attacked outside Somerville College."

Poppy dropped her teaspoon with a clatter. "Gertrude! Oh my heavens, is she all right?"

Rosie nodded. "She had a serious blow to the head, but fortunately she was found by passers-by and taken to the infirmary. She's conscious and has asked to see you."

Poppy stood up and gathered her things. "I'll be right there."

Just as the two women were leaving the hotel, the concierge called out, "Oh, Miss Denby! There's a telephone call for you from London!"

Poppy waved to him and said, "That'll be my editor. Tell him I'll call back as soon as I can. I have something urgent to attend to. Oh, and if a Mr Edward Sanforth calls, please give him my apologies and ask if he could leave a contact telephone number."

Poppy and Rosie hurried outside to an awaiting police motor car. A young male constable was driving. Rosie did not introduce them but ushered Poppy into the back seat and asked the constable to drive them to the infirmary. "I don't normally get chauffeur driven," she whispered, "but my sergeant thought a possible assault of an Oxford don merited it. And I normally wouldn't be allowed on the case, but they thought you might need a chaperone after what happened with the bicycle." Rosie's cheeks were flushed with excitement.

"You told your superiors about the bicycle?"

Rosie lowered her voice even further. "I'm sorry. Yes. After what happened to Dr Fuller, I felt that they should know. It shows a pattern of violence. I would have got into trouble if I had withheld the information any longer."

Poppy tensed. *Oh dear. So much for not getting the police involved.* Poppy gave Rosie a sympathetic look. "That's all right. I understand I put you in a difficult position asking you not to file a report."

Rosie nodded and gave a warning look to the back of the male constable's head. Poppy understood immediately what she meant and raised her voice so the driver could hear. "And well you should have. You did exactly the right thing." Then she added, "You keep saying 'possible assault', Rosie. And that Gertrude 'might' have been attacked. What do you mean by that? Was she or wasn't she?"

Rosie raised her voice to a clearly audible level. "We're not sure, Miss Denby. Dr Fuller claims she was attacked, but no one saw anything. However, there are witnesses who say that Dr Fuller was quite tipsy when she left the dinner – so there is the possibility that she might just have slipped and hit her head." Rosie gave Poppy a knowing look and added, "So we're keeping an open mind until more evidence comes to light."

Poppy realized that by "we", Rosie meant her superiors on the force rather than herself. Poppy nodded her understanding. The two women slipped into silence for the rest of the journey to the Radcliffe Infirmary, which happened to be only a little bit further down the road from the offices of *The Oxford Gazette*, and just a short distance from Somerville College. *Fortunately for Gertrude*, thought Poppy.

Two student-aged young women were sitting in the hall outside Gertrude's ward, in discussion with George Lewis from *The Oxford Gazette*, who was taking notes. He looked up as Poppy and Rosie approached. He nodded to Poppy and she smiled an acknowledgment.

"Can I have a word with you after you've finished visiting Dr Fuller?" asked the editor.

"Of course," said Poppy and she followed Rosie into the room.

Gertrude Fuller appeared to be asleep. Her head was swathed in bandages and she had a black eye brewing. Rosie pulled out a chair for Poppy and she sat down. She took Gertrude's hand and squeezed it gently. "Gertrude, it's me, Poppy. Are you awake?"

Gertrude stirred and opened her good eye. Her lips twitched into a flicker of a smile. "Poppy. I'm so glad you came. I should have got the taxi home with you last night like you said."

"Yes, you should have," said Poppy, her voice absent of any chastisement. She squeezed Gertrude's hand again. "What happened?"

Gertrude sighed. It sounded painful. "I don't know really. I left you after you got in the taxi and walked back to the college. It's only a five-minute walk. But after I crossed over the road past the Martyrs' Memorial, I started to feel uncomfortable – as if there were someone following me. But when I looked back, I couldn't see anyone. I quickened my pace, and by the time I got to St Giles I felt as if I'd shaken them. But as I approached the gates of the college, someone jumped me from behind, and as I tried to swivel around to see who it was, I felt a dizzying blow to the head. Then I fell to the ground and hit my face. I screamed for help, then curled up, hoping the bounder would leave me alone. But I got a kick to the ribs for my trouble. The doctor says one of them's broken." She stopped for a moment to take some laboured breaths.

Poppy was near to tears. How could anyone assault this lovely lady? How could anyone assault anyone? She took a deep breath. It wouldn't do Gertrude any good if she broke down.

"I understand more than you can imagine, Gertrude. I was attacked last year. Someone grabbed me from behind too – and I couldn't see his face. But I definitely had a sense that it was a man. And a sense of his size and strength. Did you? Can you say if it was male or female?"

Gertrude closed her eyes. Minutes passed and Poppy wondered for a moment if the don had fallen asleep. But she hadn't. She stirred and said, "I think it was a man. It was probably a man. I heard breathing. It was deep. And he – if it were a he – was taller than me. But then, I'm not a tall woman. But there was also a smell. I can't say what it was, but it was sharp – acidic. A strong aftershave lotion, perhaps. Or some kind of chemical. Whatever it was, it was not very feminine. Besides, women don't tend to physically grab and attack people in the street, do they?"

Poppy looked across at Rosie. "Have the police taken Gertrude's statement, WPC Winter?"

Rosie nodded. "Yes, we did. Earlier this morning. My sergeant took it. And I accompanied him." She gave Poppy one of the looks that Poppy was quickly learning was Rosie's code for: "but there's more to it than that". Poppy gave her the usual "all right, let's talk later" look and turned back to Gertrude.

"Is there anything I can get you? Anyone you want me to call?"

Gertrude shook her head gently on the pillow. Even that appeared to hurt. "No thank you. My graduate students Annabel and Martha are getting me everything I need. Are they still here?"

Poppy assumed she was talking about the two young women she'd seen outside. "Yes, they are. Would you like me to call them?"

"Yes please," said Gertrude. "I need some work brought in."

"Work?"

Gertrude cracked a painful smile. "No rest for the wicked, Poppy. I have edits to do on a journal article. If I miss my deadline, I'm in trouble."

Poppy realized it would do no good telling Gertrude to have a rest. She'd leave that to the doctors and nurses to enforce. So, she said her goodbyes and promised she'd drop in to see her again before she left Oxford.

Outside, she told the students that Gertrude had asked for them, and after they left took a seat beside George Lewis. "Would you mind waiting a few minutes?" she asked Rosie. The WPC said that was fine and went off to talk to a nurse.

Lewis nodded after her. "I see you're on first-name terms with the polis. That was quick work."

"Fate brought us together," said Poppy, and she went on to tell the editor about the accident with the bicycle.

"Goodness! And you're all right?" he asked, appraising her.

"Nothing more than a good soaking. I was prepared to believe that it might simply have been some young scallywags having a lark, but now, after what's happened to Gertrude, I'm beginning to wonder."

The editor nodded seriously. "So, you believe it's connected to the article you're writing on June Leighton? Tell me then, Miss Denby, what are you really investigating here? I know you didn't give me the full story when we spoke yesterday."

Poppy was reluctant to divulge everything to Lewis without first checking with Rollo. She was sorry to have missed speaking to him last night – and this morning when he called. But she knew she had to give the Oxford newspaperman something. He was far too shrewd to buy the "woman at work" line any longer, and besides, she did not want to make an enemy of him. So, after first ascertaining that there would be six days before the weekly paper's next edition, she decided to tell Lewis what she'd found out – and what she still needed to unearth.

By the time she'd finished, Lewis' eyes were alight with excitement. "By Jove, Miss Denby, that's a cracking story so far. But if it's murder... even better!" He grinned and then looked sheepish. "You know what I mean."

"I do," said Poppy. "I was prepared to believe it was just a story of a woman being bullied and hounded to an accidental death. According to Gertrude, June was forced to work out of hours in order to avoid her fellow scientists. And if she hadn't been alone, the accident might not have happened. Or someone could have helped her. That, to be perfectly honest, is what I've been working with. But if that's all it is, why did someone attack Gertrude and try to injure me? It suggests they're trying to – literally – knock me off the case. Someone is trying to hide something. Something illegal. Now, it still might not be murder, but I do believe June died with a secret. A secret someone – or some people – are trying to keep in the grave. And me coming here has stirred things up."

"Aye," said Lewis, his salt and pepper moustache twitching under his newshound nose, "that's all very interesting. But it could still be murder. How can we prove that?"

"Or disprove it," added Poppy.

Lewis grinned. "Of course. What would we need to do that?"

Poppy thought about it a moment and said, "I'd like to have a look at the pathologist's report and – if possible – speak to the pathologist. I would also like an independent medical professional to look at the report. Is that something you could arrange?"

Lewis twirled the end of his moustache with his finger, deep in thought, then eventually said, "Aye, Miss Denby, I think I could arrange that. Leave it to me and I'll see what I can do. I'll send word to you at your hotel when I've made the arrangements." He looked up as Rosie Winter approached.

"Are you going to be arranging protection for Miss Denby, constable?"

Rosie shrugged and said ruefully, "I am her protection, Mr Lewis."

Lewis looked from one woman to the other. "You lassies be careful then. Promise me that."

Poppy was touched by his concern. "We will, Mr Lewis, we will."

CHAPTER 20

THURSDAY 23 APRIL 1925, LONDON

Rollo Rolandson had one hell of a headache. He sat in his office chair with an ice pack wrapped in a tea towel pressed against a walnut-sized lump. Ike Garfield handed him a cup of sweet black coffee and sat down in the chair opposite.

"Are you sure you don't want me to call the police?"

"Very sure. We don't know which of them are still loyal to Easling." Rollo went on to tell Ike about his meeting with Easling the previous day and what he'd let on about sympathetic coppers in the Met in London and the Oxford City Police. "So that's why I don't want to alert the police just yet."

"You definitely think it was Easling?"

"No, not definitely. But I was clobbered after coming back from seeing him. So, it could have been him. Or someone in his pay."

"Or Lionel Saunders," offered Ike.

Rollo nodded, then regretted it as a stabbing pain shot through his head. He winced. "Yes, it could have been Saunders or one of the boys from the *Courier* – they weren't happy when I was round there yesterday. But robbery and assault aren't usually their style. We've got a robust professional rivalry, but nothing more. Saunders himself, though – I wouldn't put it past him."

Ike looked around the cluttered office thick with dust in the early morning light. "Are you sure the file's the only thing that's gone?"

Rollo patted his pocket and felt the weight of Yasmin's necklace. "Yes, it seems to be. It was in my hands before whoever it was whacked me."

"So you said it was the Sanforth Industries file... This must have something to do with Poppy's investigation in Oxford."

Rollo sipped his coffee and took a moment to allow the restorative brew to do its work. "Yes, I believe it is. And Sophie Blackburn. She is the connection here between Sanforth Industries, Lionel Saunders, and whatever he's covering up about Bert Isaacs' death. It's just too much of a coincidence otherwise. Sophie, to say the least, is obsessed with bringing Bert's killer to justice. And now, suddenly, she's got Poppy onto another mysterious death."

"Do you think Sanforth Industries is linked to Bert's death too?" asked Ike, lighting up his pipe.

Rollo shrugged and took another sip of his coffee. "Their name never came up five years ago, but I'm wondering if there is a connection between the Sanforths and the Dorchesters. They moved in similar social and professional circles. It wouldn't surprise me if there is. Perhaps Sophie has discovered that connection. But Sophie being Sophie has not come out and said it. She doesn't trust people, and she doesn't trust people will believe her if she presents evidence."

Ike sucked on his pipe until the tobacco smouldered. "Can't blame the woman after all she's been through."

"Agreed," said Rollo. "So perhaps that's why she's got Poppy onto the case. Because Poppy's reputation as an investigator is impeccable. If Poppy discovers what Sophie has already discovered, there's more chance Sophie will be believed. Just a bloody roundabout way of doing things!"

Ike gave his boss a sympathetic look. "And bloody violent. Do you think Poppy might be in danger?"

Rollo put down his cup on his desk with a clatter. "I'm worried that she might be, Ike. I was already worried after seeing Easling – the fact that he'd mentioned someone on the Oxford force had told him she was there. So, I intended to go up to Oxford this morning on the early train. But I think you'd better go instead. You've got a bit more muscle than me."

"What about Daniel?"

Rollo frowned. He was still reluctant to get Poppy's fiancé involved. "Not yet. I want Poppy to be protected but not prevented from doing her job. And Danny Boy cannot be trusted with that – for obvious reasons. Can you go? Help Poppy in her investigation, keep an eye out for her safety without worrying her too much, then get whatever information you can from Sophie. Pass on any other stories you're working on to the new lad, Cartwright. It's about time he got blooded."

"All right. I'll just have to tell the wife where I'm going. I'll also have to telephone ahead to book into the hotel, just in case I get there and someone objects to my complexion."

Rollo nodded. He knew better than to dismiss Ike's pre-emptive assumption that he might be the victim of racial discrimination. There were around twenty thousand black people in Britain at the time – far, far fewer than in Rollo's United States – and the discrimination against them was not as overt, but it was most definitely there. In 1919 there had been riots in port cities around the country after white dockers objected to black labourers being brought in from the Caribbean. Ike Garfield, of course, was a well-spoken, well-educated gentleman, but even so, if a publican or hotelier decided to turn him away, he had very few grounds for appeal. Rollo hoped that in the academic city of Oxford he wouldn't have too many problems, but it was still a possibility. "Get Mavis to call on your behalf as an official booking from the paper. She's got the details of the hotel Poppy's staying at. That should smooth things over."

"Righto. I'll get going as soon as I can. I'll take the motor down – quicker than the train, and it will create more of an impression if I arrive driving my own car." He grinned. "All right, the company car, but no one's to know."

Rollo smiled wryly back.

"What will you be doing?" asked Ike.

Rollo emptied his coffee and repositioned the ice pack on his head. "First off, I'll go see Ivan in the archive. He should be in now." He looked at his watch. It was nearly eight o'clock. He was fortunate that Ike had arrived at the office early to type up an article, and grateful that it was his senior reporter who had found him sprawled on the floor and not one of the junior staff – or his receptionist, Mavis. Ike was unflappable. Danny Rokeby usually was too, and Rollo would stake his life on the loyalty of both men, but in this case, where Poppy was involved, he was glad it wasn't the photographer who had found him. One whiff that it might be connected to the story his fiancée was working on and he would go ballistic. An even keel was needed. Rollo had already asked Ike not to mention his assault to any of the staff. He would let it be known – and look at ways to improve security in the building – at a more circumspect time. For now, he needed to get Ike off to Oxford, and to get going on the London side of the investigation himself.

Ivan Molanov would be the first port of call. He wanted to find out if he had copies of the articles he had compiled or could remember what was in them. The archivist had the memory of a bull elephant. Thereafter, he would drop home to smooth things over with Yasmin. She would be angry with him, assuming he'd spent the night at his club and failed to let her know – which, to his shame, he sometimes did; it had been hard to shake his bachelor ways. After Yasmin was mollified with the necklace, he had other plans. But much would depend on what Ivan remembered was in the file. So, he and Ike wished each other luck and parted ways, promising to telephone as soon as either of them had any information to share.

Rollo found Ivan seated at his desk, systematically reading through a pile of the city's morning newspapers. This was what he did every morning. Beside him he had a typed list of current stories that the *Globe* reporters were working on, and his first job of the day was to find anything tangentially connected in the rival papers. He also assessed and extracted any articles that were connected to prominent people or institutions that might, at some stage in the future, become useful. Some of these articles were mere gossip, many of them pertaining to socialites, and would be filed in a section of the archive nicknamed the Jazz Files. But neither Ivan nor Rollo underestimated the value of gossip. Although much of it might turn out to be untrue, there were often nuggets of gold to be found, and many a time a big story had been broken by something that could easily have been dismissed as tittle-tattle. Rollo recalled that Poppy's first big story – the Dorchester scandal – had been solved from some information in one of these files, and that Ivan Molanov himself had been reunited with his daughter, whom he feared dead, because of something else Poppy had unearthed from them. Rollo knew, because of that, he could trust Ivan with the news that he'd been attacked overnight.

Ivan looked up and stared at Rollo over his half-moon glasses. "Morning, Yankee; you look like hell."

"Thanks, Rusky; you're no oil painting yourself." The editor grinned at his archivist, but all he received was a scowl in reply. This did not bother him in the least. Ivan was a crusty old coot but loyal as the day was long. Rollo had given him a job when no one else would and protected him from deportation back to Russia where he was a wanted man.

Rollo sat down and showed Ivan the welt on his head.

"You hit your head?"

"Someone hit it for me." Rollo then went on to explain what had happened the night before and how the file the archivist had compiled had been stolen. Ivan remained expressionless.

"So, what I want to know is, do you have copies of the articles in the files? Or of the summary list? Or both?"

"Is the pope Catholic?" asked Ivan, then got up and opened a filing cabinet behind his desk. A few moments later he returned with a carbon copy of the summary document. "I always carbon my summaries. Some of those articles I kept multiple copies, some of them not. But I can track them down in the library at the British Museum if I don't have them here."

"How long will it take?"

Ivan shrugged. "An hour to get the ones I have here. Longer for the others."

"Get me what you've got here first. We don't have that much time."

Ivan grunted and got to work.

CHAPTER 21

THURSDAY 23 APRIL 1925, OXFORD

Poppy and Rosie left the hospital and declined a lift from the male police constable. "He's just here to keep an eye on us," whispered Rosie. "There's more we can do without him."

Together they had agreed a plan of action. While George Lewis was working on getting the pathologist's report, Poppy and Rosie were first going to the laboratory to see if they could speak to Sophie Blackburn. Rosie said she would also like to speak to the male scientists in relation to Gertrude's attack.

"Are you allowed to?" asked Poppy.

Rosie shrugged. "They haven't told me I can't... but I should imagine it won't be long until they do. All they told me this morning was to keep an eye on you. They didn't tell me what else I should or shouldn't be doing while I did that."

Rosie had a spring in her step, and despite the seriousness of the circumstances, Poppy couldn't help but be pleased for her new friend that she was finally getting to do some exciting police work. Poppy was, though, a little concerned that having a police officer in tow might hinder her own investigations, but for now there was nothing she needed to do without her. If that time came, however, Poppy would have to work out a way to politely lose her chaperone.

Fifteen minutes later and Poppy and Rosie were on Broad Street, outside the Science Museum. "On second thoughts, I think I'd better speak to the gentlemen on my own," said Rosie apologetically. "It will be hard to justify why you are with me on a police investigation, don't you think? I'll tell you if I find out anything pertinent. Is that all right?"

Poppy suppressed a smile. So, it was Rosie who was trying to lose her chaperone, not the other way round! Poppy didn't mind. She had already ascertained that there was a basement entrance to the crypt, so while Rosie went in through the front door of the museum and down the stairs – as she had on her first visit – Poppy decided she'd have a snoop around the unofficial entrance.

"That's fine. But if you see Sophie, ask her to come out to see me. She can make an excuse about popping out for something."

Rosie agreed and they arranged to meet in Blackwell's Bookshop later.

Poppy made a show of crossing the road but didn't go into either the bookshop or the White Horse Tavern. Instead, she waited for Rosie to go up the stairs and into the museum and then hurried across the road and down the stairs to the basement. She didn't intend to deceive, but on the spur of the moment worried that Rosie might forbid her from investigating on her own; so, Poppy reasoned, what the WPC didn't know wouldn't hurt her.

Poppy had a quick peek through the grimy window and saw an empty vestibule. She remembered from her first visit that the laboratory was a series of intersecting rooms and that the main laboratory was next door to this little entrance hall from the back door of the basement. She tried the door and was relieved that it was open. Perhaps it was kept unlocked as a fire exit while the scientists were working. She snuck in, stepping into a makeshift cloakroom with hats, coats, and umbrellas hung on a rack.

The door to the main laboratory was open just a crack and

she peeked through. She waited for Rosie to make an appearance. She expected the policewoman would speak to the scientists in one of the offices, rather than the laboratory, as she had done. Poppy wondered again why she hadn't just told Rosie she would be snooping around so the two could work in tandem – it wasn't a certainty, after all, that Rosie would have said no. Perhaps, thought Poppy, it was because she spent so much of her time trying to avoid the police – so they wouldn't stop her investigations – that it was a hard habit to break.

Poppy could see the backs of two men in white lab coats – but as far as she could tell, Sophie wasn't in the room. A pity, Poppy thought, as she had half-hoped to slip in and speak to her while Rosie was busy talking to the men. She still felt uncomfortable about breaking Sophie's confidence and wanted to smooth things over with her before Rosie spoke to her. But Sophie, as far as Poppy could tell, wasn't there.

She watched one of the men putting something in a glass tube and placing it in some kind of machine. Could this be the X-ray machine that killed June? Poppy really regretted not having someone with her on the investigation who knew what they were talking about when it came to the science. She felt like she had one of her hands tied behind her back with her lack of knowledge.

Suddenly, she saw Professor Sinclair step into the room. At his shoulder was Rosie. "Gentlemen," he said. "This is WPC Winter, and she has some unfortunate news about Dr Fuller. She was attacked last night and is in the infirmary. Would you come into my office, please? WPC Winter would like to talk to us, as we were at the dinner with Dr Fuller last night." He turned to Rosie. "I assume the police are speaking to everyone who saw Dr Fuller last night, not just us?"

"That's right," said Rosie. "My colleagues are speaking to other witnesses."

Miles Mackintosh turned off the flame of a Bunsen burner and said, "So why did we get the woman? I didn't know women police officers were allowed to investigate cases."

"I didn't know there even *were* women police officers in Oxford," drawled Bill Raines and overtly looked Rosie up and down from the top of her rimmed helmet to her black-laced boots. To Poppy's annoyance, but not her surprise, his eyes lingered on the bright row of brass buttons over the police officer's chest.

"Well, there are, and I am here to take your statements," said Rosie in an admirably professional voice. "Come with me please, sirs."

Raines and Mackintosh shared a mocking look and sauntered out of the room. Poppy breathed a sigh of relief and pushed open the door. She wasn't sure what she was searching for, but she felt she needed to have a look around. She was careful not to get too close to any of the scientific equipment – she didn't want to break anything or scupper anyone's work – but she still wanted to get a feel for the place where June Leighton had worked and died. Her eyes were drawn again to what she thought was the X-ray machine. She was once X-rayed after she had been knocked down by a motor car, so she knew what a hospital X-ray machine looked like. This was similar, but different. There was no bed for the patient and it was a lot smaller, but there was still a camera and a frame to hold a plate. The glass tube was held in a clamp in front of the camera, and inside there was a test tube with some kind of sample to be photographed. What the sample was, Poppy had no idea. There was also a microscope through which the sample could be viewed, and, tempted as she was to have a look, she refrained. Instead, she noted numerous wires and cables, the thickest one running to a plug socket in the wall. Poppy looked to see where the cable attached to the machine and noted that the wooden boxing appeared scorched. Is this where the cable pulled out on the night of June's death? Poppy could see how easy it would be to trip over the main power cable running along the floor and wondered why these clever scientists had not found a way to make it safer. It was stuck to the floor with duct tape but would still be easy to pull up if a toe or heel got caught on it – particularly the heel of a ladies' shoe. Poppy imagined for a moment the scenario as it might have played out: June working with this very machine; June getting up to do something; June's heel getting caught in the cable and pulling it out of the machine... then June tripping and grasping at something to prevent herself from falling. There were tables, chairs, and shelves to grasp. Why on earth would she grasp at the cable when she fell?

Sophie was right; only a stupid person would do that. Even she, Poppy, who had very little understanding of science, would know not to grab at a wire. For heaven's sake, if she tripped and fell at home she would not grasp at the gramophone if it were playing. It was valuable and it was run by electricity. So why would June do it? Had she been impaired in some way? Might she have been drunk? Or perhaps had some kind of narcotic in her system? If she had, it would be mentioned in the pathology report.

The other option – if accident were to be ruled out – was that someone else had been there and electrocuted June with the wire. Had she been forced to hold the live cable in her hand after it had been pulled out of the machine?

The three main suspects, as far as Poppy could tell, were currently speaking to Rosie Winter. She wondered if they had been questioned as to their whereabouts on the night of June's death and whether or not their alibis had been checked. It was basic detective work, but work that appeared not to have been done in the case of June Leighton. Why was that? Why were the police so willing to accept that this was an accident? *On the other hand*, she thought, *what if we turn this on its head? Why would the police consider that it was* not *an accident?* That was the evidence Poppy needed to find. Because it still wasn't clear – even to her – that it was, in fact, murder. It came down to motive, means, and opportunity, as every reader of detective fiction knew. The means was electrocution – but that could still be accidental. The opportunity was whoever had access to the laboratory. Was that only the three other scientists? Poppy reminded herself how easily she had managed to enter. Someone else could have snuck in as she had. Or June may even have brought someone with her that night. What if she hadn't been alone from the start?

As far as motive went, there were a few ideas coalescing in Poppy's mind, but she needed further information. She definitely needed to speak with Edward Sanforth. He had suggested a few things last night that Poppy was keen to follow up. She very much hoped he would leave contact details for her at the hotel.

For now, there was nothing more she could find out in the laboratory, so she turned to leave by the way she had come. But as she opened the basement door, she came face to face with a man in a white lab coat with the smell of cigarettes on his breath. It was a man Poppy had never met before.

"Hello there," he said, looking at her curiously. "And who are you?"

"I – well – my name is Poppy Denby."

"Ah, so you're Poppy Denby. I've heard about you. Back to speak to Prof Sinclair, are you?" He looked over her shoulder as if expecting to see the head of the laboratory. He frowned when he didn't see him. "What are you doing coming out this door?" he asked.

"I – well – Professor Sinclair is busy. I came to see him, but I discovered he was already talking to someone else. I didn't want to interrupt so I thought I'd let myself out without bothering him."

"Through this door?" he asked again.

Poppy smiled winsomely. "It seemed easier than going back upstairs and down again." It was a feeble excuse and both Poppy and the man knew it. But he let it pass.

"I don't think we've met," said Poppy.

"We haven't," said the man. "I'm Reg Guthrie, one of the laboratory assistants."

"Ah!" said Poppy, suddenly placing him in her mind's eye in the group photograph Sophie had shown her. "You work with Sophie Blackburn. Is she here? I wouldn't mind having a quick word with her, but I'm not sure where to find her."

Guthrie frowned again. "She didn't come in today. Hasn't called to say why either. Left me with a stack of work to do on top of my own. Why do you want to speak with her?"

Poppy smiled again. "Oh, I just thought that it would be nice to get a woman's perspective on June. You've probably heard that I'm writing an article on her for my newspaper."

"I've heard that's what you've *said* you're doing."

Poppy kept the smile fixed on her face, refusing to take the bait. "Well, it is. It's a pity Sophie's not here. Do you have an address for her? Perhaps I can catch her at home?"

Guthrie squinted at her, grunted, then said, "Wait here."

Poppy watched as he walked into the laboratory, fearing for a moment that he was going to tell Professor Sinclair that she was there. But she need not have worried. The lab technician returned a minute or so later with an address written on a piece of paper. She took it from him with thanks. As she did, she heard voices from the laboratory. Guthrie heard them too and turned to look. Before he could alert the professor, she gushed a quick goodbye and hurried back up the stairs, across Broad Street, and into Blackwell's Bookshop. Her heart was pounding. She knew it was just a matter of time before Guthrie told Sinclair of the mysterious visitor through the basement door.

·

CHAPTER 22

Poppy made her way to the sciences section of Blackwell's and waited for Rosie to join her. Five minutes later, Poppy heard the doorbell ring and saw the policewoman enter the bookshop. She did not look very happy. When a shop assistant approached her to ask if she could help the officer, Rosie shook her head and pointed at Poppy. Poppy smiled a welcome, but the frown did not leave Rosie's face. Poppy's heart sank. *Oh dear...* She knew what was coming.

"What in heaven's name did you think you were doing?" hissed Rosie as she drew alongside her.

Poppy cast a quick glance through the bookshop window and across the road, half expecting Professor Sinclair to be striding towards them. Fortunately, he wasn't.

"I'm sorry," said Poppy. "I thought I'd just have a look around while you were busy. I didn't expect the basement door to be open. I was just curious to see what the laboratory looked like. I wanted to see where June worked, as I hadn't had a chance to see it when I first visited." It was a small fib, but close enough to the truth for it to slip easily off Poppy's tongue.

"So, you didn't plan to use me as a decoy to draw the men out of the laboratory so you could snoop around?" asked Rosie, her voice seething.

"No! Absolutely not!" That was true. That had not been her thought process – although it had occurred to her once she was through the basement door, which she had, if she were totally honest, suspected would be open. "Look, I'm sorry, Rosie. I honestly didn't plan to use you as a decoy. But I must admit it was convenient that you drew the men away. If I had thought about it in advance, I would have mentioned it to you. But I didn't. And I apologize. Was Sinclair furious?"

"What do you think?" Rosie's good humour had still not returned. She scowled. "He accused me of working in cahoots with you. Of being deceitful and duplicitous and that he would report me to my superiors."

Poppy bit her lip. "Oh Rosie, I'm sorry. I really didn't intend to get you into trouble. I would have been in and out without anyone knowing if I hadn't run into the lab assistant coming in from a smoking break. Do you think you'll get into much trouble?"

Rosie shrugged. "Probably. I wasn't authorized to go to the Crystal Crypt or take any statements – from the scientists or anyone else. But Professor Sinclair would not have reported me – I don't think – if you hadn't been found snooping around. The interview with them went well, from their point of view. They didn't see Gertrude Fuller after she left the dinner last night. They left – together – through the Broad Street entrance of the college. They had nothing to contribute to the investigation. Or so they say..."

Poppy looked at Rosie expectantly. "So they say?"

"Yes. So they say." Rosie paused, as if for dramatic effect, then leaned in and whispered, "But I have evidence that they did not exit onto Broad Street."

Poppy's heart leaped. "You do?"

Rosie nodded excitedly. "I spoke to the porter of Balliol this morning – on the way to picking you up at the hotel – and I asked him if he recalled seeing Professor Sinclair, Dr Raines, or Miles Mackintosh leaving last night. He said that he did. He said that only Prof Sinclair had left through the Broad Street entrance, not Raines or Mackintosh – they left through the St Giles Street entrance. So they told me a blatant lie."

Poppy blinked rapidly. "Goodness, Rosie, why didn't you tell me?"

A sardonic smile twitched at the corner of Rosie's lips. "Like you've told me everything?"

"Touché," said Poppy gently. "So, what made you ask about them?"

Rosie put her hand on the small of Poppy's back and guided her deeper into the bookshop, away from the disapproving look of the shop assistant, who was growing increasingly annoyed by their ongoing whispered conversation. When they were completely out of earshot – in the history section – Rosie said, "It's because of what Gertrude said about the acidic smell on her attacker. This morning, when I spoke to her, before I came to get you, she had referred to it as 'some kind of chemical smell'. That got me thinking about the scientists. And of course, this is already connected in some way to a scientist's death. So, I had a look at last night's guest list and noticed those three were on it. I knew that you had already spoken to them and that if anything untoward had happened to June Leighton, they would be the most likely suspects. Ergo, they might also then be involved in the attack on Gertrude."

Poppy nodded, impressed by Rosie's detective work. "Oh, I wish you'd told me, Rosie, and I wish I'd told you that I was going into the laboratory. Perhaps this is a lesson to us: that we need to trust one another more. Why didn't you trust me with this information?"

Rosie shrugged. "I don't know, Poppy. I think, in a way, that I wanted to impress you with my detective work."

"Well, I'm impressed! Very impressed."

Rosie gave an embarrassed smile. "Thank you, Poppy. And I'm sorry too. I should have kept you in the loop. I suppose I just wanted to check that my hunch was right before I told you. To get all my ducks in a row, as it were. Just in case I was wrong." She gave a playful wink. "This was my chance to impress the famous Poppy Denby, and I didn't want to mess it up."

"Oh Rosie, I've messed many a thing up in my time. I can't tell you how many muddles I've got myself into."

"But you always manage to get out of them."

"So far..." said Poppy, wondering how she was going to get out of this one. If Sinclair chose to, he could lay a charge of trespass against her. She let out a long sigh. "So, what are we going to do now? Will you have to go back to the police station?"

Rosie nodded glumly. "I will."

"Will you tell them about the scientists lying about which gate they went out of last night?"

"Yes, but I can't guarantee they'll take any notice of me. They'll be too angry that I started investigating this on my own."

"But what if your investigation helps them find out who attacked Gertrude Fuller?"

Rosie shrugged again. "They're not convinced that Dr Fuller was attacked. As I said earlier, there were no witnesses to the attack, and Gertrude was quite tipsy when she left Balliol. There are plenty of witnesses to that. I wouldn't be surprised if they write this one off as an accident too. Just like June's death."

Poppy went cold. "Are you suggesting there is a deliberate police cover-up? Or that some of the Oxford City Police could even be involved with June's death?"

Rosie shook her head vigorously. "No, I'm not saying that. I honestly don't think my colleagues would do such a thing. But I do think there's been a distinct lack of interest in both cases. A lack of curiosity, if you will. They're just happy to put both down to misadventure and move on. And it's no coincidence, in my mind, that both victims were women."

"Hmmm," said Poppy, not entirely convinced. "Why, then, did they send you along to keep an eye on me when they heard about the sabotaged bicycle?"

Rosie looked at Poppy curiously. "Now that I can't tell you. But now that you mention it, I did get the impression this morning that Chief Constable Fenchurch – he's the head of the force here – thought that there *might* be a connection between the bicycle and what happened to Gertrude. Or why else would he send a car along to pick you up? But at the same time, he seemed to disbelieve Gertrude's version of events. Not to her face, of course, but afterwards." Rosie shrugged. "I honestly don't know, Poppy. But I do know I'm going to get into trouble for what happened in the laboratory. So I'd better go and face the music."

Poppy squeezed Rosie's forearm. "I'm so sorry. Would it help if I came with you? I could explain to your boss that it wasn't your fault."

Rosie shook her head. "No, best I do it myself. I will tell them I didn't know you were there – which I didn't. But I'll probably get into trouble anyway for going it alone."

"All right," nodded Poppy. "I do hope your boss will be kind to you. I shall say a prayer. Will you let me know what happens?"

"Yes, of course I will. I'll come to your hotel this evening."

Poppy smiled. "Come for dinner. Unless your boss objects...?"

"He can't tell me what to do when I'm off duty. I'll get changed into civvie clothes."

"All right. Good luck!"

"Thank you."

Poppy watched her new friend as she left the bookshop, then said the prayer she'd promised she'd say.

CHAPTER 23

Poppy was feeling peckish. It was approaching lunchtime by the time she arrived back at the Cherwell Hotel, and she planned to freshen up in her room, then come down to get something to eat. However, as she picked up her key, the concierge gave her a list of messages. The first was from Rollo, asking her to call the office. The second was from Ike Garfield, saying he was driving up to Oxford and hoped to meet with her for lunch at the hotel. She asked the concierge if Mr Garfield had arrived yet. He had not. The third note was from Edward Sanforth, saying he'd stopped by, leaving a telephone number for her to ring. She arranged to use the hotel telephone and called Edward Sanforth. He answered on the third ring.

"Miss Denby! I'm so glad you rang. I dropped by earlier, but you weren't in. Are you up for a spot of lunch?"

"I am actually," said Poppy. "Would you like to come here?"

"Tell you what, it's a lovely day. Why don't we take a punt down the river? I can pack some sandwiches—"

"A punt? Now?"

"Well, if you don't think it's too forward of me..."

Poppy did think it was forward of him. However, she also desperately wanted to speak to him and – well – a boat ride down the river would be rather pleasant. "All right," she said. "A punt ride it is. However, I hope you don't think it too bold of me to remind you that I am engaged to be married."

Sanforth chuckled. "Don't worry, Miss Denby, I noticed your ring last night. I have no nefarious intentions, I can assure you. But I would like to talk to you. In private. And it will be difficult for anyone to eavesdrop on our conversation on the river."

Poppy wondered who Sanforth thought might want to eavesdrop on their conversation, but after the goings-on with her bicycle and the attack on Gertrude Fuller, she too thought it wise to be cautious.

She received instructions on where and when to meet, then called the *Daily Globe* office. Mavis answered. Frustratingly, once again, Rollo wasn't in. He was off following up a story. Mavis told her though that Ike was driving up to see her. "He has a file for you from Ivan and Rollo. There was apparently some hoo-ha with it last night and this morning, so there's been a delay in sending it up to you, but Ike is going to bring it today."

"Oh? What kind of hoo-ha?"

"I'm not sure. Rollo didn't say, but he, Ike, and Ivan have been muttering about it all day. Something's afoot, but no one's telling me what."

Mavis sounded offended. Poppy smiled. Mavis always prided herself on knowing everything that was going on at the *Globe* office and that Rollo trusted her with so much information. Poppy wondered for a moment why she'd been kept out of the loop this time. *Anyway*, thought Poppy, *I'll find out when Ike gets here.* "What time did Ike leave, Mavis?"

"About ten o'clock. Isn't he there yet?"

"No," said Poppy, checking her watch and noting that it was already half-past one. "He hasn't arrived. It should only take him a couple of hours."

"Oh dear. He is in the old Model T. Might have had a bit of car trouble en route. I've been telling Rollo for years that he needs to get a new car! But does he listen?"

Poppy listened sympathetically to Mavis' grumbles, assuring the receptionist that she felt the same. She ended the conversation promising to tell Ike to call the office as soon as he arrived, to put Mavis' mind at rest. She also ended it without mentioning the boat ride she was about to embark upon. There were some things best left unsaid.

The last time Poppy had seen the jetty at the base of Magdalen Bridge was when she had hurtled off it on her bicycle. She shuddered at the near disaster of it all and reminded herself how lucky she'd been. *Angels watching over me...* She spotted the lanky blond frame of Edward Sanforth wearing a beige and grey sporting jacket, boater hat, and Oxford bags, chatting to the boathouse manager. He waved to her and called her over.

"Miss Denby! I'm so glad you could make it. I've hired a punt and packed a picnic." He gestured to a wicker basket and tartan blanket in a nearby punt.

"My, you pulled all this together quickly."

He smiled. "One is always half-packed for boat rides in Oxford. Besides, I live nearby. Shall we?" He reached out his hand and she took it, allowing herself to be guided into the punt and settled on a pile of cushions in the prow. Sanforth tipped his hat to the boathouse manager, who pushed the punt away from the jetty with a long boathook.

Poppy held tightly with both hands as the shallow boat wobbled from side to side. She sincerely hoped Mr Edward Sanforth knew what he was doing; she did not fancy yet another unscheduled dip in the Cherwell.

"I didn't know you lived in Oxford, Mr Sanforth. I thought you were just visiting with your mother. 'Pulling out her chair and holding her wrap,' you said last night."

Sanforth smiled down at her as he stood in the stern, pushing the punt along with a pole. They were going under Magdalen Bridge and Poppy, unnecessarily, ducked. Sanforth chuckled. "Don't worry, you're not about to lose your head. And we're not about to crash into anything; I've 'driven' one of these many times before."

"Here in Oxford?" Poppy prompted.

"Yes, here in Oxford. I'm sorry I wasn't more clear last night. I didn't mean to mislead you. I am an Oxfordian. I have my base here. I travel a lot with my work for the Foundation, and I have a small bedsit in London for when I'm down there, but this is my home."

"Your family home?"

"No, just mine. My mother splits her time between her London home and one on Long Island. That's in the USA."

"I know where Long Island is, Mr Sanforth. In fact, I visited there three years ago." She refrained from mentioning that she had in fact been held hostage – along with Delilah – in a boathouse on Long Island during a previous investigation. That would lead the conversation far away from where she wanted it to go.

"Then I'm sorry again. I did not intend to patronize you," he said.

"No offence taken. You weren't to know. So, you live here in Oxford..."

"Yes," he said, as the punt made its leisurely way out of the bridge arch and around the bend, past the Botanic Garden.

Poppy caught her breath as she spotted the bench she and Daniel had sat on when he proposed to her. She suppressed a little twinge of guilt as she remembered that he'd offered to take her punting, and she'd laughed at him and declined. Now, here she was with another man.

"I wasn't born here," Sanforth continued, warming up to the conversation, "but I studied here as an undergraduate. Then, afterwards, decided to stay. I have a house on Merton Street. Not too far from here."

Poppy noted that he hadn't mentioned his failure to graduate, or the interruption of his studies by the war and him being a conscientious objector. She decided not to mention it either. She was not here to write an interview feature on Edward Sanforth's failed academic career. But something Gertrude had said last night pricked her memory. He had read science... "It's a beautiful place," she continued. "I don't blame you for staying on. What was it you read, by the way?"

Sanforth ducked through a curtain of overhanging willow, then stood again. "Science – chemistry, to be specific."

"Like June Leighton?"

"Nothing like June Leighton."

"Oh, why's that?"

Sanforth pushed the punt closer to the left bank to allow another punt to pass on the right. "Because June was brilliant. And I wasn't." There was a tinge of sadness to his voice. Poppy wondered if it were to do with his own failings or June's demise.

"Did you share classes with her?"

He shook his head and smiled wistfully. "No. Despite these boyish looks, I'm older than I appear. I was here before the war. June was after."

"You gave me the impression last night that you knew her."

The punt rounded the bend at Merton Field, with Christ Church Meadow approaching on the right. Poppy noted with some amusement a trio of long-horned cows staring dolefully at them from between the trees.

"I did know her. I was on the panel – along with Professor Sinclair – that interviewed her for the position at the laboratory. I was there on behalf of the Sanforth Foundation. As you know, we help fund the laboratory and so have a say in the appointees.

She was clearly brilliant. On paper her credentials were highly impressive. Better than any of the male candidates. But in person – well, she shone. June was a shining light. And now she's gone."

His sharp features softened with sadness. *Golly*, thought Poppy, *he's really upset. Could his interest in her have been more than professional?*

"Yes, it's tragic," she said. "Everyone I've spoken to speaks so highly of her – professionally and as a person. Everyone from her mother to Professor Sinclair."

Sanforth snorted. "Sinclair? The bloody hypocrite! Pardon my French, Miss Denby, but Sinclair made June's life a misery."

"Oh," said Poppy, brushing aside willow fronds from her face as they passed by. "How is that?"

Sanforth stopped punting and stared down at Poppy. "You met Raines last night. You saw what type of man he is. June had to put up with that day in and day out, and Sinclair – despite his high-mindedness about respecting women's minds and professional ability – did nothing to protect her. In the end, I had to have a word with Raines to warn him off. More than a word, actually. But I wasn't there every day like Sinclair was."

Poppy wondered how it came to be that June Leighton had confided such intimate details to Edward Sanforth. She could think of only one possible answer. She dived straight in. "Mr Sanforth, were you and June Leighton involved with one another romantically?"

Sanforth bit his lip. "Yes, Miss Denby," he said quietly. "We were. But no one knew about it. We were thinking of telling our respective families when – when – she died."

"Oh, Mr Sanforth, I'm so very sorry. Do they know now?"

He nodded brusquely, then said, "Come, let's stop here and have our lunch. I don't know about you, but I'm famished."

The dreary sky of yesterday had been replaced by a canopy of blue and white. The Cherwell bubbled gently beside the Christ Church Meadow, quietly observed by a hunched heron awaiting his prey. Sanforth and Poppy had alighted from the punt and now sat on the tartan blanket, draped over a bed of daisies. Sanforth unpacked the picnic basket and opened a parcel of waxed paper to reveal a pile of chunky ham sandwiches. There were two apples and four slices of fruit cake. Then, he opened a flask and poured them each a cup of tea. It was sweeter than Poppy normally liked it, but she didn't complain. As they ate and drank, Sanforth talked. He told her about how he and June had first met, how they had punted down this very river and had picnics right on this very spot. He spoke of the beauty of her heart and her mind. His obvious love for the dead woman brought tears to Poppy's eyes. But she brushed them away, knowing she had a job to do.

"Mr Sanforth—"

"Please, Edward."

"All right, Edward. I feel that I need to be honest with you. I know I said that I am here to write an article on June's achievements, which is true, but it is not all there is to it."

"Oh?"

"Yes," she said, then took a deep breath before blurting out, "I was actually invited here to discover whether or not June was murdered."

Sanforth's hand closed into a fist around the ham sandwich. "*Murdered?*"

"I'm sorry, Edward. I don't want to alarm you, and I have not, yet, got conclusive proof that June's death was anything other than a terrible accident, but my investigation has been obstructed enough to make me believe that there is at the very least an attempt to cover up what happened. I need to find out why. Can you help me?"

"Of course, I'll help in whatever way I can. But *murdered*?"

"*Possibly* murdered."

"But who would do such a thing?"

"That's what I'm trying to find out."

"Is it Raines?"

"I don't know. He's one of a number of potential suspects."

"I bet it's Raines." Sanforth's jaw was firmly set.

"No, Edward; I can't say it's Raines. And I ask you please not to confront him. That could put my whole investigation in jeopardy. Please. Promise me that. For June's sake."

The squashed ham sandwich lay on the blanket, uneaten, and Sanforth's cup of tea remained untouched. He sighed painfully. "All right, I promise. But as soon as you have the evidence you need, you will let me know?"

Poppy nodded, making a note to herself that she would tell him, but not before she had alerted the necessary authorities. She did not want Edward Sanforth to take vigilante action against Bill Raines, no matter how despicable the man was.

Sanforth continued, "You also said you'd been invited here by someone to investigate. Who was that?"

"I'm afraid I can't tell you who it is – not yet, anyway – but I can tell you that I am making headway on the cover-up around June's death and the possible motivation of the killer. But there's a lot I still need to find out."

"Such as?"

"Such as what June was working on when she died. And what it was that she didn't want to work on. You said last night that she wasn't happy with the type of research the Sanforth Foundation wanted her to do. Can you tell me what that was and why you – as a representative of the Foundation – couldn't do anything about it?"

Sanforth nodded. "Yes, I can tell you that. Sanforth Industries – to my shame – invest heavily in the arms industry. But it's not all they do, and up until recently, the Sanforth Foundation – its charitable wing that I help run – has not had a hand in any of that. Last year, under pressure from the board of the parent company, the Foundation started to offer grants to laboratories to do research into explosives. The research involves determining the crystallographic structure of graphite. It's been hypothesized that graphite can be used to solidify and stabilize liquid explosives, making them easier to transport. I won't bamboozle you with all the science behind it – I don't understand half of it myself – but suffice to say, research into this area could be very profitable for armaments manufacturers. And if, God forbid, there's another war, profits could go through the roof.

"I argued against it, but I do not have the deciding vote. As a result, the Foundation has been approaching leading universities in the USA and here in Britain to further their research. An offer was made to Cambridge but then withdrawn, because it was discovered that a number of their scientists were pacifists and it was feared they would scupper the project. June herself, as am I, was a pacifist, and when she found out what the project entailed, she refused to work on it. Sinclair tried to convince her to change her mind, arguing that there was a domestic non-military application for the research too, but she would not be swayed. There was talk that June would be fired, but this wouldn't reflect well on the laboratory, the university, or the Foundation. So, June was to be allowed to continue her own work – a new project involving bromides – while the rest of the team worked on the graphite crystals."

"Do diamonds have anything to do with graphite?" asked Poppy.

"Yes, of course – they are both made of carbon. But diamond is the hardest form of carbon and graphite the softest. Why do you ask?"

"Because I've been told June was X-raying a diamond when she died."

"Really? I didn't know that." Sanforth picked up his cup of tea again and took a sip.

"Why do you think she was doing that?" asked Poppy.

Sanforth shrugged. "I honestly have no idea. It had nothing to do with her new research into bromides – or the project she was working on previously involving thallium."

"Could it have been something to do with the graphite project?"

"It could have been, but I can't say what. As I said, diamonds and graphite have a similar chemical composition, but they are not the same thing and diamonds would not be any use as a stabilizer. But who knows – perhaps June was working on something completely different? If she was, she never told me about it."

"Hmmm," said Poppy, picking up one of the apples and weighing it in her hand, "but that might explain why she was working on a Sunday night. Not just because she wanted to stay out of the way of Raines because he was so unpleasant to her. If she was working on something completely different and hadn't yet told anyone about it, she might want to keep it under wraps for a while. Is that something she would do?"

Sanforth nodded thoughtfully. "Yes, it would be. She was a very thorough scientist and always wanted to make sure she had sufficient evidence to support her position before sharing it with her colleagues."

"Might she have kept notes?"

"Of course she kept notes."

"Where would they be?"

Sanforth looked at Poppy apologetically. "I have absolutely no idea. I never got to see her things after she died. But I would expect they were sent to her family in London."

"Right," said Poppy, nodding, "then I'll try to arrange to see them. Would you go through them with me when I do, to help me understand what I'm looking at?"

"Of course," said Sanforth. "Anything I can do to help."

"Well, for now," said Poppy, sitting up straight, "I need to get back to town. I have a few other leads to follow up, but as soon as I am able, we can go down to London and ask Mrs Leighton to look at June's things. Would you be able to accompany me tomorrow? Or the next day?"

"Absolutely," said Sanforth. "Let me know when you're ready to go." Then, he gave Poppy his Oxford address.

CHAPTER 24

Poppy was becoming quite familiar now with the twists and turns of the route from her hotel to the centre of Oxford – with or without a bicycle. She clutched the piece of paper that the laboratory assistant had given her that morning with Sophie Blackburn's address. She had consulted her map and discovered that it was on the same street as the Ashmolean Museum, equidistant from Balliol College and Somerville College. She had a lot to tell Sophie about what she'd found out since they last spoke two days earlier in the churchyard of St Giles. Why, Poppy wondered, hadn't she kept their appointment last evening? And why hadn't she gone into work today? Had she heard about the attack on Gertrude Fuller? Did she too believe that Bill Raines and his student, Miles Mackintosh, might have been responsible? Was Sophie staying away out of fear? Poppy thought of the strongly built, strongly willed woman that she knew and dismissed that idea immediately.

Poppy crossed the road from the Martyrs' Memorial and walked past the luxurious Randolph Hotel with its top-hatted doormen and ostentatious red carpet, and onto Beaumont Street. She continued passed the impressive classical frontage of the Ashmolean Museum until she reached the residential end, lined on both sides by splendid Regency townhouses. On closer inspection, some of the townhouses had been turned into flats with multiple bells on panels at the front door. Just before she reached the end of the street, and the entrance to Worcester College, she found Sophie's address: a basement flat.

She walked down the short flight of steps and knocked on the door. She waited. There was no answer. She knocked again. After a couple more tries, she called through the letter box: "Sophie, if you're in there, it's Poppy. I need to talk to you!" Again, no answer. Poppy cupped her hands around her face and peered through the window next to the door. She looked into a small entrance hall with a hat and coat stand and a couple of pairs of shoes and boots. There was only one hat and one coat on the stand, and Poppy recognized them as what Sophie had worn to the St Giles meeting. Sophie, Poppy knew, was a woman of frugal taste in fashion. She was the type of person who would wear one coat until it wore out, then get another. She might have a summer and a winter coat, but as it was a mild spring, Poppy doubted she'd be out wearing a heavy winter coat. So, did that mean Sophie was still in the flat? She knocked again, this time on the window. Then, she saw the door from the hall to the rest of the flat quickly open and close. She did not see Sophie, but it was enough to tell Poppy there was definitely someone there. Why wasn't she answering? Poppy tried the door handle: it was locked.

Convinced now that Sophie was inside but for some reason didn't want to speak to her, Poppy decided to pretend she was leaving. She made a show of turning and climbing back up the stairs; then, she turned back down Beaumont Street. As soon as she was out of eyeshot she whipped into a side road, which she assumed would lead to the service alley running down the back of Sophie's terrace. Sure enough, there was an alley with a row of enclosed yards and small gardens. She counted her way down until she came to the back of Sophie's building. There was a wooden doorway in the high stone wall. Poppy tried the latch: it opened.

She took a deep breath and entered the yard. It was paved, with a garden bench and a cluster of pot plants, beyond which was a line of four bins. Looking up to check that no one in the flats above Sophie was looking down, she approached the basement back entrance. She tried the doorknob and it was open. What should she do? Should she call out to let Sophie know she was there? But if Sophie were hiding from her – or whoever the woman thought she was – then would she answer? Or should she just sneak in and hope to catch Sophie unawares? She decided on the latter, although she reminded herself that Sophie had the potential to be a dangerous woman. She just hoped – and prayed – that she could calm Sophie before she lashed out at her.

Poppy stepped into a kitchen. It was small and neat, just as Poppy had expected it to be. There were no unwashed utensils, so it was hard to tell what Sophie's last meal had been. Today's lunch? Breakfast? Last night's dinner? Poppy pushed open the kitchen door into a short corridor. There were four doors. She pushed open the one next to the kitchen: the bathroom. Clean and tidy with towels dry and hung up. The soap on the sink was completely dry. No one had washed their hands here recently. Poppy heard a creak of a door. Her heart jumped into her mouth. Was that inside the flat or the sound of a door opening upstairs?

She stuck her head out of the bathroom: "Sophie?" she whispered. Again, there was no reply. Had she just imagined that door opening and closing to the hallway earlier? If there was no one here, why was the back door unlocked, and why were Sophie's hat and coat still hanging in the hall? Perhaps she was overthinking things. Why on earth could Sophie not have a second or even a third hat or coat? And perhaps Sophie simply forgot to lock the back door. Poppy knew that she did, sometimes. But she was not Sophie...

She pushed open two more doors to reveal two bedrooms – both with beds neatly made. One contained a dresser of personal items, so was probably Sophie's own room; the second, clear of any personal clutter, was the guest room (which Sophie had previously claimed not to have). Sophie was in neither. There was one door left: Poppy pushed it open to reveal a living cum dining room in complete disarray. There were books and papers strewn everywhere. All the drawers and cupboards of a dresser were open with their contents spewed across the floor. A writing desk had been ransacked... and then Poppy saw the shoes. A woman's shoes sticking out from behind a sofa. Poppy rushed over to find Sophie sprawled on the floor, her clothes in disarray, her skirt hitched up around her waist, her underwear pulled down over her thighs. Her face – with her cheek to the floor – was bloodied and bruised. Her eyes were swollen shut. "Oh God! Oh God! Oh God! Sophie!"

Poppy kneeled down, fearing the worst. She gently touched Sophie's face, expecting it to be ice cold, but was relieved to feel some warmth. And then she saw other signs of life: a twitch, a moan. Sophie was alive. But just.

Unable to find a telephone in Sophie's flat, Poppy had just been about to run up the fire escape and bang on an upstairs neighbour's door, when said neighbour arrived in Sophie's kitchen, concerned that he had seen someone sneaking through the backyard. After hearing Poppy's hysterical explanation and seeing Sophie for himself, the neighbour called for an ambulance.

Now Poppy found herself, once again, at the Radcliffe Infirmary. She had been there for half an hour, anxiously waiting for the medical staff to tell her that Sophie was going to be all right, when WPC Rosie Winter and a senior male police officer arrived. He was a powerfully built man in a Chief Constable's uniform. Poppy watched them as they spoke to the doctor in charge. The doctor pointed to Poppy.

"Miss Denby," said the senior officer, "I am Chief Constable Fenchurch. And I believe you already know WPC Winter."

Poppy nodded.

"May we join you?"

"Of course." Fenchurch and Rosie pulled two chairs into a huddle facing Poppy. Rosie would not meet her eyes.

"So, Miss Denby. This is your second breaking and entering of the day, I believe," said Fenchurch, as if talking to a naughty six-year-old.

"I did not break in. On either occasion. Both times the doors were unlocked. And both times I was looking for Sophie."

"How convenient for you that the doors just happened to be unlocked."

"Yes, it was just a coincidence. And in the second instance, a very lucky one, or Sophie might have died."

"She might still," said Fenchurch, but this time he lost his patronizing tone.

"Oh Lord, no! Is that what the doctor said?"

Fenchurch nodded and Rosie slumped even lower in her chair. "They're trying their best, Miss Denby," said Fenchurch, "but Miss Blackburn has serious injuries. Do you know if she has any family?"

Poppy shook her head. "I don't think she does, but I'm not entirely sure. My editor knows her better than I do."

"Your editor – Rollo Rolandson?"

"That's correct."

"Are you here on his behest?"

Poppy looked at Fenchurch, trying to read his expression. He was impassive. "If you mean, am I here in a professional capacity, then yes. I have made no secret of my reason for being in Oxford. I am here to write an article on the late June Leighton."

"So I've been told," said Fenchurch, casting a quick glance at the WPC beside him. Rosie winced. "But what I haven't been told," he continued, "is what Sophie Blackburn has to do with it. Professor Sinclair tells me that he questioned Sophie after your first visit, and she claimed she didn't know you. But that's not the case, is it?"

Poppy realized that she could not deny it any longer. She had already mentioned that her editor knew Sophie – a slip of the tongue in fraught circumstances – so she decided to come clean. She sighed. "Sophie and I do know each other. We are not close, but her fiancé used to work for the same newspaper I do."

Fenchurch nodded. "So I believe. And you witnessed his death, didn't you?"

"Unfortunately, yes."

"That was five years ago, wasn't it? Have you and Miss Blackburn been in touch since?"

Poppy shook her head. "No. Not until recently. I met her at a lecture at the Royal Institution in London last week and she told me about June Leighton's death."

"And she asked you to come?"

"Yes."

"Then why all the secrecy? Why weren't you and Miss Blackburn above board with this?"

Poppy looked towards the emergency room where the ambulance men had taken Sophie. A nurse came out and another went in. "Because she asked me not to be. Have you ever met Sophie?"

"I have not spoken to her personally," said Fenchurch.

"Well, if you had you would understand that she is an unusual person. She can be very brusque and – what's the term psychiatrists use these days – paranoid? Yes, paranoid."

"I believe she spent some time in a mental institution."

"She did. But she was released. And was well enough to get a job at a top laboratory. I don't think Professor Sinclair would have hired her if he didn't think she was mentally up to the job."

Fenchurch nodded. "True enough. So why did she invite

you here to write an article on her former colleague? There were obituaries in the press after Miss Leighton died. Why did Miss Blackburn believe there needed to be another one, and why were you – from a newspaper that doesn't even distribute to Oxford – the person to ask?"

Poppy could have shrugged and given an excuse that Sophie thought she might be interested to write something for her Women in the Workplace column, but it was sounding hollower every time she said it. And besides, this investigation was becoming increasingly dangerous. It might be time to finally bring in a police officer who – unlike Rosie – had the power to do something. But she was still reluctant to use the word "murder". "Because," she said eventually, "Sophie believed that June Leighton's death might not have been an accident."

Chief Constable Fenchurch sat bolt upright. "Oh, did she now? And why, pray tell, didn't she report her suspicions to the police? She was interviewed after Miss Leighton's death – as was everyone who worked at the laboratory – and she had nothing to contribute. I can assure you, Miss Denby, if there was any hint that June Leighton's death had been anything other than an accident it would have been investigated thoroughly. But everyone we spoke to – including our own medical examiner – said there were no suspicious circumstances."

Poppy shrugged. "Yes, I believe that's what you were told."

Fenchurch leaned towards her, and Poppy became aware for the first time of the bulk of the man. "If you are insinuating, Miss Denby, that we did not do a proper job, then you are sadly mistaken."

"I'm not insinuating anything, Chief Constable; I'm only telling you what Sophie Blackburn told me and why she asked me to come to Oxford. She was concerned that the hypothesis of how June was electrocuted – the clumsiness of it – did not fit her character; neither personal nor professional. So, she asked me to look into it. I did come here prepared to just write an article on a remarkable young female scientist, but I was open to the possibility that there might indeed be more to the story."

Fenchurch leaned back, easing the degree of physical intimidation. "And *is* there more to the story?"

For the first time, Rosie glanced up. Poppy tried to catch her eyes, but the WPC averted her gaze.

"Yes, there is," said Poppy, turning back to Fenchurch, "in terms of the chauvinistic conditions in which June worked, plagiarism of her work, and possible ties to—" She almost said, "possible ties to some kind of weapons research" but stopped herself. She had no idea what significance, if any, June's refusal to work on the weapons research had. She hadn't yet had time to think that one through. She gave herself a quick internal shake: *Pull yourself together, old girl.*

But Fenchurch's eyes had narrowed. He leaned in again. "Possible ties to…?"

"Possible ties to an old boys' network that covered up the most shocking bullying," said Poppy, her eyes narrowing in reply.

A flicker of a smile played at the corner of Fenchurch's mouth. "But no murder."

"No evidence of murder, no." *Yet,* she wanted to add, but didn't. "However, the attack on Sophie and on Gertrude Fuller last night – just a block away from one another – as well as the tampering with my bicycle, suggests that someone is trying to stop me from finding out the truth. And that someone has a very violent streak."

Fenchurch leaned back again. "Yes, WPC Winter told me about the bicycle. She also told me that she'd been doing some detective work of her own and discovered that both Miles Mackintosh and Bill Raines were unaccounted for after the Balliol dinner."

Poppy flashed a look at Rosie, but the policewoman's eyes remained firmly focused on the floor.

"Yes," said Poppy. "WPC Winter mentioned that to me."

"She should *not* have divulged any information to a civilian. WPC Winter is now on suspension. She is only here now due to the – delicate – nature of Miss Blackburn's injuries."

You mean the rape, thought Poppy. "WPC Winter did not divulge anything to me. I tricked her into giving me the information," said Poppy. "It was not her fault." This was not in the least bit true, but Poppy felt she had to at least try to help Rosie.

"Well, tricked or not, she should not have told you. However, she has now told me and we are opening a formal investigation."

Poppy raised an eyebrow. "You are formally investigating Mackintosh and Raines for the attacks?"

"Don't put words into my mouth, Miss Denby; that's a foul journalistic habit. We are formally opening an investigation into the attacks. We are keeping an open mind at this stage and interviewing as many people as we can. Up until the discovery of Miss Blackburn, there was no corroborating evidence that Dr Fuller had in fact been attacked. We had witnesses saying they'd seen her tipsy and unsteady on her feet."

"She *told* you she was attacked. Isn't that enough?"

"Not in itself, no. She was drunk. She'd had a blow to her head. Corroboration was needed."

"And you think you have that now with Sophie's attack?"

"We have enough to suggest there might be a link. And that link, Miss Denby, is you."

At this, Rosie did look up. She was as pale as a ghost. "You're not suggesting that Poppy is a suspect in these attacks, are you, sir?"

Fenchurch snorted. "Well, I might have been if it hadn't been for the personal nature of the assault on Miss Blackburn. No, Winter, we'll be looking for a man. But Miss Denby is the obvious link between both the victims."

Poppy shook her head. "No, Chief Constable Fenchurch; I am not the obvious link. The obvious link is June Leighton. You have one dead woman and two seriously injured ones. I am just the person who poked the hornet's nest. I think you should seriously consider reopening your investigation into that so-called 'accident' in the Crystal Crypt."

The Chief Constable raised himself again to his full, seated height. "Do not tell me how to do my job, Miss Denby."

"I would never dream of it," said Poppy sweetly, but her eyes were cold.

"Good," said Fenchurch. "For now, though, I will have one of my men look after you while you are in Oxford. I do not want anything happening to you."

Oh no, thought Poppy, *that's all I need, someone watching my every move.* "That won't be necessary, thank you."

"I insist."

"And I insist that you do not."

Poppy and Fenchurch stared at one another, neither of them giving an inch. The stalemate was broken by a doctor approaching them. "Just to let you know, we've stabilized Miss Blackburn, but she's still unconscious. She won't be able to talk to anyone just yet."

"Thank you, doctor," said Fenchurch. "I'll leave WPC Winter here. If Miss Blackburn wakes up, Winter, call me immediately. Do you understand?"

"Yes sir," said Rosie quietly.

"Good. Now, Miss Denby, I shall escort you out."

"No thank you, Chief Constable. I can make my own way." She stood up.

He stood too, towering over her. She turned and walked away. She dared not turn around to see if he followed her, but she sensed that he hadn't. And she was right.

She then decided to pop into Gertrude Fuller's room.

However, Gertrude was asleep. One of the graduate students who had been there that morning was sitting at her bedside. She saw Poppy, stood, and came to the door.

"Miss Denby, isn't it?"

"It is. I'm sorry, I don't know your name."

The girl smiled. "It's Annabel. Annabel Seymour. I'm one of Dr Fuller's PhD students – and her assistant. I'm so glad you came. I went to your hotel earlier to see you, but you weren't there. I have some information…" Annabel looked over Poppy's shoulder to see that they were not about to be interrupted, then lowered her voice. "Dr Fuller said I should tell you rather than the police."

"Oh?" said Poppy, "and why's that?"

"Because Dr Fuller doesn't think the police believed her about being attacked last night. She thinks they just think she fell down. But she said that you believe her. Do you?"

Poppy nodded. "I do. But first, tell me how she is doing."

Annabel looked over at her mentor. "She seems to be all right. She's asleep now, but that's just because she's tired from working on the edits – the ones she asked me to bring her this morning. But you see, that's what I want to tell you. When I went into Dr Fuller's rooms, they were in chaos. As if they'd been ransacked. There were books and papers everywhere. Now, Dr Fuller is not the tidiest of people, but this was like a whirlwind had been through the place. I had a jolly old time trying to find the proofs she wanted. Fortunately, they were still intact in a file. But there were other pages strewn all over the place."

"Goodness," said Poppy. "That is worrying. Did you ask anyone if they'd seen anything? The fellow on the gate, for instance?"

Annabel shook her head. "I didn't, no. I was so shocked I just ran straight here and told Dr Fuller. And then she asked me to tell you."

Poppy nodded sagely. Gertrude Fuller's rooms had been ransacked. Sophie Blackburn's sitting room had been ransacked. If this was just random violence, why had he – and Poppy was now sure it was a *he* – attacked Dr Fuller and then taken the trouble to go to her rooms and ransack the place? It seemed very likely that he was looking for something. But what? In both cases it was papers that were scattered around. Was the attacker looking for papers? The only thing that connected Sophie and Gertrude – as far as Poppy knew – was an association with June Leighton. *Papers... June Leighton's papers...*

"Annabel, do you by any chance know if June Leighton left any notebooks or papers with Dr Fuller? And if she did, whether Dr Fuller kept any of her papers after she died?"

Annabel thought for a moment and said, "I don't think so. I helped Dr Fuller pack up June's things from her room and sent them off to her family in London. There were papers in there. Scientific papers, if I recall. But I don't remember Dr Fuller keeping any of them. I mean, why would she? She's not a scientist."

Indeed, thought Poppy, *why would she? Sophie, on the other hand, might very well have kept any papers she found at the lab... but if she did, why didn't she tell me?*

Poppy smiled at the student. "Thank you, Annabel. Will you please ask Dr Fuller about it when she wakes up again? And then come to the hotel and tell me? If I'm not there, then leave a note in a sealed envelope at the front desk. Can you do that for me?"

The girl's eyes were wide with intrigue. "Of course, Miss Denby. Goodness, do you think someone attacked Dr Fuller on purpose? That it wasn't just a mugging?"

"I do, Annabel, I'm afraid. So do be careful yourself. I don't want to scare you, but try not to walk around on your own. Bring a friend with you to the hotel. Promise me?"

The girl paled. "Yes, Miss Denby, I think that would be wise."

CHAPTER 25

Before she left the hospital, Poppy tried to speak to Rosie Winter – after noting that Chief Constable Fenchurch had gone – but the WPC just mumbled that she wasn't allowed to fraternize with Poppy anymore. "Sorry Poppy, I'm already in a lot of trouble. If I want to keep my job, I will have to toe the line."

"I understand," said Poppy and gave the policewoman a sympathetic pat on the shoulder. "I know it's got you into hot water, but you have been a huge help to me. And I won't forget it."

Poppy left the hospital and walked down Walton Street. As she passed *The Oxford Gazette*, she decided to pop in and see how George Lewis was getting on. The newspaperman was just coming out of the building as she arrived, pulling on his coat in a hurry.

"Miss Denby! Have you heard about the attack on Sophie Blackburn?"

"I have, Mr Lewis. I was the one who found her."

This slowed Lewis down. He whipped out a notebook from his pocket and pencil from behind his ear. "This certainly qualifies for information that directly affects Oxford – as per our agreement – so spill it."

Poppy told him what had happened but didn't mention anything about papers being searched at Sophie's or Gertrude's place. She wanted to delve deeper into that herself before going public. When she'd finished telling Lewis her story, he let out a long whistle.

"So, Fenchurch is treating the attacks as related. But he is not reopening the June Leighton case."

"That about sums it up – despite it being obvious to anyone with eyes in their head that the three incidents are related. If he is going to re-examine the Leighton case, he didn't tell me."

Lewis grinned. "That doesn't surprise me. Fenchurch is one of those men who does not like being told what to do by women – particularly young, pretty women who come up from London. But he's no fool, Miss Denby, and despite his attitude to ladies, he's one of the better fellows on the force. If his investigation into the two attacks turns anything up to justify it, Fenchurch may very well reopen June's case."

Poppy was surprised that Lewis appeared to be defending the Chief Constable. "So, you don't think Fenchurch is involved in any conscious cover-up?"

"It would surprise me if he were. However, he does not have full control of every officer on the constabulary, and as far as I know, the June Leighton incident was not his case."

"Oh? Whose was it?"

"Another senior officer called Teddy Birch. A chief inspector. He's been around for years – pre-dates Fenchurch – and is pretty much untouchable. Like the medical examiner, he's only got a few months to retirement, and no one wants to suggest he hasn't done his job properly. I reckon that's one of the things that influenced my predecessor's lack of curiosity about the case. He, Dickie Mortimer, and Teddy Birch were regular drinking pals." He shook his head. "I'm sure Mr Rolandson has already told you this, Miss Denby, but while it's good for journalists to get as close as they can to police officers, they should not get too close. There's being pally and then there's being pally to the point of losing your professional perspective. I fear that's what happened here."

Poppy nodded her understanding. "Yes, he has told me that. But how very interesting about the three of them being so pally, and how it might have influenced the Leighton investigation. Do you think I'll be able to speak with Chief Inspector Birch?"

Lewis shook his head. "Sorry, he's away on holiday. The Isle of Wight, I believe. But I have been able to arrange a meeting with Dickie Mortimer, the medical examiner. I went to see him after I left the hospital this morning. I have arranged to meet him this evening at the White Horse. And," he said, pausing for effect, "guess what? I asked him to bring the report into June's death."

Poppy's eyes widened in surprise. "That's wonderful!"

Lewis chuckled. "I have certain skills, Miss Denby."

Poppy smiled at the older journalist. "I never doubted you did."

Poppy and Lewis arranged a time to meet at the White Horse later that evening. She wasn't quite sure how appropriate it would be for a young woman to walk into the pub unaccompanied, but she'd cross that bridge when she came to it. Then, Lewis rushed off to see who else he could interview about the Sophie Blackburn story.

Poppy checked her watch and saw that it was four o'clock. Time to get back to the hotel. Hopefully by now Ike would have arrived. She'd catch up with him, telephone Rollo, then have a little rest and something to eat before meeting George Lewis and Dr Dickie Mortimer. She expected Ike might want to come along to that meeting too. She picked up her pace. However, as she passed Somerville College, she decided to pop into the gatehouse to ask the porter a few questions. He was seated in a little kiosk reading a newspaper and looked up as Poppy entered the portico.

"Can I help you, miss?"

"Hello, my name is Miss Denby. I was here the other day."

"Ah yes," he said, "the lady with the bicycle. You look a bit drier today."

Poppy smiled ruefully, expecting the smile to be returned, and she was surprised that it was not. She thought the man young for a porter. Not that she'd known many porters in her time, but those that she had – and those that she'd read about in novels – always seemed to be around retirement age. She'd be surprised if this man was even forty. He folded his newspaper and leaned forward. "So how can I help you, Miss Denby?"

"I was, well, I was wondering if you'd heard about the attack on Dr Fuller last night."

"Attack? Oh, I don't think it was an attack, miss. The police told me this morning that she'd had a fall and someone had found her and taken her to the infirmary."

"Yes, that's one theory," said Poppy. "The other is that she was attacked. In fact, Dr Fuller herself claims she was grabbed from behind by a man."

The porter raised an eyebrow. "Really? And she saw the man?"

Poppy shook her head. "No. But I do not believe she imagined it. And, I can tell you, neither do the police. I have just spoken to the Chief Constable."

The single raised eyebrow was joined by a second. "That's the first I've heard."

Poppy nodded, pursing her lips. She decided not, at this stage, to tell him about the attack on Sophie. She didn't want the conversation to be diverted. He would find out soon enough, but for now, she wanted to keep him focused on Gertrude Fuller. "So, were you on duty last night when Dr Fuller was attacked?"

"For my sins, yes. I normally don't work nights – not when I'm working the next day – but the fellow I share duties with has a touch of the flu."

"That's unfortunate. I'm sure you must be quite tired."

The man sat up straight. "Not tired enough not to do my job, Miss Denby."

"Of course not! I wasn't suggesting you were, Mr—"

"Cooper."

"Thank you, Mr Cooper. So, did you see anyone?"

Cooper shook his head. "Not out of the ordinary. It's quiet at the moment, what with Trinity term not starting until next week. There are not many students about so it's mainly just the academics."

"And town folk? You're not separate from the town here."

"That's right, we're not. But at that time of night – it was nearly eleven, I believe – there's not many townies passing the college neither."

Poppy nodded. "All right, no one passing the college. What about coming in?"

"What? At that hour? No, there were no visitors. They would have to be prearranged if there were. And there's nothing in the book." He pushed a logbook towards Poppy, then pulled it back again. From where she was standing, Poppy was unable to read anything that was written. And she had no right to ask to see it. Perhaps the police might now do so.

"So, you didn't see Dr Fuller and no one passed by or came in. Which is very curious, as I have been told that an intruder has been into Dr Fuller's rooms – possibly after she was attacked, possibly before. But definitely last night while she wasn't there."

Cooper's eyes narrowed. "Who told you that?"

"Dr Fuller's graduate student. She was in earlier to collect some notes for Dr Fuller to work on in the hospital. She said someone had definitely been into the rooms."

Cooper sat back, his arms folding over his chest. "Well, if that's the case, Miss Denby, the Beadle will have to be called."

"The Beadle?"

"University security. I'll have to call them. They already know about Dr Fuller's accident, but this is new information. And there'll have to be an investigation."

Cooper's eyes flicked down to the logbook and back up again. *Hmm*, thought Poppy, *is that a tell? Is there someone in the book that he's not telling me about?* There was no way she could find out, but she would certainly be telling Chief Constable Fenchurch about it when she next saw him.

"Well, thank you, Mr Cooper. You've been very helpful. And I'm sure you'll be just as helpful to the Beadles and the police now that you know this is more than just an unfortunate accident. However, there's one more thing I'd like to ask: yesterday, when I left my bicycle here, did anyone come in and tamper with it?"

Cooper's arms were still over his chest. "Tamper with it? Of course not! Who would do that?"

"I don't know, Mr Cooper; that's what I'm trying to find out. Because I had an accident yesterday, after I'd been here. Someone had partially sawn through my brake rod."

Cooper's eyes narrowed. "Well, it wasn't here. I would have seen."

"Yes, I'm sure you would have. You have a full view of the whole vestibule from where you are seated."

"Aye, that's right." He sat, unmoved, with his arms folded.

Poppy thanked him and left but was not able to shake the feeling that the porter knew more than he was telling. And she couldn't help noticing that he had not shown the slightest bit of concern when she told him she'd had an accident.

Time was getting on, and she wanted to get back to the hotel to catch Rollo before the end of the afternoon. She thought for a moment of phoning him from the Post Office, which was a little closer, but not that much. Still, it was a bit of a trek to the hotel, and she wished she had not shunned the use of a bicycle after her accident. She turned into St Giles Street and down to the Martyrs' Memorial, slipping into the fork in the road between the sun-soaked limestone walls of Balliol College and the gothic shadow of St Mary Magdalen's Church. But as she turned the corner into Broad Street, she noticed a man in a flat tweed cap who appeared to be following her. Was she imagining it, or had she seen him outside Somerville College too? *Well*, she reminded herself as she turned the corner, *it's no crime to be walking in the same direction*. However, she couldn't shake the feeling that he was doing more than that. A chill went down her spine and she hastened her pace, thanking God that it was still daylight and that there were people out and about. At each turn left or right, she checked over her shoulder, and there he was, not even trying to hide the fact that he was following her.

By the time she got to Magdalen Bridge she was almost jogging – and so was her shadow. When she slowed, he slowed; when she speeded up, so did he. A few times she thought of turning into a shop and asking for help, but she wondered how she would explain herself, knowing that as soon as she did, he would disappear. Then, who knew when he would reappear again? No, as long as she could see him, as long as it was daylight, and as long as there were still people on the streets, she felt safe enough to go straight back to the hotel.

Sure enough, as she turned into Cowley Place and past St Hilda's College, there he was still behind her. She ploughed on, breathless, with a stitch piercing her side, until she reached the gates of the Cherwell Hotel. As soon as she stepped across the threshold, noting that the man who looked after the bicycles had seen she was there, she turned around and shouted at her pursuer, "Who are you and why are you following me?"

The man nonchalantly stopped and positioned himself on the opposite pavement, leaning against a lamp post, and lit a cigarette. He stared at Poppy but did not answer.

Poppy's rage was bubbling over. "I say! If you don't leave me alone, I shall call the police!"

The man – who Poppy noted was perhaps in his late twenties – again said nothing and drew on his cigarette.

"Are you all right, miss?" asked the bicycle man, approaching her.

She turned to him and blurted out that she was being followed. But when she turned to point out her pursuer, the man in the flat cap was gone.

Chapter 26

Poppy was still fuming when she walked into the foyer of the hotel – too angry to be fearful. She stomped across the parquet floor towards the reception desk, ready to report the man in the flat cap. And then she saw Ike Garfield sitting in the corner with a suitcase at his side. She wanted to run to him and let him embrace her in a huge bear hug, to tell him what had just happened, and to pour out her anger and fear; but naturally, that would not be an appropriate thing for a lady to do. Poppy was getting very annoyed with ideas of what was or was not appropriate for a lady. She wished at times she could be more like Delilah. Delilah would not have given two hoots about embracing the West Indian journalist. Or anyone – male or female.

Poppy hurried over to greet him as he stood and raised his hat. "Poppy! I'm so glad to see you."

"Not as much as I am to see you, Ike! Good gracious, what happened to you? Mavis said you left London sometime this morning. It should only have taken you a couple of hours if you've got a good tailwind. I was expecting you at lunchtime."

"Sorry, Poppy. Blame Rollo for not getting a new motor. The old Model T broke down. Again."

"Oh no!" said Poppy, taking a seat as Ike returned to his.

"Oh yes. Just outside High Wycombe. I managed to walk to a nearby pub and they called a mechanic. But when he got there, he took one look at my face and drove off. I eventually got someone from the pub to go with me and tow the Ford back. It's still stuck there in the car park. I'll have to arrange to get it repaired. But the most important thing was getting here to see you. I had to order a taxi to bring me the rest of the way. But the first fellow wouldn't take me. Second time lucky though." He gave a gentle smile.

Poppy pursed her lips, then let out an exasperated sigh, her anger growing ever deeper. "Oh, for Pete's sake! What is wrong with people?"

Ike shrugged ruefully. "Tell that to the manager here."

Poppy's eyes narrowed. "Why? What's he said?"

Ike, his voice admirably calm, pointed to his suitcase. "He said they don't have any available rooms and I'll have to go elsewhere. I asked him if I could at least wait for you to return, to tell you where I'm going, and he said yes."

"Well, that's absolute poppycock!" said Poppy. "The breakfast room was only half-full this morning, and I know for a fact that there are spare rooms on my floor." She stood up. "I'm going to talk to him."

Before Ike could stop her, she stalked across the foyer to the reception desk and demanded to see the manager. He arrived, all silk cravat and onyx cufflinks. "Ah, Miss Denby. I trust you've had a fruitful day. Will you be staying for dinner?"

"I shall. A table for two, please. And a room as well for my colleague Mr Garfield. I believe you have just spoken to him."

An onyx cufflink was adjusted. "Ah yes, the negro gentleman. We unfortunately do not have any rooms available."

Poppy leaned in, fixing her bluebell eyes on the man's steel grey. She forced every bit of anger into that stare. Anger at the police for not believing Gertrude. Anger at the fellows at the Crystal Crypt for treating June so appallingly. Anger at Chief Constable Fenchurch for quashing Rosie Winter's ambition. Anger at Bill Raines for his aggression on the dance floor. Anger at the scoundrel who sabotaged her bicycle – and, finally, sheer rage at the monster who attacked poor Sophie and left her for dead. "We both know that's a barefaced lie, sir, so if you don't want unpleasant headlines in both my newspaper and *The Oxford Gazette* – because, I'm not sure if you're aware, I am on very good terms with George Lewis, the editor – then I suggest you find a room, a good room, for my colleague. Now, he and I are going to have a cup of tea, which will give you time to find something appropriate. Earl Grey please, and we'll take it on the terrace."

Poppy spun on her heel and stalked off, ignoring the stares of the hotel guests who had overheard her conversation. Ike was waiting for her, his jaw hanging agog. "Good grief, Poppy, I didn't know you had it in you."

Poppy's heart was pounding nineteen to the dozen. "Neither did I, Ike, neither did I."

Twenty minutes later and Poppy was feeling much calmer. She felt proud of herself, but also a little embarrassed. The waiter had refused to meet her eye when he brought the tea, and she did not like to think that she would now be considered a diva by the hotel staff. She was always so pleasant and amiable and personally despised people who did what she had just done: using her position of power to bully others to do her will. But, she reminded herself, she had done it in defence of someone else who was being bullied. Who had spent his life being unjustly treated simply because of the shade of his complexion. So no, she would not apologize.

Besides, there was work to be done. Ike had brought along the file that Ivan Molanov had put together. He first explained to her that it was a second attempt at compiling the file, and then told her how he had found Rollo knocked-out in his office that morning.

"Good Lord!" said Poppy, after finding out that Rollo was no worse for wear, despite a sore head. "Who do you think did it?"

Ike splayed his large hands. "We don't know for sure. Rollo went to see Lionel Saunders yesterday morning and Richard Easling in the afternoon. It could have been instigated by either of them. They both have a track record. But what it does indicate is that there's definitely a connection between Sophie Blackburn and June Leighton. Rollo asked Lionel about Sophie and did not mention June Leighton at all, yet it was the file on the Sanforths – which, as you'll soon see, also establishes a link between them and the Leightons – that was stolen. What the attacker didn't realize is that Ivan could put together another file of roughly the same material."

Poppy furiously took notes, then went on to tell Ike about what she'd discovered during her time in Oxford, then about the attacks on Gertrude Fuller and Sophie Blackburn. The West Indian journalist was stunned. "Good God, Poppy, this is serious. Rollo got a good whack on the head, but I don't think his attacker intended to kill him. But what happened to Sophie, particularly, is attempted murder."

Poppy nodded, her hand shaking slightly as she poured herself and Ike another cup of tea. "Yes, it was. Do you think it's the same person who did it? Who attacked Rollo and then Gertrude and Sophie?"

"It's possible. Rollo was attacked around seven last night, and from what you tell me, Gertrude Fuller sometime after ten. It is feasible that Rollo's attacker drove straight from Fleet Street to Oxford. What time was Sophie attacked?"

"I don't know. It could have been around the same time as Gertrude – she only lives a block away – but that doesn't account for why Sophie didn't meet me at five o'clock yesterday afternoon as we'd agreed. If it was the assault that prevented her from coming to see me, then that means the attacker assaulted her here in Oxford in the afternoon, then drove to London to attack Rollo and steal the Sanforth file, then back to Oxford to attack Gertrude Fuller. While they could have done it within the time frame given, why on earth would they? No, Ike, I think it's more realistic that there are people in London and Oxford working in cahoots."

Ike pulled out a cigarette case and selected one, asking if Poppy minded. She said that she didn't. "Yes," he said as he lit up, "I agree with you. That also ties into what Richard Easling told Rollo about the Oxford City Police being concerned that you were snooping around. He already knew you were here before Rollo told him."

"Are you suggesting the Oxford police might be involved in this?"

Ike shook his head. "No, not the police per se, but perhaps a rogue element in it. Perhaps just a single man."

Poppy thought about that for a moment, then gave Ike a summary of her dealings to date with the Oxford police. "So, in my estimation, WPC Winter is a good egg. The Chief Constable is a pompous so-and-so, but I'm not convinced he's dirty. Neither is George Lewis, the editor of *The Oxford Gazette*. But that doesn't mean there isn't someone else on the force involved in this." She then explained to Ike what she'd learned about June Leighton's death not being properly investigated and that George Lewis had set up a meeting with the medical examiner. "And after all that's been going on – and that fellow who was following me earlier – I'm glad you're going to be with me when we go out tonight. Now, let's have a look at that file. You said there's something on the Leightons in there? That'll probably be the engagement of June and Edward."

Ike shook his head. "No, that's not it. Nothing in there about an engagement. But there is something else. Have a look for yourself..."

Poppy opened the file and read through Ivan's summary, then flicked through the clippings. Sanforth Foundation Donates to Oxford Lab; Sanforth Industries in MOD Wrangle; Sanforth Industries Wins Big Defence Contract; Sanforth Industries Criticized for Weimar Investments; Sanforth Foundation Withdraws Funding from Cambridge – Pacifists to Blame; Sanforth Industries in Hostile Takeover of Diamond Mine in German South West Africa...

Poppy extracted the last article from the file and read it in detail. She could hardly believe what she was reading: Sanforth Industries – of whom the now incarcerated Lord Melvyn Dorchester was a former board member and still a substantial shareholder – had bought a South West African diamond mine in what was described as a "hostile takeover". The deal, according to the article, had been brokered by a London jeweller: Roger Leighton.

"Oh my hat! Surely this isn't—"

"June Leighton's father? I'm afraid it is, Poppy. June's father Roger not only knows the Sanforths but is in business with them. And it's also connected in some way to Melvyn Dorchester, who we all know was, and perhaps still is, Lionel Saunders' paymaster – and was once the paymaster of Richard Easling too. So, all the dots are beginning to connect. Did Edward Sanforth tell you about any of this? Of his family's connection with the Leightons?"

Poppy shook her head vigorously. "Not a word of it! He gave the impression he and June had met here in Oxford and kept their romance quiet from their families. He said he told his family about it after June's death – and I assume Mr and Mrs Leighton too – but he gave absolutely no indication that the families knew one another. All right, I never asked directly, but I think the context of the conversation should have prompted him to tell me."

"And Professor Sinclair? Did he mention it?"

Poppy shook her head. "Not a word of it. But that might explain the diamond..."

"What diamond?"

Poppy told Ike that June Leighton had been X-raying a diamond before she died and that no one could explain why. "Sophie found it odd. But she assured me it had nothing to do with jewellery theft, which was my first thought. She said it was probably an industrial diamond and not worth that much. But still, it's got to have some significance, surely? What with June's family's connection to Sanforth Industries and this diamond mine... But what, I'm not really sure. Perhaps June's lab notes will tell us – the notes that can't be found. But it seems that the attacker is searching for them."

Poppy downed the last of her tea and then stood up. "Ike, would you mind telephoning Rollo and filling him in on all this? And then ask him to go to the Leighton house to enquire about June's notes? Both Edward Sanforth and Gertrude Fuller think they were sent on to her family. Oh, and if he hasn't already, ask Ivan to see what he can dig up on the Melvyn Dorchester connection. And also if he can find anything about a" – she flicked open her notebook and found the name she was looking for – "a Chief Inspector Teddy Birch of the Oxford City Police. He apparently was the fellow who declared June's death an open-and-shut case. He's on holiday at the moment, or I'd try to speak to him myself."

Ike made some notes, then asked, "And what are you going to do?"

Poppy bit her lip. "I'm sorry, Ike. If you don't mind, I need to go and get changed before dinner. I" – she looked down at her skirt and blouse – "I've still got Sophie's blood on me."

CHAPTER 27

THURSDAY 23 APRIL 1925, LONDON

The taxi dropped Rollo outside Pentonville Prison at seven o'clock that evening. It was still an hour until sunset on an April night, and the white walls of the North London penitentiary were as bright as the towers of Camelot against the blue spring sky. Visiting hours were over, and Rollo had had to call in a couple of favours from some of his most high-ranking and confidential associates to arrange this ad hoc meeting at such short notice. However, after speaking to Ike on the telephone from Oxford, he did not feel it was something that could wait until the morning.

Melvyn Dorchester in his grey prison shirt and trousers still managed to look every inch the aristocrat, despite having been behind bars for nearly five years. That's what money would buy you: relative comfort, privacy, and protection from the riff-raff. Lord Dorchester didn't bother to get up as Rollo was shown into the interview room; he remained seated, his long legs comfortably crossed. He tilted his head and looked down his aquiline nose as Rollo took a seat opposite him.

"You're showing your age, Rolandson. Fatherhood doesn't suit you."

"From a failed father like you, I'll take that as a compliment. Has the daughter you tried to kill been in touch lately? And how is young Alfie? Still on the run from the authorities?"

Dorchester gave a tight smile. "I'm sure wherever he is he'll be doing just fine. Dorchesters always are. And how are your little sprogs? Stunted in size and class like their father?"

Rollo settled back into his chair, his feet dangling a foot off the ground. "Fortunately, they take after their mother in the class department." Rollo waited for the next jibe, aimed at his Anglo-Egyptian wife who had been on the legal team that put Dorchester away for seven years, but it didn't come. Instead, the disgraced peer and industrialist leaned forward and got straight to the point.

"So, what do you want? And what are you prepared to pay to get it?"

Rollo raised a sardonic brow. "Cash flow drying up?"

Dorchester gave Rollo a withering look, one, the editor imagined, that would have had butlers and footmen quivering in their boots in a past life. It had absolutely no impact on the caustic newspaperman.

"As to what I want," he said, "information. As to what I am prepared to pay: well, I believe you are up for parole soon. If I get what I want, I can have a word with various interested parties who might be able to sway things in your favour." He then mentioned a couple of names.

Dorchester nodded. "All right. I'll play."

Rollo nodded in return. "Dandy. What relationship do you have with the Sanforth Foundation or Sanforth Industries?"

"I think that's already public knowledge, Rolandson. You really should do your homework."

"Humour me."

"All right. I had nothing to do with the Foundation, but I was a member of the Sanforth Industries board for ten years." He gave a wry smile. "I was asked to step down after I changed my residential address."

"But you still hold shares?"

"That's correct."

"Are you still privy to business decisions made at board level?"

"I have my sources."

"Good. Then you might be of some use to me. What do you know about the acquisition of a diamond mine in the former German South West Africa? I think they just call it South West Africa these days."

"They do. And as for the diamond mine acquisition, it was completed last year."

"What was the purpose of the acquisition? As far as I can tell, Sanforth Industries has not made inroads into gemstone mining before. Why this one and why now?"

"I have no idea. Businesses diversify. It's nothing unusual."

"Oh," said Rollo, "you'll need to do better than that, Dorchester, or my offer is off the table. Why *this* diamond mine? Why now?"

Dorchester clawed his hand and examined his nails. Rollo noted that they were as well manicured as they ever were before he started his sentence. Obviously, the aristocrat wasn't compelled to participate in manual labour. Dorchester's friends went high up the food chain. Fortunately, so did Rollo's.

"Another two years in this place might not be so bad, Dorchester, but what if another ten years were added to that? Or another fifteen?"

Dorchester snorted. "On what grounds?"

"I have been informed that someone is about to turn you in for the murder of Bert Isaacs." This was a blatant lie, but Rollo delivered it with the seriousness of a judge.

Dorchester's right eye twitched. *Good*, thought Rollo. *I'm getting to him.*

"And who, may I ask, is this someone?"

"You may ask, but I don't have to tell. I could though... for a price."

"Tell me who and I'll tell you what you want to know about Sanforth."

Rollo shook his head. "Oh no, my lordship, you've got that the wrong way round. You tell me first. And if the information is helpful enough, I'll consider it. That and the word with the parole board."

Dorchester sucked at his teeth. "All right," he said eventually. "It's to do with a proxy German company. Sanforth are hoping to do a deal with Kleinmann & Co, a chemical company. As you know, rearmament of Germany is forbidden under the Treaty of Versailles, so companies like Kleinmann, who previously supplied chemicals to the German military, have been struggling for business. They have done a deal with Sanforth to sell chemicals on their behalf to the US, Britain, and France. There's nothing illegal in it, but it's not considered patriotic to do that sort of business with a German company. So business is done through a proxy company in the former German South West Africa that still has links to the Fatherland. The mine buys the chemicals – as part of their regular stock – then sells it on as surplus to various buyers."

"All right," said Rollo. "That makes sense. What, though, does it have to do with experiments into stabilizing explosives in an Oxford laboratory?"

Dorchester looked mildly surprised for a moment, then his default haughtiness returned. "Very little. But again, there's nothing illegal in weapons manufacture or experimentation. It's the rearmament of Germany that's illegal. But we all know the Weimar government are doing it on the sly."

Rollo did know this but continued with his line of questioning, hoping to get something more tangible out of Dorchester. "So, let's say, if a chemical formula were discovered to stabilize or solidify liquid explosives, and it was then sold back to Germany, that would not be illegal?"

Dorchester shrugged. "I have no idea; I'm not a lawyer. But it would be considered bad form. Not good for business if it got out."

"Ah," said Rollo. "That's what I thought. And so it might be prudent, then, to channel any resultant research through a diamond mine in Africa. Because mining requires explosives."

"I would say that's a plausible scenario. But again, I don't think it would be illegal."

Rollo wasn't so sure of that – he would ask Yazzie to find out for him – but he did accept Dorchester's theory that it might all be done to simply save face. Would, he wondered, someone be prepared to kill to keep this quiet? And if so, surely more people than June Leighton would know about it. Who else might be in danger?

A guard appeared at the door and announced they had five more minutes. Both men nodded their understanding. "So," said Rollo, "just one more thing. Do you know Roger Leighton of William Lawes & Co. in Mayfair?"

"I do. A very fine establishment."

"Are you aware that Leighton helped broker the deal to buy the diamond mine for Sanforth Industries?"

"No, but it doesn't surprise me. I should imagine a jeweller of Leighton's pedigree has lots of connections in that area."

"And are you aware too that Leighton's daughter, a very gifted young scientist, worked at the laboratory in Oxford where the research into stabilizing explosives was going on?"

"Again, no. But as I've said before, there's nothing illegal in that."

"Noted," said Rollo, checking his watch. He needed to wrap this up. "And are you aware that June Leighton died under mysterious circumstances there about a month ago?"

Dorchester once again gave a flicker of surprise. "No. But I see this is where you've been steering the conversation. I wasn't sure why you are so hell bent on digging into a non-story about non-illegal activities in the arms trade. But this is it. You're on a crusade again. Don't tell me you think I had anything to do with this girl's death?"

"I'm not sure," said Rollo. "Did you?"

"Why on earth would you think I did?"

"Because of Lionel Saunders. One of yours. He is somehow connected and that ultimately leads to you. Again."

"What do you mean, *again*?"

Rollo shook his head incredulously. "Come, come, your lordship. Don't make me spell it out. You paid Saunders to kill Bert Isaacs five years ago to try to stop the investigation into your daughter. Saunders refused to testify then, but I have it on good authority that he will now."

Dorchester sat bolt upright, then leaned across the table and lowered his voice. "If that's true, the man's lying," he hissed. "I never paid him to kill anyone. I did pay him to feed me information about what was going on inside your newspaper. But if he killed anyone, he did it on his own."

Rollo's heart was beating fast. Finally. Finally! Information that could nail Lionel Saunders and lay old Bert to rest. However, he wouldn't allow his excitement to show. Instead, he just shrugged, and asked, "Easy to say now, Dorchester. Would you be prepared to testify to that in court?"

Dorchester's eyes sparked like flint. "If it would mean getting me out of here two years earlier, you can bet your Yankee doodle dandy on it. Do we have a deal?"

"I'll have a word with a few people and get back to you."

"Make it happen."

CHAPTER 28

THURSDAY 23 APRIL 1925, OXFORD

Poppy and Ike finished their supper under the intense, unabashed stares of the other hotel guests. A middle-aged black man and a young white woman, eating together in a public place, was bound to attract attention. As work colleagues, Poppy and Ike had spent lots of time in one another's company over the last five years, but this was the first time she recalled the two of them sharing a meal in a restaurant without at least a couple of other folk from the office in tow. Poppy would have liked to have thought that it didn't bother her, but it did. She was already aware that tongues had been wagging ever since she arrived at the hotel unchaperoned, but now the level of scandal had reached boiling point. She was half expecting one of the guests to come over to them and demand that they leave. Fortunately, no one did, but she was more than relieved to say no to pudding and to head out to their next appointment. As Ike helped her into her coat, he said quietly, "I'm sorry you had to experience that, Poppy."

Poppy felt suddenly ashamed. Here was Ike apologizing to her when this was most probably what he and his wife and children had to face every day. "No, Ike, I'm sorry *you* had to experience that. On top of everything else you've experienced today. And every other day." She took her hat and pulled it firmly onto her head. "But we've got a job to do. Shall we go, sir?"

Ike grinned down at her and gestured with his arm towards the door. "Lead the way, Miss Denby."

It was dusk and the sun was setting over the Botanic Garden as Poppy and Ike turned into the High Street. As they stopped to look left and right before crossing the road, Poppy noticed – with a sharp intake of breath – that the man in the tweed flat cap was once again following her. She quietly told Ike about him, who, as inconspicuously as possible, flicked a glance behind them. "I see him. Don't worry, Poppy. I doubt he'll try anything with me here, but just to be sure, take us on the busiest and most well-lit route, will you?"

Poppy did as she was told, deciding not to take the shortcut past the Radcliffe Camera, instead taking a circuitous route down the High Street, into Cornmarket, and then right into Broad Street. Poppy pointed up Magdalen Street towards St Giles and Somerville College and told Ike that she'd take him there tomorrow. As they passed the front entrance of Balliol College, she told Ike about the porter who had given Rosie Winter reason to suspect that Bill Raines and Miles Mackintosh might have been involved in Gertrude Fuller's attack.

"Do you think those two are the main suspects in all this?" asked Ike.

Poppy nodded. "I think they're high up on the list. I want to try to speak to them both again. And I think I'd feel safer doing so with you beside me."

Ike flicked his head back at the man in the flat cap who was still blatantly following them, not even pretending to hide. "So, who's this fella then? Do you recognize him?"

"I don't, I'm afraid."

"Do you want me to try to collar him?" asked Ike.

Poppy shook her head vigorously. Ike was a large, strong man and in his youth had been a fast bowler for his local cricket team in Trinidad, but now, at fifty-something, and with too much of his wife Doreen's home cooking under his belt, she doubted he'd be a match for the fit young man who was stalking them. Ike was a gentle giant. He would try to defend himself – and her – well enough if attacked, but best not to provoke anything, she thought.

"No, he hasn't actually done anything yet, other than looking shifty. Besides, we're here." She stopped outside the White Horse and pointed across the road. "And that's the Crystal Crypt laboratory," she whispered. "In the basement of the Science Museum."

"Looks like someone's working late," observed Ike quietly, noting the lights shining from the lower floors.

"Yes, it does," said Poppy.

The man with the flat cap had by now caught up to them and leaned against a lamp post only a few yards from the entrance to the White Horse. He stared challengingly at Ike and Poppy and lit up a cigarette.

"I suggest you move on, young man," said Ike, "or I'll be calling the police on you."

The man said nothing.

"Suit yourself!" snapped Poppy. "But don't wait up for us. We're going to be a while."

Ike chuckled, opened the door of the pub, and ushered Poppy in.

Poppy's eyes adjusted to the dim, smoky light of the tavern and she spotted George Lewis near the back. He was seated with an ageing gentleman, hunched over a pint. Poppy pointed them out to Ike, and the large man made a way through the hubbub of customers waiting to be served. As expected, the mismatched couple attracted some attention, but it was short-lived. The White Horse had an eclectic mix of customers, many of them eccentric academics, so Poppy and Ike did not rate too highly on the curiosity scale.

Lewis spotted them and rose to his feet. His companion looked up but did not rise.

"Miss Denby! So glad you could make it. And your companion." To Poppy's relief Lewis smiled warmly at Ike and thrust out his hand. "George Lewis, editor of *The Oxford Gazette*."

Ike smiled back and took the Scotsman's hand. "Ike Garfield. Senior reporter, *The Daily Globe*. You were on *The Edinburgh Star* before you came here, weren't you?"

Lewis preened, obviously glad to be recognized. "I was."

"Great job you did with the Rennie exposé last year."

"Why thank you, Mr Garfield. I'm aware of your work too. That interview you did with Ramsay MacDonald earlier this year was incisive."

The man at the table gave a loud, phlegmy cough. "Can we get on with this, please? I haven't got all night."

"Sorry," said Lewis and he pulled out a chair for Poppy. "Miss Denby, Mr Garfield, this is Dr Dickie Mortimer, police pathologist. Dr Mortimer has very kindly offered to tell us about his report into June Leighton's death – although he hasn't actually brought the report along."

Mortimer took a slurp of his beer and wiped the froth off his top lip with the back of his hand. "As if I had a choice."

Poppy raised an eyebrow at Lewis. The editor gave a tight smile. "Now, now, Dickie, of course you had a choice. But as we've both agreed, best you talk about this now so other things don't have to come out into the open."

Mortimer harrumphed and leaned back in his chair, crossing his arms across his chest. "Bloody blackmail, that's what it is."

"Nonsense!" said Lewis, then turned to Poppy and Ike. "Let's just say the doctor has a colourful private life, and one of my junior reporters has been a tad enthusiastic in digging into it. I have agreed to ask him to concentrate his efforts elsewhere while Dr Mortimer here does his moral duty and tells us what he knows about Miss Leighton's death. I think it's a fair arrangement."

"Bloody lily-livered journalists," growled the doctor, but before he could continue the barman called out to ask what they'd be having.

"Same again, Dr Mortimer?" asked Ike.

The doctor gave him a bleary-eyed stare. "Aye."

Poppy asked for a lemonade – she needed to keep a level head tonight – while Ike ordered a stout and Lewis a scotch. A few minutes later the drinks arrived, and the three journalists leaned in to hear what the police pathologist had to say.

"Well," he started, "it was first thing on a Monday morning when I was called. I'd had a late night and hadn't been in bed long. But it's my job so I got up. The body had been found by one of the lab assistants who got there first to open up before the scientists arrived. He had attempted to revive her – heart massage and the kiss of life – but it was too late. Fortunately, he had sense enough not to move her from the position she was in."

"And what was that position?" asked Poppy, as the doctor took another slurp of his beer.

"She was lying on her back with her knees hitched up and her arms splayed. As if she'd been punched in the stomach and thrown back."

"Would a shock of electricity do that?" asked Poppy.

"I've never seen someone electrocuted before, but I imagine yes."

"You imagine?" asked George Lewis. "Nothing more definitive than that?"

"No," Mortimer grimaced. "But what else could have done that?"

"You're the expert, Dr Mortimer. That's why we're asking you," chipped in Ike.

Mortimer glowered at him and pointedly turned towards Lewis. "You never told me I'd be interrogated by a darkie and a floozy."

Lewis bristled. "I'll ask you to keep a civil tongue, Dr Mortimer, or our deal's off. Can you do that?"

Mortimer shrugged and took another swig of beer.

"So," continued Poppy, not allowing her annoyance with Mortimer to show, "it appears that she was electrocuted, but you can't be sure."

Mortimer slammed down his empty glass and glared at Ike. "I'll have another."

Ike shrugged, got up, and went to the bar. Poppy and Lewis had barely touched their drinks, so there was no point asking them if they wanted refills. Poppy was just about to repeat her question when Mortimer answered. "No missy, I can be sure. I can't be sure that the electrocution caused her body to fall the way it did because I've never seen someone die of electrocution before, but the effects on the body are well documented, and it was clear from the post-mortem that her body had had strong current pumped through it. That and the wires that were seared into the palm of her hand."

"Seared?"

"Yes, they were literally melted into her flesh. I have no doubt that June Leighton was electrocuted."

Ike returned with the beer and placed it in front of Mortimer. He was not thanked. The journalist pulled out his chair and re-joined the discussion. "So, she was electrocuted, but was there any evidence that it was definitely accidental, or could someone else have been involved?"

Mortimer laughed. "I'm a doctor, not a detective. I just wrote my report on the evidence presented to me by the body. Anything beyond that is up to the investigating officer."

"DCI Birch?" asked Poppy.

"That's right," said Mortimer. "You should ask him."

"He's out of town."

Mortimer shrugged. "Too bad."

Poppy looked at first Ike, then Lewis. There wasn't much to go on here. She'd hoped for more. But she had a few questions left. "All right," she said, "it's not your job to investigate the scene of the crime – if it were indeed a crime – but could you tell me if there were any cables wrapped around June's ankles or caught in the heel of her shoe?"

Mortimer thought a moment, then answered, "No. But the cable was loose. It looked like it hadn't been properly fastened down – either to the wall or the floor. I would never have allowed a piece of equipment in my surgery to be so poorly installed."

"So, you're saying it might have been a safety management issue?" asked Lewis.

Mortimer shrugged again. "Could be. Let's just say that if I were that young woman's family, I would have been asking more serious questions of their daughter's employers. And I would have been pushing for a coroner's inquest on the suspicion of gross negligence."

"And they're not?" asked Poppy. She was surprised she had not thought to ask whether or not there would be an inquest. Once more a sign that she was not quite on point with this investigation, first with the distraction of her engagement, and then with the shock of the attacks on Gertrude and Sophie. She chastised herself, reminding herself that the three victims were relying on her to unearth the truth.

"Not as far as I'm aware," said Mortimer. "They appear to have accepted DCI Birch's findings of accidental death by misadventure without complaint."

"But you're saying there might have been more to it?" probed Lewis.

"As I said before, I'm not a detective. But yes, I would have pressed for more. But I did my job and handed over my report. What happens to it after that is not my business. There was no evidence of foul play, but I do think the laboratory might have done more to prevent an accident like this from happening in the first place."

There was not much more to get out of Mortimer after that, so Poppy, Ike, and Lewis drank up and left him to it.

Poppy buttoned up her coat as she stepped out onto the street, shivering at the chill in the spring air. As she did, she noticed the young man in the flat cap going down the stairs to the basement of the Science Museum. "Well, that doesn't surprise me in the least!" she said and went on to tell George Lewis about the man who had been following her.

"Do you think he's associated with Raines and Mackintosh?" asked the editor.

"Or Sinclair," said Poppy. "Dr Mortimer in there suggested that the laboratory management might be culpable of safety breaches. And if so, ultimately the responsibility will fall to Sinclair."

"What kind of punishment do you think he would get if there were an inquest and the laboratory was shown to be negligent?" asked Ike.

"I'm not sure," said Poppy. "That's the type of thing I would ask Yasmin. Do you have any idea, Mr Lewis?"

Lewis was buttoning his own overcoat. "Basically, what you're talking about is workplace negligence. I'm unaware that there are any legal requirements for safety in laboratories like there are now for mines and heavy industry. Even if there were, I think it could still be argued that it was a freak accident. There's a loose cable, the worst that should happen is someone tripping and spraining an ankle. It was just sheer bad luck that someone pulled the cable out of the machine and grasped the dangerous end, isn't it?"

"Is it?" asked Poppy. "You see, that's what bothers me about this – why I think it might be more than just an accident. And of course, there are the attacks on Gertrude and Sophie. Why would someone do that if they were just trying to cover up a case of workplace negligence? I think someone forced June to hold that cable so that she would be electrocuted, but I have no idea how to begin proving it."

Ike nodded in agreement. "Yes, that's what I think too. But I'm also thinking Dr Mortimer in there had a point: why didn't her family push for an inquest? Even if it were just an accident? If it were my daughter, I most definitely would have."

"What I'm wondering," said Poppy, "is why Mortimer raised the issue of an inquest in the first place. If there has been any cover-up, and Mortimer himself is involved – intentionally or just by oversight – then that would come out in the inquest."

"Because he doesn't think he did anything wrong?" asked Lewis.

"Or perhaps because that's what he wants us to think," said Ike. "Perhaps Rollo might find something out about why June's parents didn't ask for an inquest when he sees them this evening."

"But he won't know to ask," said Poppy.

Ike grinned down at her. "You know better than to underestimate Rollo, Poppy!"

"True," she grinned back. The smile, though, belied her disappointment. She had been hoping for much more from Dr Dickie Mortimer – not least a look at the actual report. She now had no idea on how to progress with the investigation. She hoped Rollo might find something out about the missing papers this evening, because it seemed that unless June Leighton herself spoke from the grave, there was no way to know whether or not her death had been murder or an accident. Or... there had been another thought whispering to her quietly for a while and she had not until now paid heed to it: *suicide*. What if June had committed suicide? She mentioned it to the two men, who both looked shocked that she'd suggested it.

"Why would you think she committed suicide?" asked George Lewis.

"I don't think it; I'm just putting it forward as another theory that we haven't yet considered. It would certainly explain how she managed to grasp the live electrical cable. And is certainly more plausible than the 'she got her foot caught, fell, and grabbed at the wire theory'. Because really, the chances of that are ridiculously slim, aren't they?"

"They are," agreed Lewis. "But that doesn't answer the question of why she would do it. She was having trouble at work, yes, but she was still in a dream job for a young, ambitious scientist. And very lucky indeed to have it as a woman. And from what you've told me of her relationship with Edward Sanforth, they were very much in love and about to tell their parents of their engagement. No one else that knew her has mentioned any melancholia."

"That's all true," said Poppy. "But I still think it would be remiss of us to not consider it. Although, of course, it still begs the question of who attacked Gertrude and Sophie, and why. Someone is trying to cover something up. I think we can discount a mere accident as motivation for that. Even if the laboratory was found negligent, surely the most they'd get was a slap on the wrist. So, there is something else. Something we're not seeing."

Ike put his hand gently on her shoulder. "Perhaps we should sleep on it," said Ike. "It's been a long day for all of us."

"Aye, it has," said George Lewis. "Let's meet up again in the morning. Drop by my office for a cup of tea if you like. By then you might have heard from Rolandson in London."

Poppy agreed, and she and Ike said goodnight to Lewis and made their way back to the hotel, relieved that their "stalker" had decided not to accompany them. *Why on earth would the scientists co-opt someone to follow them?* Poppy thought. This case really was a knotty muddle.

As Poppy and Ike turned into the grounds of the Cherwell Hotel, suddenly someone stepped out of the bushes. Poppy yelped in fright. Ike pushed her back and stepped in front of her, confronting the assailant. But a moment later he relaxed when it became apparent that the "assailant" was not their flat-capped tail from earlier, but a woman.

"Rosie!" said Poppy, recognizing the policewoman in civilian clothes. "You gave us the fright of our lives!"

"Sorry about that," said Rosie grimly. "But I can't be seen with you, or Chief Constable Fenchurch will have my guts for garters. Here," she said, pushing a package towards Poppy.

"What is it?" asked the journalist, reaching out to take it, but Rosie still held it fast.

"You must swear never to tell anyone where you got this. Not even if it leads to the discovery of a murderer. Not even if a judge demands you tell him in court. Can you swear that?"

"I can," said Poppy. "We both can. This is my colleague from the *Globe*, Ike Garfield. Press sources are protected under law. We don't have to disclose where we got our information. Not even in court."

Rosie looked to Ike. "Is that true, Mr Garfield?"

"It is," he said.

"All right then," said Rosie, and she released her grip on the package.

"What is it?" asked Poppy again, her heart already racing in anticipation.

"It's the pathologist's report on June Leighton. I think you're going to be very surprised at what it reveals." And with that, the policewoman slipped back into the shadows.

CHAPTER 29

THURSDAY 23 APRIL 1925, LONDON

As prearranged, the taxi was still waiting for Rollo when the prison gates slammed shut behind him. He instructed the driver to take him to Ivan Molanov's house. There had been a time when the White Russian refugee – with no family in London – would have worked late into the night at the *Globe* office, sometimes spending the night on a sofa in the archive. But now his daughter lived with him, Ivan worked more civilized hours. But this could not wait until the morning.

The door was answered by a relaxed-looking Ivan in a smoking jacket. Inside the house Rollo could hear the sound of a gramophone playing.

"Sorry to bother you at home, old man, but I need you to get back to the office."

Ivan scowled down at Rollo. "Can't it wait until the morning?"

"No. Sorry. I'm afraid Poppy's life might be in danger." He went on to tell Ivan what Ike Garfield had told him on the telephone about the attacks on Sophie Blackburn and Gertrude Fuller. "Ike's with her and so's the editor of *The Oxford Gazette* – so I think she'll be safe for now – but I'd prefer this investigation to be wrapped up as quickly as possible."

"Shouldn't you tell her fiancé?"

Rollo felt a shudder of guilt. Yes, he probably should. But knowing Daniel, he'd rush up there and try to drag her away. Poppy wouldn't thank him. If Poppy wanted to tell Daniel herself, she could have telephoned him. She hadn't. So best he – Rollo – stay out of it. This was something the two young people would need to work out when they were married, or Poppy's days as an investigative reporter and amateur sleuth would be over. For now, Rollo felt he'd applied his duty of care towards her by sending Ike to Oxford.

"Not yet," said Rollo and left it at that. "So, I need you to search for anything you can find on a Detective Inspector Birch of the Oxford City Police. See if there is any link to Richard Easling or Lionel Saunders, the Sanforth Foundation, Sanforth Industries, or any dodgy dealings or rumours of cover-ups. And then see if you can find any dirt on some scientists. Here, I've written their names down for you." He handed the list to Ivan. "I'll come by the office later tonight. I've got somewhere else to go first. Oh, by the way, do you have a revolver to lend me?"

Ivan looked at him quizzically. "You've got your own, Yankee."

"I do. But it's at the house. And I don't want to worry Yasmin by going back to get it."

"Should she be worried?"

Rollo shrugged his shoulders. "Possibly. Whoever knocked me out last night is still out there. So better safe than sorry, eh?"

Ivan grunted, then went to get the gun. And while he was at it, he pocketed a second one for himself.

THURSDAY 23 APRIL 1925, OXFORD

Poppy and Ike huddled in a corner of the hotel lounge, drinking hot cocoa and poring over the file Rosie Winter had given them.

Poppy would have preferred to do it in the privacy and comfort of her room, but it would be a scandal too far to invite Ike to join her. The file, as far as they could tell, confirmed much of what Dr Mortimer had already told them about how the body was found and the cause of death. However, there were two pieces of information that the pathologist had failed to tell them. The first was that there were welts and bruising around June Leighton's wrists that could not be directly attributed to the electrocution. Yes, her right hand was seared and blackened by the live electrical cable, but the bruising on the wrists was unrelated. What it might be related to the doctor had not attempted – or perhaps bothered – to speculate. But to Poppy and Ike the cause seemed fairly clear.

"Her wrists had been bound," said Poppy.

"That seems the likely explanation," said Ike. "But we can't know for sure without seeing the body and getting an independent expert to examine it."

"Might this warrant an exhumation?" asked Poppy.

"I think there might be just cause to suggest it, yes. But that's not our call."

"No, it's not. I think it would be best if I went back to London tomorrow and showed this to Mrs Leighton. She can't have seen it, surely, or she would not have accepted so readily that her daughter's death was accidental."

Ike frowned. "I agree. The family deserve to know. But that's not all they'll find out from the report, is it?"

"No," agreed Poppy, sadly. "They'll also find out that their daughter was pregnant when she died." She closed her notebook and made to get up.

"What are you doing?"

"I'm going to see Edward Sanforth to find out if he knew about the pregnancy."

"It's nearly ten o'clock!"

"Then he should be in. Are you coming?"

Ike nodded and the two journalists went to collect their hats and coats.

The address Edward Sanforth had given Poppy during their picnic on Christ Church Meadow was near Merton College, a mere five-minute walk away from the Cherwell Hotel. It was a well-appointed four-storey residence that looked like it dated back to the Regency period. A butler answered the door with an air of disapproval.

Poppy apologized for calling so late and asked to see Mr Sanforth. Mr Sanforth had already had his bath, the butler told them, and asked them to call again in the morning.

"I'm sorry," pressed Poppy, "but we absolutely must see him. Please tell him Miss Poppy Denby is here, and I have some information on the death of June Leighton. It's desperately urgent that we speak with him."

The butler looked unimpressed but agreed to see if his master would entertain them. He did not invite them in and shut the door, leaving them on the step.

"Well, you can't blame the fellow," said Ike. "It is late."

"Yes, it is," agreed Poppy, stifling a yawn.

It took around five minutes – far too long for a butler to find his employer in a house this size, but perhaps just long enough for a disrobed gentleman to make himself presentable – before the butler returned. He ushered Poppy and Ike in, saying Mr Sanforth would receive them in the library. Poppy was quite surprised. Firstly, because she hadn't put Edward Sanforth down as the type of man who had a butler, and secondly that he hadn't come to the door to meet her personally. They had, after all, been punting together and shared a picnic earlier in the day. Perhaps it was Ike's presence that elicited the formal response. Poppy had no idea.

However, as they entered the house, she noted a set of suitcases lined up against the wall.

"Is Mr Sanforth going somewhere?"

"He is leaving for New York in the morning. Hence why it is doubly inconvenient of you to visit, miss. We have an early start planned."

As Poppy and Ike followed the butler, she whispered to her colleague, "Edward told me he'd be happy to accompany me to London to go through June's things. Why would he say that if he were going to New York?"

Ike nodded and raised his finger to his lips.

They were led down the hall towards the library. The butler pushed open the door and announced them. Again, the formality didn't ring true with the man Poppy had met earlier that day. But as she and Ike stepped into the book-lined room, she suddenly realized why. Seated in an armchair next to an unlit fire was the tall and erect figure of Mrs Mary Sanforth, while her son, Edward, stood behind her.

Edward stepped forward. "Good evening, Miss Denby." The relaxed use of Christian names as they floated down the river together was gone. "And this is Mr...? I'm sorry, my butler didn't catch your name, sir."

"Garfield," said Ike, stepping forward and putting out his hand. "Ike Garfield. I am a colleague of Miss Denby's from London."

"Mr Garfield is the senior journalist on *The Daily Globe*," added Poppy, feeling the need to bolster Ike's credentials. "He drove up from London this afternoon. He was waiting for me when I got back to the hotel, after..." She paused for a moment, wondering whether or not Edward had heard about the attack on Sophie Blackburn. "... after we had our meeting," she said instead. Edward and Ike shook hands. As they did, Poppy addressed

Edward's mother, who remained seated. "Mrs Sanforth, I assume. We didn't have a chance to speak last night at the Balliol dinner. I'm Poppy Denby. Miss Poppy Denby." She reached out her hand. The older woman looked at it for a moment, as if she had been proffered a wet kipper. But she eventually took it and limply shook hands.

"Sorry," said Edward, retreating behind his mother's chair, like a dog returning to heel, "this is my mother, Mrs Mary Sanforth. Mother, may I introduce Miss Denby and Mr Garfield."

Ike bowed slightly but didn't attempt to shake hands.

"You said you had some news about June Leighton," said Mrs Sanforth with a faint American accent. Edward had said she was British but spent a lot of time in the USA. She reminded Poppy of Rollo's mother, a patrician blue blood from Long Island.

Poppy was frantically trying to recalibrate her approach. She had intended to find out from Edward if he knew about June's pregnancy – and after his emotional candour during their picnic she felt it appropriate to ask him – however, she didn't want to drop him in the custard with his mother. What if he had known, and his mother hadn't? Or what if neither of them had known? Oh bother; Mrs Sanforth was a complication Poppy had not expected. Perhaps now wasn't the time... However, he was going to be leaving in the morning.

"Yes," she said eventually. "We – as in Mr Garfield and I – have come across a copy of June's pathologist's report and we felt it best that we show it to her family. I came this evening to ask if Edward – Mr Sanforth – would accompany me to London tomorrow. You said at lunchtime, Edward, you would be willing to come with me. I was just wondering if you still would? But I hear you are leaving for New York in the morning..."

"Er, yes, my mother has to make an urgent trip and has asked me to accompany her. I'm sorry, Miss Denby, I didn't know about this when I made my offer this afternoon. But perhaps Mr Garfield here could accompany you instead?"

"Can I see the pathologist's report?" Mrs Sanforth cut in.

"I'm afraid that won't be possible, ma'am," said Ike. "We were shown it in confidence on the promise that we would not divulge its contents to anyone but Miss Leighton's parents."

Oh, good save! thought Poppy.

Mrs Sanforth pursed her lips, her mouth like a drawstring bag. "And who showed you this report?"

"I'm afraid that's confidential, too, ma'am. However," he added, "it's fortuitous that you're here, isn't it, Miss Denby? Didn't you have some questions for Mrs Sanforth and her son about connections between Sanforth Industries and June Leighton's father?"

Poppy gave Ike a grateful nod. "That's right. Mr Garfield here brought up a file from our newspaper's archive in London. And in it there was an article from *The Times* about Sanforth Industries acquiring a diamond mine in German South West Africa and that Roger Leighton – June's father – was the man who brokered the deal for you. The thing is, I wasn't aware your families were connected in any way, other than through June and Edward."

"Why should you have been aware, and why does it matter whether we're connected or not?" asked Mrs Sanforth.

"Well," said Poppy, "only that your son gave me the impression that there was no connection whatsoever."

"Edward?" snapped Mrs Sanforth, her voice a whip crack. "What have you been telling this journalist about our business?"

"Nothing, Mother, nothing at all. I did not mention our business, only that June and I had been sweethearts. Miss Denby is writing an article on June – with her mother's permission – and I was helping her get a fuller picture of her. Of what a remarkable young woman she was. But I didn't mention anything about the business, as it has nothing to do with the article Miss Denby is writing. I'm not really sure, Miss Denby, what you're getting at here..."

"What I'm getting at, Mr Sanforth, is that there appears to be a lot that you have not told me. And I have also been wondering why June's mother denied that she had a fiancé. When I mentioned it to her a few days ago – that I'd heard from one of June's work colleagues that she was engaged – Mrs Leighton said there was no such relationship."

"Perhaps," said Mrs Sanforth, "she, like I, was disappointed that our children had not informed us of their engagement before the unfortunate young woman died. It came as quite a shock to me. And a sadness, that I had not had the chance to get to know my future daughter-in-law. And also, perhaps, Mrs Leighton did not think it was anyone else's business. Why on earth do you think she would want that information released in the gutter press?"

Poppy bristled at the slur but remained calm. "If she was so averse to having information about her daughter in our newspaper, why did she agree to me writing an article on her?"

Mrs Sanforth smiled coldly. "We only have your word for that, Miss Denby. For all we know you have lied to us about Mrs Leighton giving you her blessing, and you are exploiting this young woman's unfortunate death to get your name in lights. So now, if there's nothing else, I will ask you to leave. My son and I have an early start in the morning. Goodnight to you both." She reached out and pulled a bell cord. A moment later, the butler opened the door.

Poppy looked to Edward, hoping for a rekindling of the connection they'd experienced during the picnic, but he avoided meeting her eyes. *Fiddlesticks! Sorry Edward, I don't have a choice...* "Before we go, Mrs Sanforth, there is one more thing I would like to ask."

"We have nothing else to discuss, Miss Denby. Goodnight."

"Come on, Poppy, let's go," said Ike.

"In a minute, Ike," she said, more sharply than she'd intended. She shot an apologetic look at her colleague. He nodded, indicating his understanding.

"Did you know that June was pregnant when she died?"

"My God!" Edward visibly paled.

"Get out of here," hissed Mrs Sanforth.

"Did you know, Edward?" pressed Poppy.

"I – I –"

"Get out of this house now, before I call the police." Mrs Sanforth stood up, raising her arm as if ready to slap Poppy. Ike put his hand on his colleague's shoulder and pulled her back.

"Time to go, Poppy," he said. "Now."

Poppy nodded and turned on her heel. As she and Ike exited the library, she heard Edward call after her. "Poppy! Is it true? Was June pregnant?"

"Yes," she said, over her shoulder.

"GET OUT!" screamed Mrs Sanforth.

"They're going, Mother," said Edward, "and I'm walking them out."

"You come back here immediately, boy!"

"No, Mother. I will not. And I am not a boy."

CHAPTER 30

THURSDAY 23 APRIL 1925, LONDON

Rollo got out of the taxi at Berkeley Square, after switching Ivan's gun from his overcoat pocket to his inside jacket pocket. He did not want the weapon to be discovered if he gave his coat to a servant at the Leighton residence – nor did he want to be without it. He very much doubted he would be in danger at the genteel townhouse, but one never knew. The lump on his head from the attack the night before was still tender, and he thought too of the two women who had been brutally attacked in Oxford. He opened the black wrought-iron gate, flanked on either side by perfectly manicured topiary shrubs, and rang the doorbell.

It was now nine o'clock and a tad late to be calling, but he had telephoned ahead earlier in the evening to make an appointment. Roger Leighton had suggested that he come around instead to the shop in the morning, but Rollo had said that it was to do with June's papers that had been sent to the family and he would like, too, to speak to Mrs Leighton. Mr Leighton still sounded reluctant. Rollo then offered to visit Mrs Leighton separately, the next day... *No*, said Mr Leighton. So, the nine o'clock appointment was confirmed.

A few moments later, the door was opened by a maid in a white mop cap and apron. She greeted him by name; she'd obviously been briefed. He followed her in and gave her his overcoat, bowler hat, and umbrella. He then followed her into a gloriously furnished drawing room. He had never seen so many pieces of Georgian furniture or Romantic paintings outside of a stately home. Yasmin was, of course, an art collector, but her taste was far more avant-garde and minimalist. In the midst of all the antique clutter, seated side by side on an ornate Chippendale sofa, were Mr and Mrs Roger Leighton. Mr Leighton rose to his feet to greet Rollo. Mrs Leighton remained seated, her hands politely folded in her lap. They were both in mourning black.

"Ah, Mr Rolandson. Right on time. Can I get you a brandy?"

"Thank you, that would be dandy. Good evening, Mrs Leighton. I'm very sorry to bother you at this late hour. I do appreciate you humouring me."

"My husband said it was about June's papers. That Miss Denby had asked to see them."

Rollo accepted the brandy snifter from Mr Leighton and took a seat in the chair the jeweller indicated. He didn't know if it had been placed there just for his convenience, but he was pleased to see an antique footstool positioned in front of the chair, so he didn't have to clamber up in an ungainly fashion, trying not to spill his brandy.

"That's correct. In the process of gathering information for her article, she has travelled to Oxford to interview some of June's former colleagues. She was hoping to find out more about what June was working on before she died, but none of them have been able to tell her. They say that it would all be in her notes, but they haven't seen them. The principal of Somerville College – Dr Fuller – said that everything in June's room had been forwarded to you. Is that correct?"

"It is," said Mrs Leighton. "I've got them all here." She started to rise, but her husband put his hand on her forearm and gently pressed her back into her seat.

"Not yet, my dear. I have a few questions for Mr Rolandson first." The jeweller looked serious, as if he were about to launch into a man-to-man talk. Rollo prepared himself; it wasn't unexpected.

"Of course, sir. Fire away."

"I have had news from Oxford that has caused me some concern."

"Oh?"

"Yes. The first I heard about this article your reporter is writing was when I received a telephone call from Professor Sinclair, the head of the laboratory June worked at. My wife" – he cast a sharp look in her direction, at which she lowered her eyes – "failed to tell me about Miss Denby's visit on Monday or about the article. If I had known about it, I would not have given permission. I do not want my daughter's name besmirched in the press."

"It would not be besmirched, Roger," said Mrs Leighton quietly. "I have read Miss Denby's column in the *Globe* for over a year now, and I have been most impressed by the quality of her writing and the respect with which she treats her female subjects."

Rollo nodded his appreciation. "Thank you, Mrs Leighton. Yes, Miz Denby is one of my best reporters and I have absolute faith in her. She will do June justice."

Mr Leighton cleared his throat. "Be that as it may, Professor Sinclair is concerned that Miss Denby is overstepping the mark in the type of questions she has been asking."

"Oh?" said Rollo, feigning ignorance. "And what questions would those be?"

"Questions about the circumstances surrounding June's death. He said her interest appears macabre and unseemly."

"I can assure you, Mr Leighton, that there is nothing macabre or unseemly about Miz Denby. She is a perfectly proper lady. And as your wife has already said, her column is very respectful."

"Publishing the unpleasant details of June's death would not be respectful."

"I agree. And I know she would not do that."

"Then why is she asking?" This was from Mrs Leighton. "I too understood she was only writing about June's life. She didn't say anything about June's death when she came to visit me, except to offer her condolences."

Rollo thought quickly. Poppy's investigation so far had revealed that there were certainly suspicious circumstances around June's death, and the article she would write would no doubt reflect that. So perhaps now was the time to fess up. It would come out eventually. And, if his suspicions were correct, it would end up exposing a murderer. That would come as a huge shock to the Leightons. So better he control the release of information. He let out a long sigh. "I'm sorry, Mrs Leighton. I can assure you that when Miz Denby came to visit you her intention certainly was to write a story on June's life. She did not deceive you. However, in her research so far, I'm afraid she has discovered some troubling information that suggests that her employers at the laboratory have tried to cover up the circumstances around your daughter's death."

Mrs Leighton's hand went to her throat and clutched a cameo brooch. "What circumstances? There was nothing to cover up! It was an accident!"

"How do you know it was an accident?"

"That's what the police told us. What was his name, Roger, the policeman who came to see us?"

"Birch," said her husband. "Inspector Birch. And we also spoke to the pathologist who examined June's body. A Dr Mortimer. He told us there was nothing suspicious and that June had very clearly been electrocuted by the machine she was working with. It was an accident."

"Death by misadventure?" asked Rollo.

"Exactly that."

"Did you see the pathologist's report?"

"No. We didn't see the need to. It would just have made for unpleasant reading. We were upset enough as it was, as you can imagine."

"Of course. So, you took Birch and Mortimer's word for it?"

"Why wouldn't we?"

"Quite," said Rollo, "why wouldn't you?" His voice was filled with sympathy – and it wasn't an act. "So, you saw no need to question why there wasn't a coroner's inquest or to request one yourself?"

Mr Leighton cleared his throat again. "No. What are you saying, Rolandson? That our daughter was killed by someone?"

Rollo put down his brandy snifter, untouched, and leaned forward. "We can't say that for certain, sir, but Miz Denby and I – because I have been helping her in this investigation – believe that might very well be so."

Mrs Leighton let out a gasp. "Who? Who could have done it?"

"We don't know yet, Mrs Leighton, but we need your help to find out. You said you had June's papers. Miz Denby believes there may be an answer in there." He decided, for the moment, not to disturb the lady any further by telling her that two women had been attacked by someone who appeared to be searching for June's papers.

Mr Leighton was shaking his head. "Come, come, Rolandson. You will need to do better than that. Why does Miss Denby think there is foul play afoot?"

"I'm afraid I don't have the full story myself. But I shall ask Miz Denby to come and see you as soon as possible. I believe she may be coming down to London tomorrow."

"She damned well better! I would like to speak to this young woman."

"I shall bring her here myself," said Rollo placatingly. "Now, Mrs Leighton... those papers?" The bereaved mother looked shocked but rallied herself enough to get up and walk to the far side of the room. As she went, Rollo turned to her husband and said, "I know this is very upsetting for you, sir, and I can assure you that Miz Denby would not be following this line of questioning without very good reason. And I would not allow her to. Which brings me to the second reason I'm here tonight – and why I am so late in arriving. I have just been to see Lord Melvyn Dorchester in Pentonville Prison."

Roger Leighton snapped his head towards his wife, then back to Rollo. *Aha*, thought Rollo, *something he knows that he doesn't want her to know?* He must tread carefully.

"Yes. In our investigation so far, we have discovered that you and Sanforth Industries – of which Lord Dorchester was a former board member, and is still a shareholder – have some business connections."

Leighton sat up straight and cleared his throat again. *His nervous twitch*, thought Rollo.

"No secret about that."

"Quite. You helped them buy a diamond mine in South West Africa, I believe."

"That's correct."

"May I ask if June's appointment to the position at the laboratory had anything to do with that?"

"Why ever do you ask that, Mr Rolandson?" asked Mrs Leighton as she joined her husband on the Chippendale clutching a leather briefcase.

"I'm not entirely sure, Mrs Leighton, but we – Miz Denby and I – are wondering why this was never mentioned at the outset of our investigation. Not by you, or by Professor Sinclair at the laboratory."

"Why should it have been?" asked Mrs Leighton. "Miss Denby was only asking to do an article on June's life and career. Besides, if you are inferring that June got that position due to anything more than her brilliant mind and peerless academic credentials, you are sorely mistaken!"

"I am suggesting nothing of the sort, Mrs Leighton. However, our investigation has unearthed that June might have been working on something connected to this diamond mine – and weapons manufacture – which, as I'm sure you know, would have gone against her pacifist beliefs."

"Since when was June a pacifist?" asked Mr Leighton.

His wife looked at him and said, "Since she became involved with that Sanforth boy."

Rollo's ears pricked up. "You knew about June's relationship with Edward Sanforth? Poppy – Miz Denby – told me that you didn't know about their engagement."

"They were not engaged!" snapped Mr Leighton. "Not properly. Edward Sanforth had not had the courtesy to ask my permission for her hand in marriage. And, sordidly, we only found out after our dear girl died. And we only have his word that she consented. For all we know he was a fantasist; June never even mentioned him to us."

"Is that right, Mrs Leighton?" Mrs Leighton once again lowered her eyes.

"Partly, yes. And partly no."

"Oh?" said Rollo. "Can you expand on that?"

The mother lowered her chin to her chest and took a great, shuddering breath. "June never mentioned Edward Sanforth. But our son, Larry, did."

"Yes, I met your son the other day. He sold me a lovely necklace for my wife. What did your son say about Sanforth?"

Mr and Mrs Leighton looked at one another. Mrs Leighton nodded, and then Mr Leighton replied, "He said June had told him that Sanforth had been pursuing her. That she hadn't been in the least interested in him. And that – that –"

Roger Leighton couldn't finish his sentence. But his wife raised her head and said, "And that he forced himself on her. Against her will. Sadly, before we could speak to June, she died. Which, until now, we thought was a tragic accident."

"Yes," said Rollo, absorbing the news, as a few more pieces of the puzzle fell into place. "It was tragic. But I do not believe it was an accident."

CHAPTER 31

THURSDAY 23 APRIL 1925, OXFORD

Poppy and Ike stood on the doorstep facing Edward Sanforth.

"I apologize for my mother. She is a strong-willed woman and – not without some justification I'm afraid – holds the press in disdain. So best you leave; she won't settle until you're gone. But please, before you go, can you tell me where you got the information about June being with child?"

"It was in the pathologist's report. We saw a copy of it this evening," said Poppy. "Look, Edward, there's quite a lot we'd like to talk to you about. We don't want to upset your mother any more, but can you walk with us back to the hotel and we can talk on the way?"

Edward nodded, then looked over his shoulder and said, "Barnsley, tell Mrs Sanforth I'm walking Miss Denby and Mr Garfield back to their hotel. I shan't be long. And get me my hat and coat."

A few moments later, Edward, Poppy, and Ike were walking down the road, and none of them saw the flat-capped man step out of the shadows and knock on the door of the Sanforth townhouse.

"But why didn't you tell me June's father was in business with Sanforth Industries?"

"It never occurred to me to do so. We were talking about June's experience at the laboratory and what she was working on. I'm not even clear what June's father's role was. I don't have much to do with Sanforth Industries, just the Foundation. That's the charitable wing," he added, for Ike's benefit.

"I'm aware of what the Foundation does, Mr Sanforth."

"Please, call me Edward."

"All right, Edward," agreed Ike. "We suspect there is some kind of connection. June was X-raying a diamond when she died. And now we know that June's father helped broker the purchase of a diamond mine in Africa. What do you know about that?"

"Very little. And I don't think June did either. She and her father weren't very close. If she did know, she didn't mention it to me. And as for the diamond she was X-raying, as I told Poppy earlier, we might not know what that was about until we see her notes."

"My boss in London is going to see June's parents this evening," said Poppy. "He's going to ask them for the notes."

"And he's going to see someone else to try to find out more about the diamond mine and what – if anything – it has to do with work on explosives that the lab is involved in. Any idea?" probed Ike.

"I told you, no."

Poppy was walking between the two men. Both of them were tall – over six feet – and she, at five feet five, felt a bit squashed between them. She was also aware of a growing tension. Ike, normally a very phlegmatic character, was becoming increasingly combative towards Edward. She was worried that Edward might take offence and leave – before she had an opportunity to ask the questions she wanted to ask.

"That's all right, Edward, I'm sure you don't know everything about your family's business. I was just surprised when I found out that there was a connection between yours and June's family – apart from your relationship. Which, golly, I'm so sorry about June and the baby. And I'm dreadfully sorry that we had to break the news to you in front of your mother – we didn't know she was going to be there. But, with you going to New York tomorrow, I felt I had to mention it. May I be so bold as to ask if you knew?"

"I didn't, know. I – I –" his voice cracked. "June had told me she needed to speak to me. About something important. But I was away that weekend. The weekend she died."

"You were out of town?" asked Ike. "Poppy never mentioned that to me."

Because I never thought to ask, thought Poppy, chastising herself.

"Yes, I went down to London on the Friday for the weekend. So, I couldn't have killed her, if that's what you're asking." Edward stopped walking and turned to face Ike over Poppy's head.

"Can we confirm where you were?"

"You're not the bloody police!"

"No, but the bloody police should have done their job and asked you!"

"Gentlemen, please!" Poppy raised her hands to keep the two men apart. "I think the question now is, did June's killer know she was pregnant, and did that have any influence on her death?"

Edward took a step back. "June's killer? Earlier today you said you had no proof that anyone had killed her, just that you suspected. But it could still turn out to have been an accident. Are you saying you now have proof that she was murdered? My God! What evidence do you have?"

Ike put his hands on Poppy's shoulders and moved her aside so that she was no longer between him and Edward.

"There have been some developments since Poppy spoke to you at lunchtime, the first being that a second woman was attacked. This time, far more brutally."

"My God! Who?"

"Sophie Blackburn."

"The lab assistant?"

"Yes," said Ike. "And Poppy found her. She had been – well – she had been violated. She was unconscious, and still is as far as we know. So, she cannot tell us who attacked her. But three things tie it in to June's death. The first is that both Gertrude Fuller and Sophie Blackburn knew June, and both of them had been helping Poppy with her investigation. Secondly, the attacker had been searching through Sophie's papers – just like he did with Gertrude Fuller – which suggests that he might have been looking for some papers, possibly of June's. The third thing – and you'll forgive me raising such an indelicate subject in the presence of a lady – is the sexual nature of the assault. Tell me, Sanforth, were you the father of June's child?"

Edward, standing under a streetlight, looked stunned. "I – I – well, yes. I suppose that I am. June and I had been intimate on, well, on two occasions. We did not intend it to happen before we were married, but, well, you know how these things go sometimes..."

"Yes, Sanforth, I know how these things go." Ike's voice was cut through with disdain.

But there was something else bothering Poppy. "I'm sorry to interrupt, but something you said earlier today is troubling me, Edward. You told me Bill Raines had been inappropriate with June. That you had to warn him off. And after having the misfortune of sharing a dance with the man last night, I can believe that he might very well have been forceful with her. Is that what happened? Did Bill Raines force himself onto June, and if so, might the baby have been his?"

To Poppy's absolute dismay, Edward Sanforth began to cry.

It was nearly midnight before Poppy opened her hotel room door, took off her hat and coat, and flopped down onto her bed. She was exhausted. There were two notes slipped under her door. The first was a message from Rollo. *"Mr Rolandson says to expect him tomorrow. He's coming up from London and has the papers you requested. He says not to go anywhere without Mr Garfield."*

Oh goody, thought Poppy. *That might shed some light on this muddle.* But then she remembered she was planning to go down to London herself tomorrow, to see June's parents. She'd better wait until Rollo arrived. How was he getting here? Train? The note didn't say. Nor what time to expect him. She'd ring Mavis in the morning to see if she could give her some more information. And as for his admonition to not go anywhere without Ike... *It's not like Rollo to be a worrywart.*

The second note was a telegram envelope addressed to her. She opened it and her heart leaped when she saw it was from Daniel.

DEAREST POPPY. HOPE ALL WELL. MISS YOU. COME
HOME SOON. RING ME. MUST HEAR YOUR VOICE.

Poppy sniffed the paper, hoping to catch something of Daniel's scent, even though she knew he would never have touched it. She kissed it and read it again before folding it back into its envelope and holding it to her heart as she lay back onto the bed. "I miss you too, my love," she whispered. If it hadn't been after midnight, she would have run downstairs and asked to use the hotel telephone. But that, like her call to the office, would have to wait.

Would she be able to "come home soon"? How much longer would she be away from him? She had arrived on Tuesday. It was now the early hours of Friday morning, and almost a week since that love-soaked day last Saturday when he had proposed to her in the Botanic Garden. She twirled the ring on her finger and allowed her thoughts to meander to Daniel's kisses. Her body ached for him. She knew exactly what June and Edward had been through and how easy it would be to succumb to intimacy before the wedding.

Her heart sank when she thought of Edward. He had apologized for his tears, wiping them away with the back of his hand. Rather than being angry with her for suggesting that Bill Raines might have been the father of June's child, he had admitted that it might be a possibility. He confessed that he had lied when he said he hadn't known she was pregnant. She had told him a few days before she died. He said that, to his shame, instead of supporting her, he had asked the very same question: was Bill Raines the father? June had been appalled at the suggestion. She said that although Raines had been very overt in his overtures, she had resisted and there had been no sexual intercourse.

"But," said Edward, "I was madly, and irrationally, consumed with jealousy. Raines had boasted to me that he and June had had a 'roll in the sack', as he put it. And that she had been a game girl about it."

"He said she consented?" asked Ike.

"Yes. So I decked him."

"Did you believe him?" asked Poppy.

"Not at first," said Edward. "But then I began to doubt. And after June and I – well, after we were intimate – I began to wonder if it had really been her first time. I – and I don't want to be too indelicate about this, Miss Denby – but I didn't encounter what I expected, if you know what I mean."

Poppy, who had been reading Marie Stopes' *Married Love*, blushed. Edward was suggesting that June's hymen had already been broken. That she wasn't a virgin.

"I understand what you mean," said Poppy quietly. "Tell us what happened then."

"Then," Edward continued, his voice thick with emotion, "then she told me she was pregnant, and I – well – I asked her if it was mine or his. She was appalled that I had even asked the question. We had an argument. I went away to London for a few days to calm down."

"When was this?" asked Ike.

"The Friday before she died. I told the truth earlier when I said I wasn't here. Perhaps... perhaps if I had been she wouldn't have died."

Poppy got up from the bed and started to undress. As she did, she thought through the convoluted path of the investigation. After Edward returned home, she and Ike had discussed the new information and agreed that they could not be sure that he had been telling them the entire truth. He had lied before. How could they be certain that he had in fact gone down to London and wasn't in Oxford the day June died? They would need corroborating evidence of his alibi. Or the police would, if they were to reopen the investigation. Poppy toyed with the idea of going to see Chief Constable Fenchurch in the morning to tell him what she'd discovered. However, what would she say about how she knew about the pregnancy? Dr Mortimer hadn't told her. She had seen it in a stolen pathologist's report. Stolen by Rosie Winter. And she'd promised Rosie she would never tell where she got it. But Fenchurch would suspect. And no doubt demand she return the report. No, she couldn't bring Fenchurch into this, not yet. She needed to get the report to June's parents so that they could demand the investigation be reopened. Yes, that was still the way to proceed. She would wait for Rollo tomorrow, see what June's papers had to reveal, then return with him to London.

She pulled her nightdress over her head, then sat down at the dressing table to brush her hair. The hairbrush had a beautiful mother of pearl inlay and had been a gift from her mother. She wondered what her mother would have done if June Leighton had come to her for help. Poppy's mother had helped a number of young women who had become pregnant out of wedlock. But they had all been poor women from working-class families. June was the daughter of a wealthy jeweller, and engaged – if Edward were to be believed – to the heir of one of the world's great fortunes. If Edward were to be believed...

Poppy's instinct was that he was telling the truth. But how could she be sure? He hadn't been fully truthful with her and had admitted that he had outright lied. Had he really been engaged to June? They only had his word for it. June hadn't been wearing an engagement ring when she died, and they seemed to have kept it a secret from both sets of parents. Why? This had not been adequately explained. On the other hand, Sophie Blackburn had known about the engagement. She had said June had told her about it. But hadn't Sophie said that the fiancé was from London? Well, Edward *had* said he had a flat there... Poppy wondered for a moment how Sophie was doing. She must drop by the hospital before going back up to London. Rollo would no doubt want to see Sophie, too. He had a soft spot for her and still blamed himself for Bert's death. Poppy put down the hairbrush and said a prayer for both Sophie and Rollo. She asked too for God to guide her in the investigation, to find the truth about who killed June Leighton and attacked Sophie and Gertrude – and to stop him before he hurt anyone else.

After brushing her teeth and using the chamber pot, she climbed into bed. But sleep would not come. She now realized there were two main strands to the investigation which may or may not be related. Up until now she had considered that June's death had something to do with her work. Her suspicion had been that June had discovered something in her experiments that one or more of the other scientists wanted to keep quiet. Or, that one or more of the other scientists were working on something illegal or unethical related to the research into explosives, and June had found out about it. Poppy believed she had been killed to keep her quiet. She also suspected it had something to do with Sanforth Industries and their ties to weapons manufacture. But exactly what and why was still unclear.

However, there was now another possibility. What if it had nothing to do with her work and was simply the tragic result of a lovers' triangle? What if Bill Raines had killed her out of jealousy? Or to keep her from revealing that he had raped her? If in fact he had. Because there was still the outlying chance that she had in fact consented. And what if the baby was his? What if she was going to reveal that? Or perhaps the baby *was* the product of rape and June was too ashamed to admit it and was pretending – or just hoping – that it was Edward's.

But there was another possibility – one that Poppy desperately hoped would not turn out to be true: what if Edward Sanforth had not left town on the Friday before June died? Or if he had, what if he had returned on the Sunday night and confronted June in the laboratory? He had said they'd rowed on the Friday. What if they'd rowed again on the Sunday? And in a jealous rage he had killed her and the unborn child?

Perhaps Edward's sudden trip to New York was not being forced on him by his mother. Perhaps he realized that Poppy, Rollo, and Ike were getting close to the truth and he needed to get away. And perhaps his agreement to accompany them back to the hotel was not out of politeness but to find out how much they knew? How close they were to finding out the truth? And perhaps the lunchtime boat ride down the Cherwell had served the same purpose...

Poppy shivered and jumped out of bed, stumbling to the door to make sure it was locked. It was. But just in case, she pulled across a chair and lodged it under the door handle. If her thoughts about Edward were true, did that mean he had also attacked Gertrude and Sophie? He had been at the Balliol dinner. He could easily have followed Gertrude back to Somerville, knocked her out, and then gone to search her rooms. And then gone around the corner to Sophie's flat. He had said he thought June's papers had been sent to her parents. But those were her scientific papers. What if he was looking for something else? Something more personal. What if June had kept a diary, and in it she might have written about her pregnancy and who the father was. Either him or Bill Raines.

But why, then, would he have searched Sophie's flat? Why would Sophie have a private diary of June's? Yes, as a work colleague, she might have had some work notes, and that had initially been Poppy's thought on the matter, but surely she wouldn't have anything more personal? The women weren't friends...

Poppy climbed back into bed and pulled the covers up to her chin. No, it didn't add up. There were too many variables. What, for instance, did the absent Inspector Birch and Dr Mortimer have to do with it? Because, of one thing she was clear: they had helped cover something up and quash the investigation. Had they been paid to? Edward Sanforth certainly had enough money to do so. Or perhaps it was his controlling mother... she would not want the shame of the pregnancy coming out.

And what about Bill Raines and his sidekick, the acerbic Miles Mackintosh? Rosie had already discovered that they had lied about which gate they had used to leave the Balliol dinner.

Why would they do that? And why was Professor Sinclair so keen to shut the investigation down too? What was he trying to hide or cover up? Did it have something to do with the diamond in the X-ray machine? And who was the young man in the flat cap who had been following her?

Poppy looked at the travel clock on her side table. It was now ten past one... It was going to be a long night.

CHAPTER 32

THURSDAY 23 APRIL 1925, LONDON

Rollo Rolandson got out of the taxi on Fleet Street, outside *The Daily Globe*. But instead of climbing the steps and opening the front door with his key, he walked up the road and down a side alley, to get to the newspaper's back entrance. It was the day before rubbish collection day, and the overflowing bins were attracting rats. Rollo wasn't squeamish, which was just as well as one of the critters – as he called them – ran over his shoe. The back door of the *Globe* was ajar a couple of inches. He swore loudly. How many times had he told the printers to keep the door locked after six o'clock and only to open it at four in the morning when the delivery vans arrived for the early papers? But the fellas said it got too hot in there with the printers going. Which was fair enough, but then why the hell had he spent a king's ransom getting ceiling fans installed?

This, he realized, would have been how his attacker had got in last night. He pushed the door open and stepped into the basement. As expected, no one even noticed him. Any noise he made was drowned by the rumble of the machines, and all four of the men on shift were absorbed either tending to printers or binding piles of papers for collection. He thought of collaring Davey, the master printer, but decided to leave it for tonight.

He already had a blazing headache, and a screaming match with his employee would just get his blood pressure up. He needed to remain calm, as he had work to do – and Davey had to get tomorrow's edition out.

Rollo pushed the door shut behind him and bolted it, then slipped, unseen, past the printers and through the door into the main stairwell of the building. This, he thought, as he climbed the steps to the ground floor, would have been how Lionel Saunders got in when he attacked Poppy five years earlier. Rollo shuddered when he remembered it. Poppy was not just an employee; she was like a daughter to him. Poppy had come to the office alone that night – and had greeted Davey and the fellas on the way up. She had been trying to puzzle out her first murder case and needed access to a file. The file, she knew, was on Rollo's desk. Rollo, however, like half the staff at the *Globe*, was off sick with influenza. They had all feared a resurgence of the Spanish Flu of the year before, but fortunately it turned out to be just the common or garden variety. Nonetheless, he remembered, he had felt like death.

So Poppy, all alone, had gone into his office and found the file on his desk. She had read what she needed and was just about to leave when Lionel Saunders, who had recently been fired from his job at the *Globe*, cornered her and demanded the file. She refused. He then grabbed her, but she managed to fight him off by pulling down a tower of precariously stacked newspapers. In the melee she escaped. Saunders, of course, denied that he had intended to hurt Poppy, just to get the file from her. But both Rollo and Poppy believed that Saunders had been the one to push Bert Isaacs from the third-floor landing, and so rightly feared for her life.

That was when Rollo had insisted on the basement door being kept locked at night. But it rarely was. It was time to employ a nightwatchman and dog. He should have done it years ago. And now that another intruder had slipped in and accosted him last night – possibly the very same intruder, using the same modus operandi – he would get onto it first thing in the morning. Well, perhaps not first thing. First thing he would be travelling up to Oxford.

At the ground floor he got into the lift, noting as he passed the third floor on the way up that the light was on in the "morgue" – the nickname for the newspaper's archive. *Good*, he thought, *Ivan's in.*

At the fourth floor, which housed the newsroom, he took hold of the first telephone he saw and put a telephone call through to the Cherwell Hotel in Oxford. He was surprised to hear that at eleven o'clock at night, neither Mr Garfield nor Miss Denby was in. He wondered what they were up to and left a message for Poppy, telling her that he would be up to see her in the morning and not to go anywhere without Ike. Then, he got back in the lift and descended to the third floor.

He pushed open the door to the archive and looked straight down the barrel of a gun. Rollo thrust his hands into the air. "Steady on, Rusky! It's just me."

Ivan put the gun down and grunted. "Can't be too careful, Yankee." The Russian archivist, whose thick accent had softened considerably in the ten years since Rollo had known him, was surrounded by open files, boxes, and neat piles of newspaper clippings.

"Find anything yet?" asked Rollo, pulling up a chair to Ivan's desk.

"A couple of things." Ivan stabbed at a notepad with his fountain pen. "That Inspector Birch from the Oxford City Police: I've found a few references to him. The most interesting" – he pushed a clipping across the table to Rollo – "is that he was a character witness for Richard Easling at his disciplinary hearing back in 1920."

The clipping was headlined "Dirty Dicky Kicked off Force", and the article went on to detail how the once high-flying detective had fallen from grace when Poppy Denby revealed that he had been in the pay of Lord Melvyn Dorchester, helping to cover up the disgraced peer's many crimes. Rollo had a vague recollection of penning the headline himself. But he had no memory of any Inspector Birch.

"Yes," said Ivan, "seems like Birch and Easling were young recruits together back in the day and had stayed friends since. He spoke up for Easling at his hearing. Didn't do him any good though."

"Interesting," said Rollo, and he went on to tell Ivan about his meeting with Easling the previous day at the tavern near the Tower of London. "He told me then that he had friends on the force in Oxford and that is how he knew Poppy was up there investigating."

"So," said Ivan, "there is a connection between Easling and Birch. And there's a connection between Easling's former – at least we assume former – paymaster and June Leighton's family."

"A tenuous one," said Rollo. "The connection is really between the Sanforth family and June's father, Roger. Dorchester was just a shareholder on the board of Sanforth Industries."

"Still a connection though," added Ivan.

Rollo nodded, then took out his cigar case and offered one to Ivan. After the men had lit up, Rollo leaned back in his chair. "I honestly don't think Dorchester has much to do with this. He seemed genuinely surprised to hear about June's death. He did though give me some useful information that helps paint a fuller picture of the connection between Sanforth Industries and the lab in Oxford." Rollo went on to tell Ivan what Dorchester had told him about the mine in South West Africa being a front for selling weaponry and military-grade explosives to the Germans.

"Does Poppy know any of this?"

"I just telephoned, but she wasn't in. She was out somewhere with Ike. At least, I hope they're together."

Ivan nodded at his old friend. "Don't worry, Ike will stick to her like glue."

"That's what I'm betting on. I'm going up there tomorrow. I'll be taking her the papers she asked for from June Leighton's family." He patted the briefcase beside him.

"Anything useful in there?"

"I'm not sure," said Rollo. "I haven't been through it properly. But it looks like mainly scientific notes, so I wouldn't understand it anyway. I expect Poppy has found someone there who can read them." He took a few puffs of his cigar. "But back to the Easling, Birch, Dorchester connection. As I said, I don't think Dorchester is in on this one or he wouldn't have promised to testify against Lionel Saunders for his role in old Bert's death."

Ivan sat bolt upright. "He's agreed to do that?"

Rollo pulled out his cigar and grinned. "He has. In exchange for me having a word with my pals on the parole board."

"My, my, justice for Bert at last," said Ivan, looking suddenly morose. "He was a good man."

"He was," said Rollo, with equal seriousness. "Glad I can finally give him his dues."

"So," said Ivan, "you don't think Dorchester's involved. But Easling and Saunders are?"

"I think so," said Rollo. "I don't think it's a coincidence that on the day I confronted Lionel at the *Courier* I was attacked in my own office. Who else would it be, other than Lionel? He used the same modus operandi as he did the night he attacked Poppy. And Easling, well, I'm not sure exactly how he's involved, but this information about his connection to Birch – the very copper who shut down the investigation into the Leighton girl's death – seems very telling. But telling of what? Neither Richard Easling nor Lionel Saunders are actors in their own right. They're always in the pay of someone. The question is who?"

"Who has the most to gain from shutting the investigation down?" asked Ivan, rolling his cigar between thumb and forefinger.

"Well, obviously whoever killed the girl. But that we don't know. Yet."

"Maybe it's not her killing they're covering up so much as the reason she was killed."

"That's Poppy's line of thinking too. And so far, the closest we've come to that is the possible link to explosives research and the Germans."

"So, that's the Sanforths and the Leightons again," offered Ivan. "Either one of them could afford a few bob."

"I very much doubt the Leightons would cover up the death of their own daughter," said Rollo, remembering the couple's distress when he spoke to them that evening. "But the Sanforths are another kettle of fish..." He went on to tell Ivan what he'd been told about Edward Sanforth forcing himself on June and that Sophie Blackburn had also been raped. "So, for me, he's now top of the list of suspects."

"Not so fast, Yankee," said Ivan. He moved his gun from a pile of files onto his blotting pad, then opened the top file. "You also asked me to do a search for any of the male scientists who worked in the laboratory. According to the list you gave me, they are Professor James Sinclair, Dr Bill Raines, graduate student Miles Mackintosh, and a lab assistant, Reg Guthrie." He fanned out a number of clippings on the desk. "Sinclair and Raines were easy enough to find. Both of them are leading scientists. There are multiple references to them winning awards and fellowships. But here's something interesting: Sinclair has previously taught at Harvard – your alma mater in the United States. And guess who funded his research there?"

"The Sanforth Foundation?"

"Exactly. And guess what his research was into?"

"Explosives?"

"No. Synthetic diamonds."

"By Jove! Could that be what June Leighton's mysterious diamond was about? Tell me more."

"Well, he was trying to create diamonds in the laboratory, but the project was shut down after some real diamonds that he'd been using for comparative research – which had been bought for him by the university faculty – disappeared. No one ever proved that Sinclair had done it, but there was still a cloud of suspicion around him. Either he had stolen the diamonds himself or he had failed to put in sufficient security measures to protect them. But his scientific credentials remained intact, and he never lost the backing of the Sanforths. And Oxford seemed happy enough to take him back. That was before the war, and bygones seem to be bygones."

"Perhaps he was getting up to his old tricks again," said Rollo, stubbing out his cigar. "And June Leighton found out about it. If so, that puts him right at the top of the list."

"And what about Edward Sanforth?"

"That doesn't necessarily let him off the hook. Sinclair and Sanforth could have been in cahoots. Right," said Rollo, standing up, "put that all into a file for me and I'll take it to Poppy tomorrow."

"Hold your horses, Yankee," said Ivan. "I haven't showed you everything yet." He extracted one of the clippings and passed it over to Rollo. "Look who has had a previous charge of rape. The trial didn't go ahead after the victim withdrew her accusation, but it still made the papers."

Rollo took the article and skimmed the contents, his eyes resting on the name of the accused. "Good God!"

CHAPTER 33

FRIDAY 24 APRIL 1925, OXFORD

The next morning, a bleary-eyed Poppy joined Ike for breakfast. "Good grief, Poppy! You look like you've been through the wringer."

"Didn't sleep very well," she mumbled.

"Working through the case?"

"Yes, and still no clearer. And you?"

"Not too bad, thank you. But also, no clearer on the case. What's the plan for today?"

Poppy told Ike that Rollo was on his way. "I just called the *Globe*, but Mavis said she didn't know what time Rollo was planning on getting here. He'd left a message for her saying he's coming up by train but didn't say which one. So that's a bother."

"He said he'd managed to get the papers from June's family," added Ike.

"Really? Oh, that's very good. But now we'll need to get someone to have a look at them for us. I was going to ask Edward Sanforth, but I'm not so sure we can trust him now."

"I feel the same," said Ike. "He's kept a lot from us. And why would he do that if he's got nothing to hide?"

"Quite," said Poppy. "But that puts us in a bit of a bind. We can't exactly ask the other scientists in the lab, can we, as they are firmly on our suspect list. The other alternative would have been Sophie Blackburn, but she's out of action right now." Poppy frowned, aware that a headache was settling behind her eyes. "I need to go to the hospital to see how she is. I do hope she improved overnight..." She paused, waiting for her thoughts to catch up with her. "Actually, when I'm there I could speak to Gertrude Fuller to see if she can make an introduction for us to another scientist. The chaps at the Crystal Crypt can't be the only game in town, surely; this *is* Oxford University after all."

Ike nodded, pouring Poppy a strong cup of tea. "Yes, that's a good way forward. We'll go after breakfast."

Poppy shook her head. "Perhaps you should stay here and wait for Rollo. We don't want to miss him. Then you can join me at the hospital as soon as he arrives."

Ike put down the teapot and looked seriously at Poppy. "Are you sure that's a good idea? You going off on your own? We don't know who that fella is who has been following you. What if he crops up again?"

Poppy gave a weak smile, appreciating Ike's concern. "It's broad daylight. I'm sure I'll be all right. But just to put your mind at rest, I'll take a taxi from here directly to the hospital. Then, after that, I'll wait for you and Rollo at *The Oxford Gazette* – it's just around the corner from the infirmary. I'm sure Mr Lewis will be happy to host me, and I know he'd be delighted to meet Rollo."

Poppy got out of the taxi in front of the Radcliffe Infirmary and paid her fare. As she did, she looked around, searching for the man in the flat cap. She had done the same when she exited the hotel but hadn't seen him there. Who was he? Why was he following her? Could he, possibly, be the murderer and attacker? If so, he was very brazen. However, if he were the murderer, then did that mean Edward Sanforth and June's former colleagues were innocent? Or perhaps her stalker had been paid by one of them to keep an eye on her, or to simply intimidate her. That seemed far more likely. He was a paid hand. And if someone – the police, perhaps – could get him to talk, they could find out who had paid him. Poppy toyed with the idea of reporting the man to Chief Constable Fenchurch. That would have nothing to do with Rosie Winter. Besides, Fenchurch had already said that he was opening an investigation into the attacks on Sophie and Gertrude and believed they were linked to the sabotage of her bicycle. Was this the bicycle saboteur? Quite possibly. Yes, she thought, she would give a description of him to the police as soon as she had a chance, and if they brought him in for questioning, he might spill the beans on who had paid him.

Poppy went into the hospital and approached the nurses' station, asking to see Sophie Blackburn. "Is she any better?"

"She had a quiet night, miss, but she hasn't regained consciousness yet."

That was disappointing, but Poppy sent up a quick prayer thanking God that he'd seen Sophie through so far. There was a point, yesterday, when Poppy seriously wondered if Sophie would make it. But she wasn't out of the woods yet.

The nurse took Poppy to a private room. She said Sophie would be moved into a general ward when she woke up. Outside was the same police constable who had picked her up in the car with Rosie Winter the previous morning. Poppy greeted him and asked if it was all right if she went to see Sophie.

"I don't see the harm, miss," he said.

Poppy smiled at him. "Has anyone else been to visit her?"

He shook his head. "Not since I've been here. And Winter was here before that. We're taking turns, like. The chief wants us to call him the minute Miss Blackburn wakes up."

Poppy was relieved to hear that. It showed that the police were taking the attack on Sophie seriously.

Inside the room, Sophie lay battered and bruised. Her eyes were swollen shut, so even if she were awake, Poppy doubted she'd be able to see anything. Her chest rose and fell in a steady rhythm as Poppy pulled up a chair beside the bed. She took the woman's hand in hers and squeezed gently.

"Sophie, it's me, Poppy. I'm so sorry this has happened to you. We're trying to find out who did it. When you wake up, you can tell us. Do wake up, dear Sophie. Wake up soon." Sophie's chest rose and fell without interruption, giving no indication that Poppy's words had been heard. Tears came to Poppy's eyes as she started to imagine what poor Sophie had been through at the hands of her assailant. She sat there for what seemed an age, intermittently praying to God and talking to Sophie, watching for the slightest flicker of response. Then, eventually, with no miracle forthcoming, she got up to leave.

"I'll be back soon, I promise. And Rollo will be coming too. I'll see you later." She wiped the tears from her eyes with the back of her glove and left the room.

Her next stop was to see Gertrude Fuller. Gertrude looked far better than she had the previous day, and the round face under the bandaged head was in rude health.

"Poppy!" she said, sounding just as well as she looked. "They might let me go home today!"

"That's splendid!" said Poppy. "You look a tonne better than you did yesterday. How do you feel?"

Gertrude tapped her head gingerly, then placed her hand over her bandaged ribs. "Still a bit sore to the touch – and it kills me if I laugh – but I've had worse. How is Miss Blackburn?"

Poppy's face dropped. "Not doing that well, I'm afraid. She still hasn't regained consciousness."

"Oh, I'm dreadfully sorry to hear that. I hope they catch the monster who did it. When I heard what happened to her, I see

I got off lucky. I'm not too confident the police are on the right track though."

"Oh? Why's that?"

"That Fenchurch fellow was in here yesterday evening to question me again. He was very interested in what connection you, me, and Sophie had, but when I tried to suggest it had something to do with June's death, he dismissed it." The academic clutched Poppy's hand. "But it does have something to do with June, doesn't it?"

Poppy took Gertrude's hands in both of hers and held them tight. "Yes, Gertrude, I believe it does. Two of my colleagues from the *Globe* are now here helping me with it. Well, one is here already and the other is on his way. We are making progress. But I need your help. We have found June's papers at her parents' house, and we believe there might be something in there that could shed light on what she was working on before she died which might have led to her death. But we need someone who understands the science. For obvious reasons I can't ask Sinclair, Raines, and Mackintosh. And Sophie is unconscious. Do you know anyone else at the university that might be able to help us? Someone who will remain discreet and not blurt out what we are doing to the fellows in the Crystal Crypt?"

Gertrude thought for a while and said, "Yes. I think I know who I can ask. Let me get myself home first and I'll ring him then. Have you got the papers?"

"Not yet. My editor is bringing them up from London today. However, I'm reluctant to let them out of our possession. Would it be possible for us to be there when your scientist friend looks at them?"

"I don't see why not. I'll ask him. He can come round to my rooms at Somerville. When do you have in mind?"

Poppy shrugged. "I'm not sure. Possibly this evening. I hope to get down to London this afternoon to speak to June's parents myself – I have a lot to tell them. And then I'll come back. That might be tonight," she said, then wondered if she'd be able to squeeze in an evening with Daniel, "but more likely tomorrow."

"I understand. I'll let my associate know. I'll probably be too tired tonight anyway, so let's pencil in a lunch. I'll let Annabel – ah Annabel! Speak of the devil. I was just talking about you."

Poppy looked up to see the young student whom she'd met the previous day.

"Hello, Annabel."

"Hello, Miss Denby. I'm very glad you're here. I was going to pop around to see you after visiting Dr Fuller."

"Oh? Have you got something for me?"

Annabel nodded vigorously. "I have. Well, I think I have. I'm not entirely sure. I've never done any of this detecting malarkey before." She grinned. "But you see, I have been preparing the rooms for the students returning this week. The new term starts on Monday. Dr Fuller usually oversees it with the housekeeper, but she asked me to do it today for her instead. I was happy to, because you see—"

"Get on with it, Annabel! What have you found?" prompted Gertrude.

"Sorry, Dr Fuller. Yes. Well, you know that we cleared out June Leighton's room after she died and sent everything to her family?"

"Yes, yes, of course."

"Well, I was just giving it the once-over today for the new girl coming in when I noticed something we'd missed." Annabel paused for dramatic effect.

"What?" asked Poppy and Gertrude in unison.

"A letter. It had slipped behind the desk and was lodged between the skirting board and the desk leg."

"May I see it?" asked Poppy, reaching out her hand.

Annabel flushed with pride. "Oh no, I haven't brought it. I left it exactly where I found it. Just in case you wanted to take fingerprints or anything like that, Miss Denby."

Poppy blinked in surprise. *Goodness me, what kind of detective does she think I am?* But not wanting to crush the girl's enthusiasm, she said, "Good thinking, Annabel. Can you show me where it is?"

"Of course!" And with a quick goodbye to Gertrude, Poppy and the student left for Somerville.

Rollo Rolandson stepped onto the train at Paddington Station and settled down for the journey to Oxford. He had a small suitcase packed in case he needed to stay overnight, and also carried June Leighton's briefcase. He had looked through the papers after he got home last night but didn't understand much. There were diagrams and formulae and such. He did, though, notice that there were some notes on diamonds with lots of measurements of angles. There were quite a few question marks in circles, and a note: *confirm with Sinclair.* Now that Rollo knew about James Sinclair's work on synthetic diamonds at Harvard and the disappearance of the real Harvard diamonds, he was on the look-out for any supporting evidence. To his scientifically untrained eye, it certainly looked as if June had been working on diamonds and had some questions for Sinclair. Now, hadn't Poppy told him that Sophie had said June was not working on diamonds as part of her own experiments? She was working on something to do with bromides, while the rest of the team was working on graphite crystals as part of their efforts to stabilize explosives. Rollo searched through the notebooks and papers – which were dated – and found lots of references to "Br" this or that, which he assumed meant Bromide. There was a whole notebook on graphite crystals, but it was dated last year. The most recently dated entries, in the two weeks up until she died, involved, as far as he could tell, diamonds. So, he thought, did this mean the motive for June's murder was, after all, to cover up something to do with diamonds? If so, then that definitely put James Sinclair in the picture. However, his had not been the name of the man accused of rape in Ivan's news cutting last night...

He yawned. It had been a late night and early morning, and he still hadn't quite recovered from the assault from two nights before. In fact, Yasmin – who was not much of a worrier – had suggested that he didn't go to Oxford but rather send someone else instead. He had dismissed her concerns. But he was tired. Bone tired. And soon, the *chug-chug-chug* of the engine and the rhythmic rock of carriage on rail lulled him to sleep, with his arms wrapped around June Leighton's briefcase on his chest.

Sometime later, as they were pulling into Oxford, he awoke to a tugging. He opened his eyes and stared straight into the ferret-like face of Lionel Saunders. "What the hell are you doing?" bellowed Rollo and pulled the bag back with all his strength.

Lionel pulled too, snarling as he did so. "Give it up, dwarf!"

Rollo, the much smaller man, clung on for as long as he could but felt the leather slipping through his hands. But then, to his relief, he heard someone shout, "You sir! What are you doing with that little fellow's bag?"

"It's mine!" said Lionel. "The dwarf's a known thief! And a foreigner!"

"It doesn't look that way to me," said a tweed-coated gentleman with an umbrella. The gent raised his umbrella as if to strike Lionel. Lionel let go of the bag and scarpered off down the carriage.

"Call the guard! Stop that man!" shouted the man with the umbrella. But it was too late. The train shuddered to a stop at the platform, and Rollo saw Lionel leap off the train and scurry off.

"You should report it to the police immediately!" said the gentleman.

"I will, sir, and thank you very much for your help," said Rollo, who had absolutely no intention of going to the police – not yet anyway.

"You *are* foreign. American?"

"Yes sir. From New York City."

"Then I apologize on behalf of my countrymen. We're not all bounders."

Rollo smiled and tipped his hat. "No sir, you are not. And you, my dear man, are the best of British."

A quarter of an hour later, Rollo arrived at the Cherwell Hotel in a taxi and was relieved to find Ike waiting for him in the foyer.

"Where's Poppy?"

To Rollo's annoyance, the West Indian reporter told him that Poppy had gone off on her own. "Why the hell did you let her?" he snapped.

Ike mumbled an apology, explaining how Poppy had promised to go straight from the hospital to George Lewis' office at *The Oxford Gazette*. "It's literally around the corner from the infirmary," explained Ike.

"Well, we'd better get over there now then. Have you got the Model T?"

"No, it's in a pub car park in High Wycombe, remember?"

"Oh, for God's sake!" Rollo could feel his blood pressure rising. It wouldn't help anyone if he blew a gasket – least of all Poppy. "Then order a bloody taxi!"

Half an hour later a taxi dropped Rollo and Ike outside the *Gazette* office. On the way over, they had explained their respective halves of the investigation. Most important from Rollo's side was that Lionel Saunders was in town, that James Sinclair might be involved with some dodgy diamonds, and that a rapist was on the loose. They rushed into the newspaper office to fill Poppy in on all the latest developments, but instead found George Lewis alone.

"I'm sorry," said the newspaperman. "I haven't seen Miss Denby since last night at the White Horse. Was she supposed to be here?"

CHAPTER 34

Poppy and Annabel hurried to Somerville College. Or, at least, Annabel hurried, and Poppy tried to keep up. The younger woman was flushed with the excitement of the chase and ran like she was in training for the 1928 Olympic Games. They both arrived, breathless, at the arched entrance to the college to be greeted by the same scowling porter that Poppy had spoken to two days earlier. And that reminded Poppy of something. She'd been wanting to ask the porter to let her look at the logbook for the night Gertrude was assaulted and someone ransacked her rooms. But she had no authority to do so. Perhaps, though, now she had.

"Good morning, sir," she said.

"Morning, miss."

"Hold on a minute, Annabel," Poppy called after the young woman who was half sprinting through the gatehouse. "I have some questions for this gentleman first." She said it in a tone worthy of Hercule Poirot, which must have impressed Annabel because the girl slowed down and complied.

"Mr Cooper, is it?" Poppy asked, relieved that she'd remembered.

"It is, miss."

"Well, Mr Cooper, you said the other day when I spoke to you that if anyone had come into the college on the night Dr Fuller was attacked it would be in the logbook. You would not show me the logbook then. However, Dr Fuller has told me to tell you that you must show it to me. Isn't that right, Annabel?"

Annabel's eyes widened in surprise at the blatant lie, but to her credit she kept her composure. The fact is, both she and Poppy knew that Dr Fuller would give permission for Poppy to see it. They were just skipping a few steps.

"Yes, Miss Denby, it is. Cooper, Dr Fuller said you must show Miss Denby the logbook. She will be out of the hospital later today and will no doubt tell you herself then."

"Then I'll wait for Dr Fuller," he growled.

"Are you sure you want to do that? She'll be very cross," said Annabel, as if talking to a naughty schoolboy.

Cooper crossed his arms and smirked. "I'll take my chances."

Poppy was very tempted to just grab the logbook, which was visible on the counter of his kiosk, and run. But she doubted she'd get far. Annabel, on the other hand... *No.* Best they wait for Dr Fuller. But why Cooper was being so stiff-necked about it, she had no idea. *Unless...* She narrowed her eyes and appraised the man. *Unless he has something to hide. He* was *here the day my bicycle was tampered with...*

Poppy pursed her lips and turned to Annabel. "Mr Cooper is just doing his job, Annabel. We have to respect that. Now, where do I sign in?"

"Sign in?" asked Annabel.

"As a visitor to the college, don't I have to sign in? I did when I first visited Dr Fuller."

"Of course!" said Annabel, turning to Cooper with an undisguised air of triumph. "The logbook, Cooper, for Miss Denby to sign in."

Cooper smirked at Annabel, picked up a pen, and thrust it at Poppy.

Poppy took it with ironic grace and nonchalantly approached the logbook. But... *Drat it!* It was a clean page. *Touché, Mr Cooper, touché.*

Poppy and Annabel left the smug porter and entered the Somerville quadrangle. They passed Dr Fuller's rooms, went through a metal-studded door, and up a staircase to the first floor. They passed two undergraduates returning from the Easter break, hauling their trunks. Annabel greeted them both by name.

"Is it normal for women to remain in residence after they've graduated?" asked Poppy.

"You mean June Leighton?"

"Yes."

"No, it's not usually done. We're short on space and need the rooms. But June was going to be doing some tutoring and lecturing for us next term, so we agreed that she could stay on for a while until she found digs in town. She was supposed to have moved out last year already, but she never quite got around to it. June was like an absent-minded professor. She was so focused on her work that she would often forget to eat. In fact, a few weeks before she died, she fainted in the college library. Dr Fuller – who you no doubt noticed enjoys her food – was quite concerned for her. She worried that turfing her out to find her own place would not be good for June."

"I see," said Poppy, wondering if June's fainting spell had more to do with her pregnancy than skipping meals. But she kept her thoughts to herself. She very much doubted June had told Gertrude of her pregnancy, or else the principal would have mentioned it during their frank discussions about the deceased scientist. Poppy wondered if the poor girl had worried that the pregnancy would have seen her expelled from the college. *Poor June*, thought Poppy. Not only did she have to worry about how her fiancé and family would take the news of her pregnancy, but whether or not she'd lose her accommodation and, perhaps, her job. It wouldn't look good for Oxford University to be employing a pregnant, unmarried woman.

Annabel stopped outside a room and extracted a large bunch of keys from her pocket. She selected the correct one and opened the door. The room was of reasonable size, with a bay window, overlooking the quadrangle. There was a single bed stripped of laundry, a desk with a lamp, bookcase, and a single armchair. There was no en-suite bathroom, but the chamber pot peeking out from under the bed suggested June shared ablution facilities with other women on the same floor.

Annabel approached the desk – which was at a jaunty angle, pulled away from the wall – got down on her knees, and pointed triumphantly: "There!"

Poppy hitched up her skirt, got down on her knees, and crawled alongside Annabel. Sure enough, between the leg of the desk and the skirting board was an envelope. Poppy, not wanting to disappoint Annabel and her rose-tinted ideas of detection work, took a handkerchief from her pocket with a flourish and used it to pick up the envelope, between thumb and forefinger. It was addressed to Mrs Roger Leighton, 61 Berkeley Square, Mayfair, London W1J GBD. So, June had been writing to her mother...

The letter – stamped, but unfranked – might very well have been the last correspondence of June Leighton. The envelope was sealed and on the back was June's Somerville College address.

"Goodness," said Poppy, "this is quite a find, Annabel. Well done. I'm not sure what to do though. It's addressed to her mother, so perhaps I should take it to her unopened."

Annabel's face fell. "Oh. Aren't you going to open it? What if it's evidence of her murder?"

Indeed. What if it is?

Poppy was torn, not sure what to do. But the eager face of her youthful protégé spurred her on. "All right. I'll open it. But if I see it's nothing more than a personal letter, I shall re-seal it immediately. Agreed?"

"Agreed!" said Annabel, looking like a little girl on Christmas morning.

Poppy took a deep breath, took off one of her gloves, and ran a nail along the envelope.

She extracted three sheets of paper. The address at the top left was Somerville College and the date of writing, Friday 3rd April 1925 – two days before June's murder.

Dearest Mother,

Oh Mama! I don't know where to start. I shall be home next week for the Easter holidays, but I cannot wait until then to tell you what has been happening in my life. I am heartbroken. I am confused. I am ashamed. Oh Mama, please don't judge me harshly. I know that my achievements in science are the achievements you should have had. How your career in medicine was cut short by marrying Papa and having Larry and me. I am eternally sorry that your talents and abilities were so cruelly ignored, but eternally grateful of how you have encouraged me in the fulfilment of my academic and professional dreams.

So, it is with a desperately heavy heart – and with a prayer that you will forgive me and understand – that I tell you I am pregnant. The father is a sweet, sweet man. A man whom you have met. It is Edward Sanforth. We fell in love. He proposed to me and in the heat of the moment we succumbed to our bodily passions. I now carry his child. Which is a joyful thing, but sadly the joy is tainted.

Edward believes – wrongly – that the child might not be his. Remember I told you about that awful Dr Raines? How familiar he had been with me? And you told me, rightly, to spurn his advances and remind him that our relationship was professional and nothing more? Well, I did so. But he has not taken it well. He has told Edward that I succumbed to him – willingly – and that he and I had a "roll in the sack" at a scientific symposium earlier this year at University College London. Well, it's a blatant lie! But Edward isn't so sure.

I told him, today, of my pregnancy, expecting him to offer to marry me immediately, but instead he has raised this question over the paternity of our child.

I am heartbroken, Mama. I did not expect this of him. I thought he trusted me. I thought he was made of sterner stuff.

But that, I'm afraid, is not the worst of what I have to tell you. My personal circumstances aside, there is a more pressing issue I must draw to your attention, involving our family.

Remember I mentioned that Prof Sinclair had some experience in experimenting with the creation of synthetic diamonds? Well, last week – on my birthday to be exact – Larry came up to Oxford to lunch. He told me that he'd read about Prof Sinclair's previous work at Harvard and that last year he had approached him to continue the work here. The prof had declined, saying that it was a chapter of his life that he wanted to leave behind. But Larry said that he had insisted. Apparently Larry, through his jewellery trade contacts in the USA, had discovered that the prof had stolen some industrial diamonds from Harvard University and sold them on the black market. At the time it was never proven, but Larry subsequently found the proof. He told me that he was using the information he had to both further science and help our family business. He asked me to help Prof Sinclair with his experiments – to speed it up. I told Larry I wasn't interested, as I had my own work to do. Larry, as is his way, starting shouting at me, saying I had never done anything for him and the family, and that it was time I stopped being so selfish. I shouted back, we had a blazing row, and then he left.

I wasn't sure what to do. Should I speak to the prof about it? Well, I did. And to my shock, I discovered that Larry has been forcing him to continue work on the synthetic diamonds in his spare time.

I only found out about it because I have started to work in the Crystal Crypt odd hours in order to avoid that awful Dr Raines and his bratty grad student Mackintosh (remember him? The one who plagiarized some of my work on bromides?) Well, a few nights ago I came across Sinclair and saw what he was doing. I confronted him, and at first he denied it. But after I told him what Larry had told me about the Harvard diamonds, he succumbed and told me everything.

Larry is blackmailing him, threatening to present his evidence of the Harvard jewel theft to the authorities. The prof said he was very close to finding the formula and just needed a bit more time. I asked him, what was Larry's motivation? He said Larry is hoping to replace some of the most valuable diamonds in the shop with synthetics and sell the originals on the black market. And worse than that, remember the burglary we had last year when Papa lost some prize jewels? Well, it turns out Larry was the one who did it! He "borrowed" the jewels to bring to Sinclair so he could use them as comparative models.

I'm sure Larry will deny all this, and Prof Sinclair has said that he will deny it too, if questioned, so I should just keep quiet about it all. He said that if I help him, he will put forward my name for a fellowship and ensure that the Sanforth Foundation won't terminate my employment for refusing to work on the explosives project. He was so upset that I agreed, but I don't intend to keep my promise. Larry cannot continue torturing the poor man like this! Yes, he made a mistake at Harvard – all right, he committed a crime – but what Larry is doing to him, and what he plans to do to enrich himself, is just wrong. I know you'll agree with me.

So, when Sinclair was distracted, I tore some of his lab notes out of his notebook – showing what he was working on – and have enclosed them here. I am sending them to you for safe keeping and for you and Papa to decide what to do. I expect you will not want to go to the police, but rather confront Larry yourselves and release poor Prof

Sinclair from this awful bind he is in. Can we talk about it when I come home next week?

That, and of course, the baby. But please! Don't tell Papa about that. I need time to sort this all out with Edward first. Oh, and by the way, Larry knows about me and Edward (but fortunately, for now, not about the baby). I'm not sure how he knows, but he does. He's not happy about our relationship and tried to convince me to break it off. I told him to mind his own business. But of course, he won't. Just another worry to add to my growing list.

Yours with a heavy heart,

June

Poppy flipped through the pages and found a torn sheet covered in notes, diagrams, and formulae. So, *this* is what Gertrude and Sophie's attacker was looking for when he searched their rooms! The missing page from Professor Sinclair's notebook. He must have discovered it was missing and tried to get it back. Had Larry Leighton already searched for it in June's papers at his parents' house and not found it? Then, he and Sinclair decided that the page must still be in Oxford. Who was it who had killed poor June? Sinclair? Her brother? Or both of them?

Suddenly there was a banging on the door and a panicked female voice. "Annabel! Are you there? Come quickly!"

Annabel, who had been reading the letter over Poppy's shoulder, shouted to the door, "Go away, Susan! I'm busy!"

"But there's a burst pipe in the bathroom! The whole floor will be flooded!"

"Oh bother!" said Annabel, looking to Poppy. "What should I do?"

"Go," said Poppy. "There's nothing more you can do here. I've got everything I need. I'll come around and see you and Dr Fuller later. I'm going to meet up with my editor now and we'll decide what to do."

"Annabel! Come now!"

"Fiddlesticks!" exclaimed Annabel and stomped towards the door.

"Oh, and Annabel," said Poppy, "don't tell anyone else about this. Please. We need to handle this very carefully."

"You can trust me," she said, then opened the door to tackle the plumbing emergency.

Poppy wondered if she could really trust the eager student, but there was nothing she could do to control her. The sooner she met up with Rollo and Ike and then took the letter – and the pathologist's report – to June's mother in London, the better. She folded the papers, including the incriminating lab notes, back into the envelope.

As she did, the door opened again. She looked up, expecting to see Annabel, but instead – to the backdrop of screaming girls and gushing water – she saw the young man in the tweed flat cap. And suddenly she knew who he was: Larry Leighton.

She shoved the letter under the edge of the rug, hoping he hadn't seen it.

"Not so fast, Miss Denby. Give that here."

Poppy, still on her knees, didn't move.

"I said, give that here!" He took a step into the room, slamming the door behind him. There was no way out. If Poppy had been on her feet, she might have attempted to grab something – the desk lamp, perhaps – and give him a good wallop. He strode towards her. She lunged at his legs, grabbing at his calves like a rugby tackle. It worked! Knocked off balance, he stumbled, giving her just enough time to scramble to her feet and flee for the door, screaming "Help!" as she did so. But before she could make her escape, he too lunged at her and, using the same tactic, knocked her off her feet. And then he was straddled on top of her. He slapped her once, twice, in the face, the pain searing through her cheek-bones. Then, he held her throat with one hand and made a fist with the second.

"Don't move or you'll get this," he growled.

Poppy stopped straining against him. She dared not even call out lest he tighten his hold on her throat.

"Now missy," he said. "Where's your negro boyfriend?"

"He's not my boyfriend. He's my colleague. And he'll be here any minute. So you'd better let me go."

"Sure he will. Now get up, before those stupid girls figure out how to fix the pipe I wrenched." He held onto her throat but climbed off her. Putting his knee on her chest, he released her throat, then pulled off his belt and tied it around her wrists.

"Is this how June ended up with welts on her wrists before you killed her?"

"I did not kill my sister."

"Oh? Then who did?"

"Someone who went too far trying to extract information from her."

"What information?"

He looked to where she had slipped the envelope under the rug. "What I assume is in that envelope: some stolen notes."

He got to his feet, leaving her lying on her back. But with her hands tied in front of her, her chances of escape were minimal.

He quickly extracted the envelope and returned to stand over Poppy. He opened the envelope, had a quick skim of the contents, then pocketed it, muttering to himself, "Stupid, stupid bitch." Then, to Poppy, "Let's go." He pulled her to her feet.

"Where are we going?"

"You ask too many questions."

"Well, what have you got to lose by answering them? I already know what's in the letter. And I still believe you killed your sister. As will anyone else who reads it."

"Well, I didn't. I told you it was someone else."

"Sinclair?"

Larry snorted with derision. "That old fool? No, he'd never hurt June. Not even to cover up his part in all this. But the same can't be said of his lab assistant."

Poppy wracked her brain, trying to figure out who Larry meant. Then, she realized: Reg Guthrie. The man who had caught her snooping around in the Crystal Crypt yesterday. The man who had supposedly found June's body when he opened up the lab the morning after her "accident". The man who had given her Sophie Blackburn's address... *Good God!* Had he actually been in the flat waiting for her to arrive? Someone had been. Thank God the neighbour had seen her entering the back door from upstairs and come to investigate. And no doubt scared off Guthrie. "Is Guthrie working for you?"

"I needed someone to keep an eye on Sinclair. He couldn't be trusted."

"And did he attack Gertrude Fuller and Sophie Blackburn too?"

"Stupidly, yes. I just asked him to search their rooms to see if he could find Sinclair's missing notes. I hadn't realized he was such a brute. It's made things... difficult."

"*Difficult?* Difficult! Dear God! Do you know that he raped Sophie? And if what you're saying is true, he'd already killed your sister. Surely that would tell you what a brute he was. And you didn't think to report it to the police? To stop him hurting anyone else?"

Larry shrugged. "I couldn't. He would have implicated me. I paid him."

"And Inspector Birch and Dr Mortimer? Did you pay them too?"

Larry shrugged again. Poppy took that as an affirmative.

"So—" she started, planning to continue her interrogation.

"So, you should shut the hell up!" He reached into his pocket and pulled out a penknife. He flicked open a blade. "I don't want to hear one more word from you, or I'll slit your throat. It will not give me pleasure to do so; I am not ordinarily a violent man. But you – and those other women – have forced me into this. You have given me no choice. Do you understand?"

Poppy swallowed hard and nodded. Yes, she understood.

Larry loosened the belt, just one notch, and pushed it further up her wrists, then pulled down her coat sleeves to cover it. It was slightly looser, but not loose enough for Poppy to shake free.

"Now, missy, we are going to walk out of here. You are going to clasp your hands and not let on you are tied up if we see anyone. If you do, I will stab you in the kidneys. Do you hear me?"

Poppy nodded, glancing at her hands hanging awkwardly in front of her. One was gloveless.

So, with Larry walking at her side, they exited the room. Poppy looked around, desperate to catch anyone's attention, but it seemed to still be all-hands-on-deck with the plumbing emergency. Larry took her elbow as they reached the stairs and helped her negotiate them. Then, across the quadrangle to the gatehouse. She was not fool enough to expect help from Cooper the porter; by now she'd figured out he too was in Larry's employ. No doubt he was the one who had alerted Larry that she and Annabel were searching June's room. A car pulled up outside the gatehouse and Poppy's heart sank when she recognized Reg Guthrie at the steering wheel. Larry opened the back passenger door and pushed her in.

CHAPTER 35

Rollo, Ike, and George Lewis scrambled into George's car outside the *Oxford Gazette* office. Their first port of call was the Radcliffe Infirmary. Rollo, despite his short legs, hurried ahead of the other men and collared the first nurse he could find. "Is Poppy Denby here?"

"Is she a patient?"

"No. But she's visiting a patient."

The nurse looked down at him with her tri-corner hat, hovering above him like a swan about to take flight. "And what is that patient's name?"

"Blackburn. Sophie Blackburn."

"Are you a family member of Miss Blackburn? She is very poorly and we must restrict visitors."

"I – yes – I am her cousin from America."

"All right then, sir, this way."

Ike and George caught up with Rollo. "She might also have popped in to see Dr Fuller," said Ike.

The nurse looked a little perplexed. "Are you here to see Dr Fuller too?"

"We are," said George. "I'm a friend of hers."

The nurse pointed in the other direction. "She's more able to receive visitors. Third door on the left."

Five minutes later, Ike, George, and Rollo reconvened in the hospital foyer.

"Any luck?" asked Ike.

Rollo shook his head. "No. Although the policeman at Sophie's door – who wouldn't let me in – said Poppy had been to visit about an hour ago."

"Gertrude said the same. She said that Poppy had left with one of the Somerville students just over an hour ago. The girl apparently had something to show her in June Leighton's old room at the college."

"Lead the way!" said Rollo, and the men hurried back to the car.

It was just a short drive to Somerville from the infirmary. The three journalists bundled out of the car and into the gatehouse. They were greeted by a middle-aged man in a black suit and a bowler hat. "Can I help you gentlemen?"

Again, Rollo took the lead. "Can you tell us if Miss Poppy Denby and her companion – Ike, did Dr Fuller give a name?"

"Annabel Seymour."

"Poppy Denby and Annabel Seymour. Are they still here?"

The man gave Rollo a curious look. "I'm sorry, but there is no Miss Denby here. Miss Seymour left after breakfast this morning – around nine o'clock – and she hasn't returned since. She said she was off to do some shopping in town."

Rollo scowled. "We were told they were here. Is there another entrance to the college?"

"There is, but the doors are locked. This is the only way in and out. If either of those ladies were here, they would have had to have come in this way."

"Then, why is Poppy Denby's name in your logbook as having arrived at eleven o'clock this morning and, as yet, not having signed out?" Ike stood with the logbook in his hands.

"I – well – I she must have slipped in when I took a tea break."

"In that case, please lead the way to June Leighton's old room," said Rollo, his patience wearing very thin.

"I can't do that. No men are allowed in the college."

"Oh, for God's sake, man! These ladies might be in danger!"

The porter pursed his lips and folded his arms over his chest. "Rules are rules."

That was the final straw. Rollo reached into his inside pocket and pulled out his revolver.

"Rollo! What the hell?" said Ike.

"Put the gun away, man," said George. "This isn't the Wild West."

"Ordinarily I'd agree with you," said Rollo, "but there are outlaws on the loose in this town and I'm not prepared for Poppy to be their next victim." He jabbed the gun into the porter's belly. "Lead the way."

Ike and George exchanged a worried glance over Rollo's head but followed behind the American as he prodded the porter to take them to June Leighton's room. Fortunately, as term hadn't yet started, there were no students in the quadrangle, but who knew who was looking at the alarming spectacle from the windows above?

They entered a residence, climbed the stairs, and stepped onto a landing swilling with water. Two young women, armed with buckets and mops, greeted them with an air of barely contained panic. They did not appear to see the diminutive man with a gun behind the porter.

"Mr Cooper! Thank heavens you're here. Has the plumber arrived?"

"No," said Cooper, his voice taut.

Ike spoke over Cooper's shoulder. "We're looking for a lady named Poppy Denby. She was here less than an hour ago with Annabel Seymour. Are they still here?"

The girl shook her head. "No. She and Annabel were in June's old room when the pipe burst in the bathroom. The last I saw of the lady was when Annabel came to help us. Annabel left her in the room. But then, the next minute, Annabel disappeared! I was hoping she'd gone to call a plumber, but no such luck."

"Which room is June's?" asked Ike.

The girl pointed.

"Do you mind if I have a look?"

"Help yourself," said the girl and continued her manic mopping.

A minute later and Ike had returned. In his hand he held a lady's glove. "There's no one there. But I found this."

"It's Poppy's," said Rollo.

Larry shoved Poppy unceremoniously into James Sinclair's office, her wrists still tied with his belt. The professor was slumped at his desk, his pipe smouldering in the ashtray.

"Is he...?"

"Dead? No. Chloroform. But I won't bother doing the same with you. You won't be going anywhere." He pushed her down into a chair. "Ready?" he said, addressing Reg Guthrie.

"Yes."

"And Raines and Mackintosh? Are you sure they're out of town?"

"Symposium in London. So it's only Sinclair here. And her." Guthrie nodded to Poppy, his eyes like a hooded cobra.

Poppy suddenly remembered the first day she'd visited the laboratory and how she'd felt like a small animal being summed up as prey.

"Good," said Larry. "And I've dealt with the museum upstairs. Sewage leak. They'll be temporarily closing doors. The receptionist might stick around, but by the time he realizes what's going on down here, it'll be too late."

"What *is* going on?" asked Poppy, warily watching Reg Guthrie out of the corner of her eye.

"There's going to be an accident," said Larry, his voice chillingly matter-of-fact. "Prof Sinclair's pipe is going to fall into the wastepaper basket – without him or his visitor noticing – and before they know it, the room will catch fire, and unfortunately there is no telephone in the office."

Poppy's heart was beating nineteen to the dozen, her eyes flicking to the door and the only window, high above on the mezzanine floor. "But surely Professor Sinclair and his visitor would get out of the office and call the fire brigade."

"You would think so, wouldn't you? But it turns out that Professor Sinclair has locked the door from the inside, and" – he opened a drawer above the wastepaper basket and lifted out a key to show Poppy – "unfortunately he is unable to get to it in time." He dropped the key into the wastepaper basket, like a child dropping a marble into a jar.

Poppy swallowed hard. "But why would he lock the door?"

Larry shrugged. "A pretty young girl, a dirty old man... one woman has already been raped."

"Yes – by him!" shouted Poppy, pointing at Guthrie, who, alarmingly, was taking the pipe and kindling a fire in the basket. He also had a bottle of something – most probably something to accelerate the flames – and proceeded to splash it around the office. Poppy willed herself to stay calm and keep her wits about her. "When Sophie wakes up, she will tell the police who really attacked her. And who was waiting for me at her flat to attack me too."

Guthrie flashed her a quick look but didn't stop his incendiary preparations.

Larry lowered his chin to his chest and shook his head, in mock pity. "Unfortunately, Miss Blackburn will not be waking up. You may have noticed, Miss Denby, that there are an awful lot of greedy people in this town. People whose morals are left by the wayside once some diamonds are waved in their face. And I, by the good fortune of my profession, have access to a lot of diamonds. And before you ask, because, even in the face of death, you are annoyingly curious, Guthrie here arranged for a spare key for Sinclair's office. Which we will use to lock you in. Ready, Guthrie?"

The lab assistant nodded his assent as he looked on with satisfaction at the flames licking Sinclair's desk and taking hold of a bookcase nearby.

"Good work. Well, goodbye, Miss Denby. I'm sorry your article on my sister turned out to be more sensational than you first thought."

Before Poppy could summon up a retort, Larry and Guthrie were out the door and the lock turned with a deathly clunk.

"Oh God!" she whimpered. "Oh dear God!" But then she consciously took control of her breathing – just like she'd been taught to do in her ju-jitsu classes – and counted to ten. When she opened her eyes, she looked around the room, rapidly assessing her options, and made a decision.

Poppy levered herself up out of the chair, thanking God the men had not thought to tie her to it. She didn't bother trying the door; she knew it would be locked. And she didn't bother trying to get Sinclair's key – it was at the bottom of a basket of flames. Instead, she used her mouth to undo the belt around her wrists. She was making progress, but then saw the flames lapping closer to the professor. She stopped what she was doing and dragged the unconscious man to the far side of the office where the flames had not yet reached. Then, she gave a final tug on the belt and freed herself. She was relieved that she had been in this office before and had noticed the heavy antique scientific instruments on the mezzanine balcony, reached by a wrought-iron spiral staircase. Fortunately, the flames had not yet reached the stairs. She ran up them, grabbed the first heavy brass object she could lay her hands on, and swung it with all her might at the window on the mezzanine. The glass shattered. Then, she prodded at the remaining shards.

The window was level with the courtyard behind the Science Museum, facing the Bodleian Library. She took a moment to breathe in the life-giving air, clearing the smoke from her lungs, as she felt the heat of the fire at her back. She was very tempted to scramble through to safety, but she couldn't leave the professor to die in the flames. She screamed for help – once, twice! – but when no one came, she knew what she had to do. With a quick prayer for help and strength, she ran back down the stairs to get the professor, the flames nearly lapping the bottom of the staircase – but not quite yet. The air was acrid with smoke, catching in her throat. Poppy once again steadied her breathing, assessed the lie of the land, and leaped from the stairs to the chair – an island in a sea of flame – then, like a game of hopscotch, negotiated her route to the professor. Poppy grabbed him under the arms, braced herself against his weight, and dragged him to the foot of the stairs, the heat and smoke driving the air out of her lungs. She stumbled to her knees, gasping for breath, desperate not to swoon. Then, she shook her head, steadying her resolve. She needed to get out, quickly, before she succumbed, but there was no way she would be able to lift the man up the stairs. If Daniel were with her... but he was not. She had made the decision to do this on her own.

Her heart screamed. She would have to leave Professor Sinclair. She knew she was condemning him to death. But what else could she do?

"Poppy! Get out of there!"

Poppy, tears streaming down her soot-stained face, looked up at the sound of the woman's voice. And there was WPC Rosie Winter at the top of the stairs. Beside her was the student, Annabel.

"I can't lift him! Help me!"

Without any further comment, Rosie and Annabel ran down the stairs. And with the two strong, athletic women pulling, and Poppy pushing from below, they managed to manoeuvre the unconscious man up the stairs, along the balcony, and out the shattered window onto the courtyard above.

Moments later, the three women lay around the prone body of the man, gasping for air, as a group of people ran towards them. Poppy looked up, between sobs and gasps, to see Rollo, Ike, and George. And with them, Chief Constable Fenchurch.

"Oh, thank God!" gasped Rollo, falling to his knees and taking Poppy's head into his lap. "Thank bloody God."

CHAPTER 36

SUNDAY 26 APRIL 1925, OXFORD

Poppy lay back on the cushions, trailing her fingers lazily through the water. It was a beautiful spring day in Oxford, and she and Daniel were sharing the Cherwell with a mother duck and her brood. She looked up at her fiancé gallantly attempting to punt them down the river. She smiled at him, basking for a moment in the sunshine of their love.

"So," he said, eventually, "explain to me how that policewoman managed to save you. I'm not sure I've got the whole thing straight in my mind."

"Well, she didn't actually *save* me. I could have got out on my own, but she – and Annabel – helped me save the professor. The doctors say he's going to be all right. Thank God."

"Yes, but how did she know you were there?"

"Ah," said Poppy, "that's thanks to Annabel. It seems that she came back to June's room to check on me in the middle of the plumbing incident and saw that I was gone. She looked out the window, across the quadrangle, and saw me and Larry Leighton heading to the gatehouse. She knew who Larry was, as he'd previously visited his sister at the college. And she'd just read June's letter with me, which pointed the finger of blame at Larry.

"She hurried to catch up with us, but we were gone before she got there. She said the porter tried to collar her but she was too quick for him. That girl should try out for the ladies' Olympic running team!"

Daniel chuckled. "Go on."

"Well, she told me that she decided to run to the police station, and on the way bumped into Rosie Winter, who was heading to the hospital for her shift of guarding Sophie. Then, she and Rosie went looking for me. They guessed I might have been taken to the Crystal Crypt, but they weren't entirely sure. Just as well they went with their intuition!"

"Just as well," said Daniel, looking down at her, his face awash with concern. "And Sophie? I hear she's going to be all right."

"Yes," said Poppy, with relief, "she is. I told Fenchurch that Larry was planning on having her killed. He sent some officers to back up the guard at her room and wouldn't let any doctors or nurses near her on their own until they found out who was intending to harm her."

"And who was?"

"Well, Larry and Guthrie were caught yesterday afternoon in a roadblock between Oxford and London. Fenchurch had wasted no time getting the news out that they were on the run and giving out a description of the car Guthrie had been driving. It seems that they were planning on leaving the country, but Larry was going back to London first to pick up a stash of gems.

"Guthrie and Larry quickly turned on each other, and it didn't take long for the police to get the names of all the co-conspirators."

"Mackintosh and Raines?" asked Daniel.

Poppy shook her head. "Surprisingly not. Turns out their lie about leaving the dinner through the Broad Street entrance was because they had actually followed me, intending to give me a dressing down and warn me off digging any further into June and the laboratory. They didn't want their bad conduct – Mackintosh's plagiarism and Raines' sleazy behaviour – to be splashed all over the press. But by the time they got through the gate, the taxi had arrived for me."

"So why didn't they just admit they'd exited that way? No one was to know they were trying to collar you."

Poppy shrugged. "Seems like they'd got it into their heads that I was out to pin the blame on them for anything I could, and they didn't want to give me the opportunity to suggest they might have had a hand in Gertrude's attack. So they claimed they were nowhere near the vicinity at the time so they wouldn't be falsely accused." She chuckled. "They obviously had me down as the type of woman who would falsely accuse a man just out of spite." She smiled, wryly. "I suppose they were right to a point. I was trying to pin the blame on them. But in the end the real evidence didn't point to them. They told Fenchurch they feared I was trying to stitch them up."

Daniel grinned down at her. "But you're not letting them get away scot-free though, are you?"

Poppy gave a mischievous smile. "Not on your Nellie! Their despicable treatment of June will be splashed all over the press. And Gertrude is going to pursue them through the University's disciplinary channels."

Daniel smiled, joining Poppy in her enjoyment of the fact that justice would be served. "So," he said eventually, "who were the co-conspirators? Who was going to hurt Sophie?"

"Sorry," said Poppy. "That's the most important bit in all this, isn't it? It was a hospital porter. Recruited, it seems, by the porter at Somerville, who, by the way, also admitted to tampering with my brakes. They arrested both porters as soon as Larry and Guthrie spilled the beans. So, Sophie was safe. She woke up last

THE CRYSTAL CRYPT

night, and according to Rollo was able to confirm that it was Guthrie who attacked her. She's still got a long way to go in her recovery, but she's very happy to hear that Lionel Saunders will finally face justice."

Daniel ducked under a curtain of willow fronds. "Aren't we all. I was delighted to hear he'd been arrested in the newsroom of the *Courier*, in front of all his colleagues while he was gathering some files to destroy. Seems like he jumped on the next train back to London after trying to get that briefcase from Rollo. Didn't even have the sense to get out of town. Is it clear yet how he got involved with the whole June Leighton story?"

Poppy shrugged. "Rollo and I are still trying to work out all the details, but it seems that there was a dirty copper on the Oxford force – an Inspector Birch. He and the police pathologist here had been paid off by Larry. Birch is away on holiday. So, when I arrived in Oxford asking questions at the Crystal Crypt, Reg Guthrie contacted Larry. Larry sent a telegram to Birch at his holiday hotel, telling him to come home and sort me out. Birch refused to cut his holiday short and instead gave Larry Richard Easling's name in London and tasked him with trying to find out what Rollo and I knew about what was going on. When Easling heard Sophie was involved in it too, that gave him the idea to recruit Lionel to snoop around the *Globe* offices, as he had done when Bert Isaacs was murdered. He came across Rollo with a file on the Sanforths and the Leightons, and knocked him out. But stupid Lionel didn't realize Ivan would have copies of everything – and a near-photographic memory."

Daniel grinned. "It still amazes me that someone as dim as him has managed to evade justice for so long. But not anymore. I hear Lord Dorchester – and Richard Easling – are turning on him. Dorchester to get parole; Easling to have his impending sentence reduced."

"Yes, that's what Rollo told me too," said Poppy. "Justice really can be sweet."

"And what of Edward Sanforth? Did Larry implicate him as well?"

Poppy shook her head. "No. It seems the only thing Edward was guilty of was being a jealous fiancé and not supporting June when she needed him most."

"I hope you don't think the same of me, Poppy?"

Poppy looked up at him, shielding her eyes from the sun with her hand. "Why do you say that, Daniel?"

"Hold on." Daniel stopped punting and negotiated the boat to the bank. He jumped out and tied the guy rope to a tree trunk, then climbed gingerly back into the punt, trying not to lose his balance.

Poppy made room for him on the cushions and he sat down beside her. She snuggled into the crook of his arm.

Eventually he spoke. "Poppy, I know you fear I'll try to stop you doing your detection work and that Rollo thinks the same; Ivan told me. And that's why you didn't tell me everything that was going on here as you were both worried I'd rush up and interfere."

"Well, that's not exactly true…"

"Isn't it?"

"Well, all right; yes, it is. I'm sorry, Daniel. I love my work, and I love you, and it will break my heart if I can't have both, but I will give it all up for you if you want me to."

Daniel turned his head towards her so that his grey eyes looked directly into her blue. "But what if I don't want you to?"

"What do you mean?"

He smiled gently. "Oh Poppy. Your bravery and courage and curiosity and cleverness and stubbornness and relentless pursuit of the truth and justice for victims are all part of what I love about you. Yes, I worry. And yes, I can't promise I won't ever try to get you to be more careful in your investigations, but when I finally asked you to marry me – five years after I should have done in the first place – it was with the understanding that this is who you are. And that I need to love all of you, or none of you. Is that good enough for you?"

Poppy sighed, a weight of worry lifting from her heart. "Yes! Yes! Thank you, my love. That's more than good enough for me. *You* are more than good enough for me." She turned her body so that she was lying on top of him, her face hovering above his. "And now, Mr Rokeby, my husband-to-be, I'm going to kiss you."

He chuckled. "Goodness, Miss Denby. That's not what a proper young lady would do."

She smiled, then softened her lips, ready for a kiss. "Perhaps," she muttered, lowering her head, "I'm no longer that proper young lady."

THE WORLD OF POPPY DENBY:
A HISTORICAL NOTE

The genesis of this book came in late 2019 when I was finishing off writing Poppy's previous adventure, *The Art Fiasco*, and I was wondering what she would do next. The answer came through a radio show on BBC Radio 4 about the Nobel Prize-winning scientist Dorothy Crowfoot Hodgkin. To my shame, I had never heard of her, but I soon learned that she was a groundbreaking chemist who advanced the science of X-ray crystallography, eventually leading to the discovery of the atomic structure of penicillin, insulin, and Vitamin B12. She won the Nobel Prize for Chemistry in 1964 – the first, and so far only, British woman ever to do so. She had been overlooked for many years and eventually, after pressure from male nominees, appalled that she had never been honoured, was given the prestigious prize. The next day, British newspapers announced this incredible achievement: "Oxford housewife wins Nobel Prize".

The outrageous sexism enraged me – a great way to get the creative juices flowing. So, I bought a biography of Hodgkin and began reading about her life as a scientist at Oxford in the 1920s and Cambridge in the 1930s, and the battles to be recognized for her academic and professional achievements, and not just as a wife and mother. Dorothy Hodgkin, like my literary hero Dorothy L. Sayers, was a Somerville College graduate. Coincidentally, at the time, I was also reading Vera Brittain's *The Dark Tide*, set at a fictionalized version of Somerville in the 1920s. And in my parallel professional life as a children's writer, I was doing some research into the scientist Kathleen Yardley Lonsdale (who makes a cameo appearance in this book in chapter 1), who was also an X-ray crystallographer. Then, when I read that Hodgkin had a laboratory in the basement of the History of Science Museum in Oxford (opened in 1924), I knew that the murder of a female scientist in 1925 was to be Poppy Denby's next mystery.

The science of crystallography in this book was drawn primarily from Georgina Ferry's excellent biography of Hodgkin, then supplemented by information on the Royal Institution website. Real scientists must forgive any errors in my depiction or explanation of the science: I, like Poppy, am not an expert in the field, but I have done my best to translate it for the average reader.

Experiments into the stabilization of explosives were not something Hodgkin or the laboratory in Oxford were involved in, but, according to my research, were indeed something scientists at the time were working on. The atomic structure of graphite (which would become instrumental in creating more stabilized explosives) was eventually discovered in the 1930s by Sir William Bragg, who also makes a cameo appearance in chapter 1. Likewise, experiments into the creation of synthetic diamonds were not part of Hodgkin's or the Oxford laboratory's research, but this too was being explored by scientists in the first half of the twentieth century. The first successful synthetic diamond was finally created in 1955 by the American Percy William Bridgman.

The layout of my fictional laboratory is as close to the "real" laboratory in the basement of the History of Science Museum in Oxford as I could make it, while using creative licence to add in a cloakroom for Poppy to hide in when she first snoops around. Readers who visit Oxford might want to pop in there and check it out – but please note, the Crystal Crypt is a made-up name, so if you ask for directions to it, you might get some odd looks. However, across the road, Blackwell's Bookshop and the White Horse were certainly there in 1925 – and still are! Other landmarks of Oxford mentioned in the book were also there in 1925 – including Elliston & Cavell, the department store where Poppy buys her dinner outfit, which was renamed Debenhams in 1973.

The Oxford Gazette is a made-up newspaper. I have placed its office on the then Clarendon Press site (still home to Oxford University Press today) for the simple reason that there would have been a printing press and that it was close enough to Somerville College and the Radcliffe Infirmary for Poppy to walk to in a few minutes.

The only other made-up location is the Cherwell Hotel. I couldn't find a "real" hotel in 1925 that overlooked the cricket ground near where Poppy and Daniel get engaged, so I made one up. I beg the forgiveness of St Hilda's College for squeezing in yet another building on their already over-crammed road.

Somerville College is, of course, a real place, but due to the restrictions necessitated by the pandemic, the Somerville you read about in this book is mainly what I have gleaned of it from reading books set there in the '20s and '30s (including *Gaudy Night* and *The Dark Tide*), a 1920s guidebook of Oxford, my viewing of it from the outside in, and the Somerville College website. Beyond that, I have fictionalized the layout for the purposes of this story. So once again, I beg forgiveness from Somerville alumni who know the place better than I do.

Readers may also note my references to Marie Stopes, not least the quote from her book *Married Love*, at the beginning of the novel. The 1920s saw a rise in demand for better access to birth control and the first free clinics were opened by Marie Stopes in 1921. It was only in later years (from 1968 in the UK) that the Stopes clinics would offer abortion as part of their family planning services. But back in the 1920s, Marie Stopes was concerned with sex education and the provision of contraception to married women, and was personally against abortion. Although her reputation is now, retrospectively, marred by her strong eugenicist views, her two books, *Married Love* (1918) and *Wise Parenthood* (1920), broke the taboo about publicly talking about sex. By 1925, when Poppy was reading them, the first book had had thirty-nine reprints and had sold half a million copies in the UK alone.

And finally, a note on my use of the terms "autism" and "schizophrenia". Autism, as a diagnosis, was only introduced into psychiatry in 1943, by Leo Kanner. This was closely followed in 1944 by the (now controversial) Hans Asperger, who drew attention to what is sometimes referred to as "high functioning autism" or Asperger's Syndrome. It is the latter condition that I believe the character of Sophie Blackburn exhibits. However, because in 1925 neither of these terms was in use, I couldn't say Sophie was autistic or had Asperger's. Nonetheless, autistic people have been around forever, and did not just come into existence when their particular characteristics were given a name in the 1940s. I initially wasn't going to use the word autistic at all in this book, and just have Sophie be who she was without comment (as my daughter is on the Autism Spectrum – on the "high functioning" end – I felt I could do this with some authenticity). However, in my research I came across the work of Eugene Bleuler, who, as Dr Theo Dorowitz describes to Rollo over lunch, used the term back in the early 1900s to describe certain characteristics of people he was treating for schizophrenia. So I felt justified in introducing the term as a descriptor of behaviour rather than a formal diagnosis. Indeed, Dr Dorowitz is very careful to *not* give a diagnosis. Readers should also note that Dr Dorowitz's use of the word "schizophrenic" is very much of his time. What he really means is what we would today refer to as bipolar, and what Rollo thinks he means is what today we refer to as Multiple Personality Disorder. Back in 1925, there was no differentiation between the two.

As always with my books, I have endeavoured to be as historically sensitive as I can be, while aware that errors may always creep in. For those I apologize and hope they do not diminish your enjoyment of Poppy's latest adventure.

For Further Reading...

Visit www.poppydenby.com for more historical information on the period, gorgeous pictures of 1920s fashion and décor, audio and video links to 1920s music and news clips, a link to the author's website, as well as news about upcoming titles in the Poppy Denby Investigates series.

Alden, *Oxford Official Handbook*. City of Oxford & Alden & Co, Oxford, 1924.

Brittain, Vera. *The Women at Oxford: A Fragment of History*. George G. Harrap & Co., London, 1960.

Brittain, Vera. *The Dark Tide*. Grant Richards, London, 1923 (republished by Virago, 1999).

Ferry, Georgina. *Dorothy Crowfoot Hodgkin: Patterns, Proteins and Peace – A Life in Science*. Bloomsbury, London, 2018.

Hay, Mavis D. *Death on the Cherwell*. British Library Crime Classics, London, 2014 (originally published by Skeffington & Son, 1935).

Muirhead, Findlay (Ed). *Muirhead's London and Its Environs* (The Blue Guides). Macmillan, London, 1922.

Olian, JoAnne (Ed). *Authentic French Fashions of the Twenties* Dover Publications, New York, 1990.

Rose, Geoff. *A Pictorial History of the Oxford City Police*. Oxford Publishing Co., Oxford, 1979.

Sayers, Dorothy L. *Gaudy Night*. Victor Gollancz Ltd, London, 1935.

Shepherd, Janet and Shepherd, John. *1920s Britain*. Shire Publications, Oxford, 2010.

Shorter, Edward. *A History of Psychiatry*. John Wiley & Sons, New York, 1997.

Shrimpton, Jayne. *Fashion in the 1920s*. Shire Publications, Oxford, 2013.

Stopes, Marie. *Married Love*. G. P. Putnam's Sons, London, 1923 (originally published 1918).

Stopes, Marie. *Wise Parenthood*. G. P. Putnam's Sons, London, 1920.

Tsjeng, Zing. *Forgotten Women: The Scientists*. Cassell Illustrated, London, 2018.

Waugh, Evelyn. *Brideshead Revisited*. Chapman & Hall, London, 1945.

Book Club Questions

1. The Crystal Crypt was written during a global pandemic. What were your experiences of the pandemic and how, if at all, did it affect your view of science and scientists?

2. In this book, there are instances of misogyny, racism, and offensive comments about disability (physical and mental). How did you respond to them?

3. Poppy and Daniel's romance has changed and developed over the series. What are your thoughts about Poppy and Daniel's relationship now? What impact do you think it might have on Poppy's future journalistic and sleuthing career?

4. In the 1920s, career opportunities were opening for women, but many women – even if they were educated well enough to qualify – were unable to pursue these paths due to certain legal restrictions, societal conventions, and childcare constraints. Even if she could afford a nanny, would a woman be allowed to return to work (assuming, that is, that she wanted to)? What might have happened to June Leighton's career if she had lived? What might happen to Poppy? Do you have any personal experience of trying to balance your professional and personal lives? What, from Poppy's experience, can you relate to or sympathize with?

5. Nearly one hundred years later, what difficulties do women still face? How have these changed, for better or worse, from Poppy's day?

WHAT'S YOUR NEXT POPPY DENBY NOVEL?

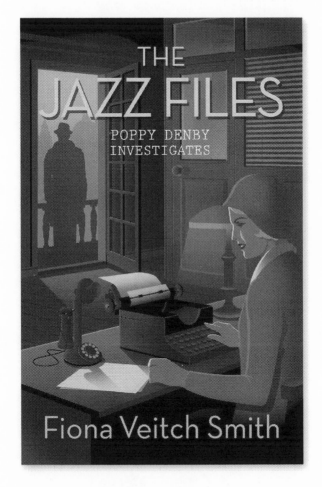

ISBN: 978 1 7826 4175 9

e-ISBN: 978 1 7826 4176 6

THE
KILL FEE

POPPY DENBY
INVESTIGATES

Fiona Veitch Smith

ISBN: 978 1 7826 4218 3

e-ISBN: 978 1 7826 4219 0

THE
DEATH BEAT

POPPY DENBY
INVESTIGATES

Fiona Veitch Smith

ISBN: 978 1 7826 4247 3

e-ISBN: 978 1 7826 4248 0

THE
CAIRO BRIEF

POPPY DENBY
INVESTIGATES

Fiona Veitch Smith

ISBN: 978 1 7826 4249 7

e-ISBN: 978 1 7826 4250 3

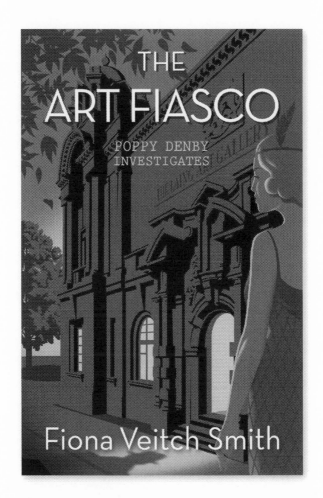

THE
ART FIASCO

POPPY DENBY
INVESTIGATES

Fiona Veitch Smith

ISBN: 978 1 7826 4319 7

e-ISBN: 978 1 7826 4320 3

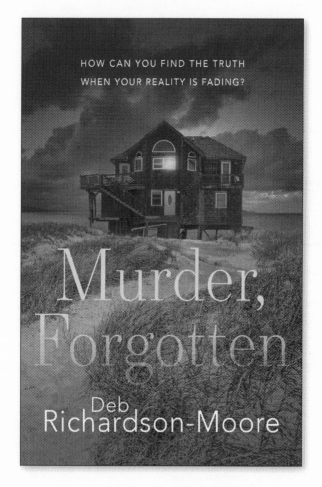

HOW CAN YOU FIND THE TRUTH
WHEN YOUR REALITY IS FADING?

Murder,
Forgotten

Deb
Richardson-Moore

ISBN: 978 1 7826 4311 1

e-ISBN: 978 1 7826 4312 8

'A delicious premise vibrantly told.'
John Jeter, author of *Rockin' a Hard Place*

A BRANIGAN POWERS MYSTERY

DEATH OF A JESTER

DEB RICHARDSON-MOORE

ISBN: 978 1 7826 4264 0

e-ISBN: 978 1 7826 4265 7

'Deb Richardson-Moore has done it again!'
Rebecca S. Ramsey, author of *The Holy Éclair*

THE A BRANIGAN POWERS MYSTERY
COVER STORY
DEB RICHARDSON-MOORE

ISBN: 978 1 7826 4240 4

e-ISBN: 978 1 7826 4241 1

'Highly recommended.'
Susan Furlong, NYT bestselling author

ISBN: 978 1 7826 4291 6

e-ISBN: 978 1 7826 4292 3

'Fun, quirky, and totally original!'
Amy Willoughby-Burle, author of The Lemonade Year

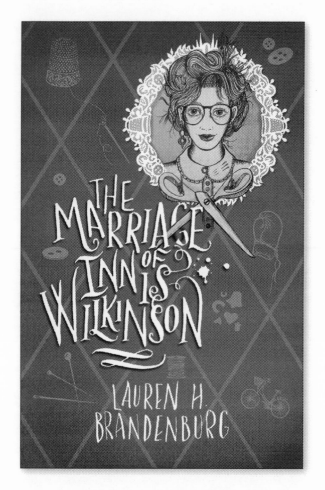

ISBN: 978 1 7826 4299 2

e-ISBN: 978 1 7826 4300 5

'Lauren is a refreshing, talented storyteller.'
Rachel Hauck, NYT bestselling author

Printed in the United States
by Baker & Taylor Publisher Services